W9-AWC-102

MARCUS BLAKESTON

RUNAWAY

Runaway

Text copyright © 2017 Marcus Blakeston
Cover image copyright © 2017 Jess Davies
All other content copyright © 2017 Bootprint

All rights reserved.

Published by Bootprint at Createspace

Second printing May 2020

This is a work of fiction. While some of the locations used
are real, all names, characters, businesses, events and
incidents are the product of the author's imagination and
any resemblance to actual persons, living or dead, is
entirely coincidental.

Marcus Blakeston would like to thank the following
for all their help with this one:

Alan Portwood
Greg Bull
Mat Harrison
Ted Curtis
Zed Tokerman

"Monsters aren't real ... but humans are."

Animal rights slogan

"An age of innocence lost without trace."

Burnt Cross, World's Fucking Insane

1

Stiggy didn't reckon much to the support band. And judging by the amount of beer and abuse being hurled at the stage, neither did anyone else in The Marples that night. It wasn't that they were young and inexperienced, although the way both the guitarist and bass player had their backs to the audience the whole way through their set, and the way the singer kept stuttering his words all the time, certainly didn't help. It wasn't even that they couldn't play their instruments properly. They were a punk band, after all, and a certain amount of rawness came with the territory. They just weren't the band Stiggy had paid his two quid to see, and he wanted them to hurry up and finish so the *Cockney Upstarts* would have enough time to play their full set before he had to leg it down to the train station for the last train home.

Stiggy didn't care much for the *Cockney Upstarts* either, but he had his own reasons for being there. The Donny punks had had nothing but hassle from skinheads for months, and he wanted to be there to back his mates up in case any trouble kicked off. And judging by the glares Twiglet kept getting from the mob of skinheads leaning against the bar, it looked like that was inevitable.

There were twelve of them in total, all dressed in regulation boots and braces with short-cropped hair and bleached jeans, like some sort of drunken regiment that wasn't too fussy about who they let in. Even the solitary bird with them was dressed the same, except in place of jeans and T-shirt she wore a short denim skirt with red braces hanging down over her bare thighs, and a pale green plaid shirt with short sleeves and buttons down the front. Her brown hair was close-cropped, just like the men, the only nod to femininity being long thin strands at the sides, and a three inch fringe that partially obscured her eyes. She stood to one side of the group, sipping from a bottle of Babycham, while the men punched the air and chanted at the support band on stage.

"Off! Off! Off!"

Their leader, a huge, stocky man at least ten years older and a good six inches taller than the others, shouted the loudest. Bulging muscles threatened to burst out of a skin-tight *Rock Against Communism* T-shirt with every jerk of his massive, tattoo-covered arm. Dangling red braces and a huge pair of black Doc Martens with white laces completed the image of someone nobody in their right mind would want to mess with.

But Stiggy wasn't in his right mind that night. He was still off his head from the bag of glue he'd had on the train down to Sheffield, and the three pints of cider he'd drunk since arriving at The Marples an hour ago gave him a sense of invincibility he never felt when he was sober. He smiled to himself as he imagined going up to the bald-headed bastard and booting him in the bollocks, then taking on the rest of his mob single-handed. Yeah, he could do that, no fucking bother.

But then someone would call the coppers and cancel the show, and Stiggy wouldn't get to find out if what it said in the newspapers about the *Cockney Upstarts* throwing a dead pig's head into the audience at the end of their set was true or not. He'd bet his mates a quid it was true, and told them he was only going with them so he could see a skinhead get smacked in the face by a flying pig's head. But that wasn't the real reason he had to know the truth.

If the *Cockney Upstarts* were using murdered animals as a form of entertainment there was nothing that would stop him bursting into their dressing room and telling them exactly what he thought of them. Then he'd write to *Crass* and tell them all about it, so they could spread the word and organise pickets outside their gigs, make sure they never played anywhere ever again. Maybe even get them kicked off their record label, or at least banned from *Top of the Pops*.

The skinhead boss draped his arm around the young girl's neck and squeezed one of her breasts while he continued chanting. She looked tiny and frail next to him, and visibly winced. Stiggy wondered what she saw in an ugly brute like that. She looked about sixteen or seventeen, whereas the bruiser she was with was at least twenty-five, maybe even older. Every now and again she would flick her head to one side to swing the fringe away from her eyes. Each time it would just flop back down again.

"This— this is our last song," the support band's singer stuttered from the stage.

The young skinheads cheered. "Make it a fucking short one, you useless cunts!" one shouted.

The older skinhead drained his lager and hurled the plastic container in the direction of the stage, then pushed the young girl away from him and ordered another drink from the barman. Released from his grip, she wandered over to the far side of the bar and leaned against it with her back to the band.

Stiggy stared at her legs and wondered again what a tasty bird like her saw in a thug like that. It just wasn't fair. Stiggy wasn't exactly handsome in the traditional sense, and he knew it — his nose was too big, the area around his mouth was riddled with acne from years of solvent abuse, and his ears stuck out like those of a chimpanzee. But at least he wasn't a fucking gorilla, like that skinhead she was with. So why didn't anyone ever fancy him instead?

Some sixth sense must have told the girl someone was watching her, because she turned around and looked straight at Stiggy. Stiggy smiled and raised his hand in greeting. The girl's face reddened, and she turned away. Stiggy shrugged to himself and brushed the dandruff from the shoulders of his *Crass* T-shirt before finishing off the last of his cider. After scrunching up the plastic container and tossing it on the floor, he leaned on the table and pushed himself upright from his stool. The small round table lurched to one side under his weight, forcing Colin, Brian and Twiglet to snatch their drinks up to save them from toppling over.

"Fuck's sake Stiggy, watch what you're doing," Brian yelled.

Stiggy ignored him and staggered over to the bar for a refill.

The support band finished their set and unplugged their instruments. Nobody clapped, nobody cared. The skinheads shouted their final insults, then turned away and ordered fresh drinks from the barman.

Stiggy sidestepped closer to the skinhead girl and waved a pound note to attract the barman's attention. The man nodded and held up two fingers while he finished off serving the skinheads — a wait your fucking turn gesture.

Stiggy pointed at the half-empty Babycham bottle standing on the bar in front of the girl. "You want another one of them?"

She shot a glance at the skinheads at the opposite end of the bar, then shook her head. Her hand trembled when she picked up the bottle and took a swig.

"You all right?" Stiggy asked. She seemed nervous about something, but he couldn't imagine what. She wouldn't even look at him, she just stared straight ahead at the optics behind the bar.

The barman finished serving the skinheads and wandered

over. Stiggy ordered a pint of cider and took a long gulp. He stared at the girl's profile, wondering what was wrong with her. Maybe she was shy or something.

"I'm Stiggy," he said.

No reply.

The skinheads turned away from the bar and glared out into the gloomy, smoke-filled room. It wasn't long before they turned their attention to Twiglet again. A chorus of monkey sounds erupted. A young lad bent forward and swung his arms from side to side, hamming it up. Twiglet stuck up two fingers and looked away. He was used to shit like that everywhere he went; being the only black punk in Doncaster always attracted unwanted attention from skinheads.

But the skinheads were looking for trouble, and Twiglet's cold shoulder routine just riled them up even more.

"You and me, cunt," their leader yelled. "We'll have our own fucking race war, right here."

The younger skinheads laughed. "Do him, Joe," one said. "Smash his fucking head in."

Twiglet glared across at the huge skinhead and sneered. "Nah, you're all right, Nazi. I wouldn't want to get my fists dirty on your ugly face."

"You what? What did you say, you fucking nigger?" The older man's eyes bulged in their sockets. His teeth ground together. He clenched his fists and took a step closer to where Twiglet sat. The younger skinheads lined up behind him with their chests puffed out, voicing their encouragement.

"Leave it out, mate," Colin said to the skinhead boss. "We're just here to see the *Upstarts*, we're not looking for no trouble."

"Well you should keep your fucking pet monkey under control then, shouldn't you?"

Twiglet's eyes blazed. He rose to his feet and cracked his knuckles, then took out his skull and crossbones ear rings and put them down on the table next to his pint. "Look after these for me, yeah? I'll be back in a minute."

"Fuck's sake Twiglet, just ignore them," Colin said. "It's not worth it."

"Maybe not for you."

Twiglet removed his studded wristband and wrapped it round his knuckles. Colin sighed and rose up next to him in a show of support. After a brief hesitation, Brian shook his head and joined them. Other punks nearby looked on with interest. Twiglet matched the older man in height, but not in build. Youth and agility would give him an advantage so long as he could dodge those huge fists of his opponent, but one thing Stiggy knew about skinheads was that they never fought fair. The others would pile in as soon as it started, they always did.

Stiggy put down his cider and stepped away from the bar so he would be ready to help even the score when the time came. The hairs on the back of his neck stood to attention, but his legs felt weak and wobbly. His stomach churned as he stared at the huge skinhead. Every instinct told him to stay out of it, let it run its course without him. But he couldn't let his mates down like that, he just couldn't.

The beefy skinhead peeled off his T-shirt and handed it to one of the others for safekeeping. More tattoos covered the man's upper body. British bulldogs, naked women, Union Jacks and Swastikas all mingled together into one technicolour mass of ink. He pulled the braces up over his bare chest and snapped them into place over his broad shoulders.

"Let's fucking have it, then, you cunts! I'll take the fucking lot of you by myself!"

Twiglet sneered at him. "Come on then, you fucking Nazi prick."

Stiggy clenched his fists, but it was more to stop his hands trembling than a show of strength. He could feel his bowels loosening. Beads of sweat dribbled from his armpits as he glanced from Twiglet to the skinhead and back again. Fuck it, he couldn't just stand by and watch his best mate take a pounding without doing anything about it. He took a step forward, ignoring the wobbly sensation in his legs. Don't think about it. Just do it.

"Oi, you two," the barman shouted. "Behave yourself, or you're out the door."

The younger skinheads glanced at the barman, then at each other. Twiglet and the bigger skinhead maintained eye contact while they continued hurling insults.

Then a high-pitched blast of feedback came from the speakers either side of the stage and everyone turned to look in that direction. The *Cockney Upstarts* stood there. The guitarist tuned up while the drummer took his seat. The bass player plugged in his instrument with a loud electrical pop and slung it over his shoulder. The singer downed a can of lager, crushed the can in one hand, and tossed it to one side.

"All right?" his amplified voice yelled as he peered out from the stage.

The young skinheads turned to their leader for guidance. He seemed to consider the situation himself for a couple of seconds, then glared at Twiglet.

"This isn't fucking over yet, cunt. I'll see you later."

"We're all fucking upstarts!" the band's singer screamed, and a wall of sound blasted from the speakers when the *Cockney Upstarts* broke into their top ten hit.

Punks and skinheads rushed for the stage, jostling to get the best position between the huge twin speakers. They leaped around together, their differences seemingly forgotten in an instant as the raucous music washed over them.

Stiggy sighed in relief as he watched Twiglet, Colin and Brian lose themselves in the swirling crowd, keeping well away from the skinheads. That had been too close for comfort. He looked at his wristwatch: half nine. That should leave plenty of time for them to finish before he had to leave for the train station. So he'd get to see if they ended their set by throwing a murdered pig's head into the audience or not. And if they did ...

The skinhead girl turned to Stiggy and smiled. Her green eyes seemed to twinkle in the harsh light illuminating the stage.

"I'm Sally!" she shouted.

"All right, Sally?" Stiggy shouted back. "You're not into all that Nazi shite as well, are you?"

Sally leaned closer and shouted into Stiggy's ear, "Am I fuck. I'm only here because Joe made me come. I don't even like this sort of music."

"Is Joe that big fucker who was hassling my mate?" Stiggy pointed into the crowd around the stage, where a group of skinheads were sieg heiling the band's singer, their leader clearly visible as he towered over them.

Sally nodded. "Yeah, sorry about that. He always gets like that when he's been drinking. Just tell your mate to stay away from him for the rest of the night and he'll be fine. Joe's that pissed up he'll have probably already forgotten about it, anyway."

Stiggy turned to watch the *Cockney Upstarts* play. It was one of their earlier songs, *Aggro Boys*, released a year before their appearance on *Top of the Pops* made them a household name and an overnight sensation. Back when they were still a punk band, and long before the skinheads latched onto them. Stiggy had heard it on John Peel's radio show at the time, and quite liked it. But that was before he found out about the pig's head.

The song ended, and the rest of the band took swigs from beer cans while the singer told the crowd about the time he was arrested and beaten up in the cells by a policeman who objected to the *All Coppers are Bastards* T-shirt he wore. It was a story most people already knew, because he had recited it word for word on their live album too, but that didn't stop them from listening in rapt attention.

Stiggy turned back to Sally, who stood toying with the Babycham bottle standing on the bar. He took another gulp of cider to bolster his confidence, then the words just blurted out of him.

"So how come you're wasting your time with an old geezer like that, anyway? A good looking bird like you could have the pick of any bloke in here, you know that, right?"

Sally turned to face him, an odd expression on her face, as if she were trying to figure out if Stiggy was just winding her up or not. She stared into his eyes. Stiggy stared back, but up close he struggled to get her into focus.

Then she smiled, shook her head, and turned away to watch the band, who had just started their next song. They watched together, side by side, sipping their drinks. Stiggy could feel the room spinning pleasantly, the cider doing its job on his already glue-fuddled brain. He bought another drink and resisted the urge to tap his foot in time to the music while he waited for any sign of a pig's head to appear.

* * *

Forty-five minutes later, the *Cockney Upstarts* gig was still in full swing and Stiggy was starting to get anxious. He would need to leave in another fifteen minutes if he wanted to catch the last train home, and there was still no sign of the pig's head.

The singer snatched the microphone from its stand and screamed into it, then dived off the knee-high stage into the audience while he sang. The crowd surged forward around him, desperate to have their go with the microphone during the chorus, to be a part of the band, even if it was only for a few seconds.

"Police scum, police scum, kill them all," out of tune voices shouted. "Line the blue bastards up against a wall. Spray them with bullets and watch them fall. Police scum, police scum, kill them all!"

The singer continued into the next verse, but was cut short when a punk with a massive red mohican grabbed the microphone from his hand. A gruff Yorkshire accent took over the vocals. The crowd pushed and shoved, closing in on the mohican to wrestle it back from him.

The band's singer stumbled in the surging scrum and

disappeared from view. Boots trampled over him in their owners' oblivious attempts to reach the punk with the microphone. The lead guitarist and bass player peered down from the stage, then stopped playing mid-song. It took the drummer a few more seconds to realise something was wrong and rise from his seat to see what was happening. The mohican punk continued singing his out of tune rendition of *Police Scum* as he dodged all attempts to grab the microphone from him.

The three band members jumped down from the stage and pushed their way through the throng, swinging punches at anyone who refused to get out of their way. Between them they managed to clear a space around the fallen singer and helped him back onto his feet. Blood poured from his mouth and nose as they led him away to the small dressing room at the side of the stage. The drunken singing continued in their absence.

Stiggy watched the dressing room door to see if the band would re-emerge with a pig's head, but the door remained firmly closed despite cries for an encore. Roadies unplugged the instruments and packed them away. The skinheads gave each other Nazi salutes while everyone else wiped sweat from their faces and headed for the bar or the toilets. Stiggy sighed. Now he would never know if the story in the newspaper was true or not.

Sally started trembling again. She bit her lip as she stared at the group of skinheads by the stage.

"You okay?" Stiggy asked.

She nodded. "Yeah. Look, you'd better go, before Joe sees you with me."

"Fuck that, I'm not scared of that wanker."

Sally looked down at her boots and shook her head. "You should be. Please Stiggy, just go while you still can."

"Are you frightened of him, is that it?"

Sally sighed. "It's best if you just go, he'll have a fit if he sees you talking to me. You don't know what he's like."

"What does he do to you, Sally?"

"Nothing. Please, you have to go now. Your mates, as well. Before it's too late."

Sally cast another furtive glance at the skinheads and edged away from Stiggy. Stiggy closed the gap once more and reached out to grip her arm. Despite his glue and cider-fuddled mind he was sure there was something about the big skinhead she was keeping from him, and it wasn't hard to guess what.

"Are you worried about what he will do to *me*, or are you worried about what he will do to *you*?"

Sally's mouth dropped open as she turned to look at Stiggy. Her jaw trembled.

"I fucking knew it," Stiggy said. "Come with me and my mates, we can save you from him."

Sally wrenched her arm free and yelled: "I don't need saving. You just need to get away from me, that's all. While you still can."

"Stiggy!" someone shouted from the other side of the room.

Stiggy turned to look. Colin and Brian were pushing their way through the crowd heading for the bar, Twiglet close behind. Colin's eyes were wide and staring. He pointed over his shoulder.

"Fucking leg it, quick!"

Then Stiggy looked beyond his punk mates at the mob of skinheads hurtling forward, knocking people out of their way as they went. The huge, bare-chested skinhead's face was purple with rage as he led the charge. He locked eyes with Stiggy and roared.

"Oi, that's my fucking bird, you cunt!"

2

Stiggy grabbed Sally's arm to stop her darting away. She struggled against him, but he held her tight. The skinheads stampeded ever closer. One of the younger skins grabbed a handful of Twiglet's afro hair and yanked it. He cried out as he stumbled backwards, his hands flailing wildly. Another ran up to Colin and smacked him in the face with such a force it sent him careening into a nearby table, knocking it over and sending an ashtray filled with cigarette butts flying. The older skinhead, Joe, barged into Brian as he ran past and sent him spinning to one side.

Stiggy tried to drag Sally to the stairway leading down to ground level, but she wouldn't budge. The skinheads were almost upon them, and had slowed their approach. They grinned as they clenched their fists and swaggered over, knowing they had him cornered.

"You've fucking had it now, you cunt!" Joe growled.

Stiggy glanced at the bar, searching desperately for anything he could use as a weapon. His eyes locked on Sally's empty Babycham bottle just as the barman pulled down shutters to cover the optics, then disappeared into a back room. Stiggy released his grip on Sally's arm and snatched up the bottle. It was too small to do any real damage, but if he shattered it on the edge of the bar he might be able to use what was left to threaten the skinheads into keeping their distance until he could make his escape. He raised the bottle by its stem and brought it crashing down against the bar. The shockwave ran up his arm, but the bottle just bounced off and remained intact. He tried again, with the same result, then gave up and put the bottle down and looked for something else to use. He saw a metal ashtray further down the bar and wondered if he would be able to reach it before they attacked.

"Don't, Joe!" Sally said. "Please. He weren't doing nothing, honest!"

The younger skinheads had stopped their advance, and just stood there watching in a semi-circle around Sally and their leader. Sally stood between Joe and Stiggy, trying her best to block him from getting any closer. She trembled before him while he glared down at her. His nostrils flared. His tattooed biceps bulged as he clenched and unclenched his fists by his sides.

"Get out of the fucking way, Sally. I'll deal with you later. It's this cunt's turn first. No fucker messes with my bird and gets away with it."

"Please Joe, just leave it. He didn't do nothing, he just—"

Without warning, Joe lashed out and slapped Sally hard across the face with the back of his hand. She cried out and stumbled back, her hand shooting up to her cheek. Stiggy reached out to catch her in his arms when she tripped, and held her upright by her armpits. Then Joe lunged forward and punched her in the stomach with so much force Stiggy felt the impact through her slim body. He staggered back a couple of steps while she doubled over in agony, suddenly a dead weight in his arms. He lowered her to the ground and snatched the Babycham bottle from the bar. Filled with rage, he raised the small green bottle above his head and ran at the massive skinhead.

Joe laughed and raised an arm to ward off Stiggy's drunken blow. The bottle bounced off his forearm and with a quick counter attack he grabbed Stiggy's wrist and twisted it up his back. Stiggy cried out and dropped the bottle. The skinhead kicked it to one side. A punch to the back of the head sent Stiggy's senses reeling, and before he knew what was happening the skinhead grabbed a handful of his spiky hair and forced him into a bending position.

"You fucking cunt!" Joe yelled as he rammed Stiggy head-first into the bar. "This is what you get for messing with my fucking bird!"

A blinding white flash filled Stiggy's vision. His legs gave out beneath him and he crumpled down to his knees.

"Cunt!"

A boot thudded into Stiggy's ribs and sent him sprawling among the discarded fag ends littering the floor. He gasped and curled himself up into a ball with his knees protecting his bollocks and his hands protecting his face while he waited for what he knew would come next.

"Cunt!"

Joe kicked out at every exposed inch of Stiggy's body while the younger skinheads cheered him on.

"Cunt! Cunt! Cunt!"

Every kick from those massive boots sent a fresh explosion

of pain through Stiggy's body. After each one he tensed himself in anticipation of the next, wondering where it would land and how much it would hurt. A boot up the arse caught him on the coccyx and sent a shockwave of searing agony up his spine. Another in his left kneecap almost caused him to remove his hands from his face so he could clutch it. It took a tremendous amount of willpower to keep them in place, because he knew if he left his head unprotected it would be the end of him. The skinhead was in a berserker rage, and he wouldn't be worried whether he did any permanent damage or not.

Then Joe roared in anger. Stiggy held his breath while he waited for the boot to thud into him once more. *Come on you bastard, just get it over with.* The anticipation of where that vicious boot would land next was worse than the blow itself. Seven seconds. Eight. Nine. Stiggy risked a gasp of air. Was it over, or was it just a trick to lull him off guard? He risked a quick peek between his trembling fingers.

Joe flailed around before him, with Brian clinging onto his back like a cowboy trying to tame a wild horse. Brian's arms were locked around the huge skinhead's neck, his legs kicking out wildly in an attempt to unbalance the older man, as well as to keep the other skinheads at bay as they rushed forward to try and grab him and pull him off. Joe twisted and turned, screaming abuse as he tried to shake Brian off him. Then Colin rushed forward and pushed Joe in the chest. The skinhead stumbled back with another roar and crashed down on top of Brian.

The rest of the pub was in chaos. Youths went at each other with fists and boots like a pack of wild animals fighting over a fresh kill. Even some of the lasses got stuck in. One hefty punk girl in a leather mini-skirt and green fishnet stockings had her meaty arm around a skinhead's neck while she punched him repeatedly in the face. Her mates cheered her on from the sidelines.

Twiglet went down in a hail of fists when four skinheads pounced on him. A punk bent down to help drag him back onto his feet and got a boot in the face for his trouble that sent him flying into the arms of three more skinheads. Another punk had a skinhead on the ground and was busy stamping on his chest until someone swung a stool into the back of his head and knocked him flat.

A hand grabbed Stiggy's wrist. He startled and rolled onto his back, desperate to get away.

"Come on!" Sally yelled. "For fuck's sake, get up, we don't

have much time."

Stiggy allowed the young skinhead girl to haul him onto his feet. He ached all over, but he could still stand, and that was the main thing. His head throbbed, and when he put a hand to his scalp he could feel a tender lump jutting up between the spikes in his hair. His ribs were on fire, and he worried they might be broken. His left knee sent a stabbing pain through his entire leg and threatened to give way when he put any weight on it. But if he could still walk, that meant he could get the fuck out of there.

Stiggy stepped forward and winced. The room spun out of control and he almost fell. Sally curled her arm around his waist and held him upright. He draped his arm over her shoulder, and shuffling one foot in front of the other he allowed her to guide him to the stairway. He paused at the top of the stairs and took one last look over his shoulder. Joe straddled Brian, laughing while he pummelled the young punk's face with his mighty fists. Colin held the skinhead around the neck from behind with both hands, trying to prise him off. Three of the younger skinheads pounced on Colin and dragged him away, then set about him with their boots.

"Come on!" Sally yelled again. "While he's not looking!"

"No, I've got to help my mates."

Stiggy tried to pull away, but Sally tightened her grip around his waist and held him in place.

"For fuck's sake Stiggy, you can't even walk properly, never mind anything else. The coppers will be here soon, let them sort it out."

As if in confirmation, the two-tone blare of a police siren sounded from the distance. As it grew louder, the fighting stopped, as if a switch had been thrown. Even the big skinhead rose up from Brian and looked around him.

"Coppers!" someone yelled.

Opposing factions squared up to each other for a couple of seconds longer, then punks and skinheads alike dashed for the stairs. Stiggy and Sally darted to one side as the first of them ran past and thundered down the steps. Stiggy still wanted to check on his mates, make sure they were okay, but found his way blocked by a huge crowd of bodies desperate to escape before the police arrived. With nowhere else to go, he had no choice but to hobble down the stairs amongst them, with Sally supporting him as best she could in the confined space. Punks in studded leather jackets barged past in their haste to get out in time, causing fresh explosions of pain in Stiggy's ribs as he was crushed against the side of the stairway. He almost lost his footing as he was swept along by them, but Sally managed to steady him before he fell.

Stiggy and Sally were half way down and had just navigated the sharp bend in the stairway when the exit door at the bottom of the steps slammed open and those at the head of the mob ran out and scattered into the street outside. The police siren grew louder and louder, causing a renewed surge from behind.

A hand clutched at Sally's shoulder. She startled and cried out, and Stiggy worried it might be one of the skinheads trying to grab her, but it was just a punk girl trying to get ahead of them in her haste to escape before the police arrived. More punks barged their way past while they continued their descent. The police siren sounded like it was getting closer and closer with every passing second, and every agonising step Stiggy took down the stairway. Sally tried to hurry him along, becoming more agitated the closer they got to the exit ahead. She kept looking over her shoulder, studying the faces of those rushing down the stairs behind her.

Then they burst through the door and out into the street. Stiggy shivered at the sudden blast of cold air after spending so much time in a hot, sweaty room. He paused to look at the punks as they ran past and disappeared into the night, hoping to catch sight of his mates. But while he recognised a few of them from Doncaster, Colin, Brian and Twiglet were not among them.

"Come on!" Sally said, trying to pull Stiggy forward. "Before Joe gets out and sees us."

Stiggy held back and looked at the doorway, from which a stream of youths still poured out. "What about my mates? I can't just leave them, I need to make sure they're okay first."

"There's no time, we need to get away before it's too late." Sally's eyes were wide and staring, her voice close to hysteria as she stared into the crowd rushing down the stairway.

Stiggy followed her gaze and noticed a mob of skinheads hurtling down in a pack. He shook his head. "I can't, not yet. Not until I know my mates are okay. That Joe of yours was giving Brian a right fucking pasting. What if he's still up there, lying injured? What if they all are?"

"For fuck's sake Stiggy, just come on! There's nothing you can do anyway, it's too late."

Sally broke away from Stiggy and hurried across the road without him just as the first of the skinheads burst through the door and ran past in the direction of the train station. Stiggy watched her go, torn over what to do for the best. With so many people still rushing down the stairs there was no way back in to reach his mates and help them get away. And the police would be there any second, so even if the blockage cleared and he could get back up there, there was no way he'd get back out again in time. He didn't like it, but Sally was right. There was fuck all he could do except save himself and hope for the best.

"Sally, wait!"

Stiggy limped across the road. Sally waited for him anxiously on the opposite side and hurried him past a row of shops that had closed for the night. He knew he wouldn't be able to go much further before his injured knee gave out. Sally looked ready to drop too. Her face was bright red, and she gasped for breath with every step.

The police siren grew even louder, almost deafening in its intensity. Then a riot van tore around a bend in the road ahead, blue lights flashing. Stiggy's heart hammered in his chest as he gaped at it. He subconsciously stepped into the shadows of a nearby building, pulling Sally with him. He expected the black van to screech to a halt at any second, for an army of coppers to surge out of the back and beat them both unconscious with their truncheons. He held his breath as it sped closer. Then let out a sigh when it flashed past on the opposite side of the road, the pitch of its siren dropping as it went by. He turned to watch it recede into the distance and screech to a halt outside The Marples, and hoped his mates had managed to get away in time.

Sally led Stiggy down Arundel Gate, past the Hallam University building, and into an indoor multi-story car park. Stiggy staggered forward another twelve paces, then slumped down next to one of the concrete supports. Sally stood gasping before him, bent forward with her hands clutching her knees. She spat a glob of white frothy phlegm on the ground between her legs.

"We ... we can't ... stay here," she said between gasps. "Joe ... the coppers ..."

"I know," Stiggy said. "I just need a minute first." He felt the lump on his head and winced at the resulting jolt of pain.

"You should ... get that checked out," Sally said. "You know, at the hospital. You might have concussion or something."

Stiggy shook his head, and wished he hadn't when he felt another sharp stab of pain. "No, that'll be the first place the coppers look for anyone who got away. I'll be okay, I've had worse than this before. But what about you? You took a bit of a walloping too, remember."

Sally straightened up and shrugged. "I've had worse too." She stared across at the car park entrance.

"Does that Joe bastard make a habit of hitting you then?" Stiggy asked. "Only I noticed you were more worried about him seeing you than getting caught by the coppers."

Sally sighed and sat down next to Stiggy with her knees pulled up to her chest. "I don't want to talk about Joe. Why do they call you Stiggy?"

"It's from that book, Stig of the Dump." When Sally gave him a blank look, he smiled. "They read it to us in junior school, it's about this caveman who lives on a rubbish tip."

Sally shrugged. "Never heard of it."

"Really? There was a TV series based on it a couple of years ago. Anyway, when the teacher showed us the pictures in the book everyone said he looked just like me, and the name kind of stuck ever since."

"So what's your real name?"

"Tony. Tony Nixon. But I prefer Stiggy."

"How long have you been a punk?"

"Pretty much since it first started, but I was only ten at the time. I was at my mate Brian's house one weekend, when his brother came home with the first *Sex Pistols* single. I'd never heard anything like it before, it was brilliant. Then my dad's newspaper started printing all this stuff about punk rockers and how they wanted to destroy society, and I knew I had to be part of it."

A thin smile crossed Sally's face. "Aw. I bet you looked really cute in your little studded leather jacket."

Stiggy smiled back. "I never had anything like that, but thanks."

"I was thirteen when ..." Sally stopped mid-sentence, then shook her head. "When *I* first got into the skinhead look."

"Never really cared much for skinheads, myself. We've had nothing but hassle from them over the last few months. One beat my mate up the other week, attacked him in the bogs while he was having a piss."

"The darkie one?"

"Twiglet? No, it was Colin. The one with the spiked up bleached hair and the *Vice Squad* T-shirt. But Twiglet gets a lot of stick off them too, for obvious reasons."

Sally shook her head. "Most skins aren't racist, it's just a small minority who are."

"Yeah, right," Stiggy said sarcastically. "Tell that to Twiglet.

Shit, I hope they're all okay back there. They were getting a right pasting from your mates."

"They're not my mates." Sally sniffed and looked away. "Besides," she said, "the police will be there by now."

"That's what I'm worried about. Fucking coppers are worse than skinheads."

The raised voices and shrieking laughter of drunken revellers came from outside. A woman in a short red skirt and matching high-heeled shoes staggered into the car park, dropped her knickers, and squatted down against one of the supports. Howls of laughter came from outside as her piss splattered against the ground and splashed over her shoes.

"Come on," Sally said, rising to her feet. "We'd best get going in case Joe comes this way."

Stiggy took the hand she offered and pulled himself up. He held onto it while she led him further into the car park and out through a side entrance. Her hand felt warm and sweaty, despite the cold night air, as he hobbled along beside her.

"Where are we going?" Stiggy asked. "Do you live round here? Only the train station's the other way."

"I live on the Shirecliffe Estate."

"Where's that?"

"Not far."

"Can I stay at yours then?"

Sally shook her head.

"Go on, I'll be no bother. I'll kip on the couch, or the floor even. You won't even know I'm there."

"It's not that," Sally said. "It's just ... well, you just can't, that's all."

"If you tell your parents what's happened I'm sure they'd be okay about me staying the night."

"I don't have any parents."

"Why not?"

Sally shrugged. "I just don't, okay?"

"Oh. Sorry, I didn't know. So who do you live with, then?"

Tears welled up in Sally's eyes. She sniffed, then wiped them away.

"Don't say you live with that fucking massive skinhead?" Stiggy stopped walking and pulled Sally to a halt beside him. "For fuck's sake, why?"

Sally looked down, avoiding eye contact. "He hasn't always been like that. He used to be quite nice."

"I find that hard to believe."

"No, he was. Still is, sometimes. He ... well, he helped me

when I needed it, that's all. I owe him a lot."

Stiggy shook his head. "The guy's a fucking psycho. I can't believe you're defending him like that."

"Yeah well, like I said, he gets a bit carried away sometimes when he's pissed up. He'll be okay in the morning, when he's sober again. Anyway, for all his faults, he was better than the alternative."

"What was the alternative? The fucking Yorkshire Ripper or something?"

Sally opened her mouth to reply, but the words were drowned out by the sudden loud blare of a police siren close by.

Stiggy spun around just in time to see the flashing blue lights tearing toward him at high speed.

3

Stiggy acted on impulse as the police car hurtled ever closer, and dragged Sally into the recess of a shop doorway. Pressed up against the plate glass door together, he could feel her trembling against him and smell the Babycham on her breath. Her eyes were wide as she stared at him, and he was sure his own eyes reflected that same fear. All he could do was hope the coppers hadn't already seen them out on the street. That they wouldn't look too closely at the shop doorways as they passed by. Because the alternative wasn't something he wanted to think about.

Flashing blue lights illuminated the shop doorway for a split second as the police car flew past. Stiggy tensed, expecting to hear the screech of brakes, followed by opening doors and the thud of rushing boots, the swish of a truncheon.

Then Sally let out a short laugh and seemed to relax against him. "It's a fucking ambulance, you daft bastard."

"What?"

Stiggy stepped out onto the pavement and watched the ambulance recede into the distance. He grinned at Sally and beckoned for her to join him.

They walked over a bridge crossing the River Don and into another shopping area before turning off and heading out of town. Sally refused to discuss her relationship with Joe any further, and kept steering the topic to more mundane matters, like who their favourite bands were and what films they liked. Stiggy learned she liked *The Specials* and *Madness*, and her favourite film was *Breaking Glass*, which she had sneaked in to see when she was twelve, despite its AA rating.

Stiggy tried to tell her about *Crass*, and how they were much more than just a band, how they formed the blueprints for a whole way of life and provided the seeds to build a new society, but he could tell from her blank expression she didn't understand a word of it.

"I like other stuff, too. You know, *Vice Squad*, *Abrasive Wheels*, *Blitz*, *Anti Pasti*, those kind of bands. And *Discharge*, of course. But *Crass* will always be my favourite."

"Never heard of any of them," Sally said.

"Not even *Blitz*? Two of them are skinheads, so I thought maybe you might like them."

Sally shook her head. "I just like the 2-Tone bands, and the old stuff from the sixties. Punk is more Joe's thing than mine. I only go to see bands like that because he makes me."

Twenty minutes later, they were walking past a row of dilapidated-looking terraced houses when they came to a small, fenced-off playing field. Opposite, next to an end-terrace house with a grimy white caravan in the front garden, was a stretch of overgrown grass with trees beyond it.

"It's just down there," Sally said, pointing at the trees.

"What is?"

"Somewhere we can stay for the night."

They crossed the field and entered the woodland. Twigs snapped beneath their feet and invisible animals scurried away in the dark. An unidentifiable bird screeched somewhere close by and made Stiggy jump. It sounded almost like a young child screaming in terror. The further away from the harsh glare of the streetlights they went, the less Stiggy could see, until he was almost walking blind. He could just about make out Sally's outline a few paces in front of him in the moonlight, and followed her footsteps as she tramped between the trees.

The smell of soil and rotting leaves reminded Stiggy of one of his favourite haunts back home, under the arch of a railway bridge crossing the River Don. He'd go there when he wanted to be alone, just to sit and think, or when he wanted to enjoy a quick bag of glue in peace, with only nature and the occasional train rattling by overhead to keep him company. It was his own private space, and he wondered if Sally had somewhere similar, and that was where she was taking him.

He was about to ask her when the trees thinned out into open grassland once more. They came to a rusting wire-mesh fence and walked along it. On the other side were what looked like lots of individual gardens, with rows of plants tied to bamboo canes. But instead of houses, the only buildings he could see by the dim light of the moon were the outlines of sheds and greenhouses.

"What is this place?" he asked.

"Allotments. Come on, it's just down here."

"What is?"

"You'll see."

Sally walked a bit further, then stopped and crouched down. She bent back a small flap someone had cut into the fence and crawled through it on her hands and knees, then stood up on the other side and brushed herself down. Stiggy crawled through and joined her.

They walked between rows of plants and hopped over a short, knee-high wooden fence into another allotment. This one had a small greenhouse at one end, and Sally entered it to pick tomatoes from the plants inside. She took one from each plant, explaining that the owner would be less likely to notice them missing that way, and cradled them in one arm. She plucked a bunch of purple grapes from a vine on the way out and munched on them while she made her way to the next allotment. Stiggy pulled a peapod from one of the plants growing alongside the fence. He slit it open with his thumbnail and scooped the peas into his mouth. They were sweet, much better than any peas he had ever tasted before. He picked more and stuffed his pockets with them before following Sally into the next allotment, determined to go back for more in the morning so he could take some home with him.

"I wish I'd known there was places like this," Stiggy said. "It'd save loads of money on shopping."

Sally smiled. "Do they not have allotments where you live then?"

"Dunno, but I'm definitely going to find out now."

"Where are you from, anyway?"

"Doncaster."

Sally made her way to a wooden shed with a sloping corrugated iron roof in the corner of another allotment and disappeared inside it. Soon after, an orange glow came from within.

Stiggy walked over and joined her. A lit candle stood on a saucer in the centre of a rickety-looking rectangular table, next to a pile of magazines about gardening, and the tomatoes Sally had picked. The candle's orange flame flickered as Stiggy closed the door behind him, casting eerie dancing shadows on the walls.

Sally crouched down next to a small paraffin heater and lit it with a box of matches from the table, then sat down on an old, beige-coloured two-seater couch set before it. Stiggy looked around the small shed, but there wasn't anything of interest. Just a few gardening tools propped up against the window on one side, and a shelf at the back that contained bottles of plant food and pesticides, along with a couple of brown boxes. He investigated one of the boxes, found it contained some kind of small blue pellets, and put it back. The other contained candles like the one on the table.

"Whose place is this?" Stiggy asked as he sat down on the couch next to Sally.

"Some old geezer, but as long as we're out by the morning he'll never know we were here."

"How did you find out about it?" He took a handful of peapods from his pocket and offered one to Sally. She took it and slit it open, then picked out each pea individually as she ate them.

"Me and my mate Trisha found it years ago. We'd run away from the home and needed somewhere to stay for the night." Sally tossed the empty peapod onto the table, leaned forward, unlaced her boots, and kicked them off. She stretched her legs out and held her feet near the paraffin heater. Steam rose from them, and Stiggy caught a whiff of sweaty socks.

"What do you mean, you ran away from the home?" Stiggy shovelled another handful of peas into his mouth and chewed them, discarding the empty pod on the floor.

"Care home. You know, for kids like me, whose parents don't want them."

"Oh, okay. So, um ... is Trisha a skinhead too?"

"No, but she is into the music. In fact it was her who introduced me and Dave to it in the first place. Dave's my other best mate, he's a skin like me now, but Trisha never really got into the look like we did. Anyway, Trisha had all these really old ska and reggae records, I think they must have belonged to her parents or something before they died, and we used to dance to them all the time in her room." She smiled to herself, as if she were reliving a memory. Then she frowned and looked down at her feet. "I don't really see her much anymore, though."

"How come?"

Sally shrugged. "I don't want to talk about it. How long have you been sniffing glue?"

Stiggy looked at her sharply. "How did you know I did that?"

"I smelled it on your breath straight away, and your clothes are covered in it."

"Oh." Stiggy looked down at his combat trousers and picked at a glob of dried glue stuck to his thigh, then gave up when it wouldn't come off. "Did you ever try it?"

"Yeah, I used to do it a lot when I was twelve. I wouldn't do it now, though."

"How come?" Stiggy leaned forward and unlaced his trainers. He kicked them off and wiggled his toes as he sat back on the couch.

"Because it fucks your lungs up. You should pack it in too,

2 6

before it's too late."

"Yeah well, maybe one day. It's not like I'm an addict or nothing, I just like it, that's all. It helps me forget stuff. You know, like how shit life is and stuff like that."

Sally frowned, then nodded. "Yeah, I know. But all that bad stuff, it's still there when the glue wears off, isn't it?"

"Yeah, I guess."

"So what's it like where you live?" Sally asked after a short pause.

"Doncaster? It's just a fucking dump," Stiggy said. "There's no jobs unless you want to go and work down the pit."

"And you don't want to?"

"Nah, fuck that. My granddad worked down the pit all his life, he died of emphysema a year after he retired. My dad said it was the pit that killed him."

"Do you live with your parents?"

"No, not anymore. I've got a flat near the town centre."

"I wish I had a place of my own."

"What's stopping you?"

Sally let out a short laugh as she shook her head. "Well, money for one thing. And then there's Joe. He'd never allow it."

"Fuck that wanker. If you want your own place, just get one, it's nothing to do with him. It's not like he owns you or anything, is it? And the dole will pay the rent for you anyway, so you don't need no money either."

"It's not that simple."

"Why not?"

Sally shrugged. "It just isn't, okay? Anyway, it's getting late and I'm tired. We need to be out of here early in the morning, so let's get some sleep, yeah?"

"Yeah, okay. Do you want the couch? I don't mind sleeping on the floor."

"No, it's okay. There's room for us both if we sleep sitting up."

Stiggy ate the rest of the peas in silence and stared at the flickering candle. All that talk of glue made him wish he had some with him. A quick bag would be just what he needed to help him relax after such a hectic night. And it would help to dull the pain from the beating he'd taken from that Joe bastard.

* * *

Stiggy ran his dry tongue around his furry mouth and moaned. His head pounded like a bass drum, and the incessant high-pitched twittering of birds close by just made it worse. He knew from experience the only way to clear a hangover this bad was to sleep it off until dinner time, then down half a pint of cider for breakfast. But someone kept shaking him by the shoulders and calling out his name, dragging him back to unwanted consciousness. His eyes, bloodshot and sticky with sleep, flickered open. He found himself slumped over the arm of a small beige couch in a strange room.

"Finally," Sally said. "I've been trying to wake you up for ages."

Stiggy looked up at her and blinked. His ribs ached, and he felt like he hadn't had any sleep at all. Where was he, anyway? It looked like some sort of shed, but what was he doing in a shed? His memory of the previous night was hazy at best, and came in short bursts. Staggering off the train with a glue bag in his hand, still tripping. Brian snatching it off him and throwing it in a bin. Seeing loads of skinheads hanging around outside The Marples and arguing with his mates whether they should still go in or not. Talking to a skinhead bird ... Sally, that was her name. Talking to Sally, and watching the *Cockney Upstarts* with her to see if they brought out a pig's head and threw it into the audience. Then some massive skinhead came over and kicked the fuck out of him for some unknown reason.

Stiggy groaned and closed his eyes. Whatever it was Sally wanted, he was too fragile to deal with it just yet. A few more hours sleep should sort him out.

Sally shook him awake again. She looked anxious, worried about something. Stiggy noticed a bruise on the side of her face and remembered the skinhead had attacked her as well, when she'd tried to defend him. He'd punched her in the stomach, too. What was his name again? He was Sally's boyfriend, although he could hardly be described as a boy. More like a grown man in his mid-twenties, at least. Sally had tried to stop him getting to Stiggy, and had taken a beating herself for the trouble. Joe, that was his name. Probably wasn't the first time he'd hit her either, thugs like that were always handy with their fists.

Sally shook him once more. "Stiggy, please! You need to wake up!"

Stiggy yawned. "Why, what's wrong?"

"We need to go, before the old geezer gets here and finds us."

Stiggy tensed. "What old geezer?" Did she mean Joe? Were they in a shed in that skinhead's garden?

Sally sighed. "The one who owns the allotment. He'll be coming soon, and we need to go before he gets here."

Stiggy relaxed again. "Oh, okay. Why, what time is it?"

"Don't know, you're the one with the watch."

Stiggy looked at his watch and couldn't believe what he saw. Just gone seven, still the middle of the night. No wonder he felt like shit. He closed his eyes and groaned once more.

"Stiggy, please!" Sally leaned over and shook him again. "We need to go. If he finds us here he'll call the police."

Stiggy opened one eye. "Do we really need to go now? My head's banging, and I could do with another hour or so of sleep."

"We don't have that long, we need to go right now. I need to go back home, and so do you. Last night was a mistake."

Stiggy shuffled himself upright in the couch and yawned as he stretched out his arms and arched his back. Something cracked, and the sudden jolt of pain made him cry out. He winced and lifted his T-shirt to find a huge purple bruise all the way down one side. More bruises covered both his arms.

"You okay?" Sally asked.

Stiggy prodded the bruise around his ribs with his fingers. "Yeah, I think so. Nothing seems to be broken, anyway." He pointed at the bruise on Sally's face. "How about you? That looks pretty sore."

Sally shrugged. "I'll survive. But come on, you need to get up. We need to go."

Stiggy remembered his left knee had been injured too as he struggled to his feet. While there was still a dull ache when he put any weight on it, he found he could still walk over to the table without too much discomfort. He picked up one of the tomatoes left over from the night before, popped it in his mouth whole, and bit into it. The sudden burst of tangy liquid in his dry mouth was like heaven, and he closed his eyes and sighed while he chewed the rest of the tomato to a pulp.

"What did you mean, last night was a mistake? We didn't do nothing, did we? All I can remember is coming here, then going to sleep."

"I shouldn't have come here. Joe will be mad at me because I didn't go home."

Stiggy pushed another tomato into his mouth and spoke around it while he chewed. "The way I remember it, you were more frightened of that Joe geezer than you were of the coppers last night. That wasn't the first time he's hit you, was it?"

Sally's face reddened. Tears welled up in her eyes.

"It wasn't, was it? Fucking hell Sally, why do you put up with shit like that?"

She turned away. When she spoke her voice had a croak to it. "I don't have no choice."

"Of course you do. Just leave him."

"You don't understand, it's not that simple."

"I'm pretty sure I *do* understand. Look, Sally, you need to get away from him before he does something even worse."

Sally sniffed and rubbed at her eyes. "That's what Trisha said."

"Well she was right then, wasn't she?"

Sally turned to Stiggy. Her cheeks glistened with tears, but her face flushed with anger.

"No she wasn't!" she yelled. "And what happened to her, it was all my fault!" She shook her head and looked down. When she spoke again her voice was softer, and full of pain. "I can't let that happen to anyone else. I just can't."

"Why what happened to her?"

Sally's shoulders slumped. "Nothing. I don't want to talk about it."

"Did Joe do something to her?"

She shook her head. "I need to go home, Stiggy. You should go home, too. Forget you ever met me."

"I can't do that, Sally. Let me help you. Please."

"You can't. Nobody can. Don't you see?"

"No, not really. What is it you are afraid of?"

"Nothing. Just forget it, okay? I need to go home before Joe goes out to work. Explain what happened last night."

"What will you tell him?"

"I don't know yet. I'll think of something on the way."

"And how do you think he will take it? You know, you staying out all night."

"Same as usual, I guess."

"With his fists?"

Sally walked over to the table and scooped up the rest of the tomatoes. "We need to get rid of any evidence we've been here. Can you pick those peapods up? We'll throw them away in the woods."

"Yeah, okay."

Stiggy knew she was just trying to change the subject, but he picked up the empty peapods and stuffed them in the pockets of his combat trousers anyway, while Sally replaced the spent candle with a fresh one from the box on the shelf. After a quick look around the shed she pulled open the door and stepped outside. Stiggy followed her out, where she was waiting for him. She closed the hasp on the door, secured it with a wooden peg, then walked away without a word.

"Sally, wait," Stiggy said. "I don't know about you, but I can't really think straight until I've had a hot drink in the morning. Is there a cafe near here? I'll buy you a coffee and we can think of a good excuse you can use together, how does that sound?"

* * *

The grimy-looking cafe Sally took Stiggy to, optimistically called Donna's Luxury Tea Bar and Grill, stood in a row of shops in a run-down commercial area on the outskirts of the Shirecliffe Estate. Two of the shops at the far end, a greengrocer and a general goods store, had long since closed down, their doors and boarded up windows covered in graffiti. A bookmakers and a newsagent sandwiched the cafe, while two charity shops and a unisex hairdressing salon made up the rest of the properties.

Sally sat down at a table by the window of the cafe, while Stiggy went up to the counter and ordered two rounds of toast and two mugs of coffee, one without milk. The fat, ginger haired woman in a dirty white apron behind the counter, who Stiggy assumed must be Donna, took the payment and said she would bring them over when they were ready. Stiggy sat opposite Sally and moved an ashtray containing a single cigarette stub onto the next table.

"You don't smoke, do you?" he asked.

Sally shook her head. "No."

"Good, because it's a filthy habit."

"What, and glue isn't?"

Sally smiled, but there was little humour behind it. She still looked worried sick about the prospect of returning home and facing Joe's wrath. It was obvious she was terrified of him, and Stiggy had a pretty good idea why. But what could he do if she was so adamant about going back to him? It wasn't like he could force her not to, it was her own decision no matter how wrong he thought that decision was.

Donna walked over with a plastic tray and plonked it down on the table without a word. Stiggy picked up the mug of black coffee and blew on its surface while Sally unwrapped the foil from one of the two butter portions provided and spread it over a slice of toast.

"They never give you enough, do they?" she said.

"You can have mine, if you want."

"You sure?"

"Yeah, I don't eat butter. I'm a vegan."

"Oh. Well, if you're sure you don't want it?"

Stiggy nodded. He watched her eat the toast while he sipped his coffee. It was weak, and tasted like it had been made with less than half a spoonful of instant granules, but it was better than nothing. Sally added a sachet of sugar to hers, and again Stiggy said she could have his too.

"Don't vegans eat sugar, either?"

Stiggy smiled. "Yeah, we do, but I don't like it. Makes everything too sweet." He picked up a dry slice of toast, tore a piece off, and dipped it in his coffee.

"How long have you been a vegan?"

Stiggy took a bite of soggy toast before answering. "About a year, ever since I heard a song about what they do to animals when they kill them."

Sally frowned. "You must listen to some really weird music if that's what they sing about. So do you eat fish, then?"

"No, fish are animals too. I don't eat eggs either."

"So what *do* you eat?"

"Nuts, vegetables, herbs, porridge, things like that. I make a mean vegetable stew when I can afford the ingredients. And there's a market stall back home that sells this stuff called Five Grain Burger Mix, I like that too. It's like a load of different seeds and stuff, in this sort of pink powder. You add water to it and fry it in vegetable oil. It's really good, you should try it one day."

Sally smiled. "I'll have to take your word on that. Don't get me wrong, I'd really like to try it, but ... well ..." Her face dropped, and she looked away, out of the window. "Joe would never buy it for me, I just know he wouldn't."

Stiggy leaned back in his chair and sighed. "It all comes back to that Joe bastard, doesn't it?" He shook his head. "You shouldn't let him control your life like that."

Sally turned to face Stiggy once more, her face blank and expressionless. "What choice have I got? You've seen what he's like."

"Yeah, I have. He's a fucking psycho. And that's why I'm telling you. You need to get away from him, before he kills you."

"And go where? He'd only drag me back again, like he did the last time."

"Why, where did you go?"

"Trisha's. She's got a bedsit on the other end of the

Shirecliffe. It only took him a day to find me again. He's got spies everywhere."

"So go somewhere he won't be able to find you. Come back to Doncaster with me. There's plenty of room at my flat until you get a place of your own. And I could help you look for one, show you how to fill the housing benefit form in when you find somewhere to live."

Sally's eyes widened. "You really mean that? You'd do that for me?"

Stiggy shrugged. "Yeah, of course. Why wouldn't I?"

"You don't even know me."

"I know enough. I know you don't really want to go back to that Joe geezer, because you're fucking terrified of him. In fact I reckon that's why you helped me get away from him last night, and why you took me to them allotments. You could've easily just sneaked off on your own while he was kicking fuck out of me if you'd wanted to. You did all that because you wanted me to help you."

Sally stared into Stiggy's eyes, as if she were searching for something hidden behind them. After a short moment she nodded, then frowned. "Yeah well, it seemed like a good idea at the time. But then when I woke up this morning, it just seemed so wrong to get you involved in that way. After what happened to Trisha ..." She shook her head. "Well, I don't want that happen to anyone else."

"You don't need to worry about me. Anyway, how could he find you in Doncaster? It's miles away, it's not like it's just the other end of the street."

"I would need to get my stuff first," Sally said after a short pause. "You know, clothes and that?"

Stiggy smiled. "Well what are we waiting for? Let's go and get it, then."

Sally shook her head. "We'll need to wait for Joe to go to work first. This is really good of you, Stiggy, thanks. I don't know what to say."

* * *

Two hours later, Sally led the way through a criss-cross of run-down council estate streets. Junk littered concreted over front yards, hidden behind broken wooden fences with the gates either missing or hanging at an angle by a single bent hinge. The doors to the houses were all a uniform red, with faded, peeling paintwork. Upstairs windows were grimy, and looked like they hadn't been cleaned in years. Dogs barked, and babies screamed for attention that never came. It all reminded Stiggy of home. The only thing missing was the prostitutes plying their trade on the street corners, but then he realised it was still too early for those to be out and about. Even Doris, by far the most eager of Doncaster's sex workers, didn't take up her pitch until lunch time.

They passed another row of dilapidated terrace houses into another street identical to the last, then down a short alleyway into a field of overgrown grass with small goal posts at each end of it. Piles of dog shit lay everywhere, and Stiggy wondered how anyone could possibly play football in a place like that. Both he and Sally looked down at their feet to avoid stepping in it as they made their way diagonally across the field.

"Oi Sally!" a gruff voice shouted from somewhere behind.

Sally stopped dead in her tracks and turned around sharply. Her eyes widened and her mouth dropped open. Stiggy turned to see for himself who it was.

A young skinhead in a white T-shirt and bleached denim jeans with dangling red braces and massive black boots ran across the field, heading straight for them.

4

"All right, Dave?" Sally said. "You okay?"

The skinhead nodded. "Yeah, I'm good, Sally." He frowned as he peered at the bruise on the side of Sally's face. "What's happened?"

Sally's hand shot up to cover the bruise. She looked down at her boots and shook her head. "Nothing. I just walked into a door last night, that's all."

Dave's eyes narrowed. "You sure? Only I heard some bother went down at The Marples last night."

"Yeah, honest. You know what I'm like, just a bit clumsy sometimes, I guess." She looked up. "Why, what did you hear?"

"That there was some big fight." He glanced at Stiggy. "A mob of scruffy punks causing trouble or something. Apparently loads of people got nicked, and a few got rushed to hospital. Baz told me about it last night, says he only just got away in time."

"Yeah?" Sally shrugged. "It must've been after we'd gone, we didn't see nothing like that. Did the coppers get Joe?"

"Dunno. Didn't he leave with you?"

"No, I left early. The music was doing my head in."

Dave smiled. "Yeah, I can imagine. I don't know what people see in that punk crap." He jerked a thumb at Stiggy. "Speaking of which, who's this wanker, then?"

"That's Stiggy," Sally said. "I met him at the pop concert last night. Stiggy, this is Dave. Me and him go way back, he's one of the good guys."

Stiggy had his doubts about that, but he kept them to himself. Everything about the young lad screamed 'thug' to him. From the Union Jack patch over the breast of his white T-shirt, to the scratchy home-made tattoo of a stick figure with a halo on the side of his neck and the small blue dot on the bridge of his nose. His left cheek had a Z-shaped scar on it, like the mark of Zorro. More jagged scars covered both arms, so he was obviously no stranger to violence. Stiggy just wanted to get away from him as soon as he could. The sooner they were on their way to

Sally's house to pick up her stuff, the better.

Dave glared at Stiggy for a couple of seconds, then turned back to Sally and shook his head. "What are you doing bringing someone like that round here? Joe will have a fucking fit when he finds out. You know what he's like about you talking to other blokes."

"Yeah well, Joe doesn't need to find out about it, does he? Not unless you tell him."

Dave held up his hands, palms out. "Hey, come on Sally, you know me better than that. I'm just warning you, that's all, in case anyone else sees you with him and tells Joe."

Sally shrugged. "I won't be here for long anyway, so it won't matter if he finds out or not."

"How do you mean?"

Sally glanced at Stiggy before replying. "I'm leaving him."

Dave sighed. "Look, Sally, I get it, I really do. You've had another barney with Joe. It's not the first time, and it won't be the last. But do you really want to go back to that other place, now Trisha isn't there to help you through it? For fuck's sake, you've only got another eight months to go, then you can do whatever you like."

Sally shook her head. "I don't think I can put up with it for another day, never mind another eight months. You don't know what it's like living with him. I hate it."

"Well he can't be any fucking worse than those other cunts."

"I'm not going back there, either. Stiggy's got his own place, I'm going to stay there for a while until I find somewhere of my own."

"And then what? Joe will only drag you back again when he finds out where you are."

"Not if I've got anything to do with it," Stiggy said.

Dave turned to Stiggy and sneered. "Yeah, I can really see a scrawny little cunt like you standing up to someone like Joe. Mate, he'd fucking flatten you with one finger."

"At least I'm trying to help her, unlike you."

The skinhead's nostrils flared. "What's that supposed to fucking mean?"

"It means what it says."

Dave's left hand shot into the hip pocket of his jeans and pulled out a vicious-looking knife with a six inch serrated blade. "You know fuck all about me and Sally, you fucking cunt!" he yelled. "You haven't got a fucking clue what I've done for her. Who the fuck are you, anyway? I'm not taking any fucking shit from a cunt like you!"

Stiggy backed away with his hands raised. His mouth gaped open and his eyes bulged as he stared at the knife. He'd been right, the skinhead was another fucking psycho. Why else would he just explode like that for no reason? And why else would he have a fucking knife with him?

"Dave, for fuck's sake!" Sally shouted. "Put it away! Stiggy didn't mean nothing by it, honest. He's a friend, okay? Don't hurt him, please. For me?"

Dave frowned, then lowered the knife and sighed. His shoulders slumped and his cheeks flushed red. He looked down and used the tip of the knife to remove dirt from under his fingernails.

"Sorry Sally," he said quietly.

Sally reached out and stroked the scars on his right arm while she spoke. "It's okay, Dave, I understand. Really, I do. But Stiggy's not the enemy. He's helping me. He's not going to hurt me, he's a friend. He's a good person, he's going to help me get away from Joe. That's what you've always wanted, remember? For me to leave Joe as soon as I can?"

Dave nodded, then put his knife back in his pocket. "Yeah, but I always thought you would come and live with me at the hostel. I can keep you safe, Sally. It won't be like last time, I'm stronger now."

"I know, Dave, but it's better if you don't get involved this time. And I need to get further away, somewhere Joe won't be able to find me."

"With him?" Tears welled up in Dave's eyes. He brushed them away before they could form properly.

"Yeah. At first, anyway."

"So where will you go?"

"It's better if you don't know. And don't let on to anyone that you've seen me, either. Because if Joe finds out ... well, he might take it out on you for not stopping me."

"Don't worry about me, I can handle myself."

"I know you can, Dave, but I'd feel better if I knew you were safe. So promise me, yeah? You won't tell anyone you saw me here, and you'll keep away from Joe?"

"Yeah. Yeah, I promise. But I'll see you again, right? You know, come and visit some time?"

Stiggy couldn't think of anything worse, but he held his tongue.

"Yeah, of course," Sally said. "And I'll phone you at the hostel every day, I promise. And once I get settled in I'll give you the address, so you can come down there and see me, tell me everything that's been going on in your life."

Dave nodded. "You'd better."

"Well that's settled, then," Sally said. "Talk to you soon, yeah?"

They hugged, and Sally rubbed Dave's back.

"Take care of yourself, Dave," she said as she broke the embrace. "And don't go doing nothing stupid, you hear?" She smiled, but Stiggy could tell it was forced. "Otherwise you won't be able to come and visit, will you? And you want to be able to do that, don't you?"

Dave nodded. "Yeah. I won't do nothing, Sally, honest. It's all good now. So I'll see you soon, yeah?"

"Yeah."

Dave turned to Stiggy. "And you'll look after her until I can make it down there, right? Make sure she's okay without me?"

Stiggy nodded. "I'll do my best."

Dave leaned in close and whispered in Stiggy's ear. "Yeah, well, you'd fucking better, you cunt. Because if anything bad happens to her I'll hunt you down and fucking kill you."

* * *

Sally's house turned out to be a normal two up, two down end terrace a quarter of a mile from the playing field. A lamp post stood directly outside, with an old car tyre looped around its base. Stiggy marvelled at the strength and skill required for such an amazing feat of hoopla. A pair of boots tied together by their laces and strung over a telegraph wire overhead paled into insignificance in comparison.

The house itself didn't look much from the outside. The whitewashed walls had yellowed with age, and the paint had cracked in a few places, but nothing out of the ordinary for the area. The small front garden was surprisingly tidy, however, with a multitude of colourful flowers surrounded by a neatly trimmed hedge.

Sally pushed open the wooden gate and walked along the stone path, but rather than heading for the front door she took Stiggy round the side of the house and into the back garden. This too was immaculately kept. It even had stripes down the lawn and brightly coloured gnomes sitting around a small fishpond, something Stiggy had only ever seen on TV before. He looked closely at the gnomes, half expecting them to have Hitler moustaches drawn on them, or Swastika armbands, but they were just normal gnomes like you would see in any posh garden.

"What do you think?" Sally asked, looking up at the rear of the house.

Stiggy followed her gaze. "About what?"

"That window up there, you think you can get through it?"

She pointed at a small window upstairs that had been left open a couple of inches. A drainpipe ran down the wall beside it.

"Why?" Stiggy asked.

"To get inside, of course."

"Can't we just go through the front door like normal people?"

"I don't have a key."

"Why not?"

Sally shrugged. "I just don't. Joe never gave me one."

"So what do you do while he's out at work?"

"I stay in until he gets back."

Stiggy sighed and shook his head. Nothing about that relationship made any sense. He walked over to the drainpipe and tugged on it. The last thing he wanted was for it to come away from the wall when he was half way up it. It seemed to be firmly attached, so he reached up and gripped it with both hands, then put his foot to the lowest anchoring point and hefted himself up. He climbed steadily up until he reached the window, then reached inside to unlatch it. He pulled it wide open and climbed through.

He found himself in a small bathroom with a pale blue linoleum floor. A toilet stood beside the bath, with a fluffy red cover over its seat. Next to it was an upright sink plunger, with several toilet rolls stacked up along the shaft of its wooden handle. Someone had drawn a little smiley face on top of the handle with a black marker pen. A mirrored cabinet hung on the wall above the sink, while a rack attached to the red door opposite contained a row of fresh clean towels. It all looked neat and tidy, apart from the muddy footprints he'd made on the windowsill climbing in, and the room smelled of lavender.

Stiggy opened the bathroom door, and noticed a glazed ceramic tile hanging on a nail on the other side. It showed a painting of a chimpanzee sitting on a toilet; in one hand the monkey held a peeled banana, in the other the toilet's flush chain handle, ready to pull it. Two red doors stood across the short landing. Both were closed. To Stiggy's right, plush red carpeted stairs led down to ground level. He crept down them cautiously, in case anyone was lurking downstairs, and winced each time they creaked under his weight.

In the hallway hung a framed photograph of an old scooter

with twin seats. Red and white in colour, it stood before a peeling brick wall bearing the spray-painted slogan *Spirit of 69*. Stiggy turned left and walked through the small kitchen to the back door, then unlatched it and pulled it open. Sally brushed past him and ran upstairs.

Stiggy watched her go, then closed the door and followed her. When he reached the top of the stairs she was already in the front bedroom. She pulled a small suitcase off the top of a wardrobe and put it down on a double bed with a plump brown duvet covering it. Stiggy walked over while she thumbed the clasps and lifted the suitcase lid. He looked around the bedroom. More photos of scooters on the walls. An empty pint glass on a bedside cabinet, next to a packet of condoms and a jar of Vaseline.

Propped up against the cabinet stood a wooden pole with a rubber grip on one end. Stiggy walked over and inspected it. The thirty-six inch long, three inch diameter shaft was pitted with small indentations, a bit like teeth marks. The end opposite the rubber grip tapered into a rectangular wedge shape, where Stiggy assumed something would be slotted onto it. Like an axe head, the type used for chopping down trees, or a pickaxe, used for digging up hard surfaces.

Sally pulled shirts, jeans and short skirts from the wardrobe, folded them, and put them in the suitcase. When it was full she crouched down and pulled out a drawer at the foot of the wardrobe containing pornographic magazines with foreign titles and lay it down on the carpet. The nude models on the covers looked very young, and all had small breasts and shaved pubic regions. Sally reached into the slot where the drawer had been, groped around at the back of the wardrobe, and took out a Boots brand C90 cassette tape with the phrase *For Sally* scrawled on the label in black felt tip pen.

"What's on that?" Stiggy asked.

"Some songs Trisha taped for me when I first moved in here." She tossed the tape into the suitcase and replaced the drawer.

"Why did you need to hide it?"

"Joe doesn't know I've got it, he'd go mental if he found out."

"Why, what sort of songs are they?"

"It's the old ska and reggae ones we used to listen to in her room, back at the home. You know, the ones I told you about last night? Joe hates it, he says it's music for ... well, you know. Coloured people."

"Oh, okay."

"Have you got something I could play it on at yours?"

"Yeah, I guess." It sounded crap, but Stiggy would give it a go. He'd recently borrowed a record by a hippy band called *The Astronauts* and had been surprised at how much he liked it once he got used to the weird sound and the violins.

Sally closed the suitcase and lifted it from the bed. "This is everything I need," she said, walking to the door. "We can go now."

"Can I use your toilet first?" Stiggy said, then felt foolish for asking such a stupid question.

"Yeah, okay. I'll wait downstairs."

Stiggy returned to the bathroom and locked the door behind him, a habit he'd gotten into while he lived with his parents, and something he still did at his flat, even though he lived there alone. He dropped his trousers and underpants, and sat down on the fluffy cover. Usually he would take something with him to read while he had his morning shit, either that week's *2000AD* or one of the music papers, but there was nothing to read in there so he just stared at the wall while he did his business.

He had just finished when a door slammed downstairs. Stiggy worried it might be Sally leaving without him, and hurriedly wiped his arse and rose from the toilet. He was about to flush it when he heard a gruff male voice downstairs.

"So you've come crawling back then, have you? Well you know what you get now, don't you, you fucking slag!"

There was no mistaking that voice. It was the massive skinhead, back home early from work. And Stiggy was trapped upstairs with nowhere to go.

5

Stiggy unlocked the bathroom door as quietly as he could and opened it a small crack so he could hear better what was going on downstairs.

"Joe, what are you doing here?" Sally's voice seemed a pitch higher than usual.

"I fucking live here, don't I?" Joe yelled. "More to the fucking point, what are you doing here and where the fuck did you go last night?"

"Nowhere, honest. I just walked around for a bit, that's all. Then I came back here, but the front door was locked. I thought the coppers must've got you, so I went round to Trisha's instead."

There was a loud slap and Sally cried out.

"You fucking liar! You were off shagging that punk bastard, weren't you?"

Another slap. Sally sobbed.

Stiggy clenched his fists and ground his teeth. The fucking cunt was hitting her again! He pulled open the bathroom door and paused in the doorway. He had to do something about it. But what? The guy was fucking massive, he'd stand no chance against him. Not unless he had a weapon to even the score.

"I saw you with him, remember?" Joe shouted. "I saw what you did, and I know you went off with him while I weren't looking."

"Nothing happened, Joe, honest. He went home, I went to Trisha's"

Stiggy looked at the sink plunger beside the toilet, and immediately discarded it. Too small, he'd never get close enough with it.

"You fucking liar! I went round to that slag's place this morning, she swore blind she hadn't seen you for months. And she wouldn't fucking dare lie to me again."

"I'm sorry Joe. I didn't mean to do it, honest. It wasn't me, it was that punk. He made me do it, I had no choice."

"Yeah right, and I suppose he fucking raped you too? No, of course he didn't, you just opened up your rancid cunt for him, didn't you? You fucking slag. So where is he now? Hiding somewhere?"

A few seconds of silence, followed by another slap and another cry from Sally. Stiggy stepped out of the bathroom and onto the landing. Fuck, he had to do something soon before it was too late. He edged toward the stairs, trying to pluck up the courage to descend. Then he remembered the axe handle in the bedroom.

"Are you fucking deaf?" Joe yelled. "I said where is he? I'll fucking castrate the bastard! Nobody fucks my bird and gets away with it."

Sally mumbled something between sobs that Stiggy couldn't make out. Had she told the skinhead he was upstairs, hiding in the bathroom? He wouldn't blame her if she had, but that would mean Joe would be heading upstairs to get him in a matter of seconds. He crept into the bedroom, hoping none of the floorboards would creak, and picked up the solid wooden handle.

A door slammed back on its hinges downstairs.

"If you've been fucking him in my bed I'll kill the both of you."

Stiggy made his way back to the stairs and stood behind the banister. He raised the axe handle over his shoulder and waited, ready to send the bald bastard tumbling back downstairs as soon as his ugly mug appeared.

Another door slammed.

"What the fuck's this? Where the fuck do you think you're going with that?"

"Nowhere, honest, Joe."

"Well why is it here then?"

"It's ... your dirty washing. I was going to take it to the laundrette for you."

The clasps of the suitcase clunked open. "You fucking lying bitch!" Joe screamed. "It's all your fucking shit in here!" The suitcase hit the floor with a dull thud. "You're running off again, aren't you? With that fucking punk bastard, this time!"

"No, Joe, honest. I haven't seen him since the concert last night, and I don't know where he is now. And I didn't fuck him, I wouldn't do that to you."

"You think I'm fucking stupid? He's waiting outside, isn't he? Hiding in the garden like a fucking coward. Well he's welcome to you, I've had enough of you and your bullshit. If you want to go you can fucking go. But don't expect me to carry on paying for you, and you're not taking any of my stuff with you. And that includes this."

Something ripped. Sally cried out.

"One other thing before you go," Joe said. "You're going to fucking pay for showing me up in front of my mates last night. Now get in there."

"No Joe! Please! Don't! I'm sorry! I'll stay with you! Just please don't do that again!"

"Shut up, you fucking slag. You've brought this on yourself, and you know it."

Stiggy had heard enough. Whatever Joe was up to now, it had Sally absolutely terrified — he could tell from the hysteria in her voice. He tiptoed downstairs, avoiding the steps that creaked, and paused halfway down to listen. Sally's crumpled clothes littered the hallway. The open suitcase lay upside down near the front door. The cassette lay in tiny pieces, ground into the carpet. Tape spooled out from it like curly brown hair.

An ear-splitting scream came from downstairs. Stiggy raised the wooden handle over his shoulder and hurried down the rest of the stairs, not caring how much noise he made. He peered through the half-open living room door, and what he saw inside made his blood run cold.

Joe, dressed in the same *Rock Against Communism* T-shirt and bleached jeans he had been wearing the night before at the Cockney Upstarts gig, held Sally bent over the arm of a leather couch with one hand clasped around the back of her neck. Her back was bare and bloody, the pale green plaid shirt she wore little more than rags hanging from her shoulders. Joe raised a doubled-over leather belt and swung it down with a grunt. The metal buckle slammed into Sally's back and she screamed once again as she convulsed in agony.

"You fucking slag, showing me up in front of my mates like that!" Joe's face was a mask of pure rage as he raised the belt once more.

Stiggy kicked open the door and ran into the living room with a roar. Joe turned to face him with a confused look just before the axe handle smacked into the side of his head with a dull thud that sent shockwaves up Stiggy's arms. The skinhead's eyes bulged as they locked onto Stiggy.

"You! You fucking ..."

Joe swayed on his feet. His eyes seemed to gloss over as they continued to stare at Stiggy. Then he stumbled back a couple of steps before toppling face first into a smoked-glass coffee table with a deafening crash. Glass shards flew into the air and thudded down onto the cream shag pile carpet around him. Joe moaned and pushed himself up from the table frame with his fists. He raised his head and glared at Stiggy. Blood dripped down his face from dozens of tiny slithers of brown glass embedded in it. Then he let out a rasping sigh and rolled onto his back to stare up at the ceiling. Blood continued to pour from the cuts to his face and soaked into the carpet around his head, staining it a dark crimson colour. His eyelids flickered and then closed. Stiggy lowered his weapon and turned his attention to Sally.

She lay slumped over the arm of the couch like a rag doll, tears streaming from her eyes. Her shoulders jerked with hitching sobs. Her bare legs glistened with wetness, and Stiggy caught a whiff of urine coming from them. His heart went out to her. The poor girl had been so scared by the ordeal she had pissed herself. Her back was a bloody mess. Along with the fresh, weeping wounds Joe had just inflicted on her with the belt were a criss-cross of old scars; some faded with time, others much more recent. A lump grew in Stiggy's throat as he stared at them in horror. Fuck. No wonder she wanted to get away from the bastard. How long had that been going on for?

"Sal—?" Stiggy's voice hitched with emotion. He cleared his throat and tried again. "Sally ... it's okay, he can't hurt you anymore."

He walked over and placed a hand on Sally's shoulder. She flinched away from him and cried out. Stiggy stepped back, his palms raised to reassure her, even though she wasn't even looking in his direction.

"Sally, it's okay. It's just me. Stiggy." He glanced at Joe to make sure he wasn't about to get up again, then went into the hallway and picked up one of Sally's crumpled shirts from the floor. She flinched again when he draped it over her shoulders. Dots of blood seeped through the thin material.

"Sally, it's over. He can't hurt you again. But we need to get going before he wakes up. Do you understand? We need to go, right now."

After what seemed like ages, Sally rose up and turned to face Stiggy. A swollen purple bruise over her left eye forced it shut. Snot poured from her nose and dripped from her lips onto her exposed breasts. Tears still rolled down her ashen cheeks, and her bottom lip trembled. With shaking hands she drew the shirt around herself and held it in place with her arms folded over her chest. She looked beyond Stiggy at Joe and her one good eye widened. She whimpered and drew back.

The hairs on the back of Stiggy's neck prickled. He spun in

alarm and raised the wooden club to strike out at the skinhead he felt sure was looming up on him. But Joe still lay on the floor where he had fallen, unmoving except for the gentle rise and fall of his chest.

"It's okay," Stiggy said. He lowered the axe handle and turned back to Sally. "He can't hurt you now. It's over."

"No it isn't!" Sally screamed. "It will never be over!"

Sally's shirt flapped open to reveal her breasts again as she reached out and snatched the wooden handle from Stiggy. Before he could react she raised it above her head in both hands and brought it crashing down into Joe's face with an animalistic grunt. His nose disintegrated into a bloody mess of skin, cartilage and gristle as it splattered across his face. His eyes shot open. His hands flew up to protect himself when Sally raised the wooden pole once more, but he wasn't quick enough. She swore as she swung it down into his mouth with a sickening crunch. Joe let out a gurgling rasp. His head lolled to one side. Blood and broken teeth dribbled from between his pulverised lips. His fists clenched and unclenched by his sides.

"You fucking bitch," he said in a feeble, choking voice. "I'm going to fucking kill you."

"No you're not!" Sally screamed.

She raised the wooden shaft and swung it down with another grunt. Joe's right eye flew from its socket with the impact, and flopped down against what was left of his nose, held in place by stringy tendons. But Sally still wasn't finished. Stiggy watched in open-mouthed horror as she raised the weapon once more. This time it landed with a wet squelch, and seemed to disappear deep into Joe's skull. Blood and gore splattered up and showered Sally's face and chest. Joe's body shuddered, then lay still. Sally stood over him panting with exertion for long seconds, then dropped the axe handle and fell to her knees in a pool of blood and sobbed into her hands.

Stiggy stared down at Joe's body. There was no doubt in his mind the skinhead was dead; nobody could survive injuries like that. The side of his head had caved in, and there were bits of pinkish-grey brain matter seeping out of it. His right eye still hung down from what was left of its socket. It seemed to stare back at Stiggy accusingly, and he found it impossible to look away.

What the fuck had Sally just done?

And more to the point, what the fuck was he supposed to do now?

6

Stiggy paced the room, trying not to look down at Joe's corpse. At the shattered skull and the pink mush seeping out of it. All the blood soaking into the cream carpet. At the eye that he knew was still staring at him as if it was all his fault. He didn't notice he was leaving a trail of bloody footprints all over the cream carpet, and couldn't hear the broken glass crunching beneath his trainers over the sound of Sally's constant sobbing.

Every instinct told him to run, to get the fuck out of there and not look back. This was Sally's mess, not his. Jesus fucking Christ, she'd gone and killed him. And Stiggy had struck the first blow, so that made him just as guilty as she was. Especially with his fingerprints all over the murder weapon. Fuck! He'd get twenty-five years, minimum, for his part in it. He'd be an old man in his forties before they let him out.

If they ever did.

He went over it all in his mind. If he hadn't spent so long in the toilet him and Sally would have been gone before Joe arrived. If he hadn't knocked Joe out, Sally wouldn't have been able to finish him off the way she did. The skinhead had already said he would let her go after she took her beating, so maybe Stiggy should have just stayed upstairs and let him get it over with.

But no, Stiggy wasn't like that. He'd been brought up knowing you should never hit a girl, no matter what the provocation. He couldn't just stand back and do nothing while Joe beat her like that. He'd made the right decision to intervene, and what happened to the bastard as a result was his own fault. He got what he deserved, that's all.

But that didn't mean the police would see it the same way. They would twist everything, that's what coppers always did. Make everything look far worse than it really was. Not that it would be difficult in this case. Fuck. Why did Sally have to go and do that? They could've just legged it while Joe was unconscious, then everything would've been okay. Once they were safe at his flat in Doncaster there would be no way the bald-headed bastard could ever find her.

Stiggy stopped pacing and looked down at Sally, torn over what to do for the best. She was still kneeling beside Joe's body in a pool of blood, sobbing into her hands while more blood dribbled down her arms. Talk about being caught red handed. The coppers would make mincemeat out of her if they saw her in that state, and there was no telling what she might say to them. Stiggy couldn't risk that happening, couldn't risk them finding out about his part in all this. He had to get her away from there, it was the only option. Besides, Sally was the real victim, not that skinhead bastard. What he'd been doing to her when Stiggy came downstairs ... nobody should have to go through that. Ever.

"Sally," he said softly. "Sally, we can't stay here. You know that, right?"

Sally didn't seem to hear him, so he called out her name a little louder. She looked up. Joe's blood was smeared across her face. Her good eye was wide and staring, the other clamped shut by a huge purple swelling.

"Oh God, what have I done?" she said. She looked down at Joe's body and recoiled. "We need to phone an ambulance."

Stiggy shook his head. "It's too late for that. He's dead."

"The police, then."

"We can't do that, either."

"But if we tell them what happened, what he did to me ..."

"They won't believe us. Coppers never do."

"But it was self defence. You saw what happened, right? He said he was going to kill me."

"Sally, none of that matters because we can't prove it. If we get caught here, with ..." Stiggy gestured at Joe's corpse with his hand. "... well, we just can't be here when the coppers come, okay? We have to go. Stick to the plan, yeah? Go back to my flat and stay there. Nobody knows we've been here, so—"

"Dave knows we were coming here."

"Shit!" With all that had happened, Stiggy had forgotten all about the young skinhead on the playing field. "Would he say anything to the coppers?"

"I don't think so."

"You don't *think* so?"

"I've known him for years, and he's always looked out for me before."

Stiggy pointed at Joe's body. "He didn't do anything about what that cunt was doing to you though, did he?"

Sally sniffed. "Only because he didn't know."

"You never told him? For fuck's sake Sally, why not?"

"Because then Dave would've gone for Joe, and Joe would've put him in hospital, or worse. After what Joe did to Trisha, I didn't want that to happen to anyone else."

"Why, what did he do to Trisha?"

Sally let out a sob. "He ... he slashed her face up. I told her what Joe was doing to me, and she made me stay at her bedsit. Only Joe found out where I was, didn't he? And he said if I told anyone else he would do the same to them."

"Christ." Stiggy shook his head. "Why didn't you go to the coppers, tell them what he'd done to you and Trisha?"

"It wasn't that simple."

"Why not?"

Sally shrugged. "It doesn't really matter now, does it?"

"No, I guess not. So what was that stuff Dave was saying about you only having eight months left?"

"Nothing. He ..." Sally looked away and shook her head. "Well, you know. It was just ... a joke, I guess."

Stiggy frowned. "Right, okay." It didn't sound to him like Dave was joking about anything, but it was obvious Sally didn't want to discuss it any further, and there were more pressing matters to attend to anyway. "Well, nobody else knows we've been here apart from that Dave geezer, right? So if we just fuck off out of here, then the coppers won't be able to pin it on us, will they?"

"What about fingerprints? I got done for shoplifting a couple of years ago, so they'll have them on file. They'll know it was me."

"Sally, you live here. It's obvious your fingerprints will be everywhere."

"Not officially, I don't."

"What? What do you mean, not officially?"

Sally looked down at the floor. "Nothing, forget I said it. It doesn't matter."

"Right, well, whatever. If the coppers come asking, you were with me all last night, yeah? And that woman in the cafe, she'll remember us from this morning, so there's nothing to say you've been here since, is there? Well except for that Dave, but he won't say anything, right? So it's going to be okay, yeah?"

Sally nodded. She sniffed, then wiped her nose with the back of her hand, but all she succeeded in doing was smearing snot and blood across her cheek. Stiggy held out a hand to help her to her feet. She gripped his hand and he grimaced at the warm, sticky texture of the blood coating it.

"You need to get cleaned up before we go," Stiggy said. "Have a shower or something. I'll sort everything out down here."

Sally looked down at her bloody breasts, then drew the shirt around herself to cover them up. It was hard to tell with all the blood on her face, but Stiggy thought she might have blushed just before she turned away and headed for the living room door. He followed her into the kitchen, where she washed her hands and face in the sink before heading upstairs. Stiggy found a roll of black plastic bin liners in a cupboard under the sink. He tore one off while the sound of running water came from the bathroom.

Back in the living room, Stiggy picked up the blood-stained axe handle and dropped it inside the bin liner. The remains of Sally's torn shirt followed it, then he looked around for the leather belt. What was a skinhead doing with a belt anyway? They always wore braces, not belts. It made no sense, but he didn't have time to worry about that. He found the belt near where Joe lay, and dropped it into the bin liner before looking around the room for any other evidence of his and Sally's presence.

The carpet under the arm of the couch was sodden with Sally's piss, but there wasn't anything he could do about that. Or the bloody footprints he had made on the carpet himself. He wondered briefly if it was possible to trace someone from things like that, but it was a chance he would have to take. He got a damp dish cloth from the kitchen and wiped down every surface he could remember touching. After a final look around the living room, he used the dish cloth to close the door behind him and dropped it into the bag with the other evidence.

In the hallway he gathered up the rest of Sally's scattered clothes, stuffed them back in the suitcase, and left it by the front door. He picked up the spool of cassette tape and the fragments of broken casing and dropped them into the front right pocket of his combat trousers. As he did so he noticed a black Crombie coat with red lining hanging on a coat hook near the stairs, and walked over to investigate it. In the pockets he found a pewter Swastika keyring with three keys, and a bulging brown leather wallet with the initials JH stamped on it in gold lettering. He took out the wallet and opened it. Along with a photograph of an old, grey-haired woman, there was more money than Stiggy had ever seen before, well over four hundred quid in crisp five, ten and twenty pound notes fresh from the bank. He wondered where the skinhead had got it all from while he stuffed the wallet into his back pocket. No point leaving that for the coppers to find, when he could put it to good use.

"Sally, are you ready to go yet?" he called out from the bottom of the stairs.

"Nearly." The reply was muffled, and accompanied by splashing water.

"Hurry up, yeah? We need to go before anyone comes."

Stiggy paced the hallway while he waited. This was taking too long. Someone could come at any minute and catch them there. One of the neighbours might have heard something, they could be on their way to investigate right now. Or maybe they called the police instead. He checked the front and back doors were both locked, then went back into the living room and closed the curtains so nobody peering through the windows would see Joe's bloody corpse lying on the carpet. When he returned to the hallway Sally still hadn't come downstairs, so he went up to see what was taking her so long.

"Sally?"

"In here."

Stiggy pushed open the bathroom door with his foot, after wiping the handle with his T-shirt. Sally sat upright in six inches of pinkish-red water in the bath, scrubbing her legs with a green sponge.

"Shit, sorry," Stiggy said. His cheeks flushed red as he looked away.

A fresh pile of clothes lay on top of the fluffy toilet lid, while Sally's blood-stained denim skirt and the shirt he had wrapped around her shoulders lay in a heap on the pale blue linoleum flooring underneath the sink. Her boots, also covered in blood, stood next to the toilet.

"Can you pass me a towel?" Sally asked.

Stiggy pulled a towel from the rack on the back of the door and held it out for her, trying not to look at her naked body as she rose up from the bath and took it from him. She wrapped it around herself, stepped out into the cramped space, and turned her back on him while she rubbed herself dry. Spots of blood seeped through the towel.

"Shit, Sally, are you okay?" Stiggy asked. "Your back's still bleeding."

Sally glanced over her shoulder. "Can you fix it up for me?"

"Um ... yeah, okay. What do I need to do?"

Sally pointed. "There's some antiseptic and stuff in there."

Stiggy turned to the cabinet above the sink Sally had indicated and yanked it open. Bottles and toothbrushes clattered into the sink. On one of the shelves he found a half-empty box of Elastoplast and a tube of Germolene that had been squeezed from the middle. There was also a bottle of TCP, a roll of muslin bandage, a bottle of painkillers, and a bag of cotton wool balls. Whoever stocked that cabinet had obviously planned in advance for situations like this, and that made Stiggy seethe with rage as he grabbed the cotton wool balls and TCP and turned back to Sally.

She stood facing the bathroom wall with the towel held around her waist, her scarred back exposed. Drops of blood formed around the fresh wounds, and Stiggy felt a fresh wave of anger as he watched them join together and dribble down her spine. What sort of evil bastard would do something like that to a defenceless girl? His hands shook as he screwed the lid off the TCP bottle and dabbed some of the liquid onto a cotton wool ball. He reached out and pressed it against her back. Sally winced and cried out.

"Shit, sorry." He pulled the cotton wool ball away.

"It's okay," Sally replied. "It needs to be done."

"How long has he been doing this to you?"

"Does it matter?"

"Well, yeah. Some of these scars look pretty old, so ..."

"Two years," Sally said. "It started soon after I moved in with him."

"Fuck. Why didn't you tell the coppers? They could've locked him up and put a stop to it."

"It's not that simple."

"You keep saying that, but what does it mean?"

"Nothing, it doesn't matter. Anyway, I deserved it."

"What? Fuck off, nobody deserves this."

"Yeah well, you don't know what I did."

"I don't care what you did, there's no excuse for this."

"I could've wrecked everything. No wonder he got so mad."

"What do you mean?" Stiggy asked, but Sally didn't reply. She just stared at the wall while he continued cleaning the wounds on her back as best he could. After he finished he handed her the muslin bandage to wrap around herself, and went back downstairs. He took all the medical supplies he could find with him and put them in the suitcase, knowing he would need them over the next few days to stop those wounds from going septic.

Sally joined him a few minutes later in a white polo shirt with black and red stripes around the neck and sleeves, and a small black wreath design embroidered over the left breast. She'd swapped the denim skirt for a pair of bleached jeans with the bottoms turned up to show off her Doc Marten boots, which had been wiped clean of blood and still glistened with wetness. Stiggy wasn't sure if the red braces hanging from her hips were the same ones from earlier, or if they were a different pair.

"What did you do with your other clothes?" Stiggy asked.

"I left them upstairs in the bathroom."

"Okay, wait here and I'll go and get them."

Stiggy picked up the bin liner and took it upstairs into the bathroom. He used his fingertips to pick up Sally's discarded clothes from under the sink, being careful not to get any blood on himself, and dropped them in the black bag. There was a bloodstain on the linoleum flooring where the clothes had lain, and he mopped it up with the bath sponge. He spotted his muddy footprints on the windowsill and wiped those away too, before turning his attention to the bath. A red tide mark coated the sides of it, along with a trail of red along the bottom that led to the plug hole. Stiggy turned on both taps and used the sponge to rinse the last of the blood away. Finally satisfied there was nothing left for coppers to find, he dropped the sponge in the bin liner, washed his hands, and went back downstairs.

"Do you know how to drive?" Sally asked.

"Um ... I dunno. Yeah, sort of, I guess. I went joyriding with my mates a few times when I was twelve, I had a go at it then, so I know basically how to do it, but that was years ago. Why do you ask?"

"Joe's van will be out the front, I thought maybe we could go in that."

Stiggy remembered the Swastika keyring he saw in the skinhead's coat pocket and went to get it. It was a good idea to use the van, it would be quicker than walking into town and getting the train. Safer, too, than carrying around a bin liner full of torn and bloody clothes and a pickaxe handle covered in someone's brains. Plus a van outside would advertise Joe's presence in the house if any of his skinhead mates called round. If it wasn't there they would just assume he was out somewhere, beating up ethnic minorities or whatever it was he did in his spare time. And with a bit of luck, he and Sally would be long gone before anyone discovered Joe's body and raised the alarm.

Stiggy opened the front door and checked none of the neighbours were watching before he stepped out with the bin liner. Sally followed with the suitcase and closed the door behind her. A white transit van bearing the insignia *Hawkins Landscaping Services, no job too small* stood on the road outside.

"What's landscaping?" Stiggy asked as he walked up to it.

"It's a posh way of saying gardening," Sally said. "He looks after the gardens at the care home I ... *used to* live at, that's how I met him."

"How old were you at the time?"

Sally shrugged and looked away.

Stiggy unlocked the back of the van and pulled the door open. It was full of expensive-looking gardening equipment — a petrol lawnmower, electric hedge cutters, a jumble of rakes and spades, and a few more specialised items he didn't recognise. He tossed the black bin liner inside and slammed the door, then unlocked the passenger side for Sally to get in with the suitcase.

"Wait here," he said.

Sally looked at him sharply. "Where are you going?"

"There's something I need to do before we go, I'll just be a minute."

Stiggy went back through the gate and round the side of the house into the back garden. He used his handkerchief to pick up one of the gnomes and hefted it through the downstairs window. The glass shattered with an almighty crash. Somewhere nearby a dog barked, setting off the rest of the dogs in the neighbourhood. Stiggy ran back to the van and climbed into the driver seat.

"What did you do that for?" Sally asked.

"To make it look like a burglary."

Stiggy put the key in the ignition and twisted it, then revved the engine when it rumbled into life. He ground it into first gear and took his foot off the clutch. The van shot forward, jerking them both back in their seats, then stalled abruptly and threw them forward again. Something in the back tumbled with a clatter. Sally cried out in pain. Stiggy shot her a quizzical glance, then realised what had happened. The sudden jar to her injured back must have been excruciating.

"Shit, sorry," he said as he depressed the clutch and restarted the engine. "I'll be more careful from now on."

"Are you sure you know how to drive?" Sally winced as she leaned forward and gripped the front edge of the seat.

Stiggy let out the clutch more slowly this time, and the van rolled forward. "Yeah, but like I said, it was years ago now, and I only did it a few times. I guess I just need a bit more practice."

Stiggy kept to first and second gear while he weaved his way through the council estate roads and got used to the way the van handled. He misjudged a junction and the front left wheel bounced up onto the kerb, then back down again. Sally bounced with it, gripping the front of the seat tight. By the time he reached the main road Stiggy felt more confident and moved up to third gear, being careful to stick to the thirty mile per hour speed limit as he peered at the road signs and tried to get his bearings. He found his way onto a dual carriageway leading to Rotherham and accelerated up to forty as he drove down it.

Then a flashing blue light in the rear view mirror caught his attention.

"Fuck!"

"What is it?" Sally asked. Her mouth dropped open when she saw the police car pulling alongside the van. The officer in the passenger seat gestured for Stiggy to pull over. Sally slumped back in the seat and swore. "They've found Joe's body, haven't they? And they know we did it."

Stiggy shook his head. "No, it's too soon for that, it must be something else. Let me do the talking, yeah?"

Sally gaped at him. "You're not going to stop, are you?"

"I'll have to, there's no way we could outrun them in this. Not on a straight road, anyway."

Stiggy brought the transit van to a halt. The police car overtook and parked in front at an angle, blocking any escape attempt. An officer stepped out of the passenger side and swaggered up to the driver's side of the van with a cocky leer on his face. The other stayed behind the wheel and spoke into a radio. Stiggy wound down the window as the policeman approached, then gripped the steering wheel tight to stop his hands shaking. Sally turned away and stared out of the passenger side window, hiding her bruised face from the copper's direct line of sight.

"Can you switch off the engine, please?"

Stiggy twisted the key and regained his grip on the steering wheel. The van fell silent, save for an occasional *tink* from the engine as it cooled down.

"Is this your vehicle ..." the policeman paused, then added with a surly voice as he stared down at Stiggy: "*Sir?*"

Stiggy cleared his throat and swallowed before replying. "Yeah, why?"

"Do you know why I have stopped you?"

Stiggy shook his head.

"Your nearside brake light isn't working. Were you aware of this fault?"

Stiggy let out an involuntary sigh. He almost laughed, and just managed to stop himself in time. "No, I wasn't, honest. It was okay yesterday, so it must have only just stopped working."

"I see. Do you have your documents with you?"

"Um ... I don't know, maybe."

Stiggy opened the glove compartment and rummaged around inside. He found the van's log book, Joe's driving license, and what looked like an insurance document and passed them all through the window. The policeman took them without taking his eyes off Stiggy.

"Can you verify your name and address for me?"

"Um ... you what?"

"Your name and address. Can you verify them for me?"

"Joseph Hawkins," Sally said, without looking away from the window. "Forty-two Morgan Avenue, Sheffield."

The policeman glared at the back of her head. "I wasn't asking you, I was asking the driver."

"Joseph Hawkins," Stiggy said. "Forty-two —"

The policeman held up a hand and interrupted. "Never mind." He glanced down at the documents, passed them back to Stiggy, and said: "Do you have any other form of identification with you, Mr Hawkins?"

"Like what?"

"Passport, trade union card, library card, utility bill?"

"No, those are all at home."

"I see. Can you both step out of the vehicle, please?"

"What for?" Stiggy asked.

"Because I've told you to."

Stiggy frowned. Was all this fuss normal for a broken light, or did the copper suspect something? Was there something in his or Sally's behaviour that gave them away, or was he just being paranoid? He glanced at Sally and shrugged. It wasn't like either of them had a choice. Even if they could get past the patrol car and outrun it, the copper would reach through the window and grab him before he even managed to twist the key in the ignition.

Sally opened the passenger door, climbed out, and stood beside the van, looking down at the pavement. Stiggy sighed and joined her.

"Been in a fight, have we?" the officer asked, looking them both up and down. "Anything to do with what happened at The Marples last night?"

Stiggy gaped at him. Shit, with everything that had happened at Joe's house, he'd forgotten all about the *Cockney Upstarts* gig. No wonder the copper had taken so much interest in a punk and a skinhead travelling together. Especially with the state of Sally's face. But what was the worst they could do? Arrest them for being beaten up? They would need to prove they were there first, and Stiggy certainly wasn't going to confirm it for them.

"Don't know what you're on about," he said, "we were both at home last night."

A sneer crossed the policeman's face. "Then how do you account for the state of your girlfriend? Walk into a door, did she?"

"I did, actually," Sally said.

"I see. And your name is?"

"Sally Carter."

The cop took out a notebook and wrote in it. "Well, Miss

Carter, I'm not satisfied with your answer, so you will need to accompany me to the station for further questioning." He turned his attention to Stiggy, his eyes flicking down to the large *Crass* logo on the front of his T-shirt before they settled on his face. "But before we do that, maybe you can tell me what you have got in the back of the van?"

A shiver ran down Stiggy's spine when he thought about the pickaxe handle with bits of Joe's brain stuck to it. The one with both his and Sally's fingerprints all over it.

"Um ... nothing. Just gardening stuff, that's all."

"Well you won't mind if I take a look then, will you?"

"Um ... no, I guess not."

Stiggy glanced at Sally. Should they run, or would that just make it worse? He hadn't put any thought into hiding that bag of evidence when he slung it in the back of the van, and couldn't remember if it had landed behind any of the equipment already in there or not. And if the copper saw it, would he want to look inside?

With a feeling of dread, Stiggy retrieved the keys from the ignition and walked around to the back of the van. The police officer followed him, and stood a few paces back with one hand covering his truncheon. Stiggy's hand shook as he inserted the key into the rear door and twisted it. He pulled open the door, fearing the worst, and looked inside. The black polythene bag lay near the centre, the knot he'd tied in the top of it clearly visible between a lawnmower and a petrol chainsaw. No way could the copper miss it. Any second now he would reach in and pull it out, tear it open to see what was inside. And all that effort Stiggy had gone to in covering their tracks back at Joe's house would be for nothing. All because of a fucking broken brake light.

The policeman grunted. "Thank you, you can close it now."

Stiggy exhaled audibly, realising he had been holding his breath the entire time the copper had been peering over his shoulder. He slammed the door and reached for the keys. But before he could take them from the lock, the police officer held up a hand to stop him.

"Just a minute, sir." He lifted the pewter Swastika hanging from the bunch of keys and turned it over in his fingers so it faced the right way. "Is this yours?"

Stiggy groaned inwardly. If he denied it was his, the copper would want to know why he had it and whose keys they were. Whereas if he confirmed it, everyone at the station would think he was a Nazi and it would probably earn him an extra kicking in the cells as a result. So he was fucked either way. He scratched the back of his head and nodded. Doing anything else would just cause further suspicion, and the last thing he wanted was a more thorough search of the van's contents.

The policeman locked eyes with him, nodded once, then stepped back. "I see. Well good day to you, sir. Make sure you get that brake light fixed at your earliest convenience. And drive carefully."

"Um ... yeah. Yeah, I will. Um ... thanks."

Stiggy watched the uniformed man return to the police car and climb inside. The car drove away, leaving him wondering what the fuck had just happened. Why had the copper just changed his mind about taking them both in for questioning?

* * *

Stiggy manoeuvred around his neighbour's three-wheeled motorcycle and parked outside the dilapidated mid-terrace house on Broxholme Lane that contained his ground floor flat. Sally peered out of the passenger window at the broken down washing machine someone had dumped in the concreted over front yard several months ago, while Stiggy kept an eye on Doris as she picked up her rucksack and wandered over to the van.

"Are you looking for business?" she asked.

Stiggy's cheeks flushed as he shook his head. Doris pulled a face and returned to her regular pitch on the corner of nearby Glynn Avenue. Stiggy wondered if she attracted many customers this early in the day, or if she was only there because she had nothing better to do. She wasn't as pretty as the other working girls who hung around Doncaster's red light district, and at thirty-five years of age she was by far the oldest of them all, but what she lacked in looks she certainly made up for in enthusiasm and experience.

"Who's that?" Sally asked.

"Um ... you what?" Stiggy realised he had been smiling to himself while he continued staring at Doris. He shook his head to clear the memory from his mind. "Um ... nobody. Come on, let's go inside. I'm gasping for a drink."

Sally picked up the suitcase and climbed out of the van. When Stiggy joined her on the pavement he found her staring at the motorcycle.

"Whose is that?" she asked.

"My neighbour, John. He's a good bloke, you'll like him."

Sally frowned. "Not if he's a Hells Angel, I won't."

"How come?"

"Because they are always beating skins up. Everyone knows that."

Stiggy shook his head. "Nah, John's not like that, he wouldn't hurt anyone. In fact one time me and my mates were getting a load of hassle from a bunch of bikers outside this pub they all drink in, and he came out and told them to leave us alone. They haven't bothered us since."

Stiggy took out his house keys and headed for the front door. One of the other tenants had left it on the latch when they went out, something that always irritated him. It was like they were just asking to be burgled or something. He waited for Sally to join him in the hallway, then thumbed the knob on the Yale lock before he closed the door behind them. Two doors, both made of cheap plywood with an even cheaper mortice lock as their only means of defence against intruders, stood on the right hand side. Stiggy directed Sally to the door at the far end of the hallway, next to an uncarpeted wooden stairway leading up, and unlocked it.

Sally sniffed as she walked into the flat. Stiggy caught a whiff of stale glue masking the smell of damp and decay coming from the living room. It was funny he'd never noticed it before, but maybe that was because he'd never been away from it for so long. He flicked a switch beside the door and the single bare 40 watt light bulb hanging from the ceiling cast a dim light over the squalid interior.

"Coffee?" he asked.

Sally shook her head. "I'd rather have a cup of tea, if that's okay?"

"Yeah, no worries."

Stiggy headed past the sideboard containing his stereo system and a jumble of records and tapes, and down a couple of stone steps into the adjoining kitchen. He filled two mugs with cold water, poured them into a kettle, and put it on the small Calor Gas camping stove on the worktop to boil.

"Do you like soya milk?" he called out.

"Never tried it."

"I don't have any sugar, but I could go and get you some if you want?"

"No, it's okay, I'll have it without."

Stiggy opened the fridge door and reached inside for the half-empty carton of soya milk on the top shelf. The light was off, the fridge silent. He swore under his breath as he opened a cupboard door above the fridge and pulled out the margarine tub he kept a stash of fifty pence coins in. He fed a couple into the electric meter under the sink, and the fridge hummed into life once more. He cursed himself for not topping it up before he left for Sheffield the day before, and hoped it hadn't been off for too long, or all his frozen vegetables would have melted and gone soggy.

When Stiggy returned to the living room with the drinks, he found Sally sat on the edge of the battered armchair by the door, leaning forward with her hands on her knees. She took one of the mugs and cradled it in her hands.

"What are we going to do, Stiggy?"

Stiggy shrugged. "What do you want to do? We could listen to some records, or see what's on the telly? Or we could go into town if you like, after you've unpacked? I'm not really fussed, you can decide."

Sally flicked her head to one side. Her fringe fell back into place almost immediately. "I don't mean that, I mean what are we going to do about Joe? I killed him, we can't just pretend it didn't happen. When the police find out they'll come looking for me."

"You can hide here until it all blows over."

Sally shook her head. "This isn't something that will just go away, Stiggy. And that van outside, it'll lead the police straight here."

"Yeah, I guess. I hadn't really thought about that. We'll need to get rid of it, but I can do that later. Trust me, yeah? It'll be okay, I promise."

"What if someone sees me and tells the police?"

"Why would they? Nobody round here knows who you are, or what you did. And even if they did know, they wouldn't care, and they certainly wouldn't be talking to no coppers. Everyone keeps themself to themself, that's one of the things I like about living here. Besides, the coppers will think it was a burglary, so they won't even be looking for you, will they? What I'm saying is—"

"What about the ones who stopped us in Sheffield?"

Stiggy sighed. "What about them?"

"What if they followed us here?"

"Why would they? It's just a broken light. Anyway, they—"

Then a loud knock on the front door made them both startle. The mug dropped from Sally's hands, its contents splattering over the threadbare carpet by her feet. Her mouth gaped open as she stared up at Stiggy in absolute terror.

Stiggy put his coffee down on the sideboard and opened the

flat door to see who it was.

"Don't answer it," Sally whispered. "It might be them."

Stiggy frowned. Hadn't she been listening to anything he said? "It's more likely to be whoever left the front door unlocked. Or one of my mates calling round to see if I'm okay from last night."

"But you don't know that. Why take the risk?"

The knock came again, much louder this time. More insistent.

A copper's knock!

Stiggy hesitated. What if Sally was right? The way that police officer in Sheffield changed his mind and let them go hadn't made any sense at the time, and it still didn't. Was it just to lull him into a false sense of security? Could he have told the driver to follow them all the way to Doncaster?

Stiggy stared at the front door, half-expecting it to burst open at any second.

8

Stiggy held his breath while he continued staring at the front door. The handle depressed, and the door rattled in its frame when someone outside pressed their weight against it. Another loud knock. Then footsteps receded away.

Stiggy exhaled with a loud sigh. Relief coursed through him, and he felt stupid for thinking the worst and letting Sally's paranoia rub off on him. Of course it wasn't the police. How could it be?

"Well whoever it was, they've gone," he said, turning to Sally. "Like I said, it was probably just one of my mates."

Sally shook her head. "You don't know that. Not for sure."

"Who else could it be? Coppers wouldn't just give up like that."

Stiggy thought about telling Sally if it was the police coming to arrest her they wouldn't have knocked, they would have just kicked the door down and stormed inside with truncheons raised. But he knew planting that idea in her head would be a bad idea. So instead, he closed the flat door and locked it.

"Look, Sally, you need to listen to me, okay? You're safe here, nobody's coming to get you. And I'll get rid of the van, yeah? Then there won't be nothing to lead anyone here. And if any coppers do come, you've been with me all the time, right? We left The Marples together last night, and you haven't seen Joe since. I'm sure he's got loads of enemies, a wanker like that, so it's not like they will be short of suspects, is it?"

Sally seemed to consider this for a few seconds, then nodded. "Yeah. Yeah, he has. I hadn't thought of that."

"Well there you are, then. Once the van's gone we'll be okay, won't we?"

Sally attempted a smile, but it looked forced. She nodded. "Okay. So what are we going to do with it?"

"Leave that to me, I'll sort it."

"Can you do it now?"

Stiggy sighed, then nodded. "Yeah, okay. Just as soon as I've drunk my coffee. You stay here, yeah? Make yourself at home, there's a pan of potato and carrot stew in the fridge if you get hungry, it just needs warming up. I'll be back as soon as I can, maybe about an hour or so?" He picked up Sally's mug from the floor. "I'll go and make you another cuppa. Try and relax, yeah? There's no point worrying about stuff like that. They probably haven't even found him yet, and when they do they won't be looking for you anyway."

* * *

Stiggy drove the transit van down Market Road and onto Church Way, turned off onto Chappell Drive, and parked at the back of the town's slaughterhouse. He hated that place, and any other time it would make him feel sick at the thought of what sort of brutality and torture went on inside those grey walls, the sheer terror flowing through the minds of the innocent victims just before they were murdered. But that day he had more pressing matters on his mind, and barely gave it a thought as he took the black bin liner containing Joe's pickaxe handle and Sally's torn, bloodstained clothes from the back of the van and carried it down a footpath leading to the River Don.

Danny and Steve, two fourteen-year-old punks Stiggy knew from when he lived in the Wheatley area of Doncaster with his parents, sat under an arched bridge that carried gas pipes across the river. Their eyes were glazed as they breathed into plastic bags, their minds so far away in dreamland they didn't even notice his presence. Solvent fumes filled the air, fuelling Stiggy's urge to join them for a quick bag of glue to settle his nerves and take his mind off his troubles. But he knew he needed a clear head for what he had in mind, so that would need to wait until later. There would be plenty of time to get off his head once the job was finished, but he would do that somewhere else, far away from any witnesses who might spot him down by the river.

Stiggy walked far enough beyond the bridge so Danny and Steve wouldn't notice him if they came round from their glue dreams, and stepped down to the river's edge. He weighed the bin liner down with stones, then hurled it as far as he could into the murky water. It landed with a splash and sank down to join the shopping trolleys, bicycle wheels, broken household appliances and other assorted junk littering the bottom of the river. Where, Stiggy hoped, it would remain forever.

He glanced at Danny and Steve as he passed under the bridge once more on the way back to the van. They were still oblivious to his existence, lost within their own little worlds. Danny mumbled something about Old Mother Riley's second hand old boots being full of spiders. Stiggy wondered if he made as little sense as that when he was glued up.

Back in the van, Stiggy drove around the outskirts of town and onto Beckett Road. He stopped off at a second hand shop half way down and sold all the gardening tools to a weasel-looking bald man behind the counter. He only got fifty quid for them all, which seemed very low considering how specialised some of them were, but no questions were asked about where the tools had come from and Stiggy was just happy to dispose of them. That just left the van itself, but Stiggy knew the perfect way to get rid of that, as well as have a little bit of fun while he did it.

He drove all the way down Beckett Road to the bus terminus and parked outside a row of shops servicing the block of flats where his parents lived. A bunch of kids Stiggy remembered from when he used to live there were sat outside the fruit and veg shop, just like he'd been hoping they would be. A *Duran Duran* song blared out of a portable cassette player beside them, the tinny sound distorted by the small speaker being pushed beyond its limit. They looked a bit older than he remembered them, maybe twelve or thirteen, but just as bored as they had always been. When Stiggy parked the van opposite the fruit and veg shop they all looked up and stared, as if it was the most interesting thing they'd seen all day. Which it probably was.

Stiggy wiped the steering wheel and gear stick with a handkerchief and climbed out, slamming the door behind him to make sure he kept their attention. As he walked away he faked a loud sneeze into the handkerchief and dropped the keys on the pavement.

"Oi mate," one of the kids called out.

Stiggy stopped walking and turned to look, thinking he might need to revise his plans. But then one of the others elbowed the speaker in the ribs and told him to shut up. Stiggy suppressed his smirk.

"Yeah?" he said. "What do you want?"

The boy shrugged. "Nothing, mate. I thought you was someone else, didn't I? All you punks look the same to me. You know, scruffy fuckers." The other kids laughed.

Stiggy smiled to himself as he made his way to the hardware store on the corner. Like they had some need to talk, in their worn out hand-me-downs and charity shop specials. At least he had an image, they just looked like future tramps in the making. Destined for a life on the dole, just like him.

Stiggy paused outside the shop and pretended to look in the window, positioning himself so he could see the van's reflection in the glass. One of the youths walked over and picked up the keys, just like he knew they would. He glanced over at Stiggy, and Stiggy took the cue to enter the shop and head straight for the adhesives section. As he picked up a tube of Evo Stik, the sound of van doors slamming came from outside. An engine revved. Tyres squealed. Stiggy ran to the shop doorway just in time to see Joe's transit van shoot past, accompanied by the sound of juvenile laughter and the sight of several two finger salutes waving at him through the windows.

"Oi, that's my fucking van!" Stiggy yelled. He turned to the shopkeeper, a fifty-year-old man in brown overalls. "Can you believe that? I only left it a few seconds."

"Sign of the times, kid," the man said. He looked at the tube of glue in Stiggy's hand and sighed. "I suppose you'll want a plastic bag to go with that, will you?"

Stiggy nodded. "Yeah, cheers."

Stiggy handed over a fifty pence coin and left the hardware store with a broad grin on his face. He walked around the back of the shops and sat down in the alleyway near the entrance to the block of flats, then looked out at the Kingfisher Junior School playing field opposite while he screwed the lid off the tube of glue. Just a quick bag to help him relax, then get the bus back into town. With all the money he'd made from the gardening tools, along with the wad of cash in Joe's wallet, he could easily afford a few bottles of cider on the way home to keep the buzz going. He'd get some Babycham for Sally, too. Getting pissed was always the best way to take your mind off your troubles.

* * *

Two hours later, his eyes red, his nose still streaming from the after effects of the glue, Stiggy arrived back at the flat on Broxholme Lane. The portable black and white television set resting on top of a stack of upside-down empty milk crates in the corner of the room was playing to itself, the volume turned down low. The room itself was empty.

"Sally?"

No reply. He put the carrier bag filled with bottles of cider and Babycham down on the sideboard, next to his record player.

"Sally, it's me. I've sorted it."

Assuming she must be in the kitchen, Stiggy locked the door to his flat and went to find her. The kitchen was empty too.

"Sally?"

He checked the small bathroom in the corner of the kitchen, but she wasn't in there either. Then he noticed the back door was open, so he went into the yard to see if she was out there. The gate leading to the alleyway at the back was open too.

But there was no sign of Sally.

She had gone.

9

Stiggy put his new *Discharge* album on the record player and slumped in the armchair with a bottle of cider while he listened to it. He thought about Sally and sighed. She must have been using him all along. He'd helped her to literally get away with murder, and now she'd just fucked off, never to be seen again. And without so much as a thanks for all the trouble he'd gone to for her.

He screwed the lid off the cider bottle and took a swig. No gratitude, some people. She could've at least left a note or something. Oh well, fuck it. At least he still had Joe's cash to spend. Maybe he'd treat himself to a new record player, one of those posh ones he'd seen in Barker & Wigfalls that cost two hundred quid. Or one of those Sony Walkmans you could record with, so he could take it to gigs and make his own bootlegs. Or maybe he could put down a deposit on a colour TV and a video recorder instead, and pay the rest off monthly from his Giro money. Then he could tape all the punk bands on *Top of the Pops* and *The Old Grey Whistle Test*. *Crass* were sure to be on one of those shows sooner or later, and when they were he'd be able to watch it over and over again.

He tapped his foot rapidly to the *Discharge* record while he drank the cider. Yeah, that's what he'd do. Go on a shopping spree. No point having money if you don't spend it. He yawned and stretched out his arms. His head was still mashed from the glue earlier, and the cider was just making him sleepy. He decided to get up and go for a walk into town to clear his head, see if any of his mates were hanging around outside Woolworths. Then he could check they were okay, and find out if any of them had been arrested at The Marples before he hit the shops. He remembered something the skinhead on the field had said about people being rushed to hospital, and hoped it was nobody he knew.

As he headed for the kitchen to lock the back door, he noticed Sally's suitcase standing upright on the floor at the foot of the bed. He walked over and picked it up, surprised at how light it was. He put it down on the bed and thumbed the catches. Empty. That made no sense. What would she have put her clothes in when she left?

A sudden thought popped into Stiggy's fuddled mind. He went over to the wardrobe and pulled both doors open. The jumble of T-shirts, jeans and underpants at the bottom of the wardrobe had been folded and neatly stacked in separate piles, next to his stash of *2000AD* back issues in the corner. Sally's shirts hung on wooden coat hangers on the rail above them, next to his studded red canvas jacket and the cut-off black denim waistcoat he had spent hours covering in band patches he'd bought from the market.

An unexpected sense of relief flooded through him. If Sally's clothes were still here, that meant she couldn't be far away. But where would she have gone to? It wasn't like she knew anyone in Doncaster. Had someone come to the door and spooked her enough to make her run away? That was possible, but it wouldn't explain why she hadn't come back yet.

Stiggy hurried through the kitchen and out the back door. He looked up and down the alleyway, but there was no sign of her lurking out there.

"Sally!" he shouted, but the only reply he got was from a dog barking in the next street.

He went back inside and made himself a coffee to counteract the effects of the glue and cider, then put the *Discharge* album back on while he waited. He hadn't had it long so he didn't know all the words yet, but he sang along with the lines he did remember and hummed the rest.

He was just flipping the record over to play side two when the back door slammed and Sally walked into the living room from the kitchen. She wore the green camouflage cap he'd sewn a *Crass* logo patch onto a few months ago, with the peak pulled down low to cover the bruises on her face and her black eye. Stiggy had given up wearing that hat soon after he'd decorated it, because his mates kept swiping it off his head and throwing it over the balcony in The Arndale Centre. But he had to admit, it did look good on her.

"Where have you been?" he asked as he dropped the tonearm onto the record.

"You didn't have no—" Sally frowned when she was interrupted by a loud discordant guitar wail from the record player speakers. Stiggy turned the volume down. "You didn't have no milk, so I went and got you a bottle."

Stiggy shook his head. "That's because I don't drink milk. I already told you, I'm a vegan."

"Well I know you said you don't like butter, but you never said nothing about milk."

"Butter is made out of milk, so it's all part of the same thing; torturing animals for profit. I don't want no part in that. I don't wear leather or use any products that are made out of murdered animals, either."

Sally looked down at Stiggy's combat trousers and sniffed. "Isn't glue made out of animals?"

"Don't be daft, it's just glue. Chemicals and shit."

"No, I'm pretty sure it is. I read about it somewhere."

Stiggy picked at one of the fresh glue stains on his trousers and wished he'd kept the empty Evo Stik tube so he could check the ingredients printed on the back. What if Sally was right? He'd better check up on that as soon as he could, just to be sure. Inhaling murdered animals would be just as bad as eating them.

"What's wrong with milk, anyway?" Sally asked. "I would have thought it would be cruel not to milk the cows. Wouldn't their udders explode or something?"

"No, cows are like people. They only make milk when they have babies. So the farmer gets them pregnant, then kills the baby so it won't drink the milk. Then when they stop making milk, they get them pregnant again."

Sally frowned. "Oh. So what should I do with the milk? Throw it away?"

Stiggy shrugged. "That's up to you and your own conscience. By paying for it you've already become complicit in the suffering, so whatever you do with it won't make any difference at this stage."

"I didn't actually pay for it," Sally said. "I found it on a doorstep."

"Yeah well, whatever. The damage is already done. But how come it took you so long? I've been back over half an hour, it doesn't take that long just to pinch a bottle of milk off someone's doorstep."

Sally looked down at the carpet. "There was something else I needed to do. Did you get rid of the van?"

"Um, yeah, it's gone now. But what do you mean there was something else you needed to do?"

Sally looked up at Stiggy and bit her lip. "I had to find out if they'd found Joe yet or not."

Stiggy's eyes widened. "What? How?"

"I phoned Dave."

Stiggy gaped at her. "What? For fuck's sake, why would you

do something like that?"

"Because I promised him I would, so I could let him know I was okay. And I couldn't just sit here and worry about whether anyone had found Joe or not, could I? I had to know."

"What, so you asked that Dave geezer? Fuck, how's that going to look, you knowing Joe's dead before anyone else does?"

"We just talked about normal stuff, I figured if they'd found Joe that would've been the first thing Dave would've said. But he didn't, so I guess that means they haven't."

"Fuck, you didn't tell him where you were, did you?"

"No. He did ask, but I didn't tell him. I thought it best not to."

Stiggy exhaled audibly. "Well that's one thing, I guess. But you still shouldn't have phoned him."

"What, so I can't talk to my friends anymore?"

"No. I mean yeah, of course you can, but ... well, you know. It's not a good idea, is it?"

"Dave wouldn't snitch on me if that's what you're worried about."

"I'll have to take your word for that, but why risk it? He saw us on the way to your house, so once he finds out what happened to Joe it won't take him long to figure out the rest. And he's not exactly stable, is he? He tried to fucking stab me, remember?"

Sally shook her head. "That was just because he didn't know you."

"What, so he stabs everyone he doesn't know? What is it with these fucking skinhead mates of yours? Are they all fucking psychos or something?"

"Dave's not a psycho, he was just looking out for me, that's all."

"What, by waving a knife about?"

"You don't need to worry about Dave, he's more likely to hurt himself than anyone else."

"What's that supposed to mean?"

Sally shook her head and looked away. When she spoke her voice was barely a whisper. "Nothing, it doesn't matter. Forget I said it."

"Are you okay?" Stiggy asked. He reached out for her hand, but she jerked away from him. "Look, Sally, it's best if you don't phone him again, okay? When they do find Joe's body ... well, even if Dave doesn't tell the coppers he saw us they will still want to talk to you because you used to live there. So the less people who know where you are now, the better, yeah?"

Sally frowned, then looked down at her boots.

* * *

Later that night, Stiggy lay on the bed and stared up at the cracked ceiling while *Crass's Penis Envy* album played on the record player. He'd chosen it for Sally, thinking its feminist lyrics would appeal to her and bring her out of the morose mood she seemed to be in, but she just sat there on the edge of the armchair, staring into space with her hands on her knees, her head twitching to one side every now and again.

The record ended and Stiggy crossed the room to put the other side on. Sally watched him, and a frown creased her face when he flipped it over and put it back on the turntable.

"Have you got anything that isn't about violence?" she asked.

"Like what?"

"Any 2-Tone? You know, *Madness* or *Specials*?"

Stiggy shook his head. "No, I don't like that sort of stuff." Then he remembered the broken cassette tape he'd picked up from the hallway at Joe's house. He pulled spools of brown tape from the pocket of his combat trousers and showed it to her. "I've got this, though."

"What is it?"

"It's that tape of yours. You know, the one with all your songs on it?"

Sally huffed. "What use is that now? Might as well just throw it away."

"Nah, I can fix it for you, I've done it before with my own tapes. It just needs putting in a new case, that's all. There'll be some dropouts where it's got all twisted, but most of it should play okay."

Sally's eyes widened. "Really? You'd do that for me?"

"Yeah, course I would. Not tonight though, I'm too pissed and knackered. But tomorrow, yeah?" He put the spools of tape down next to the record player so he would remember.

"You're a good man," Sally said.

"Um ... thanks. You're not too bad yourself."

"No, I mean it. What you did for me, after ... well you know ... what happened, and that. I owe you a lot."

Stiggy shrugged. "Don't worry about it, any bloke would've done the same."

"No, they wouldn't. Most would have just left me there."

"Yeah well, you're ..." Stiggy struggled for the right word, then sighed and shook his head when he couldn't think of one. "Well, I suppose I like you, I guess." He looked down at his feet, suddenly embarrassed. "Besides, you're kind of cute."

Sally gave out a short laugh. "Hardly. I look like I've gone ten rounds with Muhammad Ali."

Stiggy looked up and stared at the puffy bruise forcing her left eye closed. He thought about the scars on her back and clenched his fists. He hated that Joe bastard more than he had ever hated anyone before. Even more than he hated Thatcher.

"What that cunt did to you ... fuck, it was just plain evil. Nobody should have to go through anything like that. If you ask me, he got what he deserved, and you shouldn't feel guilty about it."

Sally stared into his eyes. "I'm sorry about this morning," she said after a short pause. "I shouldn't have gone out and did what I did."

"What do you mean?"

"When I phoned Dave. I didn't know it would make you angry, honest. If I did, I wouldn't have done it."

Stiggy shook his head. "Don't worry about it, there's no harm done. And I guess I kind of over-reacted, but I was just worried you might tell him where you were, that's all."

"I didn't, honest."

"Yeah, I know. Like I say, I over-reacted. I don't mind, honest. We just need to be careful, that's all. Because the less people who know where you are the better."

Sally nodded, then bit her lip. "There's something else I haven't told you. I used one of your fifty pence coins to phone him, I found them in the kitchen. I know I should have asked first, but you weren't here. I'll pay you back, honest."

"Sally, it really doesn't matter. Just forget about it, it's not a big deal."

Stiggy took the *Crass* album off the turntable and put it back in its wraparound sleeve. "So if you don't like *Crass*, what do you want to listen to instead?"

"Anything, really. You decide."

"What about *Discharge*?"

"Never heard of them."

"That's what was playing when you came back from phoning Dave this morning."

"Oh." She looked down at the carpet and shrugged. "Not really my kind of thing."

Stiggy flicked through his collection of singles for inspiration, and came across a *Fatal Microbes* one he'd bought mail order from a shop in London a couple of years ago, after reading in *Sounds* that it was *Honey Bane's* first band. He didn't care much for it himself because it was too slow and it didn't sound anything like her single on *Crass Records*, but he put it on anyway in case it was the sort of thing Sally would like.

Sally frowned. "This one is about violence as well."

"No, if you listen to the words it's about how violence grows from violence, so it's more of an anti-violence song. Most of my records are, it's the Oi! bands who glorify that sort of thing."

Stiggy followed up the *Fatal Microbes* song with singles by *The Mob* and *Zounds*, handing Sally the wraparound posters to look at while she listened. While she said they were both okay, she expressed a preference for *Zounds*, and asked Stiggy if he had anything else by them.

"No. They did an LP last year, but I was skint at the time so I couldn't afford to get one, and they'd sold out by the time my next Giro came. I've been hoping it'll turn up in the second hand record shop in town, but nobody seems to want to get rid of it."

Then Stiggy remembered an album he had borrowed from a friend the previous week and pulled it out.

"This is the same sort of thing, though. And oh yeah, I forgot, there's a sort of ska type song on it, too."

Sally looked up with interest. "Who is it?"

Stiggy held up the red and black sleeve. "*The Astronauts*."

"Never heard of them."

"Neither had I, until my mate borrowed me it. He got it when they played in Doncaster a few weeks ago. I thought it were crap at first, but it kind of grows on you after a while, and the songs are really good. In fact I need to tape it before I give him it back."

Stiggy put on side two of the album, which opened up with the ska song, and stepped back to watch Sally's reaction. She smiled and tapped her foot.

"You like it, then?"

Sally nodded. "Yeah, it's nice."

The ska song ended, replaced with a more folk-sounding acoustic guitar number. Stiggy headed for the record player to skip to the next track like he usually did when he played it, but Sally stopped him.

"Don't turn it off, I want to hear the rest of it."

"There isn't no more ska songs on it, there's just that one. The rest of it's more like hippy stuff than anything else. You know, with violins and shit."

"I don't mind, I still want to hear it."

"Oh, okay. Well don't say you weren't warned."

Stiggy returned to the bed and lay down with his hands clasped behind his head. The song didn't seem as bad as he remembered from the first and only time he'd played it, although he couldn't help yawning. Sally yawned in sympathy.

"You tired?" Stiggy asked.

"Yeah."

"You want to go to bed, then?"

Sally gave him a startled look, and Stiggy realised his mistake straight away. He sat up and held out his hands.

"I don't mean with me. Well, um ... not unless you want to, that is. I can kip on the chair instead if you like?"

"You don't mind? It's your flat, and I don't want to put you out."

"No, it's fine. I've slept in worse places than that before now. Besides, it's not like you could sleep in the chair, is it? What with your back and everything. How is it, anyway?"

"Sore."

"You want anything? More pills or whatever?"

Sally shook her head. Stiggy switched off the music, then went for a piss in the small bathroom attached to the kitchen. When he returned Sally was lying on her stomach in the bed, with the covers folded down so they weren't touching her back. She still wore the white polo shirt with black and red stripes around the neck, but her boots, socks, and bleached jeans lay on the floor beside the bed. Her head rested on the pillow, facing him, and she smiled when he walked in.

"You're a good man," she said.

Stiggy smiled. "You already said that, but it's no bother, honest. Night, then, Sally. I'll see you in the morning, yeah? Then after breakfast I'll fix that tape for you."

Stiggy reached for the light switch beside the door. But before he could flick it off, Sally bolted out of bed and screamed at him.

10

Stiggy startled and spun toward Sally. His eyes flicked down to her red knickers of their own volition, and he had to force them back up to her face. Her good eye was wide and staring, her other still clamped shut by the purple swelling around it. Tears streamed from both as she trembled before him.

"Don't turn it off!" she yelled.

Stiggy's forehead creased. "Why not?"

"Because ..." Sally's head jerked to one side. Her bottom lip quivered.

"Sally? Sally, what is it? What's wrong?"

Stiggy walked over to comfort her and she melted into him, her arms wrapped tight around his waist. Stiggy raised his arms to return the embrace, then remembered the cuts on her back and lowered his hands to his sides while she sobbed into his chest.

"Sally, it's okay, I can leave the light on if you want me to, it's not a big deal. But whatever this is really about, you can tell me, you know that, right?"

Sally didn't reply. After another minute her tears subsided and she sniffed. She released Stiggy and backed away from him. Her cheeks were wet, and snot dripped from her nose down to her upper lip. She wiped it away with the back of her hand, then sat down on the edge of the bed and stared down at the carpet.

"You okay?" Stiggy asked.

Sally nodded, then lay down and curled up into a foetal position on her side. Stiggy walked over and picked up the covers from the floor. He draped them over her bare legs and gazed down at her.

"What is it, Sally? What's wrong? Whatever it is, you can tell me, you know?"

"I can't," Sally said, avoiding eye contact.

"Why not?"

"I just ..." Her voice hitched. "I don't want to talk about it. I just don't like the dark, okay?"

Stiggy nodded, but he knew there was more to it than that. It had been pitch black in those woods they had passed through on the way to the allotment in Sheffield, and that hadn't seemed to bother her at all. But he didn't want to press the matter any further because he could tell she was close to tears again. He crouched down to her level and nodded once more.

"It's okay, Sally. Really. You get some sleep, yeah? And don't worry about coppers coming for you or whatever, if that's what this is about. You're safe here, I promise."

"And you'll stay here with me, you won't go anywhere?"

Stiggy shook his head. "Of course I won't. Where would I go?"

"Can you move the chair closer, so I'll know you're still here?"

"Yeah, if you want."

* * *

Stiggy cried out and shrank back into the armchair, his hands raised in a futile attempt to ward off the pickaxe handle flying toward his face. His breath came in short gasps, and his heart hammered so fast it felt like it was trying to force its way out of him. Mere seconds passed, but it seemed more like an eternity while he waited for Joe's corpse to cave his head in before he risked a glance between his trembling fingers.

"Fucking hell," he whispered to himself.

Just a nightmare, that's all. But it had seemed so fucking real.

Stiggy leaned forward and held his head in his hands, trying to force the image from his mind. The small globs of brain matter slithering out of Joe's shattered skull as he stamped across the room with the pickaxe handle raised above his head in both hands. Joe's bloodshot eyes straining at the tendons anchoring them to their sockets, like a snail's eyestalks, as they stared straight at him. Blood and teeth spraying from what was left of Joe's pulverised mouth as he roared and swung the pickaxe handle down onto Stiggy's head.

Stiggy shivered. The clothes he had slept in clung to his body like a wet sponge. Sweat still poured from every gland. He knew he had to think of something else, or that nightmare would haunt him for the rest of the day. He glanced at the bed beside the armchair, ready to apologise to Sally if his scream had woken her. But the bed was empty, the covers crumpled up at the bottom.

"Sally?" he called out.

"In here."

The voice came from the kitchen. Stiggy rose from the

armchair and stretched. His back ached from sleeping in a sitting position, and his ribs still felt tender from the kicking he'd received at The Marples. He picked up a fresh pair of underpants, a *Varukers* T-shirt, and a pair of yellow and black tiger-print trousers from the wardrobe and padded into the kitchen with them.

Sally sat at the kitchen table, nursing a mug of tea. "Are you okay?" she asked when Stiggy entered.

Stiggy nodded on his way to the small bathroom in the corner of the kitchen. "Yeah, why?"

"I heard you shout something, and you look really pale."

"Just a bad dream, that's all."

Stiggy closed and locked the bathroom door behind him and switched on the shower before peeling off his sweat-drenched clothes.

"The kettle's just boiled if you want a drink?" Sally called out.

"Yeah, I could—" Stiggy almost said he could murder one, but managed to stop himself in time. "Thanks, a coffee would be great. No sugar, though."

"You hungry?" Sally asked.

"Yeah, a bit."

Stiggy stepped under the warm jet of water and let it rinse the stale sweat from his body while he urinated into the plughole. Outside in the kitchen he could hear cupboards opening and closing.

"You've only got porridge left, is that okay?"

"Um ... yeah, porridge is fine. I'll go to the shop later, so if there's anything you want, let me know."

"How long will you be?"

"Not long. It's only a few streets away, so ten minutes, maybe?"

"Can I come with you?"

The question took Stiggy by surprise, and he glanced at the closed bathroom door before replying. After the way Sally had reacted when someone came to the flat yesterday, her wanting to go outside was the last thing he expected.

"Um ... yeah, if you're sure you want to. Are you not worried about people seeing you, then?"

"No. I've been thinking about what you said, and you're right. Nobody takes any notice of me. Well, no more than usual, anyway. Besides, they haven't found Joe yet."

"How do you know?"

"Because I ... well, you know. I watched the morning news

on the telly, while you were asleep."

"Oh, okay. Yeah, good idea. We should probably keep an eye on the news, just in case." Stiggy picked up a bar of vegetable soap and lathered himself down. "But if you don't mind going out, maybe we could make a day of it, then? We'll go into town, then I can introduce you to my mates and show you the local sights. Not that there's much to see, but I could show you all the places where I hang out, if you want?"

There was a moment's pause, then: "Maybe at the weekend. Let's see how it goes today first."

"Okay, yeah."

After he finished showering, Stiggy rubbed himself dry with a towel, put on the fresh clothes, and spiked his hair up with the soap before opening the bathroom door.

Sally stood before the Calor Gas camping stove, stirring a pan of porridge on the single hob. Stiggy dropped the towel and his dirty clothes into a basket, then got the margarine tub from the cupboard above the fridge and fed a couple of fifty pence coins into the electric meter under the sink before sitting down at the table. He noticed his camouflage cap on the edge of the table as he picked up the mug of coffee Sally had made him, and wondered why it was there. He was sure he'd put it back in the wardrobe last night, but maybe he was mistaken.

Sally spooned thick globs of congealed porridge into two bowls and put them down on the table. She sat opposite Stiggy and bit her lip as she looked at him. "I've never made porridge before. I followed the instructions on the box, but I think it must have gone wrong. Sorry."

Stiggy shrugged. "It looks okay to me." He sprinkled salt on the surface and used the back of his spoon to press it into the almost-solid lump of oats. It was so thick you could spread it on bread and have it as a sandwich. Sally frowned as she toyed with hers, then took a tentative taste and grimaced. Stiggy smiled. "I take it you don't like porridge, then? I was thinking of getting some muesli from the shop, if you want to wait for that instead. Or some corn flakes or whatever?"

"No, it's okay, I don't want to put you to any trouble." Sally jabbed her spoon in the porridge and left it standing upright in it, like King Arthur's sword sticking out of a stone, then leaned back in her chair and sighed. "I can't do anything right, can I?"

"You just need a bit more practice, that's all. The first time I made some it went wrong, too." Stiggy got up and fetched a carton of soya milk from the fridge. "Mix some of this with it, then it'll be fine."

"I just feel so useless. And I'm sorry about last night, too. You must think I'm a right nutter."

Stiggy shrugged. "It's understandable enough. We were both pretty frazzled over what happened."

"It's just ... well, you know." Sally looked away. "Like I said, I don't like the dark."

"Did Joe let you leave the light on, when you were staying at his place?"

"No, he took the piss out of it all the time, and called me a baby. But there's a street lamp just outside the bedroom window, so it wasn't too bad. I just waited for him to fall asleep, then opened the curtains."

Stiggy nodded, remembering the lamp post with the car tyre looped around its base. It seemed odd that someone Sally's age would still be afraid of the dark, but after everything she had been through with that Joe bastard he wasn't going to push it.

"Look, Sally, it's not a big deal, honest. I don't mind having the light on all night if it makes you feel better."

"Thank you. For everything, I mean. I don't know what I would have done without you."

Stiggy gazed at Sally's bruised face, at the purple swelling forcing her left eye closed. He thought back to Joe holding her over the arm of a chair and beating her with a leather belt, and wondered what else he had done to her. What sort of life she would have had living with a monster like that. No wonder she had taken such brutal revenge on him when she had the chance. Anyone would have done the same, and helping her get away with it was the right thing to do. Sally didn't deserve prison for killing Joe, she deserved a fucking medal for ridding the world of scum like that.

"Stiggy?"

"Um ... yeah?" Stiggy blinked, his mind returning to the present.

"It's okay me staying here, isn't it? You don't mind? I don't want to get you into trouble with the police."

"No, don't be daft. It's good to have you here, and like I keep saying, you don't need to worry about no coppers coming looking for you."

Sally reached across the table and placed her hand on top of Stiggy's. "Thank you."

Stiggy grinned at her. "No worries."

* * *

Four days later, Sally waited in the hallway while Stiggy locked the flat door. She had taken to sleeping in one of his old *Discharge* T-shirts, and he couldn't help wishing she was still wearing it for the Saturday afternoon trip into town to meet his mates instead of the pale green plaid shirt she'd chosen instead. How would everyone react when they saw she was a skinhead? Colin, Brian and Twiglet didn't like skinheads at the best of times, and what happened at the *Cockney Upstarts* gig would have only made matters worse. But he was sure he'd be able to convince them Sally was different, once they got over the initial shock.

Stiggy pocketed the keys and opened the front door. John Spedding, his next door neighbour, sat on the kerb outside the house, working on his three-wheeled motorcycle. Tools and engine parts littered the cracked paving slabs. A puddle of oil lay on the tarmac under the trike's engine, where he had taken off the side panels. Spedding glanced over his shoulder when Stiggy slammed the door, then stood up and turned to face him.

"All right, kid?" he said. "How's it going?"

Although only thirty-two years of age, Spedding looked a lot older due to his prematurely greying hair, which was tied back in a ponytail, and the long, scraggly beard that covered most of his pock-marked face. His right arm was missing from the elbow down, the result of a motorcycle accident in his teenage years that had also left him with a pronounced limp. His jeans were filthy and ragged, the old leather waistcoat he wore covered in stained biker patches. Winged skull tattoos decorated both the man's shoulders.

"Aye up, John," Stiggy said with a nod. "Pretty good, yeah. How's it with you?"

"Can't complain, kid, you know how it is." Spedding looked at Sally and cocked his head to one side. "So who's this, then?"

Sally stood in the front yard and gaped back at the biker.

"This is Sally," Stiggy said. "She's ... a friend. Sally, this is John."

Spedding nodded to Sally. "How do, Sally?"

Sally nodded back, but didn't say anything.

Spedding turned back to Stiggy and grinned, revealing a row of uneven and yellowed teeth. "Bit shy, is she?"

Stiggy smiled back. "Yeah, I guess. Anyway, we'd best get off. See you, John."

"Yeah, see you, kid. Bye Sally, nice meeting you."

Sally edged past the biker and set off down Broxholme Lane

at a brisk walk. Doris watched on from her regular spot on the corner of Glynn Avenue when Stiggy hurried to catch her up, then stepped out in front of him.

"Are you looking for business?"

Doris held her hands behind her back and thrust out her chest. Her eyes were vacant, her voice a monotone. Stiggy glanced down at her exposed cleavage before shaking his head and walking onto the road to get around her. Doris huffed, then returned to her rucksack and leaned against the wall next to it. Stiggy had often wondered what she carried around in that bag, and had even gone as far as asking her one night, but she had just told him to mind his own business. Whatever it was, she guarded it closely and never let it leave her sight.

"See, I told you John was okay," Stiggy said when he caught up with Sally half way down Glynn Avenue.

Sally shrugged and continued walking.

"He might look a bit rough, but he's harmless enough." Stiggy smiled. "Get it? He's armless."

Sally either didn't get the joke, or chose to ignore it. "Yeah well, I don't like Hells Angels, the way they beat skins up all the time for no reason. And they never fight fair, do they? It's always three onto one with them."

"Yeah? That's the sort of thing skinheads do to us punks, it's always three onto one with them, too. Either that or they'll sneak up on you from behind so you've got no chance of fighting back."

Sally gave Stiggy a sharp look, but didn't say anything.

"But like I say, you don't need to worry about John," Stiggy continued. "He's not like that, he's a good bloke if you give him a chance. He's always done right by me, anyway, ever since I moved in next door to him."

"Yeah well, I don't want to take the chance. He might be all right on his own, but what about when there's a gang of them?"

Stiggy shook his head and sighed. "It wouldn't make any difference if there was. You've got him all wrong, he isn't like that. And I've met some of his mates, they're okay too. They're just into bikes, that's all."

* * *

Stiggy checked all the regular town centre places punks hung out on Saturday afternoons, but there was no sign of any of his mates anywhere. They weren't in the Maple Leaf Cafe playing on the Space Invaders, they weren't hanging around the wool market, they weren't outside Bradley's Records taking the piss out of the middle-aged winos who congregated there, and they weren't sat next to the fountain statue in the Arndale Centre.

He checked the cafe in Woolworths too, but none of the people sitting at the Formica tables were punks. It was as if they had all vanished from the face of the earth since his last trip into town just over a week ago. He wondered briefly if he might be missing something good, maybe the annual Smokey Bears Picnic in Hexthorpe Park where local bands played to an audience of stoned hippies and bemused parents with young children. But that was usually in September, still another couple of months away. So where was everyone?

Stiggy bought a pot of tea and shared it with Sally while he puzzled it out. She asked if he could buy her some toiletries while they were in town, and he said yes without hesitation. After all, the money in Joe's wallet was as much hers as it was his. He'd told her about it two nights ago, while they listened to the John Peel show on the radio. She had been surprised when she saw how much it contained, and said she had no idea he made that much from his gardening business. She wanted some boot polish too, to shine her Doc Martens with. Stiggy didn't have any in the flat because he had no use for it. Since becoming a vegan he only wore canvas trainers, having given his old leather boots a decent burial and paid his respects to the cow who gave up her life to provide them.

After they finished off the tea, with still no sign of his mates, Stiggy decided they might as well go and get the stuff Sally wanted and head off somewhere else. Wilkinsons, the next shop along to Woolworths on the upper deck of the Arndale Centre, sold DIY and household goods, so he was sure they would have most of it. Then a quick trip to Fox's Records for some blank tapes, down to WH Smiths to pick up that week's *2000AD* and see if the new *Punk Lives* magazine was out yet, and he'd be done. After that he'd take Sally down to the River Don, maybe walk along it down to Hexthorpe Park, and get the bus back into town.

It was as they were walking out of Woolworths that Stiggy heard peals of laughter. Three young skinheads sat at the bottom of the steps leading up to the car park on his left, sharing a two litre bottle of Strongbow cider between them. They were staring straight at him, nudging each other and grinning. Stiggy tensed at the sight of them, and hurried across to the Wilkinsons entrance door.

"All right?" one of the skinheads called out.

Sally turned and nodded. "Yeah, not too bad."

She paused, like she was deciding whether to go over and talk to them or not, but Stiggy knew from experience that entering a secluded area with a bunch of drunken skinheads would be a huge mistake. He had been walking through a subway late one night when he had been jumped by two skinheads loitering there. They had seemed friendly too until they grabbed him, otherwise he would have turned and ran as soon as he saw them. He wouldn't make that same mistake again.

He ushered Sally into Wilkinsons, keeping an eye on the skinheads to check they weren't about to follow. Once inside he relaxed. No way would they cause any trouble with so many witnesses around. Sally picked up a shopping basket and made her way down the aisles. Each time she found something she wanted she asked Stiggy if it was okay to have it, and seemed surprised when he said yes. A battery operated hair clipper, a tin of black boot polish, a packet of tampons, shampoo and shower gel, a spray-can of deodorant, and various other bits and pieces went in the basket.

At the checkout, after the middle-aged woman in the red uniform had rung up all the items and put them in a carrier bag, Stiggy handed her an extra five pound note along with the payment, and asked if it could be changed into fifty pence coins for the electric meter. There had only been four left in the margarine tub in the cupboard above the fridge that morning, and while he didn't mind leaving the light on all night for Sally, it did seem to be eating through his stash of meter coins at a rapid rate.

A wolf whistle came from one of the skinheads at the bottom of the car park stairway when Stiggy and Sally left the shop. Sally turned and smiled. Stiggy hurried her away and took her on a circular trip around the upper floor of the Arndale Centre, pointing out places of interest as they went and telling her stories of his exploits in each one.

The electric organ shop he and his mates were banned from after they all piled in one day and made a tuneless racket on one of the display organs while they tried to figure out how to play *Anarchy in the UK* on it. The DIY shop on the corner that had banned all punks from entering after one got caught shoplifting a tube of glue. British Home Stores, where he and his mates had been banned for throwing the women's hats at each other. And Boots, the first shop Stiggy had ever been banned from when he was eleven years old, for asking the teenage girl behind the record counter if she had *The Snivelling Shits*.

"It was a single," he explained when Sally gave him an odd look. "*Terminal Stupid*, I think it was called, or something like that, by a band called *The Snivelling Shits*. I never heard it, I just saw it advertised in *Sounds* once, but it has to be the best name for a punk band ever, don't you think? She went mental and called the manager to chuck me out. Even now, they still won't let me back in."

"Are there any shops you're not banned from?" Sally asked.

Stiggy smiled. "Yeah, there's still a few left." He pointed at Fox's Records on the opposite balcony. "They still let me in, but probably only because I spend half my Giro in there."

Stiggy paused outside Boots and leaned over the handrail to look down at the fountain statue below to see if any of his mates had turned up yet. Two punk girls, Tina and Shaz, sat there, looking bored while a group of young trendies pointed and laughed at their matching bright red Mohicans, and leered at their torn fishnet stockings.

"Oi Tina," Stiggy shouted. "Where the fuck is everyone?"

Passing shoppers glanced at him and tutted. The punk girls both looked up.

"Don't know," Tina shouted back. "Not seen anyone all day."

Stiggy frowned and drummed his fingers on the balcony handrail. This was getting stupid now. On a Saturday afternoon the Arndale Centre should be packed out with punks, it was the one day of the week everyone turned out for. So where were they? The only other thing he could think of was they'd gone down to the Speedy Bar Cafe at the other end of town to torment the mods who hung out there, but they would only go mob handed if they were at war with them again. And he'd only been out of the social loop for a week, so that seemed unlikely.

Stiggy looked up and spotted the three skinheads sauntering over to the escalator on the opposite balcony, closely followed by a security guard who had no doubt caught them lounging on the car park steps and moved them on. He expected the guard to order them onto the escalator, and maybe have a colleague waiting downstairs to eject them from the premises; that was what usually happened when punks were caught drinking in there. But the skinheads walked straight past the escalator in the direction of Fox's Records, and the guard didn't seem to care. Stiggy watched them pass the record shop. If they continued on that route without any interference they would end up where he stood now, and he couldn't risk that. He glanced at Sally. She hadn't noticed the skinheads yet, she was too busy looking down at the nude statue rotating in the centre of the fountain.

"Come on, let's go," he said, and took Sally back the way they had come, past British Home Stores and the DIY shop, and round to the escalator. He kept an eye on the skinheads the whole time to make sure they kept their distance, and watched them enter C&A on the opposite corner. He smirked. It was the shop all the mods bought their suits and parkas from, a place he would never dream of going, even if he wasn't already banned from there for calling one of the YTS shop assistants a trendy wanker within earshot of the manager.

Stiggy took Sally into Fox's Records and browsed through the punk albums to see if they had anything new, while Sally wandered over to the 2-tone section and flicked through those. He came across an album by *The Mob*, something he didn't know existed until he saw it, and placed it on top of the stack of records to his left while he carried on looking. There was no way he was going to miss out on that, like he had with the *Zounds* LP.

He also found a new *Bullshit Detector* and pulled that out to inspect it. They'd jacked the price up since the last one, but it was a double album this time so it seemed reasonable enough. Stiggy had been alone among his circle of friends in liking the original *Bullshit Detector* compilation on Crass Records. Everyone else dismissed it as amateurish crap, but he knew better. It was the message that was important, not technical ability or recording quality. One track, by someone with a northern accent who called himself *Andy T*, had even inspired Stiggy to write his own poetry, which he planned to record himself reciting and send to *Crass* for their consideration. But he soon gave up on the idea when he struggled to think of anything that rhymed with Thatcher.

Stiggy picked up the two albums he had chosen and went to join Sally, who was still looking through the 2-Tone section.

"Look what I found," he said, holding up the *Mob* album.

Sally glanced at it and went back to flipping through the stack of records. "Who is it?"

"*The Mob*. You know, that band you said you liked." He hummed the intro to *I Hear You Laughing* and sang the chorus to her.

"Oh yeah," Sally said, "I remember. I wouldn't exactly say I liked them, I just thought they were better than that *Crass* and *Discharge* stuff you keep playing."

Stiggy grunted, then gestured at the 2-Tone records. "Is there anything you want, while we're here?"

Sally turned and gawped at him. "Really? Are you sure? You've already got me loads of stuff, are you sure you can afford it?"

Stiggy patted the back pocket of his combat trousers, where Joe's wallet full of cash resided. "Yeah, of course I can. Like I said, it's your money as much as mine. So if there's anything you want, just let me know."

Sally turned back to the records and pulled out an album by *The Selector* almost immediately, as if she knew precisely where it was. "I've always wanted this one, ever since I saw them on *Top of the Pops* once, when I was back at the home. Joe would've had a fit if he knew I liked them."

Stiggy smiled when he looked at the band photo on the back of the sleeve. It wasn't hard to figure out what Joe would object to; there was only one white face in the entire band. He took the three records to the counter and paid for them, along with a pack of five blank C90 cassettes, and made his way to the exit with Sally grinning by his side.

Then stopped dead in his tracks when he saw the three skinheads standing outside the shop.

They were staring straight at him.

11

One of the skinheads pointed at the Fox's Records carrier bag in Stiggy's hand, but his question was directed at Sally. "Did you get anything good?"

Sally smiled. "*Too Much Pressure*."

The skinhead smiled back. "Yeah? Good choice, I love that band."

"Me too," Sally said.

"Bollocks," one of the other skinheads said. "I was hoping you might've been into Oi, meself."

Sally shook her head. "No, not really."

"Told you she weren't an 'erbert like you, Tom," the first skinhead said. "That's a quid you owe me."

"Yeah, yeah. Whatever." The second youth, Tom, reached into the hip pocket of his bleached jeans and pulled out a crumpled pound note, then handed it over. "But you're getting the first drinks in at the weekend."

"Stiggy likes Oi," Sally said.

All three skinheads turned to Stiggy and waited for a response. He shrugged, still standing in the shop doorway. "I like all types of punk. Except that fucking Nazi shite. *Skrewdriver* or whatever."

The first skinhead grinned and cracked his knuckles. "Good to hear it, we've got no time for them Nazi wankers either." He turned back to Sally and jerked his head at Stiggy. "So is this your bloke, then?"

Sally locked eyes with Stiggy and smiled. "Yeah, I guess so."

A thrill ran down Stiggy's spine as he grinned back. Did she just say what he thought she said?

"That's a shame," the skinhead said. "So what's your name, then?"

"Sally."

"I'm Mark." He pointed a thumb at each of his mates in turn. "That's Paul, and that's Tom. We thought we knew all the skins round here, but we've not seen you before."

"I only moved here last week."

"Yeah? So where you from, then?"

"Sheffield."

Stiggy groaned inwardly. What did she have to go and tell him them that for?

"Really?" Mark said, his eyes widening slightly. "So what made you move to Donny, then? Me, I'd take the big city any day over a dump like this. At least there's jobs in Sheffield, there's fuck all round here."

Sally opened her mouth to speak, but before she could say anything an overweight security guard approached and told them all to move along. The skinheads sighed and shuffled away. Sally started to follow them, but Stiggy grabbed her by the arm to stop her.

"We're going this way."

"Oh, okay," Sally said. "Bye then," she called out to the skinheads. "Nice meeting you."

"You too Sally," Mark replied. "See you again, yeah? All the skins hang out at The Black Bull in the market on Friday nights if you fancy coming down to see us some time. They've got a boss jukebox in there, you'll love it. The barmaid's an original skin too, from the olden days."

"They seemed nice," Sally said as she and Stiggy headed for the escalator.

Stiggy nodded. "Yeah, I guess. I think that's the first time I've ever met any skinheads who didn't want to beat me up. Well, except for you, anyway."

Sally smiled and bumped her shoulder against his. "I told you, we're not all like that. And we're not all Nazis either, like you were trying to make out back there. It's just a small minority, like ..." She frowned.

Stiggy stepped onto the escalator and turned to face her while he travelled down. "Like Joe?"

"Yeah." Sally clutched the escalator handrail and walked onto the step above.

"What about that Dave?" Stiggy asked. "Is he a Nazi?"

Sally shook her head. "Dave's no more racist than I am. How could he be when he likes Jamaican music?"

"Yeah, I never thought of that. I guess it wouldn't really make much sense, would it? It'd be like a Rasta being into *Skrewdriver*. So how can you tell which ones are the Nazis if they all look the same?"

Sally smiled. "What, so all skins look the same to you? That's racist, that is."

Stiggy laughed as he stepped off the escalator on the ground floor level. "You know what I mean. They all wear the same clothes."

"I don't know, talk to them, I guess?" Sally gestured at the shoppers milling around them. "I bet you at least one of these people voted National Front at the last election. Can you tell which one it is?"

Stiggy looked, but nobody stood out to him. They all just looked ... normal. Not a jackboot or Swastika armband to be seen. "No, I guess not."

"Well there you are, then. Why would it be any different with skins? You should judge people by who they are, not what they wear. I bet you get a lot of funny looks, walking around dressed like that, don't you? They all think you're some sort of monster because of what they read in the newspapers."

Stiggy nodded. It was something he had got used to, so he didn't really take much notice of it anymore. Even now, people were staring at him with barely concealed disgust as they walked by. But was it really any different to Sally's views on Hells Angels? John Spedding was a good man, despite what he looked like, and what Sally thought of him.

"Well it's the same with skins," Sally continued. "People make assumptions based on how we look. They see a cropped head, boots and braces, and think Nazi." She shook her head. "It's just bollocks, and it pisses me off that you think that way too."

Stiggy frowned. "Yeah, I can see that. But to be fair, those are the only sort I've ever come in contact with until now. And it's usually my face coming into contact with their fists, or my ribs coming into contact with their boots."

"You just haven't met the right skins yet, that's all. Trust me, I know what I'm talking about, and I don't make stuff up. There's good people and bad people, the clothes they wear don't come into it at all."

Stiggy nodded "Yeah, maybe you're right. Now you mention it, a bunch of punks came down from Rotherham one weekend last year and attacked me and my mates for no reason. They just ran up to us shouting 'Exploited barmy army' and one of them went straight for Twiglet. Maybe he was a Nazi too."

"Well there you are, then. And I bet you couldn't tell them apart from normal punks, could you?"

"Well yeah, that was pretty easy, they all had *Exploited* skulls painted on the back of their leather jackets, and they all had red mohicans."

Sally frowned. "Yeah, well, the point is, it's not being punks that makes them bad people, is it? Same with skins, there's good ones and bad ones."

Stiggy held up his hands. "Okay, okay, you win. Not all skinheads are bad." He grinned. "Just most of them."

"Oi!"

Sally went to punch him on the arm, but she was grinning too. Stiggy darted out of the way, just in time.

"So what you said back there to that Mark geezer, did you mean it, then?"

"Did I mean what?" Sally asked.

"That I'm your bloke."

She shrugged. "Do you want to be?"

"Yeah." Stiggy nodded. "Yeah, I think I'd like that."

Sally looped her arm through his. "Good. Well that's settled then. So what are we doing now?"

"A bit more shopping, then there's a place I want to show you before we go back home."

* * *

Sally paused on the bank of the River Don to watch a green houseboat chug by. A middle-aged man in a tweed jacket stood at the rear with his hand on the tiller, while a young woman in a yellow bikini sunbathed on the roof. The man glared at Stiggy and Sally with barely concealed disgust as he floated past.

"Do you think they live on it?" Sally asked.

"I doubt it. Probably just something they pose on at the weekends."

"If I had something like that you'd never get me off it. I'd sail across the sea in it, go round the world."

"I wouldn't," Stiggy said. "I went on a boat with my mum and dad when we went to York once, except it was a lot bigger than that one. It scared the fuck out of me the way it kept lurching to one side every time people went to gawp at whatever the tour guide was telling them about. I kept screaming at them to keep still, but they wouldn't. I were sure it were going to sink."

Sally laughed. "That's daft. They wouldn't let people on them if they weren't safe."

Stiggy smiled. "Yeah well, I was only six at the time. Put me off boats for life, though."

The houseboat continued at a leisurely pace, water lapping at its sides. As it passed under the arched bridge carrying gas pipes across the river a stone thudded against its side, and a voice shouted out: "Fucking rich bastard!"

The woman in the bikini sat up in alarm and folded her arms over her chest. The man shouted back: "Oi, clear off out of you little shit, it or I'll call the police on you."

Another stone whizzed through the air, just missing the man's head. "Fuck off, you rich cunt!"

Stiggy smiled. He recognised that voice. Steve, one of the young punks he often shared a tube of glue with by the side of the river. His mate Danny was with him under the bridge, laughing at the houseboat owner's red face as he fumed back at them. The young woman grabbed a towel, wrapped it around herself, and disappeared inside the houseboat. Her face glared out from one of the windows.

"You mad bastards," Stiggy said with a grin as he approached the bridge.

"All right Stiggy," Danny said. His eyes were glazed, the pupils huge, and his breath smelled of chemicals when he spoke. "You got any glue?"

Steve looked and smelled the same, and held a plastic bread bag in one hand. A rolled up tube of Evo Stik lay against the wall of the bridge behind him.

Stiggy smiled and shook his head. "No mate, but it looks like you've already had some to me."

"All gone, innit? Can you lend us fifty pence, then?"

Stiggy patted his hip pocket. "No, I'm skint."

Danny pointed at the Fox's Records carrier bag in Stiggy's other hand. "How come you can afford to buy records, then?"

"That's why I'm skint. So if you want some more glue you'll have to go and nick some, won't you? But that reminds me, I don't suppose you know what glue is made out of, do you?"

Danny shrugged. "Cows and horses, innit. Everyone knows that."

"Shit, really?" Stiggy's grin dropped. A lump grew in his throat when he thought about all those poor animals he'd inhaled since he became a vegan. Why did the glue factories have to ruin something that was so much fun in that way? They would be putting bits of murdered animals in cider next.

"Told you," Sally said.

Danny and Steve both gaped at Sally, as if they had only just noticed she was there.

"Oi Stiggy," Steve said, "what you doing bringing a fucking skinhead down here?"

"This is Sally," Stiggy said. "She's my bird."

"I thought you hated skinheads. You always said they were a bunch of cunts."

Stiggy's cheeks flushed. He glanced at Sally and shook his head. "Yeah well, that was before I met Sally, wasn't it? They're not all bad."

Steve spat on the ground. "Tell that to Brian. That's if you ever see him again."

"What do you mean?" Stiggy asked.

"What, haven't you heard? Some cunt bottled him at the *Cockney Upstarts* gig, didn't they?" Steve glared at Sally. "One of your lot, apparently."

Sally's face reddened. She looked down at her boots and shuffled her feet.

"What?" Stiggy said. "Is he okay?"

"Still in the hospital, isn't he? Nearly fucking died, I heard. The cunt left him in a right fucking state. Blood everywhere, according to Twiglet. He got battered, too. Loads of people did."

Stiggy thought back to that night. When he'd left with Sally, Joe had been beating Brian senseless. Had he left him unconscious for one of the other skinheads to finish him off? Or had he grabbed a bottle and done it himself? He was almost afraid to ask the question.

"So what did he look like, this skinhead?"

Steve shrugged. "Don't know, we just got told he were a skinhead."

"Did the coppers get him?"

"Did they fuck," Danny said." Fucking coppers are useless, aren't they? Probably don't even care, Brian's only a punk so he don't matter." He smiled. "So we have to take care of it ourselves, don't we?"

"Too fucking right," Steve added.

"How do you mean?" Stiggy asked.

"Everyone's gone down to Sheffield to find the cunt, haven't they?" Danny said. "We would've gone too, only we haven't got no money for the train, have we?"

Stiggy nodded in sympathy, but it was probably for the best that Danny and Steve hadn't joined the lynch mob in Sheffield. They were too young and skinny to be any use in a fight, and would have just got in the way or ended up in hospital themselves.

"So what records did you buy, then?" Danny asked after a short pause.

"The new *Bullshit Detector*, and an LP by *The Mob*."

Danny's eyes widened. "What, them that did that single on *Crass*? I didn't even know they'd done an LP. Can you tape it for me?"

"And me," Steve said.

"Yeah, no worries. Anyway, we'd best get off."

"Where you going, like?" Danny asked.

Stiggy nodded down the river bank. "Just for a walk down here. See you later, yeah? And watch out for coppers, that bloke on the boat looked like he were going to explode so he's bound to call them sooner or later."

"Fuck him," Steve said. "Rich bastard. How's he going to phone any coppers, anyway? It's not like there's any phone boxes on the river, and it'd take him hours to get anywhere at the speed he were going."

"Yeah well, watch out for them anyway, yeah? You know what your mam will be like if she has to pick you up from the cop shop again. See you, then."

"Yeah, laters Stiggy," Seve said.

"You sure you haven't got no glue?" Danny asked as Stiggy and Sally walked away.

Stiggy turned and smiled. "Positive. In fact, as of now, I've officially given it up."

Danny laughed. "Yeah, right. You'll be saying you're giving up the cider next."

"So all skins are a bunch of cunts then, are we?" Sally said once they'd left Danny and Steve behind.

"Shit, Sally, that was before. You know I don't—" Stiggy noticed she was smiling. He smiled back. "Yeah, okay, fair point. How about *some* of them are cunts?"

"Yeah, that will work for me." Her smile faded. "I'm sorry about your friend Brian. I hope he'll be okay."

"You think it might have been Joe who did it?"

Sally shrugged. "It wouldn't surprise me. And it's definitely something he's capable of, you don't need me to tell you that."

Stiggy thought about the scars on Sally's back. No, he didn't need anyone to tell him what that bastard was capable of. "Fuck. I should've stayed and helped my mates fight back."

"Then it might have been you in the hospital instead. Or down at the cop shop with the others who got arrested. And I'd be back in Sheffield with Joe." Sally looked down and sniffed. Tears welled up in her eyes.

Stiggy grabbed her hand and pulled her to a stop. He looped his arms around her and stroked her back, tracing the ridges of the scars beneath her shirt with his fingers. "There's no point thinking like that, Sally. Joe's ... well, he's gone now, and he can't hurt you again."

"I know. And thank you for what you did. You know, after ..."

"Don't be daft, anyone would have done—"

Sally silenced him with a kiss. Stiggy's eyes bulged when her tongue darted into his mouth. Nobody had ever kissed him like that before. Certainly not Doris. In fact Doris made it clear from day one that kissing wasn't part of the deal. Not that he would want to kiss her. Her breath always smelled rank, like she'd been eating mouldy fish or something.

"No they wouldn't," Sally whispered when they parted.

She took Stiggy by the hand and continued down the river bank. Stiggy felt like he was walking on air. Other than Doris, who didn't really count, he'd never had a girlfriend before. He had friends who were girls, but none of them had ever fancied him in that way. It was always Brian, with his pretty-boy looks, who had the girls flocking around him, and Colin and Twiglet who scored the leftovers. Stiggy never stood a chance with his big nose and his chimp ears. The one time he had plucked up the courage to ask a girl out, she just laughed in his face and told him not to be so daft. Something his self confidence had never recovered from.

A couple of minutes later Stiggy and Sally came to an open stretch of ground strewn with worn out furniture and rusting household appliances, bricks and other building rubble, empty bottles and cans, and dozens of black plastic bags filled with rubbish. Stiggy often wondered how it all got there, so far away from the main road, but there was always something new each time he went. He'd even found a clapped out moped there once, with all its lights and mirrors smashed and its tyres slashed. He'd pushed it all the way back into town and took it to a scrap yard over the North Bridge, where he got five quid for it, enough to buy a litre can of glue and three bottles of cider. The cider disappeared down his neck that day, but the glue lasted him over a month.

Stiggy guided Sally across the unofficial rubbish tip to another arched bridge and sat down under it, on an old car seat he had found on a previous visit and transported there for that purpose. He shuffled to one side to make room for Sally, and she sat next to him while they watched the murky water float by and chatted about their respective pasts.

Sally told Stiggy about the first care home she lived in, and what little she remembered of the time before that. How her mother had never wanted her, and only saw her as a burden. Being left on her own at night when she went out drinking, then finding strange men in the flat when she woke up the next morning. Being screamed at all the time, but not knowing what she had done wrong to deserve it.

"Then one day, I think I must have done something really bad but I don't remember what, but she just wanted to get rid of me. This lady came, a social worker I guess, and two policemen, and they took me away. She was still screaming at me, even then. I can remember her banging on the window of the car they put me in and shouting abuse at me. The police had to grab hold of her and pull her away so she couldn't get to me."

"Fucking hell." Stiggy shook his head. "I don't know why people like that have kids. How old were you when that happened?"

"Dunno. Three or four, maybe?"

"Did you ever see her again?"

"No, and I didn't miss her either. It was good back then, that first home they put me in. Kids would come and go, but there was always someone to play with. And toys and books and stuff, and nobody ever yelled at you if you made a mess. I'd never had anything like that before, so it was like going to heaven."

"What do you mean, kids would come and go?"

Sally shrugged. "I suppose thinking about it now, they must have been adopted, or gone to a foster home or whatever."

"But you weren't?"

"No. I guess nobody else wanted me, either. So I stayed there until I was ten, then they moved me to another home for big kids. That's where I first met Dave. He'd been living in care all his life too, so I guess we had that in common." Sally sighed. "I don't know what I would have done without him. Or Trisha, come to that. I don't think I would have been able to ..."

Sally's voice trailed off as she stared across the river at the graffiti on the opposite side of the bridge. Stiggy sensed a sudden change in her mood, and reached out and squeezed her hand. She turned to him and smiled, but it looked forced.

"So what was it like for you growing up?"

"Pretty normal I guess," Stiggy said. "The early years, at least."

He told her about sunny day trips to Skegness, building sandcastles and going donkey riding. The long months spent waiting for July to come around, because that meant the annual holiday in Cleator Moor at Uncle Bert's house. Playing with his dog, a daft cocker spaniel that was obsessed with carrying stones around in its mouth. Visiting dead relatives in the town's cemeteries and hearing outlandish stories about each one.

Getting drunk on shandy made from real beer, and posing by the fountain next to the library while the locals gawped at him as if they'd never seen a punk before. Skimming stones across the river at the outskirts of town. Not a murky dead river filled with pollution and abandoned shopping trolleys like the one in Doncaster, but one so fresh and clean it even had live fish swimming in it.

"But then my dad got made redundant, and it all went a bit crap after that. We lost the house and ended up in this little council flat miles away from my mates, so I only got to see them at the weekends. And we couldn't afford to go on holiday no more, not even for a day trip."

"I've never been away on holiday," Sally said.

"What, never?"

"No. Never even been out of Sheffield until now."

"Really?" Stiggy turned to face her. "So if you could go anywhere in the world, where would it be?"

"Spain, I guess. Joe went with his football mates last year for the world cup, he said it's brilliant over there, sunny all the time, and there's lots to do and the beaches are really clean. You should've seen the tan he had when he got back."

"Why didn't he didn't take you with him?"

Sally shrugged "He said I would've just got in the way when the fighting started. But I think that was just an excuse, he's never been that bothered about me being there when he's fighting any other time."

"Yeah well," Stiggy said, "fuck him. I'll take you to Spain."

Sally smiled and shook her head. "You don't have to, it's just a dream, that's all. I know I'll never go there."

"No, I mean it, I'm going to take you to Spain. In fact we could go and live there right now, if you want. Fuck off out of England forever. What's to stop us?"

"I haven't got a passport. Don't even know how to get one."

"Do you need a passport for Spain?"

"Yeah, I think so."

"Oh. I haven't got one either." Stiggy looked down and bit his lip, then looked up and stared across the river. "But I'll still take you there one day, even if it means we have to sneak onto a boat or something."

Sally laughed. "Wouldn't you be worried about it sinking?"

* * *

On the way home, Stiggy called in at Patel's Corner Shop on Thorne Road to pick up a bottle of cider for the night and a loaf of bread for the weekend. He liked to support local businesses as much as he could, preferring to spend his money in those than the large, impersonal supermarkets in town, even if everything did cost a couple of pence more. A bell above the shop door pinged as he pushed it open and stepped inside. Mr Patel glanced up at him, then turned his attention back to one of the newspapers spread out on the counter before him.

Stiggy headed to a row of shelves lining the right hand side of the shop while Sally paused in the doorway and put the bag of toiletries down by her feet so she could browse through the magazines placed there on a rotating rack. He bent down to squeeze all the wholemeal loaves and check the dates printed on their packaging before choosing one from the back of the shelf, then took it to the counter and put it down on top of the newspaper Mr Patel was still engrossed in.

"And a bottle of Strongbow and two bottles of Babycham, please."

The shopkeeper looked up and frowned. "Hey you," he said when he noticed Sally. "No skinheads, can't you read? Get out of my shop or I will be calling the police."

"It's okay," Stiggy said, "she's with me." He'd forgotten about the sign on the door banning skinheads from entering. It had appeared several months ago, but he didn't know what had prompted it.

"I don't care who she is with, I won't be having hooligans like that in my shop again. All they do is cause trouble and never buy anything."

"She's not like that," Stiggy said, "she's different to the others." But Sally had already put the magazine back on the rack and left the shop. He sighed and repeated his order.

Mr Patel retrieved the drinks from a shelf behind the counter and put them in a carrier bag with the loaf of bread. "What a world we are living in," he said as he placed the bag down on the counter. "First skinheads, and now this."

"You what?" Stiggy asked.

"This." Mr Patel slapped his hand down on the newspaper he had been reading. "If you are not even safe in your own home, what hope is there for any of us?"

Stiggy glanced down at the newspaper the shopkeeper indicated. It was the *Doncaster Evening Post*, a local rag his father used to buy every Thursday for the job vacancies before he gave up all hope of ever finding employment again. Stiggy cocked his head to one side and squinted at the upside down headline.

MURDER VICTIM FOUND ON SHEFFIELD ESTATE

Underneath, taking up almost half the front page, was a grainy black and white photograph of Sally's house, cordoned off by crime scene tape. A uniformed police officer stood guard in front of the gate.

The ground seemed to lurch to one side under Stiggy's feet, and he had to grab hold of the counter to steady himself. He snatched up the newspaper and stared at the front page. His hands trembled as he read the headline once more.

"Oh fuck," he said under his breath.

12

"Shall I be adding that to your bill?" Mr Patel asked.

Stiggy heard the man speak, but he was too busy reading the newspaper report for the words to register.

Police were called to a home in the Shirecliffe area of Sheffield this afternoon, after neighbours complained of a putrid smell coming from a broken window at the rear of the property. Police officers forced entry to the house and found a decomposing body in the downstairs living room.

"I said, shall I be adding that to your bill? This isn't a library, you know."

"Yeah, whatever." Stiggy continued reading.

It is thought the body belongs to twenty-eight year old landscape gardener Joseph Hawkins, who took over tenancy of the property after the death of his mother five years ago, but this has not yet been confirmed. Police are appealing for any witnesses to come forward, and believe the victim was bludgeoned to death with a heavy object that has yet to be found. Detective Inspector Brady, who is leading the investigation, declined to comment when asked to speculate on a possible motive for the attack.

"That will be two pounds and sixty-eight pence, please."

"What?" Stiggy looked up from the newspaper.

Mr Patel held out his hand. "Your bill. Two pounds and sixty-eight pence, please."

"Um ... oh. Yeah, okay."

Stiggy pulled a five pound note from Joe's wallet and handed it over, then folded the newspaper in half and stuffed it into the carrier bag. The glass bottles inside clinked together when he picked the bag up and turned to head for the exit.

Had anyone seen him leave that house? Would that skinhead on the field keep quiet, like Sally said he would? Thank fuck he'd got rid of the van when he had the chance. But what about the man in the second hand shop he'd sold all the gardening equipment to? He'd seen the van when he helped carry it all into the shop, and he must have noticed the writing on the side of it. Hawkins Landscaping Services. Joseph Hawkins. He would be sure to make the connection sooner or later.

"Are you not wanting your change?" Mr Patel called out.

Stiggy paused as he reached out to open the shop door. He turned to stare at the Indian man behind the counter for a couple of seconds before it registered what he was saying. He blinked and nodded, then went to get the two pound notes and loose change Mr Patel held out for him.

"Thank you, come again," he said as Stiggy walked away once more.

Sally stood outside the shop, waiting for him. "Is there something wrong?" she asked when he joined her.

Stiggy thought about lying to her, but it was obvious from the way she looked at him that she suspected something. He took the newspaper from the bag and showed her the headline. Her face paled as she read it.

"Oh," she said. She glanced at the telephone box on the opposite side of the road, then bit her lip.

"What should we do?" Stiggy asked.

Sally shrugged. "What *can* we do? We both knew they would find him sooner or later."

"Yeah, I guess. I was kind of hoping they wouldn't, though."

Stiggy thought about coppers trawling through the house, looking for evidence. Would they find anything that put him at the scene? He was pretty sure he'd wiped everything down before he left, but there was always a possibility he had missed something. And all it would take to implicate him would be a stray fingerprint somewhere.

But then again, Stiggy realised with a flood of relief, he didn't have a criminal record, so his fingerprints wouldn't be in the system anyway. He'd had a few close scrapes while joyriding when he was a kid, and he'd been taken home by coppers a couple of times when he was off his head on glue while he was still living with his parents, but he had never been arrested for anything. So even if the coppers found his fingerprints somewhere in that house, they still wouldn't know who they belonged to.

Back at the flat, Stiggy found a note pushed under the door. He put the bags down on the sideboard and picked it up while Sally went into the kitchen with the bag of toiletries she'd bought. He unfolded the note and sat in the armchair to read it.

Stiggy, where the fuck have you been? Nobody's seen you since the Cockney Upstarts, so I came round to see if you're okay. Don't know if you heard about Brian or not, but he's getting better now, thank fuck. They reckon he'll be coming home next week, so we're all planning a get together round his house when he does if you want to come along. Anyway, see you soon. Colin. PS have you finished with that Astronauts record yet? I said I'd do Brian a copy, and it'd be good if he could have it to listen to as soon as he gets home.

Stiggy smiled. Well at least that was one less thing to worry about.

"Sounds like Brian's going to be okay," he said.

"That's good," Sally replied from the kitchen.

She came back into the living room, switched on the portable black and white television set on top of the stack of empty milk crates, and knelt down on the floor in front of it. On the screen, Giant Haystacks tried to pull Kendo Nagasaki's mask off while a mob of middle-aged women cheered him on.

"Don't you want to play your new record?" Stiggy asked.

"No," Sally said. "I want to watch the news."

Stiggy glanced at his watch. "News won't be on for another half an hour."

"I don't care, I need to see it. I need to find out what they know."

Sally picked at her lips through the rest of the wrestling, followed by the day's football results and a list of all the score draws for people checking their pools coupons. Then it was on to the racing results, and how much you would have won if you picked the right horses in the ITV Seven, before the sports reporter finally bade everyone a good evening.

The discovery of a murdered body in Sheffield was given a brief mention on the national news, but it wasn't until the local news bulletin covered it in more detail that Stiggy and Sally learned anything new. The victim was confirmed as being local businessman Joseph Hawkins, and an old school photograph of a fresh-faced young boy with dark, shoulder length hair was shown on screen. Stiggy leaned closer to the television to peer at the photo, wondering why they had chosen that one. He started to ask Sally, but she shushed him with a wave of her hand.

A man in a pinstripe suit, identified by a caption at the bottom of the screen as Detective Inspector Brady, gave the basic facts of the case and appealed for any witnesses to come forward. When pressed by reporters for a possible motive for such a brutal attack he said early indications pointed to a burglary gone wrong, and that Mr Hawkins must have arrived home early and confronted the intruder before being bludgeoned to death.

Hearing this, Stiggy exhaled audibly. His plan had worked, and he and Sally were in the clear. He smiled to himself and got up to switch off the television set. Sally continued staring at the screen as it shrank down to a tiny white dot in the centre, then faded away to nothing.

"That's good news, right?" Stiggy said. "They think a burglar did it."

Sally shook her head. When she turned to face him there were tears in her eyes. Stiggy crouched down before her and placed a hand on her shoulder.

"Sally? What is it? What's wrong? This is a good thing, it means they won't be looking for you."

Sally sniffed and brushed the tears away with the palms of her hands. "Until they find my fingerprints everywhere."

"Why would that make any difference? Yeah, they might want to talk to you to see if you saw anything, but that's all. It's not like they will think you broke into your own home, is it?"

"They will want to know why I was there."

"Well yeah, but then you just tell them you used to live there. Your neighbours will be able to confirm that."

"They never saw me."

"What? But you said you lived there for two years, how could they have not seen you?"

"Joe said if anyone ever saw me there I would have to go back to ..." Her voice trailed off. She looked down and shook her head once more. "They just didn't see me, okay?"

Stiggy frowned. The more he heard about her and Joe's relationship the more fucked up it seemed.

"Okay," he said. "Well there's always your mate Trisha, she knows you lived there, right? And that skinhead on the field, what's-his-name, he'll back you up too, yeah?"

"Dave? Yeah, I guess. But I don't know if they would believe him or not, he's been in a lot of trouble with the police."

"Anyone else who can confirm it? Joe's mates or whoever?"

Sally nodded. "Yeah, they all knew I lived there as well. But what if they saw me leave with you that night at the pop concert?"

"Why would that matter?"

"They saw you fighting with Joe, remember?"

"Yeah, so?"

"So what if they think you killed him in revenge for what he did to you? If they told the police, that would make you a suspect too."

Stiggy stiffened. He hadn't thought of that. "Okay," he said after a short pause. "Well maybe it's best if we just keep out of it then, yeah? Nobody knows you're here, right? I mean, you didn't tell that Dave geezer where you were when you phoned him, did you?" Sally shook her head. "Right, well, so we just lay low here then, yeah? Wait and see what happens. I mean, it's not like anyone's going to come looking for you here in Doncaster, is it?"

* * *

Stiggy sat in the armchair and finished off a bottle of cider while he listened to his new *Mob* album for the third time that evening. It was everything he had hoped it would be, even better than their *Crass* single. Sally was in the bathroom, cleaning her teeth and shaving her scalp with the battery-operated razor she'd bought. He could hear it buzzing away in the short gaps between songs. She'd been quiet and withdrawn all night, just like she had been that first night she moved into the flat, and Stiggy didn't know what to do about it. The *Selector* record she'd bought hadn't done the trick, she just stared into space all the way through it. She was still worried about the police, that much was obvious, but what could they do if they didn't know where she was?

Just as the record ended, Sally entered the living room wearing Stiggy's *Discharge* T-shirt. It was big and baggy on her, just long enough to cover her naked thighs, and the torn off sleeves and the rips in the worn out fabric gave tantalising glimpses of what lay beneath. Stiggy couldn't help staring as she walked over to the bed. It looked good on her, much better than the skinhead gear she wore in the daytime. If only he could get her to wear clothes like that more often, then he wouldn't need to worry about what his mates thought of her.

Sally pulled back the covers and sat on the edge of the bed with her hands on her knees. Stiggy smiled when she looked across the room at him, but she didn't smile back.

"You okay?" he asked.

"Yeah. Will you do something for me?"

Stiggy nodded. "Yeah, of course."

"I don't want to be on my own tonight."

"You won't be," Stiggy said. He patted the arm of the chair. "I'll be right here, same as always."

"I mean in here. In the bed. I want you to be in the bed with me. Will you do that for me? Please?"

Stiggy's eyes boggled. As if anyone would say no to an offer like that from a beautiful bird like Sally. He grinned. "Um ...

yeah. That's if you're sure you want me to. So, um, should I take my clothes off first?"

"I don't mind, it's up to you."

Sally lay down and scooted over to the far side of the bed, next to the wall, before pulling the covers over herself. She lay on her side facing him, her head resting on the single pillow.

Stiggy pulled off his *Crass* T-shirt and dropped it on the floor, then rose from the armchair. His hands trembled in anticipation at the thought of what was to come as he unbuttoned his combat trousers and pulled down the zip. But just as he was about to let them drop to his ankles and step out of them, a sudden panic came over him. What if his cock was too small, and Sally just laughed at it? He had no idea what she was used to with Joe, or how he would compare. The skinhead had been massive, so what if his manhood was in proportion to the rest of his body? And what if Stiggy was just no good at shagging, anyway? With Doris he was paying for a service so it didn't matter if he was rubbish at it or not. But with Sally it was different, and he didn't want to disappoint her. He bit his lip as he gazed across the room at her.

She was looking straight at him.

Stiggy's cheeks flushed red. He turned his back on her and dropped his trousers, then crab-walked over to the bed with his hands covering his crotch to hide the bulge in his underpants. Should he take his socks off, too? He sat down on the edge of the bed and peeled them off, then turned to look at Sally and ran a hand through his spiky hair.

"Um ... are you sure about this?"

Sally gazed into his eyes. "Yeah. That's if you don't mind."

Stiggy climbed into bed beside her and lay on his back, wondering how he should start this. With Doris he just hopped on and got straight down to business, but this was different. He wanted Sally to have a good time, too. Maybe he should let her take the initiative, then just go along with whatever she wanted?

Sally took his hand in hers. "Night then," she said.

"Um ... what? Oh. Um .. yeah .. night, Sally."

Still holding his hand, Sally drew up her knees and closed her eyes. Ten minutes later her breathing slowed and she fell asleep.

* * *

The next day Stiggy woke to the sound of the lunchtime news bulletin on the portable television. Sally sat in the armchair, clutching her knees to her chest as she stared at the black and white screen. She still wore his *Discharge* T-shirt, stretched over her legs like a cocoon so only her feet were visible. Stiggy smiled. It was good to see her still in it, that meant she hadn't been up long so she might come back to bed for a quick cuddle if he asked her to. Then he noticed her pale face, her trembling bottom lip. He bolted upright, convinced something bad had happened, and turned to face the television. But it was just some nonsense about the Pope visiting Poland. So what had put her on edge like that?

Unless it was something he had missed while he was asleep.

"Have they said something about Joe?" he asked, almost afraid to hear the answer.

Sally glanced in his direction, then turned back to the television. "No, not yet."

The news moved on to sport, then the national weather forecast. Sally bit at the fingertips of one hand while she waited for the local news to start.

Joe's murder was the lead story. A coroner had estimated his time of death to be the sixteenth of June, and Stiggy wondered how they could guess it so accurately. The newsreader went on to say police had reason to believe Joe's white transit van had been stolen by the perpetrator, along with a quantity of gardening tools contained within it. The registration number and a description of the van were read out, and an appeal was made for anyone who may have seen it on or around the sixteenth of June to come forward.

Stiggy thought about the man in the second hand shop. Would he make the connection, and give the police a description of the person who sold him those gardening tools? What if someone had seen the van parked up by the abattoir? That would make the likely dumping site for the murder weapon pretty obvious, and if they dredged the river they would be sure to find it.

"Police are also appealing for this person to come forward to assist with their enquiries," the newsreader continued. "Miss Sally Carter, who recently absconded from the Masbury Residential Care Home in Sheffield, is believed to have visited the home of Joseph Hawkins prior to his brutal murder and may hold information crucial to bringing the perpetrator to justice."

Stiggy's mouth gaped open. His eyes boggled as he stared at the photograph of Sally on the screen. She stood in front of a Swastika-daubed brick wall, giving a Nazi salute to the camera. He turned to face her in horror.

"What the fuck? You're a fucking Nazi?"

13

Tears welled up in Sally's eyes. She shook her head. "Joe made me pose like that, honest. You know what he's like, I didn't have no choice." She buried her face in her knees and sobbed.

Stiggy ran his hand through his hair and sighed. It seemed plausible enough, given what he knew about their life together. He frowned, then nodded. "Yeah, okay. Sorry. I should have thought of that, of course he would make you do it. I guess it was just a shock seeing you like that, you know?"

Sally looked up, tears still streaming down her cheeks. "Joe was in that photo too, standing next to me, but they must have cut him off it."

"Why would they do that?"

"Don't know."

"And why use that photo of him when he were a kid?"

Sally shrugged. "Don't know, I've never seen that one before."

"It's like they don't want anyone to know what he was really like, or something."

"What are we going to do, Stiggy?" she said after a short pause. "They know who I am."

"Yeah, I know. But they don't know you're here with me, do they? For all they know you're still in Sheffield, so that's where they'll be looking for you. It'll be okay, yeah?"

Sally bit her lip and nodded, but didn't say anything.

"So what do you want to do today?" Stiggy asked, trying to change the subject. "You know, after dinner? I thought maybe we could go down the river again, walk all the way down into Hexthorpe Park this time. I used to go there all the time when I was a kid, but I haven't been for years."

Sally shook her head. "I can't go out. Not now, not ever. Someone might recognise me and call the police."

"Yeah well, there's always a way round that."

"Like what?"

"Well, I've been thinking. That photo they showed, you were wearing your skinhead stuff, yeah? So what if you wore something else?"

"What do you mean?"

"Well, you know … if you looked like a punk instead of a skinhead, nobody would recognise you, would they?"

Sally's brow furrowed. "You mean stop being a skinhead?"

"Well, yeah, I guess. At least for now, anyway."

Sally stared at him for a couple of seconds, as if she were trying to figure out if he was joking or not. Then she shook her head and looked away. "I am what I am, Stiggy. How would you feel if someone said you had to stop being a punk?"

"Well yeah, but it's not me the coppers are looking for, is it? And at least it would mean you didn't have to hide away in here. Look, it doesn't need to be forever, Sally. It's just a disguise, right? You know, like when you were at school, and you had to wear a uniform?"

Sally lowered her feet to the ground and folded her arms over her chest. "I didn't go to no posh school like you did."

Stiggy smiled. "You make it sound like fucking Eton or something, it was just a normal high school. But the point is, it doesn't matter what you wear on the outside, you're still the same person inside. Does that make sense? Besides, you'd look good in anything."

Sally gave out a short, humourless laugh. "Hardly."

"No, I mean it. You're fucking beautiful."

Sally looked away again. "Fuck off, no I'm not."

"Of course you are." Stiggy got up from the bed and crouched before her. "Look, Sally, I don't know what sort of shit Joe's filled your head with, but I can probably guess. I had a PE teacher like that at school. He was always picking on me, saying how I'd never amount to anything, yeah? People like that, they just want to pull you down to their level. They get in your head and make you feel worthless, but it's all just bollocks. You're a fit looking bird, don't let anyone tell you otherwise. You just need to believe in yourself, that's all. For fuck's sake, I'm lucky you would even notice someone like me, never mind anything else."

Fresh tears welled up in Sally's eyes. She turned to face him and attempted a smile, then shook her head. "No, I'm the lucky one. I don't know what I would do without you. And I'm sorry about last night. I could tell you wanted to, but … well, it hurts, you know?"

"What does?"

"Fucking."

"Oh." Stiggy's face flushed. "Does it? I didn't know, I've only ever done it with..." He almost said a prostitute, but managed to stop himself in time. It didn't seem to hurt Doris when he fucked her, but maybe she was just good at hiding it. It was her job, after all. He shook his head and sighed. "Look, Sally, I don't mind, I really don't. And to be honest I'm kind of nervous about it myself, it's not like I'm an expert or anything. I'd probably just end up disappointing you."

"You won't," Sally said. She reached out and placed her hand on his arm. "And I will let you do it to me soon, I promise. It's the least I could do for you after everything you've done for me."

Stiggy shook his head. "Sally, you don't need to do anything for me. Last night, it was ... well, yeah, it was weird, but it was nice too, just being there with you. And anything else ... well, you know. That's up to you, and I don't mind waiting until you're ready, however long it takes."

"Yeah well, we might not have much more time left before the police catch me."

Stiggy frowned. "There's no point thinking that way, Sally. You're safe here, I promise. Besides, what's the worst that can happen if they do catch you? They pull you in for questioning, you tell them you don't know nothing, then they let you go. We've already been through this, remember? We left the gig before the trouble started, we slept in that shed at the allotments — both our fingerprints will be there to confirm that — then we went to that cafe for breakfast and came straight here. Whatever happened at your ... at Joe's house, it's nothing to do with us and nobody can prove otherwise."

* * *

Two nights later, Stiggy lay on the bed while the ska tape he had salvaged for Sally played on the stereo. The music was awful, but it was worth putting up with it just to see a smile back on her face as she bobbed her head along to it. She still wore her skinhead gear, he hadn't managed to talk her out of that yet, but things were definitely moving in the right direction. She hadn't used the battery operated shaver since they showed her photograph on the news, and the hard stubble on the back of her head had turned into a soft brown fuzz. The fringe and the long strands at the sides were still there, but Stiggy was convinced it was only a matter of time before they went. Then she could grow her hair out properly, maybe even dye it and spike it up to complete the image.

He decided he would have another go at convincing her to

wear some of his punk clothes in the morning. Then she might feel confident enough to go with him the next time he went out for supplies, instead of hiding away in the flat. Once she realised the disguise worked, and the streets weren't full of coppers waiting to grab her, things could go back to the way they were before. They could be a normal couple again, and he could show her off to his mates.

Sally got up from the armchair and switched the tape off. Stiggy glanced at his watch and groaned when he saw what time it was. Five to ten. He'd been hoping she would forget, or not realise what time it was until it was too late, then he'd be able to listen to John Peel on the radio instead. There hadn't been anything on the local news about Joe's murder since the day they found his body, but that didn't stop Sally from watching each bulletin religiously. She headed for the television resting on top of the milk crates in the corner of the room and switched it on.

An advert for a toilet cleaning product faded into view, the voiceover actor shouting the words to make sure everyone got the message about the danger of germs lurking in the u-bend. Sally returned to the armchair and sat on its edge, leaning forward with her hands on her knees. The smile had evaporated, replaced with worry lines. Why did she have to torture herself like this?

"It'll be okay," Stiggy said. "You'll see."

Sally glanced at him and forced a smile before turning her attention back to the television.

The News At Ten opening sequence played, the camera panning across Westminster to close in on the Big Ben clock tower. The first clang of the giant bell sounded. The photograph of Sally giving a Nazi salute flashed on screen.

"Police hunt teenage neo-Nazis for the murder of Sheffield businessman," a voice announced.

Sally let out a gasp and covered her mouth with one hand. Stiggy bolted upright and swore. Sally's hand trembled as she bit at her fingertips. She flinched with each crash of the bell punctuating the remaining headlines, before a grey-haired newsreader stared out from the screen.

"Good evening," he said. "Police were called to a residential home in Sheffield three days ago, where they discovered the body of local businessman Joseph Hawkins. At first it was thought Mr Hawkins had been bludgeoned to death after confronting a home intruder, but in a shock twist this evening South Yorkshire Police have now announced they have fresh evidence which suggests Sally Carter, a teenage girl who recently absconded from a care home in the city, along with an unknown associate of hers, may have been responsible for his death. Miss Carter, who is believed to be a member of a far right neo-Nazi skinhead gang notorious in the area, was previously wanted for questioning after her fingerprints were discovered in the deceased's council home on the Shirecliffe Estate in Sheffield. Detective Inspector Brady, who is leading the investigation into Mr Hawkins' murder, had this to say earlier."

Detective Inspector Brady sat behind a desk while cameras flashed and clicked around him.

"Earlier today, the burnt out remains of a white transit van registered to the victim were discovered by a dog walker in a remote area of Sandall Beat Wood in Doncaster. I can also reveal that Miss Sally Carter, along with an unknown male, were stopped for a routine traffic violation whilst driving Mr Hawkins' van near the scene of the crime earlier this week, on or around the date the coroner estimates to be his time of death. We believe Miss Carter may now be hiding out in Doncaster, possibly with this unknown accomplice, and would urge anyone who thinks they may have seen her to come forward. For their own safety, members of the public are urged not to approach either of these individuals themselves, but to contact the police immediately."

Stiggy clasped the top of his head and looked up at the ceiling. Fuck. This changed everything. And thanks to those coppers who pulled them over in the van, they knew about him too. They should never have taken that van, they should have got the bus instead. Why had they been so fucking stupid? Then he'd gone and made everything worse by letting those kids outside the fruit and veg shop drive off with it. He should have got rid of it himself, driven it up to Derbyshire or something, dumped it as far away as possible and got the train back. Now he'd led the coppers straight to them.

"The man we are searching for," Brady continued, "is described as white, approximately eighteen years of age, of medium build and height, dressed in attire consistent with those who follow the punk rock craze. He was last seen wearing green camouflage trousers and a black T-shirt with a circled white cross symbol on it. The officer who issued him with a warning for the traffic violation says it was clear from his dishevelled appearance and the bruising on his arms that he had been involved in some altercation, as was Miss Carter. We are issuing this photofit of the man, and would urge anyone who thinks they may know his identity to come forward."

Stiggy stared at the composite photograph of himself. They had his protruding ears right, and the acne around his mouth, but the rest of it didn't look much like him. The hair was too short, the nose was too small, the shape of his head was all wrong, and the eyes they had given him just looked creepy, like they belonged to a serial killer or something. They had even got the *Crass* logo on his T-shirt completely wrong, it was just a plain white cross inside a circle. More like a sniper's crosshairs than the symbol of anarchy and peace it represented.

Stiggy turned to Sally when the news moved on to other matters. Her face was ashen, her eyes wide and staring. He didn't know what to say. What could he possibly say to reassure her when he knew deep down himself that their situation was hopeless? His throat tightened, like someone was strangling him, and it hurt when he swallowed. He clasped his hands together to stop them shaking.

But worse was to come.

The local news following the national bulletin devoted its entire ten minute slot to the story. They showed the schoolboy photograph of Joe and described him as an honest businessman cut down in the prime of his life by crazed fascists. They ran the same video clip of Detective Inspector Brady, and followed it up by showing the photofit of Stiggy alongside the photograph of Sally giving a Nazi salute.

A sociology lecturer from Sheffield University pointed out that the circled cross symbol shown on the photofit was widely used by supporters of *British Movement*, a far right political organisation who called for the enforced repatriation of all non-whites from the United Kingdom.

"It is highly likely Joseph Hawkins' death was politically motivated," he said. "To neo-Nazis such as these two individuals, anyone who doesn't see the world through their own narrow prism is considered a traitor to the white race, and therefore an enemy to be disposed of without a second thought. There is no doubt in my mind that, if these individuals are not apprehended soon, they will kill again."

The newsreader interviewing the lecturer nodded, his face a mask of indignant outrage.

"Miss Carter had a very troubled upbringing," he said, "is it possible this may be responsible for her extremist views toward immigrants?"

"Well, as we now know from a report by her social worker,

she spent most of her life in the care of the local authority. It's highly likely her own self-loathing at being abandoned by her parents is being projected onto ethnic minorities as a form of coping mechanism. This, combined with her history of solvent abuse, may indeed have been the catalyst for her numerous violent outbursts, culminating in the cold-blooded slaughter of Mr Hawkins."

"You sound like you are trying to make excuses for her actions."

"No, not at all. I am merely postulating on events that may have led her down such a violent path. Miss Carter is solely responsible for her own actions. She chose to join a neo-Nazi skinhead gang in order to terrorise ethnic minorities. Just like she chose to bludgeon Mr Hawkins to death."

"I've had enough of this fucking shit," Stiggy said. He got up from the bed and headed over to the television to switch it off.

"No, leave it on!" Sally yelled. "We need to know what they're saying."

Stiggy turned to face her. "What's the point? It's just fucking bollocks. They've got you down as some sort of raving Nazi, when it was Joe who was the fucking Nazi. All that shit they're saying about you, they should be saying it about him."

"I know, but we still need to hear it."

Stiggy sighed. He ran his hands through his hair, then sat down on the arm of the chair next to Sally. He could feel her trembling as she leaned against him. He stroked the side of her head. "It doesn't matter what they say Sally, we both know the truth. And so does everyone who knew him. Sooner or later, someone will come forward and tell them what Joe was really like. You'll see."

"Well, earlier this evening," the newsreader said, "we spoke to Simon Watkins, manager of the Masbury Residential Care Home in Sheffield where, until she absconded several days ago, Sally Carter resided for the last five years. This is what he had to say about her."

Stiggy was about to ask what 'absconded' meant, when Sally let out another gasp. She jerked back into the armchair as if she had been physically thrown there, then looked away and covered her ears with her hands.

The man on the television screen looked to be in his late thirties and had a neatly trimmed goatee beard and moustache. Stiggy wondered what it was about him that had caused such a reaction in Sally.

"Sally Carter was already a deeply troubled young girl when

she entered my care," he said. "She would regularly truant from school, and on the rare occasions when she did attend she was violent to both teachers and pupils alike. At the age of twelve she began experimenting with solvents and her attitude toward authority worsened. Her violent outbursts became more frequent. One night she threatened a visitor to the care home with a knife, and had to be restrained by members of staff for her own safety."

Stiggy glanced at Sally. She was shaking her head, her hands still clasped over her ears. He couldn't believe she would do something like that, despite what he saw her do to Joe with that axe handle. If she did threaten someone with a knife, she must have had a fucking good reason because in normal circumstances she was the most timid person he'd ever met.

"Soon after that incident Miss Carter ran away from the home with another girl, and we were forced to alert the police and report what she had done in case she attacked them, too. When apprehended she made up wicked stories about me to justify her actions, stories deliberately designed to ruin my professional reputation. Fortunately the police saw through her lies, and no further action was taken against me. Sally Carter, meanwhile, was issued with a police caution for threatening behaviour and wasting police time. We had hoped she would calm down after that, but if anything it just made her behaviour even worse."

"Why is he saying all that stuff about you?" Stiggy asked.

Sally removed her hands from her ears and clenched her fists. Her nostrils flared as she stared at the man on the black and white screen. "Because he's a fucking bastard!" she said through gritted teeth.

"At the age of thirteen," Watkins continued, "Sally joined a neo-Nazi skinhead gang and adopted their far right views. Her behaviour deteriorated even further from then on, as she became more and more embroiled in her own fantasy world in which everyone was out to get her. One little Pakistani girl in our care was left traumatised when she was told she should, and I paraphrase here for the sake of decency, go back to her own country."

"You fucking liar!" Sally shot up from the armchair and bolted over to the television.

"We tried our best to keep her on the straight and narrow, but she was simply out of control and we just couldn't cope."

"Fuck off, you fucking bastard!" Sally yelled, her face inches away from the flickering screen.

"With the type of people she was associating with at that time, people with no real moral code, it wasn't long before she—"

Sally jabbed at the off switch so hard Stiggy thought it would send the portable television crashing off the upturned milk crates it rested on, but instead it just rocked backwards and forwards precariously for a couple of seconds. Sally turned to face Stiggy. Her fists were clenched, her eyes blazing in anger. She breathed audibly through her mouth in short gasps.

Stiggy stared from Sally to the white dot in the centre of the now silent television, and back again. His mouth dropped open. What the fuck was that all about? And what was Watkins just about to say about her before she switched it off?

14

Stiggy got up from the armchair and padded over to Sally.
He reached out for her, and at first she flinched away from him,
but then she melted into his arms and returned his embrace.

"What happened to you at that home?" he asked. "That
geezer on the telly, did he do something to you?"

Sally struggled in his grip, but he held her tight.

"What did he do to you, Sally?"

Her shoulders slumped. "Nothing."

"You wouldn't have reacted like that when you saw him if
he didn't do nothing."

"Just forget it, okay?"

"Is it something to do with Joe? I just want to understand,
that's all, because none of it makes any sense to me. You said
you were still living at the home when you first met him, so
you must have only been about fifteen at the time. Did Watkins
know about it? Did he encourage it?"

"I don't want to talk about it."

"What he said about you threatening someone with a knife,
is that true?"

Sally shrugged. She struggled against him again, and this
time he let her go. She walked over to the bed and sat down on
it.

Her hands trembled as she unlaced her boots and kicked
them off.

"Who was he?" Stiggy asked.

Sally shook her head. "I don't know. I never knew his name.
Just one of the men who used to visit, that's all." She peeled off
her socks and put them inside the boots.

"What did he do?"

Sally looked up and stared at Stiggy for several seconds,
then looked away. She stood up and turned her back on him
while she unbuttoned her shirt and took it off. A lump grew in
Stiggy's throat as he stared at the criss-cross of old scars on
her back. He couldn't help thinking back to Joe pinning her
down to that chair, lashing out at her. The pain she must have
endured through all those beatings. No wonder she flipped and

bashed his brains out.

"Sally, I know you. You wouldn't wave a knife at someone for no reason. He must have done something to you first."

Sally picked up the *Discharge* T-shirt lying at the bottom of the bed and threw it on before turning round to face him.

"Does it matter?" she asked.

"Well, yeah. I just want to understand it better."

Sally sighed again and shook her head. "It's in the past, Stiggy, let's just leave it there, yeah? I don't want to talk about it. I don't even want to think about it. Let's just go to bed, yeah? We might not have many more nights together, so we should make the most of them, not worry about things we can't change." She pulled the T-shirt down over her thighs and peeled off her jeans, then climbed into bed and shuffled over to the far side, next to the wall.

Stiggy wanted to press her for more information, but it was obvious he wouldn't get any answers from her. Maybe she was right, and they should just make the most of whatever time they had left before the coppers caught up with them. Sally watched as he undressed down to his underpants and tossed his clothes onto the armchair. He stood before the bed and gazed down at her.

"I'll think of something," Stiggy said. "Just because they're looking for us in Doncaster, it doesn't mean they'll find us. Maybe we'll be okay. And like I said the other day, you could always wear some of my punk clothes. Then once your hair grows out properly nobody will recognise you, will they?"

Sally pulled back the bed covers and patted the mattress beside her. "Let's just forget about all that stuff for now. It's not like we can do anything about it tonight. Just come to bed and hold me. Please?"

Stiggy got into bed and pulled the covers over them both. Sally snuggled up against him and held the back of his head while they kissed. Stiggy draped his arm around her waist and pulled her lower body closer. Her tongue forced its way into his mouth. Her right leg hooked over him and she drew up her knee so the crotch of her knickers rested against his swollen manhood. Fingertips ran up and down his spine, sending him wild with desire.

He knew she would pull away from him soon, she always did, but he was determined to make the most of it while he still could. He caressed her thigh, and her knee inched higher. She murmured, and squirmed against him. He toyed with the elastic of her knickers, then when she didn't object he slipped his hand inside them and felt his way along the cleft between her buttocks. She broke the kiss and gave out a little gasp. Her cheeks were flushed, and he could feel her body trembling against him. But she made no attempt to disentangle herself from him, like he expected.

"Have you got any johnnies?" she whispered.

Stiggy stared back at her. It took him a second to realise the implication of her question. His eyes boggled. "Um ... yeah, I think so. Are you sure?"

"Yeah."

Stiggy grinned at her, all thoughts of impending doom gone from his mind. "I'll go and get them, then."

He jumped out of bed and headed for the kitchen. He couldn't believe this was happening. He'd fantasised about this moment for so long, and now it was really here. Or was it? Halfway across the living room he stopped and turned back to face Sally.

"You're definitely sure this is what you want? I don't want to force you or nothing."

Sally sat up in bed and pulled the *Discharge* shirt over her head. She smiled as she tossed it to one side. "Just go and get the johnnies, yeah?"

Stiggy stared at her breasts for a couple of seconds, then ran into the kitchen to do as he was told.

* * *

The following morning Stiggy woke to the aroma of coffee and porridge wafting out of the kitchen. He smiled to himself as the memory flooded into his mind. Sex with Sally had been nothing like what he did with Doris. That was just mechanical and businesslike, with Sally it was tender and loving. Afterwards they lay together in each other's arms, and Stiggy had never felt so content before. Nothing else mattered. Not Joe, not whatever it was Sally was keeping from him, not even the threat of coppers bashing the door down and beating them both senseless.

"Was it okay?" he asked as he traced the scars on her back with his index finger. "Did I do it right?"

"Yeah," Sally whispered.

Then he remembered something she'd said soon after moving in, and propped his head up on his elbow so he could look into her eyes when he asked her. "Did I hurt you? You know ... like you said it did with Joe?"

Sally smiled and snuggled up against him. "No, it was nice. I didn't know it could be like that. It never was with any of the others."

Others? Stiggy felt a sudden pang of jealousy. What others? He'd assumed Joe was the only one she'd slept with, so who else was there? Presumably Dave, the skinhead she kept going on about all the time, would be one of them, but who else? And how many others?

Then Sally rolled onto her back and held Stiggy's hand while she drifted off to sleep, just like she did every other night, and he forgot all about it. Whoever they were, they weren't as good at shagging as Stiggy was, and that was all that mattered.

Stiggy lay there daydreaming for as long as he could before his bladder insisted he needed to get up and empty it. He slipped on a fresh pair of underpants, picked up the used condom from the floor with his thumb and forefinger, and padded into the kitchen to dispose of it.

Sally sat at the kitchen table wearing a *Sex Pistols* T-shirt along with her bleached jeans and red braces. It was a shirt Stiggy had bought for himself when he was thirteen, back when they were still his favourite band, long before he discovered *Crass* and *Discharge* and went off them. It was too small for him now, and he had forgotten he had brought it with him when he moved out of his parents' flat, but it seemed to fit her well. And there was no denying it, it did look good on her the way it hugged her pert breasts.

Sally looked up and smiled as Stiggy headed for the toilet in the bathroom. "Morning. I was just about to wake you."

"Why, what time is it?"

"Just gone eleven."

Stiggy grunted in reply, still lost in his memory of the night before. His mind registered there was something different about Sally other than the clothes she wore, but it wasn't until he dressed in his combat trousers and *Varukers* T-shirt and sat down opposite her at the table that he realised what it was. She'd cut off the fringe and the long strands at the sides, to make her hair a uniform half an inch in length. Stiggy wondered if he should say something about it, compliment her on how much better it looked. She might think he hadn't noticed, otherwise. Like his dad once, after his mother came back from the hairdresser. That had caused a blazing row that went on for hours. He picked up the mug of black coffee Sally had poured for him and took a sip while he composed his words.

"I've had an idea," Sally said before he had chance to think of anything. "What if we went away somewhere? Somewhere nobody knows us, and where nobody would ever think of looking for us."

"What, you mean like Spain or something?"

"No, I was thinking more about that place in the country you told me about. You know, where you used to go on holiday."

"What, Cleator Moor?" Stiggy grinned. Why hadn't he thought of that? "You know, that's not a bad idea at all. We could stay at my uncle Bert's house until we found somewhere of our own."

"Do you think he would mind?"

"No, why would he? I haven't seen him for years, he'll be dead chuffed when we turn up at his door."

"Maybe you should phone him first, just to make sure?"

"He's not on the phone. Or at least he wasn't the last time I stayed there. Don't worry, he'll be fine with it."

"And he won't mind me staying there, too?"

"Nah, don't be daft. Why would he, a beautiful bird like you?"

Sally smiled and shook her head. "Is it far away?"

"Yeah, couple hundred miles, at least, and you have to change trains loads of times, so it'll take all day to get there. And there's no train station at Cleator Moor, so you have to get off at Whitehaven and go the rest of the way by bus; and those only run every couple of hours or so, if you're lucky. But that's what makes it so perfect, nobody ever bothers going there because there's nothing to do once you get there. It's just fields and hills wherever you look, and there's no coppers as far as I remember. I never saw none, anyway. The people who live there are dead friendly, too. Even in my punk gear I never got any hassle while I was there. Well, except for this old bloke who said people like me should be put in the army, but he'll probably be dead by now."

Sally smiled. "Sounds nice. So when can we go?"

"Whenever you like. After my next Giro comes would be best, then we'll have a bit more money to keep us going while I make a fresh claim."

"When's that?"

"Next Friday. But I'd like to see my mates again before we go. You know, to say goodbye and stuff, and give them back the records I've borrowed off them. There's this pub in town they all go to on Friday nights, The Juggler's Rest it's called, and they usually have a local band playing there. I thought maybe we could go along to that? Then we could set off the next day, after dinner. The train's less likely to be packed out by then, so we won't have to stand up."

Sally nodded. "Sounds good to me. Saturday it is, then."

Later in the afternoon, Stiggy went to Patel's Corner Shop for a loaf of wholemeal bread while Sally looked after a pan of stew he'd left to simmer on the Calor Gas camping stove. His mind buzzed with anticipation as he walked up Broxholme Lane to Thorne Road. It would be a struggle fitting all his belongings into a suitcase, and he would need to make some hard decisions about what to leave behind. But they were only possessions, and they could be easily replaced once he and Sally got settled into their new life in the country.

He couldn't wait to show her around Cleator Moor. He'd take her up Dent Fell, the giant hill dominating the landscape for miles around. The River Ehen on the outskirts of town, and the picnic area next to the hump-backed bridge. The row of shops that all closed early on Saturday afternoons, and the two pubs — one for old people and farmers, the other for youths closer to their own age. They'd make new friends, settle into a life of leisure in the countryside. Get a flat somewhere, and claim Housing Benefit to cover the rent. Pick blackberries and

—

Stiggy stopped dead in his tracks on the corner of Broxholme Lane. A skinhead in a green bomber jacket sat on the bench next to the telephone box opposite the corner shop. Stiggy felt the same spike of adrenalin he always felt when he saw skinheads. He'd been attacked by them too many times in the past for anything Sally said about them not all being violent thugs to make any difference. Maybe they weren't all bad, like she said, but why take the risk? He decided to head back down Broxholme Lane and go into town instead. While he was there he could find out how much the train tickets would cost, then see if any of his mates were in the Arndale Centre. Find out what happened when they all went down to Sheffield looking for skinheads last Saturday, see if they found any or not.

Doris stood on the corner of Glyn Avenue, her rucksack leaning against a wall beside her. Her hair was matted, her face grimy.

"Are you looking for business?" she asked as Stiggy approached.

Stiggy shook his head. "No, sorry. I've got a girlfriend now."

"Oh." Doris looked almost disappointed. She frowned, then said: "Can I use your shower?"

"Um ... what?"

"Your shower. Is it okay if I use it?"

"Why, what's wrong with yours?"

Doris shrugged. "It's busted."

Up close, she did smell pretty ripe. Doris had never been much of a one for personal hygiene at the best of times, but in the blistering heat of the early afternoon sun she absolutely stank of stale sweat and ... was that piss he could smell, too?

Stiggy sighed. He wanted to help, but what would Sally think if he took a thirty-five year old woman back home with him so she could use the shower? Especially one wearing such revealing clothing. That would lead to some awkward questions he didn't want to answer. But he did still have fond memories of his times with Doris, dating right back to the night Twiglet hired her for him as a flat warming present when he first moved into Broxholme Lane. It was the night he lost his virginity, and even though it only lasted twelve seconds it was something he would never forget, and something he would always be grateful for.

Doris scratched her head as she stared at Stiggy and waited for an answer. Specks of dandruff and what looked like soil rained down onto the shoulders of her low-cut PVC top.

"Um ... yeah, okay, I guess it won't hurt. But it will need to be later, I'm heading into town now."

"Will you be back soon?"

"I don't know. Probably an hour, maybe? I'll come and find you."

"You're a good kid," Doris said.

Stiggy walked down Glyn Avenue and onto Christ Church Road, heading into town. He picked up a wholemeal loaf at the Kwik Save supermarket on the corner of Park Road, called in at the amusement arcade on Silver Street to change a couple of pound notes into fifty pence coins for the electric meter, then continued through town to the train station.

Three uniformed police officers with clipboards stood outside the main entrance. The sight of them made Stiggy's skin crawl. Whatever they were up to, it couldn't be anything good. One was busy talking to a couple who had just stepped out of a taxi with a suitcase, while another had his back turned, looking inside the station. The third stared straight at Stiggy.

Stiggy slowed his pace as he headed across the car park toward them. Every instinct told him to turn around and run, get the fuck out of there in case he'd been recognised from the photofit. But doing that would just make him look suspicious, and cause them to give chase. So instead he looked down at his trainers as he shuffled closer. Maybe he could slip by without being stopped. Without any of them getting a closer look at him.

"Just a minute, son," the copper said. He held up one hand, as if he were directing traffic.

Stiggy stood before him, still looking down to avoid eye contact. "Yeah?"

"I wondered if you might have seen either of these two individuals in the area recently."

He held out the clipboard. Stiggy's cheeks flushed as he stared at the stack of leaflets it contained.

They showed Sally giving a Nazi salute in front of a Swastika-daubed wall.

The photofit of Stiggy with the sinister eyes and the weird circled cross symbol on his chest.

Along with a caption that promised a five hundred pound reward for information leading to their arrest for the murder of Sheffield businessman Joseph Hawkins.

15

"Um … no, I don't think so."

If the copper heard the squeak of panic in Stiggy's voice he didn't comment on it. Five hundred quid! Just about everyone he knew would shop their own granny for that sort of money.

"Take your time, son," the policeman said. He tapped the photofit of Stiggy with his index finger. "Does this one look at all familiar to you? We believe he may live locally, and his manner of dress suggests he might be one of your lot."

Stiggy's ears burned. Would the copper notice they stuck out the same way the ones on the photofit did?

"My lot?" he asked.

The hint of a sneer crossed the officer's face. He glanced down at Stiggy's glue-stained combat trousers, then back up at his Varukers T-shirt before regaining eye contact. "Punk rockers."

Stiggy shook his head and looked away. "No, never seen him before."

"Are you sure?"

"Yeah, I said so, didn't I?"

"Perhaps you should look again. This is a serious matter, and it deserves serious attention."

Stiggy made a point of studying the photofit for several seconds, then shook his head again. "No, don't know him, honest. Or the other one."

"You do realise, aiding and abetting a murder suspect is a serious offence?

"Well I can't tell you nothing I don't know, can I?"

The officer sighed. He pulled the top sheet from the clipboard and held it out to Stiggy. "Well if you change your mind, or if you do happen to run into either of them, call the number at the bottom immediately."

"Yeah, okay."

Stiggy took the sheet of paper, folded it up, and stuffed it in his back pocket. He turned and headed through the glass door into the train station foyer with a sense of relief mixed with a feeling of dread. The bastard hadn't recognised him from the photofit, but there was no way he and Sally could escape by train if they were guarding the station like that. Even if Sally was in disguise it wouldn't stand up to close scrutiny. And if they were watching the train station, there was a good chance they would be watching both the north and south bus stations, too.

"Just a minute, son." The copper followed Stiggy into the foyer.

"Yeah?"

"What's in the bag?"

"Some bread."

"Mind if I take a look?"

Stiggy shrugged and held open the carrier bag. The copper looked inside, prodded the bread with his finger, and grunted.

"Turn out your pockets."

"What? Why?"

"Because I told you to."

Stiggy sighed. He pulled his hanky and the fifty pence coins out of his left pocket and held them out for inspection, then turned his pocket inside out to show there was nothing else in there.

"Now the other one."

"There's nothing in that one."

"Prove it."

Stiggy pulled out the lining of his right pocket.

"Anything else on you?"

Stiggy thought about Joe's wallet in his back pocket. Was there anything in it that would link it to its previous owner? There was the photograph of the old woman, but that could be anyone. Other than that he couldn't think of anything. The skinhead's driving license and other identifying documents had been in the transit van when he dumped it.

Stiggy felt his face flush as he pulled out the wallet and presented it. The gold initials JH stamped in the corner seemed a lot bigger than he remembered them. Impossible to miss. Sweat dribbled from his armpits as the copper snatched the wallet from him and opened it up. He looked inside, flicked through the notes it contained, then looked up at Stiggy with his head cocked to one side.

"Is there a reason you are carrying this much money around with you?"

"Um ... yeah."

"Which is?"

"It's ... well, it's Giro day, isn't it? And I've just cashed my rent cheque as well."

The copper frowned. Stiggy wasn't sure if he'd believed him or not.

"I see." He closed the wallet, held it up with his thumb and forefinger, and waved it in the air. "And your name is?"

Was this a test? Had he seen the initials? Stiggy had to think fast. "Um ... John. John ... Hanky."

"Well, Mr Hanky, I would recommend you deposit your money in the bank until you need it, it's not safe to carry this sort of amount around with you."

Stiggy nodded. He smiled as an immense feeling of relief coursed through him. "Yeah. Yeah, I will. Good idea, thanks."

The copper turned and walked away, back through the glass door to join his two colleagues. Stiggy closed his eyes and sighed. Fuck, that was close. He sat down on one of the benches opposite the newsagents kiosk and scratched the top of his head between the rows of spikes. He would need to rethink his plans, and quick. The more of those photographs the police distributed, the more people would be looking for him and Sally so they could cash in on the five hundred quid reward. So the sooner they got out of Doncaster and headed for the country the better.

But how?

Stiggy thought briefly about stealing a car from somewhere, but soon dismissed the idea as being too risky. Once it was reported stolen, every copper for miles around would be on the lookout for it. All it would take would be for one patrol car to recognise the registration number and that would be the end of everything. He would rather take his chances by hiding out in the flat than let that happen. Buy up enough food, cider, and other essential supplies to keep them going until he could come up with a new plan. Or just wait it out until the heat died down.

But sooner or later the police would be going door to door with those leaflets, and when that happened it was only a matter of time before someone shopped them in order to claim the reward.

Stiggy sighed. Whichever way he looked at it they were well and truly fucked. He wondered what sort of sentence he would get for his part in it all. Maybe if he persuaded Sally to give herself up they might go easy on him? But there was no getting away from what Sally had done to Joe. That would mean serious jail time for her, so even if he was lucky enough to get a suspended sentence for himself he'd probably never see her again. And just the mere thought of that happening made his chest ache.

No, they were in it together, and they would fight it all the way. The coppers would have to drag them kicking and screaming from that flat. He'd barricade the door, push all the furniture up against it. Arm himself with a knife and stand and fight. Defend their liberty from an army of blue bastards and demand a TV news crew so he and Sally could tell their side of the story. What Joe was really like, and what he had done to her. Then the whole world would know the truth.

But Stiggy knew deep down it was all just a fantasy. When the coppers came for him and Sally there would be nothing he could do to stop them. He wouldn't last ten seconds against a mob of thugs with truncheons, and he knew it.

Stiggy rose from the bench and wandered over to the newsagents kiosk so he could check what the coppers outside were doing in the reflection of its plate glass window. While one of them had already seen him, it would be best if the others didn't get too close a look in case they recognised him. He'd wait until all three were busy, then slip past with his head down. Maybe wave the sheet of paper at them, so they would know he'd already been checked.

The station tannoy announced the arrival of a train from Sheffield on platform 3B.

Stiggy smiled. Perfect timing. With a bit of luck there'd be a crowd of people disembarking, and he could lose himself among them when they left. One of the coppers was looking in his direction, so he went inside the newsagents and browsed the magazine covers while he waited for the crowds to arrive.

He remembered he hadn't picked up that week's *2000AD* yet, and crouched down to check the comics on the bottom shelf to see if they had any left. They had one dog-eared copy sandwiched between *The Beano* and *The Dandy*. He picked it up and took it to the counter. While he rummaged in his pocket for twenty pence to pay for it, he glanced down at the newspapers spread out before him. Then gaped at one of them in particular.

MEET SALLY CARTER, THE TEENAGE NAZI KILLER! the headline screamed in two-inch high block capitals. Below it was the same photograph of Sally giving a Nazi salute he had seen countless times before. He snatched the paper up and unfolded it, then read the brief introductory text on the front page with a feeling of despair.

Full and exclusive details on pages two, three and four! it promised at the bottom. *How a history of violence and hate turned a young girl into a killer!*

Grateful it was only the local newspaper and not one of the nationals, Stiggy bought a copy along with the *2000AD* and dropped them both into the carrier bag with the loaf of bread. No way could he let Sally see that, it would just push her over the edge. But he had to know what the coppers knew about her, and what it was she was keeping from him, and the newspaper was sure to give him those answers. Maybe when he knew what it was that was wrong with Sally he would be in a better position to help her get through it.

People were starting to drift through the ticket barrier and head for the train station exit. Not as many as Stiggy had hoped, but it was his best chance to slip away unnoticed before any of the coppers spotted his resemblance to the photofit they were handing out. He tagged along behind a young woman pushing a pram, and walked straight through the exit with his head down. Once safely out of sight, he crossed the road and headed into the Arndale Centre to find a spare bench to sit on while he studied the newspaper for clues about Sally's past.

Joe's schoolboy face smiled out at him on page two. The article described him as an honest, hard-working businessman cut down in the prime of his life and speculated on why he had been targeted by neo-Nazis like Sally Carter and her gang of skinheads. Glowing character testimonials from several of Joe's landscaping customers were printed, including one from Simon Watkins, the manager of the care home Sally had lived at when she was younger. Even an elected member of Sheffield City Council had nothing but praise for the murdered skinhead, calling him a close personal friend who he had first met at a business club function he attended several years ago.

Sally, meanwhile, was portrayed as a far right fantasist with proven links to a prominent neo-Nazi skinhead gang known to be active in the Sheffield area. This gang, it said, had recently infiltrated a pop concert at The Marples and caused a riot that resulted in several people being hospitalised, including one almost-fatal wounding with a broken bottle.

Stiggy assumed they meant the *Cockney Upstarts* gig. That would make his mate Brian the almost-fatal wounding.

It went on to say Sally Carter was most likely the instigator behind the violence that night, and made reference to a police caution she received for threatening behaviour after an unsuccessful attempt to stab a visitor to the care home in which she resided at the time.

The inference that Sally was responsible for stabbing Brian with a broken bottle wasn't lost on Stiggy. Except that was just bollocks, because she had been with him the whole time and she wouldn't do anything like that anyway. He wondered how the newspaper could get everything so wrong. Sally was no fucking Nazi, and if she did wave a knife at someone when she lived at the care home she would have had a fucking good reason for it. And why weren't they telling people Joe was a skinhead too? He had been wearing skinhead gear the day he died, and he even had a Swastika tattoo on his chest, so they must have known what sort of person he was. But there was no mention of any of Joe's far right political beliefs, or his own violent past. The old school photograph they showed of him with shoulder length hair and an innocent smile distanced him even further from his true nature. So what the fuck was going on?

Sally's personal history, presented on page three, made for uncomfortable reading. Some of it Stiggy already knew from the television news report and from what little she had told him herself, but there were extra details that both surprised and sickened him. Sally's teenage mother suffered from clinical depression most of her young life, and this, combined with the abject poverty she lived in and the lack of any apparent father figure, was seen as reason enough to take Sally into local authority care for her own protection.

Stiggy looked up from the newspaper and stared into the distance. So Sally's mother hadn't given her away, after all. She'd had no choice in the matter, and Sally must have remembered it wrong. She wouldn't have been shouting abuse at Sally, she would have been shouting at the social workers and police, trying to stop them from taking her. He should tell Sally about it, maybe it would change the way she felt about herself. Stop her from feeling so worthless and unwanted. He looked down and continued reading. Maybe it would say where Sally's mother lived, so he could reunite them before they left for the country.

Sally's mother sought treatment for her depression and spent the next three years fighting to get her daughter back, mounting appeal after appeal with the help of a junior solicitor sympathetic to her plight. Each time, the judge hearing the case decided in the favour of Sheffield Social Services and she was denied any contact. At the age of nineteen, following one such court hearing, she threw herself off the balcony of her high-rise flat and ended her life.

Stiggy let the newspaper drop to his knees and stared into space once more. Anger flared through him. Those bastard judges. It was all their fault. Sally could have had a normal life with her mother if it wasn't for them. Instead, she had ended up living with some fucking monster, and now she was on the run because of it. How could he tell her the truth now? If Sally's mother was still alive, it would be different. But to find out her mother had wanted her after all, and then killed herself because of some heartless judge? It would be kinder to just keep it all from her.

Stiggy sighed, and lifted the newspaper once more.

The article went on to detail Sally's experiments with solvent abuse at the age of twelve. This, it said, was when her behaviour first started to deteriorate. Where she had once been a bright student with above average grades, well loved by everyone, she became more and more disruptive. It described her as being out of control, and related several instances of unprovoked attacks on other children, both in the playground and during classes. One involved a black boy being scarred for life after she hit him in the face with a brick. Another said she poured a bowl of scolding soup over a boy's head one dinner time because, she said, he was looking at her in a funny way. There were also reports of racist graffiti being daubed on toilet walls. Although the culprit was never caught, the newspaper said, in light of recent events it seemed obvious who was to blame.

Stiggy shook his head. None of this sounded anything like Sally. He just didn't recognise the friendly, timid girl he knew from the violent racist thug portrayed in the newspaper. But there was worse to come.

A sociologist said it was Sally's propensity for violence that first attracted her to the skinhead cult. Skinheads, he explained, were a youth subculture with a history of extreme violence dating back to the late 1960s. It went on to describe several racially motivated attacks on ethnic minorities in the Sheffield area, including one Asian family's home being burnt to the ground while they were asleep upstairs. It didn't specifically say these acts were carried out by skinheads, or that Sally had taken part in any of them, but again, the inference that she had been involved was clear.

"Fuck off, you lying bastards!"

Stiggy threw the newspaper down in disgust. He'd had enough of all their bollocks. Passing shoppers glared at him, but he didn't care what they thought. Was any of it true? He shook his head and stared down at the scattered pages by his feet. He wanted to rip them into tiny pieces, then march down to the newspaper offices and throw a brick through their window. Grab whoever made up all that stuff about Sally and slam his head against a desk until he admitted it was just a pack of lies.

He leaned forward and spat on the photograph of Joe grinning up at him, then ground the sole of his trainer into his face. It was all that bastard's fault. If he hadn't been beating Sally, none of this would have happened. She could have just moved into Stiggy's flat with him, then everything would have been perfect. But instead of that, now everything was —

"Pick that up!" a gruff voice ordered.

Stiggy looked up at the security guard standing over him. The man stood with his arms folded, glaring down. Stiggy glared back for a couple of seconds, then sighed and bent down to pick up the sheets of newsprint spread out in front of the bench. It just wasn't worth the hassle. He snatched up the page with Joe's photograph on it first, and screwed it up into a ball before slamming it into the bin at the side of the bench. The security guard watched on while he gathered up more pages and stuffed them where they belonged, with the other rubbish.

Then something caught Stiggy's eye among the classified ads at the back of the newspaper. He grinned. Of course! It was the obvious solution. He picked the page up, checked it didn't have anything about Sally on the other side, then folded it up and put it in his back pocket.

"Now get out!" the security guard said, pointing at the nearest exit. "And don't come back for the rest of the day."

"I were going anyway," Stiggy said. "This place is a fucking dump, and the sooner I'm out of here the better."

* * *

Turning onto Glyn Avenue on the way home, Stiggy remembered his promise to let Doris use the shower in the flat. He had intended to think of some way of explaining it to Sally without raising any suspicions, but with everything that happened at the train station he had forgotten all about it. He debated whether to turn round and head up to Thorne Road so he could sneak into his flat from the other side, but what would be the point? Chances were Doris would still see him anyway.

But as he walked closer he saw Doris wasn't standing in her usual spot on the corner. She was otherwise occupied in the back alley behind Stiggy's flat, servicing one of her clients.

Stiggy glanced at them as he passed by. Doris was on her knees, the backpack clutched in one hand while she sucked off an old man sitting on top of a dustbin with his trousers around his ankles. Stiggy hurried by before either of them noticed him, and entered his flat.

"Where have you been?" Sally asked as soon as he opened the door. "I thought you were just going for some bread, but you've been ages."

"Yeah, I, um ..." Stiggy didn't want to tell her he'd been spooked by a skinhead, she would think he was pathetic. "They'd sold out at Patel's, so I had to go into town for it."

"Oh, okay. Well you could've come back and told me, I got worried."

"Yeah, sorry. I never really thought."

Stiggy went into the kitchen to check on the pan of stew he'd left Sally in charge of. She'd done a good job with it, and it smelled great. He gave it a quick stir with the wooden spoon she'd left in it, then tasted a bit. Perfect. Not too soggy, and not too stiff, just the way he liked it. He opened up the wholemeal bread and dipped a slice into it before making a sandwich with lumps of potato, carrot and swede and stuffing it into his mouth.

Sally walked into the kitchen and sat down at the table. Stiggy poured two bowls of stew and sat down opposite her. He pulled the newspaper page from his back pocket and unfolded it on the table.

"I've had an idea," he said, tapping one of the columns of classified ads. He grinned as he spun the page round so Sally could read it. "What do you think?"

Sally peered at the columns of newsprint. "About what?"

Stiggy reached across the table and indicated with his finger. "Vehicles for sale."

"Yeah, so?"

"We could get one. You know, for when we go to Cleator Moor at the weekend."

"Why, what's wrong with the train?"

"Well, um ..." Stiggy wondered if he should tell her about the coppers guarding the station, and decided against worrying her. "You know. All the times you have to change, and that. This would be easier, and we could take all our stuff with us. And once we get settled in at my uncle Bert's house we could go for trips out in it. It'll be great, you'll see."

"Is there enough of Joe's money left to buy something like that? They look pretty expensive."

"Well it would need to be a cheap one, but yeah. I don't see why not." Stiggy pulled Joe's wallet from his back pocket and counted out the cash. "Three hundred and twenty quid. Plus another fifty when my Giro comes on Thursday. We'll need to keep some back to live on until I can sort out a fresh claim at the dole office when we get there, but we should be able to get something decent with that much." He spun the newspaper page back to face him and traced his finger down the column while he scanned the adverts. Most were way out of his reach, with prices in excess of four hundred pounds, but there were a few possibilities.

"How about this one?" Stiggy said. "It's only a hundred quid. 1972 Hillman Avenger, needs attention, ideal restoration project."

"Sounds like a wreck," Sally said.

Stiggy frowned. "Yeah, I guess. This one, then. 1966 Morris Minor, good runner but no MOT."

Sally laughed. "It's older than me, it'll be on its last legs. Let me have a look." She spun the page back round. "How much do you want to spend?"

"About two hundred, two-fifty tops."

Sally bit her lip while she studied the adverts. "This one sounds okay," she said after a short pause.

Stiggy got up and walked around the table so he could read the advert over Sally's shoulder.

Much loved VW Campervan in need of a new owner. Reluctant sale due to circumstances. Tax/MOT, £300.

"That wouldn't leave us much to live on."

"Yeah, but you might be able to get the price down a bit when you go and see it. That's what Joe did when he needed a new van. And at least it's got an MOT, so it'll be safe. That's more than you can say for any of the ones you picked out."

"You think I should go and have a look at it, then?"

Sally shrugged. "Up to you, it's your idea. I'd be happy enough going on the train."

* * *

Stiggy paused outside one of the drab, grey prefabricated buildings along Exeter Road and checked the address he had written down. He'd got it from the campervan's owner when he called him from a town centre phone box, then got the Beckett Road bus down there. He had originally planned to use the phone box opposite Patel's Corner Shop, but the skinhead in the green bomber jacket had still been loitering on the bench outside it and he didn't want to take the risk.

It was the right address, so Stiggy pushed open one side of the rusting wrought iron gates and walked across the concreted over yard to the front door. Like the other ramshackle dwellings on Exeter Road, the corrugated walls were stained and dirty and showing their age. Some residents had made an effort to spruce them up with hanging baskets filled with brightly coloured flowers, others hadn't even bothered to remove faded graffiti that looked like it had been there for decades. The house Stiggy stood before was one of the latter, and had the phrases 'Wogs out' and 'Vote NF' spray-painted on the wall between the front door and the downstairs front window, along with a crooked Swastika.

A baby started crying when Stiggy knocked on the door. The downstairs curtains parted, and he caught a quick glimpse of a dark brown face staring out at him before they shut again. Then a female voice sang a lullaby while the baby continued to cry.

Stiggy waited, and when nobody came to answer the door he knocked again. He was about to knock a third time when a sash window slid open above him.

"What do you want?" a male voice demanded.

Stiggy stepped back and peered up at the window. A black guy in his early thirties with a massive afro leaned out and glared down at him.

"I've come about the van," Stiggy said. "I phoned about half an hour ago, you said to come round?"

The man at the window grunted. "You got the money with you?"

"Yeah, but I want to see the van first, make sure it works okay."

"Wait there."

The face disappeared, and a moment later the front door opened.

"You by yourself?"

He wore a pair of blue tracksuit bottoms and a faded red sweatshirt with a white stain on one shoulder. His feet were bare, and he held a baseball bat in one hand. Stiggy gaped at the baseball bat and nodded as he backed away with his hands raised.

"I don't want no trouble, I'm just here for the van, honest."

The man looked up and down the street as if he were searching for something, then leaned the baseball bat against a table inside the hallway and stepped outside. He closed the door behind him and, after another quick glance up and down the street, gestured for Stiggy to follow him around the house into the back yard.

Like the house, the Volkswagen campervan had seen better days. Originally red and white in colour, the red paint had faded with age to a dull pink and had flaked off in several areas, revealing dented bare metal beneath. Rust had eaten through the wheel arches and the area above the rear bumper, and Stiggy counted several large, jagged brown holes gaping open near the undercarriage. The chrome wheels and both bumpers were a dull yellow, pitted with rust and decay. Bird shit covered its rusting, once-white roof and spattered down the sides. It certainly didn't look 'much loved' like the advert had said. It looked more like it had been abandoned on a rubbish tip for years, with kids throwing stones at it the whole time.

Stiggy cupped his hand over one of the rear windows to look inside, but there was so much dirt and grime coating the surface he couldn't see anything. He pulled the handle on the side door to slide it open, but it was locked. His hand came away covered in dirt, and he wiped it down the leg of his combat trousers.

"Wait there, I'll go and get the key," the man said.

While he waited, Stiggy pulled out a handkerchief and wiped a small porthole in the dirt covering the back window to look through. There wasn't much in there, just a red padded bench along one side, and a brown Formica worktop on the other. The worktop was littered with crushed beer cans, empty pizza boxes, chip wrappers, and an ashtray overflowing with cigarette butts. The bench had been repaired in several places with what looked like black masking tape.

The van's owner returned with a key, and opened up the driver side door. When he stepped inside, the van lurched to one side under his weight, despite his slight build. The starter engine made a chugging, whining sound for several seconds, then there was a loud bang that made Stiggy jump.

"It's been stood for a few months," the man offered by way of explanation, "but it runs like a dream once it gets going. You'll see."

He twisted the ignition key again, and after another round of undulating whines and another bang the van's engine spluttered into life. Black smoke belched out of the rusting exhaust as he revved the engine.

"You getting in then, or not?"

"Er, yeah, okay."

Stiggy climbed into the passenger seat. The inside of the

van smelled musky, like it hadn't been used in years, and the worn seat gave out a sigh as he settled into it. A spider's web stretched from the gear stick to the cassette player built into the dashboard, and the driver wiped it away with the back of his hand before putting the campervan into gear and reversing past the side of the house. He got out, opened both the wrought iron gates, then reversed onto the road. Something grated against the kerb as the van bumped down it. Stiggy wondered how the man could see anything through all the dirt on the windscreen as he drove down to the end of Exeter Road, round the roundabout onto Norwich Road, then back onto Exeter Road again to park up outside the house.

"You see?" he said, switching the engine off. "I told you it runs like a dream. So are you wanting it then, or not?"

Stiggy thought about it. Despite its outward appearance, the van did at least seem to work okay, and that was all that really mattered. He didn't have time to be fussy, he needed something quick so he and Sally could make their escape before the coppers started going door to door with a five hundred quid reward and someone grassed him up. But at the same time, he knew it wouldn't pay to seem too eager. And the less he spent on the campervan, the more he would have left over for when they got to his uncle's house in the country.

"Yeah, maybe," Stiggy said. "Price seems a bit steep, though, for the state it's in. How about a hundred quid for it?"

The driver looked at Stiggy and shook his head. "Hell, no, it's worth more than that in scrap. And it's still got a month's tax and MOT, that's gotta be worth fifty notes all by itself."

Stiggy shrugged. He couldn't care less about tax or MOT, he just wanted the van. "Hundred and fifty, then."

"Bullshit, a hundred and fifty. Add another ton, then maybe we've got ourselves a deal." He tapped the dashboard with his hand. "You'll not find better at that price, and I'm already robbing myself."

Stiggy sighed. Two hundred and fifty quid seemed way over the top for something in that condition, but he really did need that van. He nodded. "Yeah, okay. I suppose I could stretch to that."

The van's owner grinned, flashing a set of perfect white teeth. "It's a deal, then. Come on inside and I'll get you the paperwork."

Stiggy followed the man through the front door and into the living room. It smelled of shit and stale tobacco smoke, the sparse furniture inside as old and worn as the junk in Stiggy's flat. A young black woman with braided hair crouched over a baby lying on a sheet of newspaper on the settee, a stained disposable nappy on the floor beside her. She looked up at Stiggy when he entered, and her mouth dropped open at the sight of him.

"Who the hell's this?" she asked, her eyes wide and staring.

"Relax, he's come to buy the van off me, that's all."

"Oh."

She went back to wiping the baby's arse with tissues from a box lying beside it, but still kept one nervous eye on Stiggy.

The stink was making Stiggy's eyes water, so he stepped as far away from the couch as he could in the small room, and stood by the window wishing he could open it and lean his head outside to get some fresh air. The man rummaged in a drawer and pulled out some sheets of printed paper, then waved them at Stiggy.

"You got the money then? Two hundred and fifty notes, like we agreed?"

The woman looked up again, but didn't say anything.

Stiggy nodded and pulled Joe's wallet from his back pocket. He counted out the money and handed it over in return for the van's log book, MOT certificate, and the key.

"You'll need to fill the log book in and send it off to Swansea so they'll know who to send the tax bill to next month."

Stiggy nodded as he stuffed the paperwork into his pocket, but he had no intention of ever doing so. They could fuck their tax, there was no way he would ever volunteer money to a corrupt war monger like Thatcher. Other than VAT, which he had no choice over, he had never paid a penny in tax all his life, and he wasn't about to start now.

* * *

Stiggy drove down Broxholme Lane and brought the campervan to a spluttering halt outside his flat. John Spedding sat on the kerb outside his house, polishing his trike's paintwork with a yellow cloth soaked in T-cut. He looked up and waved with the stump of his right arm when Stiggy climbed out of the van and slammed the door behind him.

"Planning a trip, kid?" he asked with a grin.

Stiggy nodded. "All right, John? Yeah, something like that. Thought I might get away for a few days, take me bird somewhere nice while we've still got the weather for it, you know?"

Spedding's grin grew even wider. "Yeah, that's probably

not a bad idea right now, what with you and that bird of yours being wanted for murder and everything."

16

"You what?" Stiggy's mouth gaped open. He looked down at the pavement to avoid Spedding's steely gaze. He shook his head, then looked up. "I don't know what you're on about, mate."

Spedding tapped his nose with a finger, the grin still in place. "Sure you don't. And I'm the fucking Queen of England."

"No, really. I haven't got a clue what you're on about."

Beads of sweat formed on Stiggy's brow. His mouth was suddenly dry and he struggled to swallow. How long had Spedding known? And more importantly, who else knew? He glanced up and down the street, expecting to see all the neighbours staring at him while they phoned the coppers to claim the five hundred quid reward. But there was nobody watching. Except Doris, on the corner of Glyn Avenue. He bit his lip and turned back to Spedding. How the fuck was he going to talk his way out of this one? It was obvious the biker knew everything.

Spedding scratched his beard and grinned while he shook his head. "You wouldn't make a good poker player, you know that, right?"

"You what?"

"Your face, kid, it's gone bright red. You look like you've been caught with your hand down a nun's knickers." He laughed. "Relax, kid, it's none of my business. But murder though, yeah? That's pretty fucking heavy. I've done some serious shit in my time, but I've never offed anyone. That's some proper class, that is."

"What, you mean you're okay with it? You won't tell anyone?"

Spedding shrugged. "Who's there to tell? So this bird of yours, is she really a Nazi then?"

"No she isn't, that's just some bollocks the newspapers made up. That photo, she were forced to pose like that."

Spedding nodded. "Yeah, I thought so, kid. She didn't look the type when I saw her the other day, and I've come across a fair few in my time." He smiled. "Boneheads, we call them, on account of their skulls being completely fucking solid. Best times of my life were spent rucking with them bastards. Probably caught a few innocent ones too, but who cares, right? If it looks like a duck, and all that. So anyway, this Joseph Hawkins geezer, I take it he deserved it then, did he? He weren't as squeaky clean as the papers make out?"

"Yeah, you could say that. He's the fucking Nazi, not Sally. And he's been beating her for years, you should see the scars on her back. Fucking pervert too, if you ask me. He's loads older than her, and she was still living in a kids' home when he first got his hands on her, so she probably would've only been about fifteen at the time."

"Yeah? Sounds like you did the world a favour, then." He gestured at the campervan with his stump. "So now you've got yourself some wheels to make your grand escape then, yeah?"

Stiggy nodded, glad of the change in subject. Spedding wandered around the van, shaking his head.

"I hope you're not planning on going far, because it looks like it's about to fall to bits any minute. And from the sound of the engine when you pulled up, I'd say you'll be lucky to get more than a couple hundred miles or so before it conks out for good. You pay much for it?"

Stiggy's face reddened again. "Um ... no, not really."

"Just as well. I reckon whoever sold you that hunk of scrap saw you coming. You should've said you were looking to get some wheels, I could've gone with you and checked it out first, saved you buying a dud."

"Yeah, well, too late now. You think it'll be okay for another couple hundred miles, though, yeah?"

Spedding shrugged. "If you're lucky, and don't thrash it too hard. But that's just a guess, so don't hold me to it."

Stiggy frowned. That wasn't what he wanted to hear, but at least there was a chance the van would survive the journey to Cleator Moor. Or at least most of it. They could always get the train the rest of the way if they had to. It would mean abandoning most of the stuff he planned to take with him, but that couldn't be helped. And maybe they would be lucky, after all. He and Sally were due a bit of luck, after all the shit that had happened lately.

"Cheers John," Stiggy said. "Thanks for letting me know. And thanks for not saying anything about ... well, you know."

Spedding took a pack of cigarettes from his hip pocket, flipped up the lid, and pulled one out with his teeth. "No worries, kid, we're all on the same side here. So when are you off?"

"At the weekend. There's some stuff I need to sort out first."

"You got somewhere safe in mind?"

"Yeah."

"Well best of luck with it then, kid. If I don't see you before you go, you take care of yourself, yeah? And if you ever need anything, you know where I am."

"Yeah, cheers John, I really appreciate that. See you around, yeah?"

Spedding nodded, then walked away into his front garden. As soon as he had disappeared into his house, Doris picked up her rucksack and wandered over.

"Can I use your shower now?"

Stiggy sighed. "Yeah, go on, then."

Stiggy opened the front door and Doris followed him into the hallway. The *Selector* album was playing on the stereo, the sound drifting through the door to his flat. Sally sat in the armchair, and looked up when he entered.

"Did you get it?" she asked. Then she saw Doris and frowned. "What's she doing here?"

"She, um ... well, she got caught short, and I said she could use our toilet. You don't mind, do you?"

Doris squeezed past Stiggy and headed into the kitchen with her rucksack. Sally watched her go, then shook her head and smiled.

"You're too kind for your own good, you know that, right?"

Stiggy smiled back. That had gone a lot better than he thought it would. "Yeah well, me mam always taught me I should treat people the way I would want to be treated myself."

"Remind me to thank her for that, one day. So did you get the van, then?"

"Yeah. Do you want to come and have a look?"

"Okay."

"It's a bit grubby, but I can clean it up before we go."

Stiggy took Sally's hand and pulled her to her feet, then led her through the hallway to the front door. He smiled as he gestured at the campervan parked outside.

"So what do you think?"

Sally frowned. "It doesn't look as good as it sounded in the advert. Does it run okay?"

Stiggy thought about what Spedding had said about the van being on its last legs, but didn't see any point in worrying Sally unnecessarily.

"Yeah, of course it does. I drove here in it, didn't I? I know it doesn't look much from the outside, but it's perfect for what we need. There's loads of room in the back for all our stuff, and there's like a bench and a table in there as well, for when we go on day trips. Come on, I'll show you."

Sally hesitated in the doorway while Stiggy walked up to the van and slid open the side door. He turned and gestured for her to follow him.

"Come on, there's nobody about if that's what you're worried about."

Sally glanced up the street, then hurried over and climbed into the back of the van. She brushed the padded bench with her hand and sat down on it.

"You weren't kidding when you said it was a bit grubby."

"Yeah, but wait until I clean it up, you'll love it." He pointed at the worktop. "We could put the camping stove on there, with the gas bottle underneath. Then we could have some stew or something, and a hot drink on the way."

"Won't your landlord notice it missing?"

Stiggy shrugged. "Who cares? The gas bottle's mine, anyway, it cost me twenty quid so I'm not leaving that behind. Anyway, the council will still be paying the rent for another couple of months until the Housing Benefit needs renewing, so we'll be long gone before he even notices."

"Well I suppose we'd best make a start on it then, hadn't we?"

Sally got up from the bench and started gathering up the empty beer cans littering the floor of the van.

"It's okay, I can do that tomorrow," Stiggy said. He peered out of the van door and watched Doris leave with her rucksack to take up her regular spot on the corner of Glyn Avenue. "Come on, let's go back inside, I'm starving."

* * *

Stiggy spent most of the next day clearing out the rubbish from the campervan and sprucing up the interior. He filled a bin liner with chip wrappers, pizza boxes, fag ends and crushed beer cans, and tossed it into the front yard of a boarded up house further down Broxholme Lane. He washed the grime off the padded bench with a cloth soaked in lemon-scented vegan washing up liquid and replaced the masking tape covering the holes with some more durable duct tape he bought from Patel's Corner Shop. Then he wiped down the Formica worktop, mopped the floor, walls and roof, and started on the front of the van. By the time he finished, the whole of the interior smelled of lemons, rather than the musky odour it had before.

He stepped out of the van and closed the door behind him, humming the intro to *Tube Disasters*, then set about the external paintwork with the mop. He thought about heading into town to get some cans of spray-paint to cover up the worst of the rust, but decided there was no point. If what John Spedding had said about the van only lasting another couple of hundred miles was right, it would just be a waste of money. So instead he started making a mental list of which records he would tape so he could listen to them on the way. His new *Mob* album, of course, along with *Stations of the Crass* and a selection of singles. And the *Astronauts* one, before he gave it back to Colin on Friday night.

He tried to remember what else he had borrowed from his mates and not returned yet. There was a couple of *Vice Squad* singles Brian had lent him a few months ago, but he couldn't think of anything else. And if there was, he could always take it round to Twiglet's house before he set off for the country.

The thought of never seeing any of his mates again brought a lump to Stiggy's throat. He, Twiglet, Colin and Brian had been through so many good times together, and it seemed like he'd known them all his life. From hanging out together in Hexthorpe Park and terrorising the park keeper when they were little kids, to their first pint together when they looked old enough to pass for eighteen. They'd lost touch for a while when Stiggy's parents had their home repossessed and he had to move into a council flat miles away, but they'd soon reconnected, and had been inseparable ever since they left school. They'd even discovered punk together, something that went on to define the rest of their lives.

They'd been at Brian's house, playing with his dog in the front garden one Saturday afternoon when Brian's older brother Simon came home from town with a Bradley's Records carrier bag. They followed him into the house and watched him pull out a single with a plain black sleeve.

"Who's that?" Brian had asked.

"Mind your own business," Simon had said. "Now push off, you little brat, and take the other brats with you."

But when Simon put the single on the record player in the living room, Stiggy stared at the speakers in amazement. He'd never heard anything like it before. So much power. So fast. And such strange words. He had to know more about it, what it all meant. What was this 'anarchy' the singer was going on about, and why did he want to be in it? Then the singer swore, and the song ended. Brian's brother put it back on again, and flung his arms around while he jumped up and down. Stiggy joined in, shouting "Get pissed, get pissed, get pissed," over and over again until he was forcibly ejected from the room along with Colin, Twiglet and Brian.

After that, Brian's brother started wearing a studded dog collar, complete with an engraved nametag hanging from it, and insisted everyone should call him Simon Rotten. He came home with new records every Saturday, spending his entire pocket money on them, and Stiggy always made a point of being there when he arrived so he could hear them. *Sex Pistols, The Clash, The Damned, The Jam, The Stranglers, Johnny Moped*, they all seemed to have such silly names. But the songs they sang, they all had meaning behind them, unlike the crappy nonsense Jimmy Savile introduced on *Top of the Pops* every week. This was Stiggy's music, and he knew it was what he had been waiting for all of his life.

A year later, Simon Rotten announced that punk was dead, and became just plain old Simon again. He threw out all his punk records and bought a parka with a huge target on the back of it. The records he started buying were all shit in comparison, but by then Stiggy, Twiglet, Colin and Brian all had pocket money of their own to spend on proper music. And then along came *Crass*, and everything changed once again.

After he finished washing the outside of the campervan, Stiggy went inside to clean himself up. His hands and face were covered in grime, his clothes filthy. Sally was in the living room, packing up the clothes they wouldn't need before the weekend into a pair of suitcases laid out on the bed. Her hair was over an inch long now, and with her new punk look he doubted anyone would recognise her from the photograph in the newspapers.

She looked over and smiled as Stiggy kicked off his trainers and padded into the kitchen to run a shower. While the water warmed up he peeled off his dirty clothes and put them in a basket near the back door, ready to wash in the sink when he had some spare time. He realised that was something else he would need to find time to do before they set off at the weekend, and added it to the list.

Stiggy opened the transparent glass shower door and stepped under the jet of hot water. He closed his eyes and scratched the dirt from his hair before lathering it with vegan soap. Water and bubbles cascaded down his face and shoulders. He tilted his head up and rubbed the soap from his eyes, then lifted each arm in turn and scrubbed at his armpits before moving on to his chest and legs. He hummed to himself while he showered, enjoying the warm spray of water against his skin. Then the soap slipped out of his hand and he crouched down to pick it up. As he straightened up he saw Sally walk past the open bathroom door.

"Are you coming in?" he called out.

Sally reappeared in the doorway, holding the basket of dirty washing. "I thought I'd wash these for you, and peg them out to dry."

"I can do that later. Come on, while the water's still warm."

Sally's eyes drifted down to his cock, and he felt it twitch as it began to swell. She smiled. "Is there even room for two of us in there?"

Stiggy shrugged. "Only one way to find out."

Sallly's cheeks flushed red as she put down the basket and unbuttoned her jeans

* * *

The following Wednesday morning, Stiggy got up early for his eleven-thirty appointment to sign on at the dole office. Sally was already up and about as usual, and was in the same cheery mood she'd been in for the last few days, as if she didn't have a care in the world. Seeing her like that made Stiggy happier than he could remember ever being before.

After the hatchet job on Sally in the local newspaper, along with the glowing testimonials about how wonderful a person Joe Hawkins was, articles about the murder case had dried up and concerns had moved on to more pressing matters, like the upcoming by-election and the general state of disrepair of the area's roads and byways.

Stiggy knew the investigation would continue in the background, but if there had been any fresh leads on Sally's whereabouts it would have been reported by now. And no news was good news, as far as he was concerned. So they spent their days listening to music in blissful ignorance while they finished off the packing and enjoyed each other's company while they waited for the weekend and the journey down to the countryside to start their new life together.

After breakfast Stiggy left Sally at the flat and headed up to Thorne Road. He saw the skinhead in the green bomber jacket sitting on the bench beside the telephone box straight away, but this time there was no jitter of nervousness. Everything in the world was perfect, and nothing could spoil that. The skinhead wasn't even looking in his direction anyway, he was staring across the road at Patel's Corner Shop. Stiggy walked past behind him and continued down to Christ Church, and into the Social Security Office at the back of the Gaumont cinema.

He joined the long, winding queue and hummed to himself while he waited. People turned and stared, but he didn't give a fuck. Even the SS officer's scowl as he approached the counter didn't bother him. He pitied her more than anything else, being forced to work on such a lovely day while he was free to do whatever he wanted. He tossed his tattered UB40 onto the counter. She picked it up and inspected it with barely concealed contempt.

"You're ten minutes late," she said, and scowled once more.

Stiggy smiled. "Yeah well, I got here on time, it's not my fault there's a big queue, is it? Blame Thatcher, she's the one who put everyone on the dole, not me."

The sour-faced woman grunted. "Have you done any paid work in the last two weeks?"

Stiggy grinned and shook his head, and after another scowl the SS Officer pushed a form across the counter.

"Sign here."

Stiggy picked up a pen chained to the counter and signed his name. The woman glanced at his signature, scowled for a fourth time, then put the form on top of a huge pile of identical forms.

"Next!" she yelled as Stiggy walked away.

Stiggy hurried home. His chest ached when he was away from Sally, even for short periods like this, and he couldn't wait to get back there to be with her. The skinhead was still sitting on the bench as he approached. The lad looked vaguely familiar, but Stiggy couldn't quite place where he'd seen him before. All skinheads tended to look the same to him. There were fat ones, thin ones, tall ones, short ones, some with tattoos, and some without, but that was about the extent of their differences as far as he could tell. This one had slightly longer hair than most, almost half an inch in length; and short bristles covering most of his face, like he hadn't shaved for a couple of days.

He was also staring straight at Stiggy.

Stiggy kept an eye on the youth as he walked closer, ready to turn and run if he had to. He didn't want any hassle, he just wanted to get back to his flat so he could be with Sally. Maybe this was one of the good skinheads, and he just wanted to say hello. Maybe one of those he'd met in the Arndale Centre last Saturday, and that's why he looked so familiar.

The skinhead rose from the bench and cocked his head to one side.

"It's Stiggy, isn't it?"

Stiggy stopped dead in his tracks. He looked the skinhead up and down, still trying to place where he knew him from. There was a blue dot tattooed on the bridge of his nose, and a stick figure with a halo on the side of his neck. Again, Stiggy was sure he'd seen them before, but couldn't remember where.

"Um ... yeah, why?"

Before Stiggy knew what was happening, the skinhead ran straight at him and punched him in the stomach with such a force it sucked all the air out of his lungs and doubled him over in agony.

"You fucking cunt!" he roared. "I told you what I'd do to you if anything bad happened to her!"

17

Stiggy dropped to his knees and clutched his stomach. He couldn't breathe. His mouth gaped open and his eyes bulged in their sockets. A sudden thought hit him, and brought with it a surge of panic: what if the damage was permanent, and he would never breathe again? He would die, right there on the pavement with some skinhead glaring down at him being the last thing he ever saw.

Stiggy thrashed his head from side to side, willing his lungs to start working again. He slumped over onto his side, then rolled onto his back and stared up at the clouds. Then, just as he thought he was about to pass out, his muscles relaxed and he sucked in a lungful of air with a gasp. He coughed and spat, then clutched his stomach with one hand while he held the other up in surrender.

The skinhead leaned over him, fists clenched, staring down, his face a mask of pure hate. Stiggy stared at the Z-shaped scar on his left cheek, partially obscured by the stubble of facial hair, and knew straight away where he'd seen him before. It was Sally's friend, Dave, the one they'd met on the field in Sheffield just before they'd gone to Joe's house. The psycho who'd pulled a knife on him for no fucking reason. And now here he was in Doncaster, less than a hundred yards away from Stiggy's flat. How the fuck had he found out where he lived? Stiggy sat up and raised both hands. Sally must have told him, it was the only thing that made any sense. But if that was the case, why hadn't he just gone straight round to the flat and attacked him there?

"Well?" Dave said. "Anything to say, before I beat you to a fucking pulp?"

"I've not done nothing to her. She's okay, honest."

"Okay?" Dave laughed, but without any humour. "She's wanted for fucking murder because of you. You killed Joe, and now you've got her taking the blame for it, you fucking cunt."

"You've got it wrong," Stiggy said. "It wasn't like that."

"Bollocks! I've read the papers, I know what you did." Dave grabbed Stiggy by the shirt and dragged him to his feet. He held him in place and drew back his fist. "You caved his fucking head in and now everyone thinks it was Sally!"

Stiggy flinched, but the fist stayed where it was.

"So here's what's going to happen," Dave continued. "You're going down to the cop shop right now, and you're going to tell them it was you who killed Joe, and Sally had nothing to do with it. You understand me? You're going to clear her fucking name, you cunt, then you're going to pay for what you did. You can either do it now, or you can do it after I kick your fucking head in. Your choice."

"It wasn't me," Stiggy blurted out. "I didn't do it. It was Sally, she killed him."

"Fuck off, you lying bastard."

"It's true. Sally killed Joe, and I helped her get away with it. I've been helping her ever since, I swear."

"Fuck off, Sally's no fucking killer," Dave said. "I've known her for fucking years, she doesn't have it in her."

"She had no choice, he was beating her with a leather belt. He has been for years."

"You fucking liar!" Dave yelled. His nostrils flared and his eyes blazed, but his fist still hovered in the air. A sudden look of doubt crossed his face.

"You knew him," Stiggy said quickly, "so you must've known what he's like. Sally told me what he did to Trisha."

"Now I know you're lying. Joe didn't do fuck all to Trisha."

"What? He slashed her face up. He's a fucking psycho, and he's been beating Sally for years. That's why she did it. She had no fucking choice, he would've killed her otherwise."

"Bollocks. Trisha got mugged by some druggy, she told me herself. And if Joe ever hurt Sally I'd know about it, because she'd tell me. You're just trying to save your own worthless skin."

"It's true, and I can prove it."

Dave's eyes narrowed. "How?"

"Her back. It's covered in scars. Let me up and I'll take you to her, then you can see them for yourself."

"If you're lying I'll fucking kill you, and take what's left of you to the coppers myself."

Stiggy shook his head. "I'm not lying. I wish I was, but it's all true. And that bruise Sally had on her face that day you saw her with me? Joe did that to her too, only she didn't want you to know in case you went for him and he put you in the hospital. You know, like he did with Trisha. They probably didn't tell you what really happened to her for the same reason."

Dave frowned, and seemed to consider it. He lowered his fist, and when he spoke the anger had gone from his voice, replaced with grim resignation. "Tell me where she is."

"It's not far. I'll take you there."

Stiggy was hoping the young skinhead would release him so he could leg it, but Dave must have anticipated this because he kept a firm grip on Stiggy's shirt.

"Where?"

Stiggy pointed. "Just down that road."

Dave dragged Stiggy by his shirt down Broxholme Lane and into the house he indicated Sally was in. Stiggy unlocked the flat door and pushed it open. The living room was empty.

"Sally," Stiggy called out, "there's someone here to see you."

Sally appeared from the kitchen. She gaped at Dave for a full three seconds before speaking. "Dave, what are you doing here?"

Dave's eyes widened as he took in Sally's new punk look. He glared at Stiggy for a second, then pushed him away and walked over to her.

"Is it true, Sally?"

"Is what true?" Sally looked from Dave to Stiggy and back again.

"I've told him," Stiggy said. "About what Joe did to you and Trisha."

Sally's mouth dropped open. "What? Why would you do that?"

The look of pained betrayal on Sally's face brought a lump to Stiggy's throat. He shook his head and looked down, avoiding eye contact. "I had no choice. I'm sorry, but I had to tell him."

"Is it true?" Dave repeated. "What he says Joe did to you and Trisha?"

"Show him your back," Stiggy said. "He needs to see it for himself."

"What? No, I won't." Sally shook her head. "And you can't make me." She turned and ran back into the kitchen. Stiggy and Dave both followed her.

"Please, Sally," Stiggy said, "it's the only way he will understand why you did it. He'll turn me in to the coppers, otherwise. He thinks it was me who killed Joe."

Sally turned to face the skinhead. Tears welled up in her eyes. "Dave, no, you can't. It wasn't Stiggy, it was me. I killed him. It's all true."

Dave shook his head. "I don't believe you, Sally, you're just covering for this cunt here. Why would you do that to Joe, after everything he did for you? It just doesn't make any fucking sense."

Sally let out a sob. Her shoulders slumped and she seemed to shrivel up inside. She turned her back on Dave and pulled the *Sex Pistols* T-shirt loose from her bleached jeans, then lifted it up to her shoulders. "This is why."

Dave stared at the criss-cross of scars running down Sally's back. His mouth dropped open, and his voice croaked with emotion when he spoke. "Sally, why didn't you tell me what he was doing to you? I could've done something about it, saved you from him."

Sally let the shirt drop and turned back to Dave. Tears rolled down her cheeks, and her bottom lip trembled. "How could I? You've seen Trisha's face. Joe did that to her, because I told her what he was doing to me." She shook her head and looked down at her boots. "Don't you see? She'll have those scars for the rest of her life, and it's all my fault." Then she looked up, directly into Dave's eyes. "I couldn't let Joe do the same thing to you, I just couldn't. Not after everything we've been through together."

Sally broke down and sobbed into her hands. Stiggy went over to comfort her but she brushed past him and rushed over to Dave instead. Dave's arms circled around her waist. Seeing them together like that brought a fresh lump to Stiggy's throat. Why had she gone to him instead? And what did she mean about everything they had been through together?

"Sally," Dave said, "it weren't your fault. It was him. Fucking Joe. He did that to Trisha, not you. And if I'd known what he was doing to you, I would've fucking killed him myself. Look, maybe there's a way out of all this, so you can come back to Sheffield with me. Then we can both look after each other, like we used to."

"What do you mean?" Sally asked.

"Well, what if we go to the coppers together, and I say I was there too? We could say the punk did it. It'd be our word against his, so they'd have to believe us. You'd be in the clear."

Stiggy gaped at Dave. Sally would never go along with something like that. Would she?

Sally stiffened. She drew back from Dave's embrace and stared into his eyes. "Dave, we ... we can't. Stiggy didn't do it, I did. I couldn't let him take the blame, it wouldn't be right."

"Well what if we went away somewhere, then? Manchester or whatever. We could have new names, so nobody would know who we are."

Sally shook her head. "I can't get you involved in all this, Dave, I just can't. It's too much. If we were caught, they'd send you to prison."

"I don't care about that, I can handle prison if I have to. And I'm already involved, just by being here. Fuck it Sally, I just want to help you."

"I know you do. And you'll always be special to me, you know that, right? You helped me through some really bad times when we were kids."

"Not as much as you helped me," Dave said. "I wouldn't even be alive if it weren't for you."

"I know, but ... don't you see?" Sally shook her head. "We could never be together, we would remind each other too much about what happened."

"What did happen?" Stiggy asked, but they both ignored him.

"Sally, it doesn't have to be like that. We could make it work, I know we could. I love you, I always have."

"I know. But ..." Sally's voice hitched. "... it just wouldn't be enough, would it? I'm sorry, Dave. Stiggy makes me happy, he helps me forget about ... all that stuff. And that's what I need right now, to forget. You understand, don't you?"

"I could make you happy, and I could help you forget. Fuck it Sally, I need you to be in my life. I can't cope without you, and you know that."

Sally rubbed Dave's arm. "Dave, don't do this to me, please. If things were different, if I wasn't with Stiggy, and none of this had happened ... yeah, maybe we would have ended up together after I'd spent my time with Joe, who knows? But Stiggy's helped me in so many other ways, too. I can't just leave him. I don't want to. I'm sorry."

Dave seemed to deflate, and if Stiggy wasn't so overjoyed at what Sally had just said he might have even felt sorry for him. Dave slumped down at the kitchen table and held his head in his hands. He sniffed, then rubbed his eyes and looked up.

"Sally, there's something else you need to know. I didn't just come here to turn him over to the coppers, I came to warn you. Joe's mates are coming for you, they're all heading down here and they're coming tooled up. They say they're going to do to you what you did to Joe, then they're going to turn you over to the coppers."

18

"How do they know where we are?" Stiggy asked. "Have you fucking told them?"

Dave shook his head. "Have I fuck. They know she's in Doncaster, everyone does. It's all over the fucking news, for fuck's sake, so it's not like it's a fucking secret." He glared at Stiggy. "And they know she's with some jug-eared punk bastard, so it won't take them long to find out who you are and where you live." He turned back to Sally. "You need to be a long way from here when that happens, Sally. Because if I can find you, then so can they."

"How *did* you find us?" Sally asked. "I still don't understand how you are here."

Dave shrugged. "It wasn't that hard, really. After you phoned me that first time, I just called the operator and asked for the number you rang from. I thought maybe I could use it to talk to you when I needed to."

"What, and they just gave you it?" Stiggy asked.

"Yeah well, they weren't going to at first. But then I said the hostel kept getting threatening calls from some druggy who got kicked out and we needed a number to give the rozzers, so they did in the end." Dave turned his attention back to Sally. "Only when I phoned it to tell you what happened to Joe, it turned out to be some fucking phone box, didn't it? Some other cunt answered it, said he'd never heard of you, so I asked him where it was and came straight down here. I thought maybe if I hung around that phone box long enough you'd turn up eventually."

"You mean you've been there all this time?" Sally asked.

"Well, yeah. You'd stopped phoning me by then, and I had to warn you, didn't I? You know, about Joe's mates coming for you."

Stiggy glanced at Sally. So she didn't just phone Dave once, it was a regular thing? That would explain where all the fifty pence coins were disappearing to. But did she really think he would have minded if she told him? And when was she doing it, anyway? As far as he could remember she hadn't left his sight the whole time, except when he nipped out to Patel's Corner Shop for a few minutes every other day, and she couldn't have been doing it then because that was where the nearest phone box was and he would have seen her. Unless it was early in the morning, before he woke up? That would make sense, she was always dressed when he got up, but surely he would have heard her go out?

Then he thought of something else.

"Wait," he said to Dave. "If you've been here since they found Joe, how do you know his mates are coming for her?"

Dave turned to face Stiggy. His fists clenched. "You calling me a fucking liar?"

"No, just wondering how you would know. Sally wasn't even a suspect until about three days later."

"I just fucking know, okay?"

"No, that's a good point," Sally said. "Who told you they were looking for me?"

Dave frowned at Stiggy, then turned to Sally and shrugged. "I heard it on the estate a couple of nights ago. Everyone were talking about how you'd killed Joe, and they were going to make sure you paid for it."

"So you haven't been here all the time, then, like you said?" Stiggy asked.

Dave scowled. "I've been here every day, that's what matters."

"Have you seen Trisha lately?" Sally asked, changing the subject.

Dave nodded. "Yeah, I went to see her straight after I found out about Joe."

"How is she?"

"Yeah, she's good, considering. Doesn't go out much, though. Says people keep staring at her face." Dave shook his head. "You should've told me who really did it to her, Sally. And what he was doing to you. I would've fucking battered the cunt if I'd known."

"That's why we didn't tell you. Trisha wanted to, but I made her promise not to."

"Yeah well, at least I can protect you from Joe's mates. That's all I'm bothered about now."

"Well thanks for warning us," Stiggy said. "But you might as well go now, because I've got this covered."

Dave folded his arms. "No chance. I'm staying right here so I know she's safe."

"The fuck you are. This is my flat, and there's no way I'm

having you staying here."

"I'm not leaving Sally on her own, not with Joe's mates after her."

"She wouldn't be on her own," Stiggy said. "I'm here."

Dave gave out a snort. "Yeah, and a fat lot of use you'll be when they show up here."

"Why, what are *you* going to do? Fucking stab them all?"

"You fucking cunt!"

Dave's left hand shot into the pocket of his bomber jacket. He jumped up from his seat, his eyes blazing as he pulled out a knife and pointed it at Stiggy. But before he could lunge forward, Sally rushed over and stood before him, her hands raised.

"Dave, please, don't be like this, not now. I need you both here, okay? But you need to put the knife away, yeah? Stiggy didn't mean nothing, honest. He's just looking out for me, the same as you. You understand, right? You want me to be safe, don't you?"

Dave nodded. After a brief hesitation he put the knife back in his pocket. "Yeah. Sorry, Sally. It's just all this shit, it's getting to me, you know?"

"I know. But none of it is Stiggy's fault, is it? He's been helping me. Keeping me safe."

"Yeah, I know." Dave slumped down into the chair and held his head in his hands, his elbows resting on the kitchen table.

Sally turned to Stiggy. "Is it okay if Dave stays here with us?"

Stiggy shook his head. "We don't need him here, Sally. We're okay on our own."

"I want him here," Sally said. "I'd feel safer if you were both here looking out for me. Besides, it's only for a couple of days."

Dave looked up. "Why, what happens then?"

"We're leaving," Stiggy said. "And you're not coming with us, before you ask."

"Where are you going, like?" Dave's question was addressed to Sally.

"Nowhere you need to know about," Stiggy said.

"A place in the country called Cleator Moor," Sally said. "Stiggy's got an uncle there, we're going to stay with him for a while."

Dave folded his arms. "Yeah well, we'll see about that."

"It's already decided," Stiggy said. "We're going at the weekend, and there's nothing you can do to stop us."

"Are you going to let him control your life like this?" Dave said to Sally. "Look what he's done to you, that stupid get-up he's got you wearing. And look at your hair. Fuck, Sally, you're a skin, not some fucking smelly punk bastard."

Sally looked down at her feet. "It's for the best," she said. "And it was my decision."

"Yeah, right, sure it was." Dave glared at Stiggy. "And I bet it was him who stopped you from phoning me, wasn't it?"

"I haven't made her do nothing she didn't want to do herself," Stiggy said. "Like she says, it's for the best. The coppers are looking for a skinhead, not a punk. And it's because they're looking for her that we have to move away, to somewhere they won't be able to find her."

"Yeah well, until that happens I'm staying right here so I know she's safe."

Stiggy shook his head. "There's no room for you here."

"I don't care, you'll just have to make room for me, won't you? Because I'm not going nowhere."

"Please, Stiggy?" Sally said. "He could kip on the chair, and he'll be no bother, honest. And if Joe's mates do turn up here, we'll need someone on our side."

Stiggy sighed. He knew this was an argument he'd never win, not when it was two against one. But there was no way he was going to have that skinhead bastard watching him and Sally in bed together like some old perv. Especially with that knife of his.

"Look, Dave," he said, "you want to be here in case Joe's mob come for Sally, yeah?"

Dave nodded. "Yeah."

"Well if you were outside in the street, then you'd be the first to know when they showed up, wouldn't you? Then you could warn us before they had a chance to get her."

"You can't make him stand guard outside all night," Sally said.

"I weren't thinking of that. I were thinking he could sleep in the van."

Sally shook her head. "No way. You can't make him sleep in that thing."

Stiggy shrugged. He turned to Dave. "Best I can offer, take it or leave it."

"Yeah okay," Dave said. "It's a good idea, Sally, he's not as daft as he looks. I'll stay in the van and keep watch from outside. If anything happens I'll sound the horn, give you chance to escape out the back before they get in."

* * *

A little after midnight, Stiggy had to practically force Dave out of the flat and into the campervan so he could get some alone time with Sally. He'd had enough of sitting in the armchair by himself with a bottle of cider while Dave and Sally jabbered on together in the kitchen about people and places he'd never heard of before, so it was a relief to be finally rid of him. It was even worse listening to Sally shave his head with the battery operated razor, and hearing Dave trying to convince her she should let him shave hers, too. The last thing they needed was Sally going back to looking like a skinhead again, especially now it wasn't just coppers looking for her. But at least Sally had remained firm, and hadn't let Dave talk her into it.

Sally had been so engrossed in Dave's company she even forgot about watching the evening news, and Stiggy didn't see any point in reminding her about it. All it ever did was make her anxious, even when they didn't mention anything about Joe or the ongoing murder investigation, so he was more than content to just sit and listen to the John Peel show instead.

Sally was in a cheery mood after Dave left, and initiated sex when they retired to bed for the night. Stiggy had a feeling it was just her way of making up for ignoring him all night, but he was more than happy to oblige. After they finished they lay in each other's arms, and his thoughts returned to the conversation with Dave in the kitchen. There was something the skinhead had said, along with Sally's reply, that was playing on his mind. He stroked her hair and stared into her eyes while he considered the best way to bring it up. She smiled back at him, then nuzzled her cheek against his chest.

"You said a while ago that you've known Dave since you were ten?" Stiggy asked eventually.

Sally yawned and stretched against him. "Yeah. He would have been eleven at the time, same age as Trisha. We've been friends ever since."

"So I guess you trust him, then?"

"With my life. He's not a bad person, Stiggy. I wish you two could get along, it would mean a lot to me if you did."

"He doesn't exactly make it easy for me. That's the second time he's waved a knife at me."

"Once he gets to know you like I do it'll be different. You'll see."

"Do you love him?"

Sally lifted her head from Stiggy's chest and stared into his eyes. "What sort of question is that? I'm here with you, aren't I?"

"Yeah, I know. But there was something you said to him earlier. About how if it wasn't for me, you and Dave would be together after you'd spent your time with Joe? Well, it got me thinking, that's all."

Sally smiled and shook her head. "You don't need to be jealous, you know that, right?"

"It's not that. Dave said something similar on that field we saw him on, too. Something about how you only had to spend another eight months with Joe, then you would be free. What did he mean by that?"

Sally stiffened. Her gaze darted away from Stiggy's eyes and onto something across the room. The flat door, Stiggy guessed, where she had last seen Dave less than half an hour ago. Then she relaxed once more and shook her head.

"Nothing. I guess he thought ... well, you know ... that I would leave Joe one day and be with him."

"Eight months seems pretty specific. Almost as if you and him had planned it in advance."

Sally shrugged.

"You and Dave seem pretty close," Stiggy said after a short pause.

Sally settled down on the pillow beside him and smiled. "We are. Him and Trisha, they're my best friends, I'd do anything for them."

"But you never got together with him? You know, like this? Like you do with me?"

"No. I don't really see Dave in that way. He's more like a big brother than anything else."

"I think he wants more than that. He says he loves you."

Sally frowned. "I know. I think I've always known he felt that way. The way he's always looked out for me, and the way he tried to protect me from ..." Her voice trailed off, and she bit her lip.

"From what? The stuff you want to forget?"

"Yeah."

"What happened, Sally? What is it that you want to forget? Was it something Joe did to you? I know you said you were living at the home when you first met him, so you must have been pretty young at the time."

"Please Stiggy, I don't want to talk about that."

"Did he touch you up or something, is that it?"

Sally's eyes widened. "What? No, of course not. He saved me."

"What? What do you mean, he saved you? Saved you from what?"

"From ..." Tears welled up in Sally's eyes. Her bottom lip trembled. She shook her head. "I ... I can't tell you."

"Why not?"

"Because it will ruin everything. Don't you see?"

Sally broke down and sobbed into Stiggy's chest. He stroked the back of her head and thought about everything Joe had done to her while he waited for the tears to subside. He couldn't think of anything worse than regular beatings, so what could he have possibly saved her from?

Then he remembered Sally's reaction to seeing Simon Watkins, the care home manager, on the television. All the vile things he had said about her. About her threatening someone with a knife, and running away before she could be punished for it. The violent outbursts and all the Nazi crap she was supposed to have been involved in. The glue, the fights, the racist attacks on other children. Why would he say all those things about Sally, and yet have nothing but gushing praise for a violent racist thug like Joe Hawkins? Whatever it was Sally didn't want to talk about, both Watkins and Joe had to be involved in it somehow.

"Sally," he said, "it's okay, you can tell me, there's nothing you can say that will ruin anything, I promise. If it's not Joe, is it something to do with that Watkins geezer on the telly?"

Sally stiffened in his arms once more, and that was all the confirmation Stiggy needed. His mind raced with possibilities. She'd told him she used glue to help her forget, but then all the bad shit and pain was still there when the effects wore off. Had Watkins been beating her, too? Some sort of punishment for the knife incident, and running away from the care home, all the fights she got into at school? Was Watkins responsible for at least some of her older scars?

Living with Joe was better than the alternative, Sally said that night he first met her. But she would have left the care home by the time she moved in with Joe, so maybe she was referring to something else? The hostel where Dave lived, perhaps. A place he imagined to be filled with druggies, criminals, and the dregs of society. Maybe Sally had lived there too for a brief period after she left the home, and something bad had happened while she was there? Something involving Dave? There was something he had said earlier that night, about how he wouldn't even be alive if it wasn't for her. And then Sally said Dave and her couldn't be together because they would remind each other too much about what had happened. But just what was it that had happened?

Stiggy realised with a jolt he didn't know much of anything about Sally's past, only the few short glimpses she had allowed him. *It will ruin everything*, she said. *It will ruin everything if you know what happened.* What could she have done that would be so bad for her to think that?

He didn't want to consider it, but what if Joe wasn't the first person Sally had killed? Or at least maimed in some way. What if all that stuff in the newspaper about her violent past was true? Maybe some drugged up crazy at the hostel had attacked Dave, and she'd gone to his defence and got carried away, like she did with Joe. But then again, if something like that had happened it would have been reported to the police and the newspapers would have mentioned it as part of their hatchet job on Sally. The hostel wouldn't cover it up, would they? Not unless someone like Joe forced them to. Was that how Joe had saved her? By threatening the hostel manager and making it all go away?

"Sally, please. I need to know what you did. I need to know what Joe saved you from."

"I can't tell you. I just can't. Please Stiggy, I don't want to think about it. It's in the past, just leave it there."

"I can't, Sally. Not now. I need to know what you did."

Sally shook her head. "I can't tell you. I won't."

Stiggy pushed Sally off him and sat up in the bed. "Fine, then. I'll go and ask Dave instead, and I'll make *him* tell me."

Sally bolted upright beside him and grabbed his arm. "Stiggy, no! Don't do that! Please! He'll stab you, and I don't want that!"

Stiggy turned to face her. "Well tell me what Joe saved you from, then. Because if you—"

"It was the men, okay? He saved me from the men who came in the night and raped me! There. Are you happy now?"

19

The words hit Stiggy like a sledgehammer to the chest. The bed seemed to lurch to one side beneath him. His mouth dropped open and he stared at Sally as the tears streamed down his face. Oh God, not that. Anything but that. He reached out for her but she slapped his hand away and flopped back down on the bed.

"Sally, I ..."

The hurt look on Sally's face brought a lump to Stiggy's throat, and choked off the rest of his words. Sally sobbed as she turned away from him and curled herself up into a ball. Stiggy stared at the scarred ridges on her back, made more prominent by the taut skin. No wonder she thought that was a price worth paying to get away from it all. He wanted to rage and scream. Track down those bastards who had done that to her and kill them. But all he could do was hold his head in his hands and weep as he imagined what it must have been like for her. *It hurts*, she'd said. *It hurts when people fuck me.* Now he knew what she meant by that.

"Sally," he said. "Sally, I ... I don't know what to say. What you must have gone through ..." He shook his head. "Fuck, I had no idea. I'm sorry. I thought you'd ... well, I thought it was something else. I wish it had been. God, that's terrible. Who were they, Sally? You can't let them get away with it, you need to tell someone what they did to you."

Sally uncurled herself and turned to face him. Her eyes were red and puffy, her cheeks damp with tears. Her breath came in hitching gasps. Stiggy lay down next to her and reached out for her again, and this time she melted into his arms and he held her tight.

"We tried," she said. "Me and Trisha. You know, that day we ran away and the police took us back? Only they didn't believe us, did they? And Watkins said we were always making stuff up, just to cause trouble for him, so they just left us there."

"The fucking bastards. So was Watkins one of the men who ... who did that to you?"

"Sometimes. But mostly he just watched, and took photos.

And it was different men each time, I don't know who they were. One looked really familiar, like I'd seen him before somewhere, but I don't know where. He was really old and fat, and he liked it rough. His breath stunk of smoke, and when he stuck his tongue in my mouth it tasted horrible. He was the worst of them all. Everyone hated him because of what he did to them."

"So it wasn't just you it happened to?"

"No, it was all of us. Some of the boys, too."

Stiggy's eyes widened. "Shit, you mean Dave?"

There was a long pause before Sally replied, as if she were deciding whether to tell him or not. Then she sighed.

"After that first time ... when they brought me and Trisha back ... well, I guess Dave knew there was something wrong. When I told him, he held me and said he would fix it so it never happened again. He started staying in my room at night, sleeping in the bed beside me so he could protect me when they came. I'd hold his hand while I fell asleep, so I'd know he was still there. He hid a knife under the pillow, I think he must have stolen it from the kitchen or something. He said if any bloke tried to rape me he'd cut their bollocks off with it. But ... well, he wasn't strong enough, none of us were. It was the fat one, you see. There was nothing he could do."

Sally gripped Stiggy so tight her fingernails dug into his back and he almost cried out from the pain.

"Dave went for him with the knife, but Watkins was too quick. He grabbed his arm and twisted it up his back, and he dropped it. The fat man, he picked it up, and ... and he ... he held it to Dave's throat and said if he didn't do what he wanted he would kill him."

Stiggy's heart sank. He was almost afraid to ask the question. "What did he make him to do?"

A fresh wave of Sally's tears dampened Stiggy's chest.

"He had to pull down his pyjamas and ... and ... and they made me watch while ... Watkins held him bent over ... while the fat man ... he kept hitting him on the arse with his shoe, and then he ... he ... he pulled his own trousers down and ..." She choked back a sob. "And then he ... and then Watkins ... they both ..."

"Fucking hell," Stiggy said under his breath. "It's okay, I don't need to know the rest. That poor kid."

"I ... I didn't know they liked boys too, Stiggy, honest I didn't, or I never would have let Dave stay in my room like that. It was my fault he was in there. My fault they did that to him. He ... he was never the same after that."

"Sally, no. What happened to Dave ... it was horrible, but it wasn't your fault. You said it yourself, you weren't strong enough. There was nothing you could have done."

"You can't tell Dave I've told you," Sally said. "It would destroy him if he found out you know. He's so ashamed of it there's no telling what he would do to you."

"I won't, I promise. And I'll try not to wind him up, too. Fuck, Sally, I had no idea. I thought he was just another thug. That knife he carries ... I mean ... well, you know. He's pretty quick to pull it out. I guess ... well, I guess now I know why."

"He cuts himself with it. He's been doing it for years. When he first started, he said it was to make himself ugly, so the fat man wouldn't want him anymore."

Stiggy thought about the Z-shaped scar on Dave's cheek, and the dozens of jagged scars on his arms. He'd always assumed they were the result of a fight, he never once thought they might be self-inflicted.

"Only it didn't work, did it?" Sally continued. "Because he just kept coming, and he didn't seem to be interested in anyone else after that. Dave's room was at the opposite end of the corridor from mine, but I always knew when he was there because I could hear them through the walls. You know ... the fat man hitting him, and Dave crying out, and then sobbing while he ... Only there wasn't anything I could do, was there? Except ... well, you know. Just listen, and try to comfort him the next day. But then one night ... Dave was really screaming, so I knew it must be worse than usual. So I waited until I heard the fat man go downstairs and out the front door, then went to see if Dave was okay. Only ..." Sally's fingernails dug into Stiggy's back again. "Only he wasn't okay, was he? He ... I don't know if he did it on purpose or not, but ... he was just lying there naked with a knife in his hand, and ... and there was dozens of cuts all over his chest. I think maybe he must have done some of them too deep or something, because there was blood all over him, and the bed was soaking wet from it too. I'd never seen anything like it before, it was horrible. I thought he was going to die. He was just lying there, staring up at the ceiling, and he didn't even seem to know I was there."

"Christ," Stiggy said. "So what did you do?"

"I didn't know what to do, so I went and got Trisha. I must have been screaming too, because everyone came out of their rooms, and Watkins came upstairs to see what was going on. He swore when he saw Dave lying there, and told us we had to stay away from him and go back to bed. That he was dead, and there was nothing we could do about it, and how he would call the police in the morning and they would come and take him away. Trisha told him to fuck off, that it was all his fault Dave had done that to himself, and she went downstairs and phoned an ambulance. Then she came back with the first aid kit and bandaged him up while we waited for them to get there. They said she'd done the right thing, and that she'd probably saved his life."

"So Watkins would have just left him to die?"

Sally shrugged. "Maybe he thought he was already dead. Or maybe he was just scared of what Dave might tell people if he wasn't."

"And did he? You know, tell people? Doctors or whoever?"

"No. And he made me and Trisha promise not to tell anyone, too. He said he didn't want anyone to know what they'd been doing to him, because he was too ashamed of it. He didn't want people to think he was gay."

"Fuck, that's just stupid. It's not like he had any choice in it. He was just an innocent victim, same as you."

"Yeah well, that's the way he saw it. And he still does, so you can't let on that you know, and you can't tell anyone else about it."

"I won't, honest."

"Promise me, Stiggy."

"I promise, I won't say anything to anyone. Why would I, anyway? So what happened after the ambulance took him away?"

"They kept him in the hospital for three weeks while he got better. I skipped school to go and visit him every day, and while he was in there it was like he was getting back to normal again. But then they said he had to go home, and he just wouldn't stop crying. He wanted me to go and get him a knife, so he could cut his stitches open again, just so he could stay there longer. I told him the council and the police had been round wanting to know what had happened and why nobody had seen it coming, and that Watkins had been suspended while they investigated it. That someone else had taken over, and that it had all gone back to the way it was before Watkins arrived."

"So that was the end of it?" Stiggy asked. "Those men ... they didn't come back?"

"Not for another six months, no. Watkins came back a month later, I think the council must have decided he didn't do anything wrong. But the others ... I guess they must have been spooked by what happened with Dave, because it was a long time before they started coming again. And after the fat man came back ... well, Dave went a little bit crazy after that."

"Did he start cutting himself again?"

"Yeah. But it wasn't just that. It was like ..." Sally sighed and shook her head. "He got into a lot of fights at school. He'd just go up to people and punch them for no reason. Usually the bigger kids, too. It was like he wanted them to batter him, or something. I'd never seen him like that before, and it scared me. He just didn't seem to care what happened to him. Then one day, he ... it was horrible ... he just seemed to snap and bashed a kid's face in with a brick. He just kept hitting him and hitting him with it, I thought he was going to kill him. One of the teachers managed to drag him off, otherwise I think he would have."

"Wait, what?" Stiggy remembered the newspaper article, how it said Sally had hit someone with a brick. "This kid ... was he coloured?"

Sally gaped at him. "How did you know that?"

"Um ... just a guess."

Sally shook her head. "Dave's not like that, Stiggy, I already told you. It could have been anyone. That kid, he was just in the wrong place at the wrong time, that's all. It was nothing to do with what colour he was."

"It's not that, it's just that ... well, I wasn't going to say anything, but it was in the paper the other day. Only they said it was you who bashed him with a brick."

"What? Why would they say that?"

"I don't know, to make you look bad, I guess. They said you joined a Nazi gang and started beating up immigrants, and he was one of your victims."

Sally's eyes widened. "We weren't even skinheads back then. And there *was* no Nazi gang, that's just stupid. Half of Joe's mates aren't even racist. Not properly, anyway. Not like him. And I wouldn't do something like that anyway, I just wouldn't."

"Yeah, I know. And I didn't believe it, either. Sally, it has to be that Watkins geezer telling them all that stuff, it's the only thing that makes any sense. He said it was you who threatened someone with a knife, too. And that was why you and Trisha ran away, because you knew you would get in trouble for it."

"That wasn't how it happened, it's all in the wrong order. After that first time ... I didn't go down for breakfast the next day, I just didn't want to see anyone. But Trisha came looking for me, and as soon as she saw me she knew what had happened.

They'd been doing it to her, too, only she was better at hiding it than me. That's when we ran. She could tell I couldn't cope with it like she could, and she knew that running away was the only way to stop it happening to me again. We ended up sleeping at those allotments I took you to, and Trisha had this idea about hitching down to London and finding somewhere to live together the next day. Only the guy whose allotment it was found us there the next morning while we were still asleep and called the police. Dave didn't find out about what they did to me and Trisha until they took us back there, and it was another month after that before they came for me again while Dave was in my bed, and he got ... well, you know. And it was another couple of years after that before I met Joe and got into the skinhead look. Dave was gone by then."

"Where to?"

Sally sighed. "He got three years in borstal for smashing that kid's face in with a brick, they only let him out a few months ago. He was smiling when the police took him away. I think maybe that's what he wanted all along. Like he saw it as his only way out, or something."

"Christ."

"They wouldn't let me visit him in there, it was too far away, but he used to write to me all the time. And I think maybe he was happy there. And at least he was safe."

"But you weren't though, were you?"

"After Dave had gone I blocked most of it out with glue. There was a few of us doing it back then, but I don't remember who came up with the idea first. Trisha tried it once, but it freaked her out too much and she never did it again. She used vodka instead, she was always better at shoplifting than me. Anyway, when Joe started doing the gardening at the home, I think he must have been able to smell the glue on my breath or something, because the first thing he ever said to me was that I should pack it in before it kills me."

"Did you tell him why you were doing it?"

"No. Not at first, anyway. I just said I didn't care if it killed me or not. Joe seemed nice back then. We talked a lot, and he let me help him out with the weeding and stuff like that. He told me all about skinheads, and how nobody ever messes with them because of the way they dress, and their tough reputation. How they look out for each other, like it's a big family or something. And then one day he showed me this magazine with photos of skinbyrds in it — that's what they call skinhead girls, he said — and they looked really cool, you know? And I said I wish I could be a skinbyrd, so nobody would be able to mess with me again. So then, at the weekend, he took me to this shop in town and bought me an outfit of my own, then took me to the barbers and I got my own feather cut."

"Feather cut?"

"That's what they call the hairstyle, but I don't know why. Anyway, I wrote to Dave and told him all about skinheads, how they look out for each other and don't let anything bad happen to you, and sent him a photo of me that Joe had took with my new gear on. He wrote back a few days later, and said he would be a skinhead too as soon as they let him out. He said they'd already shaved his hair off anyway, so he was already half way there."

"So when did you tell Joe what they were doing to you?"

"He got it out of me a few months later. I guess he could tell I was upset one day, after ... well, you know. I didn't think he would believe me, but he did. He said not to worry, he would sort it."

"What did he do?"

"He gave me his address, said I could go down there any time I needed to. You know, somewhere to escape to when things got really bad. I asked if Trisha could come too, and he said yeah. So we started spending a lot of time down at his house, hanging out with the other skinheads who turned up. You know, drinking cider and listening to music and stuff, talking about football and what they get up to, that kind of thing. And sometimes, when we got really drunk, we'd stay over for the night and sleep on the couch. We thought we'd get in trouble for it, but Watkins didn't seem to care. I think maybe Joe must have had a word with him, or something. Only ... well, it didn't stop the other stuff from happening, did it? And when I told Joe they were still doing it, even though I was a skinbyrd, he said I could move in with him if I wanted to. I didn't think it would be allowed until I was sixteen, that I would need to stay at the home until then, but he said not to worry about that because he had an idea how to get around it."

"Wait, what? Why, how old were you when you moved in with Joe?"

"Thirteen. And a half, nearly."

"Thirteen? Fucking hell Sally, he just wanted you for himself, that's all. Can't you see that? He was no better than those other perverts."

"Yeah well, nothing comes for free, does it? There's always a catch. But at least there was only one of him, and he wasn't as rough as the others were."

"What? Come off it, I saw what he was doing to you, remember? And those scars ... he must have been beating you for years."

"Yeah well, that didn't start until later. He wasn't like that at first, it was just when he got mad at me. And that first time, it was my own fault, anyway."

"Sally, none of it was your fault. It was all him." Stiggy almost spat the word: "Joe! Joe fucking Hawkins, king of the skinheads." He shook his head. "Nazi fucking prick, more like. And a fucking rapist too, if you ask me. You were just a kid, he was a grown man, for fuck's sake. What he did to you ... it was just pure fucking evil. He didn't save you, he just fucking abused you even more."

"No, you don't understand. It was me, I made him like that. I got caught shoplifting, I could have wrecked everything. After the police charged me, they took me back to the home because that's where I had to say I was living. When Joe came to pick me up, Watkins said if he couldn't control me properly then the deal was off. He put the price up, said he wanted extra because of the police turning up like that, asking questions and making him look bad."

"What do you mean, he put the price up? Price for what?"

"For not reporting me missing, and not telling anyone where I was. I would have had to go back there if he did."

"Are you saying Joe bought you off Watkins?"

Sally shrugged.

Stiggy sighed. "Fucking hell, Sally, this just gets worse and worse. You need to report all this, someone needs to do something about it. You can't let them get away with it."

"It's in the past, it's done with."

"For you, maybe. But what about all those other kids who still live there?"

"There's nothing we can do. Even if they would believe me, it's not like I can go to the police now, is it? Not after ... what I did to Joe."

"I wasn't thinking about the police. Come next door with me and tell John about it."

"The Hells Angel?"

"Yeah. He knows people who can make sure it never happens again. But he would need to hear it from you, he wouldn't just take my word for it. Not something like that. He'd need proof."

Sally shook her head. Tears welled up in her eyes. "I can't, Stiggy. It's bad enough telling you, I couldn't tell someone like that, too. Don't make me, please. I just want to forget what happened. And I want you to help me do that, like you did before you knew. Don't you see? It's the only way I can move on, and leave all this stuff behind me. But I'm scared, Stiggy. Scared that now you know all this ... that it won't be the same again. That it will always be there between us ... like with Dave ... and you won't be able to leave it behind."

"Don't you want justice?"

"I just want to forget it ever happened. And I don't want to talk about this ever again, because I can't forget if you keep reminding me. That's why me and Dave would never work. Please Stiggy, let's just go to that new place at the weekend and leave it all behind us. Because I don't want to have to think about all that stuff ever again."

Stiggy sighed. He didn't like it one bit, but what else could he do but go along with it? At least for now.

"Okay. If that's what you want."

"It is."

"Just one more thing, then I won't mention it again."

"Stiggy, please."

"What happens in eight months? Why did Dave say you only needed to stay with Joe for another eight months?"

"That's when I'm sixteen. I would have been able to leave Joe, and they wouldn't be able to take me back to the care home. I would have been free, just like Dave and Trisha."

20

Stiggy bolted upright, taking the bed covers with him. There was someone banging on the flat door, but with the curtains closed and the bare lightbulb glaring down from the ceiling he didn't know if it was day or night. Sally sat up beside him and gaped at the door. Her eyes were wide and staring, a look of terror on her face.

Stiggy swore under his breath. His first thought was that the coppers had found them. One of his neighbours must have seen Sally and grassed them up for the reward. Then he remembered what Dave had said the day before. *Joe's mates are coming for you, Sally. They're going to do to you what you did to Joe. Then they're going to turn you in to the coppers.*

Stiggy didn't know which would be worst, a gang of angry skinheads or a mob of truncheon-happy coppers. The end result would be the same either way — a good kicking, followed by a cell door slamming behind them. He rubbed his eyes and shook his head, trying to wake up properly so he could think what to do to stop that happening. If it was coppers, they would have the back of the house surrounded too. But if it was just Joe's mates, maybe there was still a chance of escaping through the back alley.

Stiggy started to rise from the bed, but Sally reached out and grabbed his arm and stopped him. The constant hammering on the flimsy plywood door made it rattle in its frame. It sounded like someone was kicking it, and it didn't look like it would take much more of that sort of punishment before it splintered and burst open.

"Open the fucking door!" a gruff voice yelled.

Sally let out a sigh and released Stiggy's arm. She bent down, picked up the *Discharge* T-shirt she'd dropped beside the bed the night before, and slipped it on.

"What the fuck are you doing?" Stiggy whispered when she got up and headed for the door. Was she going to let them in? Try and reason with them, or something?

Sally unlocked the door and swung it open. Dave swaggered in, carrying a bottle of milk.

"About fucking time. All right, Sally?" Dave grinned as his eyes drifted down to Sally's bare legs, the hem of the over-sized T-shirt only just covering her thighs. Then he looked up and sneered. "Fucking *Discharge*? They're fucking shite they are, have you heard them? It's just a load of noise with some cunt shouting over the top of it."

"Is it bollocks," Stiggy said. He reached over to the bedside cabinet, picked up his watch, and squinted at it. Half six? Who gets up that early?

Sally blushed. "I just wear it as a nightie, that's all."

"Yeah well, they're still shite." Dave held up the milk bottle. "Any chance of a cuppa? I'm spitting fucking feathers here."

Dave gave the milk bottle to Sally and slumped down in the armchair. After a quick glance at Stiggy, Sally went into the kitchen and filled the kettle from the tap.

Stiggy looked at Dave and thought about everything Sally had said about him. How he'd tried to save her from some fat old pervert, then been beaten and raped because of it. The months of abuse he must have suffered at that man's hand before he decided to take his own life. And when that failed, the only way he could see to escape was to get himself banged up in borstal. No wonder he was such an angry young man. Despite the skinhead's constant brusque and antagonistic attitude toward him, Stiggy couldn't help feeling sorry for the lad. He wondered how he would have coped himself if he had gone through all that as a kid, but he just couldn't imagine it.

Dave must have sensed Stiggy staring, because he looked over and scowled. "What are you fucking looking at?"

Stiggy shook his head and looked away. "Nothing. Just wondering why you're here so early, that's all."

"Milk float woke me up, didn't it? Made a right fucking noise, all that clattering about and shit. And the seats in that van of yours aren't right comfortable, are they? Not like this one." He patted the arms of the chair with his hands, causing clouds of dust to fly up. "If I'd kipped on here instead I'd probably still be asleep, so it's not like it's my fault you got woke up early, is it?"

Stiggy sighed. He knew what the skinhead was angling for, but he wasn't going to let himself be drawn into an argument like that. He thought about getting up to go and sit in the kitchen out of the way, but his clothes were on the floor beside the armchair and he didn't want Dave to see him naked. So instead he just lay back down and stared at the ceiling. He yawned. It didn't seem like he'd had any sleep at all. He'd tossed and turned all night, going over it all in his head. Thinking about all those children Dave and Sally had left behind, the ones who were still suffering, and what he could realistically do about it. Which was pretty much nothing at all if Sally refused to confirm any of it.

He thought about Sally's age, too. Fifteen, still legally a child. Did that make Stiggy a pervert, just like Joe and those other men who'd abused her? He didn't feel like one, and he certainly hadn't forced himself on her like they had. Besides, he was only a couple of years older himself, and she wasn't that far off sixteen anyway. But that wouldn't be how the police saw it if they ever caught up with him.

Sally came back with three mugs of tea balanced on a dinner plate. She moved Stiggy's records and tapes to one side and put the plate down on the sideboard next to the record player, then gave one of the mugs to Dave before walking over to Stiggy with another.

"I made you some tea," she said, standing before the bed. She looked off to one side, avoiding eye contact, and her hand trembled as she held out the mug by its handle.

Stiggy sat up and reached out for it with both hands. He cupped one hand around the hot mug, and stroked Sally's arm with the other. She glanced at him, then looked away.

"Thanks," Stiggy said. "I'll have it later."

Sally started to move away, and Stiggy clasped her hand to stop her. She turned to face him and bit her lip.

"It's okay, you know?" Stiggy said. He smiled. "You know, what we talked about last night? It's going to be okay, I promise. It won't change anything, and we don't need to talk about it again."

Sally gave a quick smile, then glanced at Dave before turning back to Stiggy. Stiggy put the mug down on the bedside cabinet and took both her hands in his. He shook his head, guessing what Sally was worried about. *I won't*, he mouthed, and Sally visibly relaxed. *Thank you*, she mouthed back, then retrieved her own mug from the sideboard and sat at the bottom of the bed while she sipped from it.

"So what are we doing today then, Sally?" Dave asked.

"Today hasn't even arrived yet," Stiggy said, lying back down. "It's still the middle of the night."

The bedsprings creaked when Sally got up from the bed. "Come on, let's go in the kitchen. Stiggy needs his beauty sleep."

Dave laughed. "You're not wrong there, Sally. From the look of him I'd say he needs at least a fucking month's worth, just to sort those ears out."

Stiggy didn't rise to it. He pulled the bedcovers over his head and rolled over onto his side.

"You got anything to eat?" Dave asked. "I'm fucking starving."

Cupboard doors opened and closed in the kitchen. Stiggy imagined Sally reaching up to remove things from them, the shirt rising above her thighs when she stretched up on her toes. Dave must be getting a right eye full. She wasn't even wearing any knickers.

"Fucking porridge?" Dave said. "Who the fuck eats that crap outside Scotland?"

"It's not too bad when you get used to it," Sally said. "There's muesli as well, if you want that instead?"

"That's fucking rabbit food, that is. Haven't you got no bacon and eggs?"

"No, Stiggy doesn't like it. He's a vegan."

"A what?" Dave laughed. "Now I've heard it all. He hasn't turned you into some sort of fucking lettuce muncher as well, has he?"

"No, he says it's up to me and my own conscience what I eat."

"Good. Well I'll go and get you some bacon later, then we can have some proper butties for breakfast tomorrow. I'm not eating no fucking hippy crap."

Stiggy frowned. No way was that happening in his flat, it would stink the place out. If Dave wanted to cremate murdered pigs and then eat them, he could do it somewhere else.

Dave and Sally talked together in the kitchen for the next hour, reminiscing about the old days. The time Trisha stole a bottle of Cinzano Bianco from the off license and all three of them got absolutely plastered in the park and threw up all over the bowling green. Days spent collecting glass bottles so they could line them up on a wall and throw stones at them. Nights spent listening to records in Trisha's room and dancing together on her bed. Going on the dodgems and eating candy floss and toffee apples when the fairground came to town. Dave showing off and jumping on the waltzer while it was spinning round and nearly breaking his leg when he fell off. Each story was punctuated with laughter, followed by shushing from Sally because she didn't want to wake Stiggy up. Which just made Dave laugh even louder, and stamp his feet on the kitchen floor.

Stiggy smiled to himself while he listened to it all. At least they had shared some good times, they weren't all bad. And whatever he thought about the young skinhead, at least Dave's presence made Sally happy. And after what she had told him last night, that could only be a good thing. It amazed him how she could go through all that and come out the other side the way she had. How she could even function at all with those painful memories swirling around in her head. Stiggy knew he wouldn't have been that strong if it was him. He would have been more like Dave — damaged beyond repair, raging against the whole world. Dave and Sally were polar opposites in the way they coped with their shared past. And yet there was a bond between them that Stiggy could never hope to understand.

Sally needed Dave in her life just as much as Dave needed her. That was why she'd carried on phoning him, despite the risks. And it was why Dave had gone looking for her when she stopped calling him. Why he'd refused to go back home once he knew she was okay. It wasn't just the threat of Joe's skinhead mates turning up that made Dave want to stay and protect her, it was a lot deeper than that. How would they both cope when they were separated by hundreds of miles?

Stiggy didn't want Dave following them down to Cleator Moor, but he knew Sally would need to keep in contact with him somehow, for both their sakes. He decided he would try and make peace with the skinhead before they left, show him there were no bad feelings on his part. Maybe share a bottle of cider with him after dinner, tell him how much they both appreciate him looking after Sally the way he does. If he and Dave could part on good terms, it would mean a lot to Sally. And if not, it certainly wouldn't be for want of trying on Stiggy's part.

* * *

On Friday afternoon, Stiggy boxed up all his non-essential belongings and loaded them into the back of the campervan, while Sally and Dave listened to the *Selector* album and chatted in the living room. Sally had offered to help, which was more than Dave did, but Stiggy told her he could manage by himself. It would be Sally and Dave's last day together, so it would be best if they made the most of it.

While sorting through his records the night before, Stiggy picked out a few of his favourites along with the ones he'd borrowed from his mates over the last few months, and copied them onto cassettes so he could listen to them on the long journey north. He backed Colin's *Astronauts* album with the

new *Mob* one he bought on one cassette, taped all his *Crass,
Conflict, Flux of Pink Indians* and *Dirt* singles onto another,
while a third tape contained Sally's *Selector* LP on one side,
and *Discharge's Hear Nothing See Nothing Say Nothing* on
the other for a bit of variety.

Dave was his usual surly self, and glowered at Stiggy every
time he went back in the flat for some more stuff. Stiggy didn't
rise to it, even when Dave came out with one of his sarcastic
comments about the things he treasured.

"Fucking *Crass*? They're shit, they are."

"Fucking comics? What are you, a fucking kid or something?"

Stiggy took it all in his stride. Tomorrow morning he and
Sally would be heading off to the country to start their new life,
and Dave would be back in Sheffield where he belonged. Fuck
him. It wasn't like Stiggy hadn't tried his best to get along with
the young skinhead for Sally's sake, but there was just no
penetrating that wall of hate he'd built up around himself. Sally
seemed to be the only person he would let in, so how was he
going to cope without her? Stiggy couldn't help feeling a little
bit guilty about that, but it wasn't like he and Sally had much
choice in the matter. They had to get as far away from Doncaster
as possible before the police closed in on them, it was their
only option and their only chance of remaining free. Even Dave
must agree that keeping Sally safe was the main priority.

By early evening, the campervan was mostly packed and
ready to go, with just a few more things left to add the following
morning — a fresh set of clothes each to replace the ones that
would almost certainly be drenched in sweat and beer by the
end of the night; the portable television so he and Sally could
watch late night Hammer Horror films in bed together at his
uncle's house; and the camping stove and half-full Calor Gas
canister from the kitchen so they could make cups of tea and
coffee by the roadside when he needed a break from driving.
They wouldn't need the camping stove once they reached his
uncle's house, but they could always sell it and get a few extra
quid to tide them over until the dole money started rolling in.
Which made more sense than just leaving it behind for the next
tenant.

Stiggy slumped down in the armchair and sighed as he wiped
the sweat from his brow with the back of his hand. It was too
hot for strenuous work like that, and he needed a rest before he
and Sally headed out for the night to see his mates at The
Juggler's Rest. He'd take all their records back and say his
goodbyes, watch the band together, and get pissed up with

them one last time. Make it a night to remember.

Sally and Dave sat on the bed together and looked across at him. Sally smiled, while Dave just scowled. She had on a black *Vice Squad* T-shirt Stiggy had bought for her from the market earlier that morning, showing the whole band decked out in studded leather jackets with Beki Bondage standing front and centre. It looked good on her, much better than his own baggy shirts did, and showed off her curves in all the right places. Especially with the short denim skirt she'd chosen to match it with. He couldn't help smiling as he gazed at her, and looked forward to having her all to himself for a few hours. Dave would still be there when they got back from the pub, but by then Stiggy would be too drunk to care.

When it was time to leave for The Juggler's Rest, Stiggy gathered up all the albums and singles he'd borrowed from his mates and put them in a carrier bag next to the record player so he could take them with him. He'd wanted to spike Sally's hair up with soap to match his own, but she had refused, saying she wasn't ready for anything like that yet. The way Dave cracked his knuckles and smirked when she told him made Stiggy think the skinhead had something to do with her reluctance, but it wasn't worth starting an argument over it. Lots of punks didn't bother doing anything with their hair, so it was no big deal.

Stiggy waited while Sally finished lacing up her boots, then picked up the carrier bag of records and opened the flat door. Dave rose up from the bed and put on his green bomber jacket.

"You don't need to wait in the van," Stiggy said. "You can stay here if you want, until we get back."

"Fuck that, I'm coming with you. Joe's mates are still looking for her, remember?"

"What? You can't, it's a punk pub. There's no telling what might happen if you turn up looking like that. Especially with all the hassle we've been having with skinheads lately."

"Well maybe Sally shouldn't go either, then," Dave said. "If it's not safe, you'd best leave her here with me and go on your own."

Sally shook her head. "No Dave, I want to go. I've been looking forward to it, I haven't had a proper night out since ... well, you know. For ages." She gestured at her clothes. "Besides, looking like this nobody will know I'm a skin, will they? Maybe you could borrow some of Stiggy's clothes, then you'd be okay too."

Dave pulled a face. "Fuck that. You might not mind walking

round like some sort of freak, but there's no way I am."

"Well stay here then," Stiggy said.

"No chance. If Sally goes, then so do I."

"Well don't say you weren't warned."

Dave shrugged. "I can handle myself if I need to."

"I don't want you attacking any of my mates," Stiggy said.

"Well that's up to them really, isn't it? If they don't fuck with me, I won't fuck with them."

"Please, Stiggy?" Sally said. "Can he come with us? He'll be no bother, honest." She turned to Dave. "*Will* you?"

"As if."

Stiggy sighed. "Okay, fine, whatever. But he can't let on to my mates he's with us, okay? He has to keep away and pretend he doesn't know us."

"That's not fair," Sally protested.

"No, it's okay Sally," Dave said. "I don't want to spend time with a bunch of smelly punks anyway, all I'm bothered about is making sure you're okay if Joe's mates show up. I'll just stay at the bar and watch out for you from there. And if no cunt hassles me, I won't need to smack them, will I?"

* * *

Danny and Steve were standing outside The Juggler's Rest, peering through one of the windows with their hands cupped over their eyes. Even from a distance, Stiggy could smell the solvents wafting off them. It brought with it a brief feeling of nostalgia, and a yearning for a quick bag of glue himself. But then he thought of all those innocent cows and horses who had been tortured, murdered and mutilated to make it, and just felt shame and regret about all the years he had been complicit in that.

"Right," Stiggy said to Dave. "You go in first, we'll follow a few minutes later. And remember, keep your distance, I don't want my mates to know you're with us. And keep an eye on the door, in case Joe's mob show up."

Dave shrugged. "Yeah, whatever. You just make sure she's safe in there from your smelly mates."

Stiggy and Sally hung back while Dave swaggered over to the pub. Danny and Steve both turned and gawped at him as he passed them by. Loud music blared out when he pushed open the door, then faded away as it closed behind him. Stiggy waited until he thought enough time had passed, then took Sally by the hand and walked over to the two young punks.

"All right, Stiggy?" Danny said. "Got any glue?"

Stiggy shook his head. "No, mate. I packed it in, remember? Are you two coming in then, or what?"

"Got no money, have we?" Danny said. "And they probably wouldn't let us in, anyway. Not old enough, are we? So we thought we'd watch the band from out here."

"I doubt there's many people in there over eighteen anyway," Stiggy said. "I don't think the landlord's that bothered, to be honest, as long as he makes his money. So you might as well come in with us instead of standing out here all night. You'd be safer, too."

"How do you mean, like?" Danny asked.

"I heard there might be some skinheads in town tonight."

"Well, duh!" Steve said. He pointed at a photocopied flyer in one of the pub's windows. It showed a grainy photo of a skinhead sticking up two fingers as he was dragged off by two police officers.

Razor Wire, the accompanying text said. *Barnsley's only proper Oi band. Entrance fifty pence.*

Stiggy frowned. Would his mates even be in there if they knew there was a skinhead band on? After all the grief they'd had from skinheads over the last six months they'd hardly want to walk into a pub full of them. He looked through the window. A mass of shaven-headed youths crowded around the bar. Some were in shirts and braces, others wore green bomber jackets identical to the one Dave had on. Stiggy wondered if any of Joe's mates were among them, waiting to pounce on Sally as soon as she entered. But then he realised there would be no way they could have known where he would be taking her tonight. And if they were there, Dave would have come back out to warn them by now.

Punks occupied the nearby tables, far outnumbering the skinheads at the bar. Stiggy recognised most of them, but others he hadn't seen before, and assumed they must have followed the band down from Barnsley. Then he spotted Colin and Brian sitting on chairs at a table near the stage. Their girlfriends, Becky and Kaz, sat opposite them on a padded bench adjacent to the wall, but there was no sign of Twiglet anywhere. Maybe he'd decided not to risk it after being battered at the *Cockney Upstarts* gig because of the colour of his skin. Stiggy couldn't really blame him for that. Even though he now accepted that not all skinheads were raving Nazis, he still felt a little bit queasy around them. Especially around large numbers of them in a confined space, with added alcohol. But everything inside the pub seemed peaceful enough, and it would be his last chance to see his mates before he left for the country, so he decided to chance it.

"Come on, then," he said to Danny and Steve. "I'll pay for you to get in, but if the landlord catches you and chucks you out, you're not with me, okay?"

"Cheers, Stiggy," Steve said.

"Yeah, cheers, Stiggy," Danny added. "We'll pay you back when we can."

Stiggy pushed open the door and gave two pound notes to the casually-dressed youth sitting at a table inside. *Someone's Gonna Die* by *Blitz* blared out of the jukebox. Punks and skinheads alike shouted along with the chorus: "Oi! Oi! Oi!" Stiggy hoped it wasn't a prophesy as he walked into the lounge with Sally. Danny and Steve hurried to a quiet corner, out of the landlord's direct line of sight. Danny picked up a half-empty glass of lager from one of the tables while its owner wasn't looking, and took it with him.

Stiggy glanced at the ram-packed bar and decided against joining the mob of skinheads clamouring for the landlord and his solitary barmaid's attention. He nodded to faces he recognised as he and Sally made their way over to the table where Colin and Brian sat with the two punk girls. Sally spotted the three skinheads they'd met outside Fox's Records in the Arndale Centre last week, and went over to say hello to them. They gave her a bit of a ribbing about her new punk look, but it was just light hearted banter and she laughed along with them, telling them it was only temporary.

"Stiggy!" Colin yelled. "Where the fuck have you been?"

Stiggy smiled as he walked over to the table. "All right, Col? Aye up, Bri. This is Sally."

"All right?" Sally said.

Colin nodded. "Aye up, lass."

Brian cocked his head to one side as he peered at Sally. A jagged line of stitches on his neck stretched tight. "Don't I know you from somewhere?"

Sally blushed and looked away. "Dunno, don't think so." She sat down on the padded bench next to Becky and Kaz and said hello. They asked her what bands she liked, if she had ever seen any of them play live, and how long she had known Stiggy for. Brian stared at her with a frown on his face the whole time.

Stiggy's heart sank. The last thing he wanted was for someone to recognise Sally from the photograph on the news. He'd hoped her appearance had changed enough for that not to happen. He held up the carrier bag to attract Brian's attention away from her.

"I've brought your records back."

Brian turned to look as Stiggy spread the records across the table.

"Cheers Stiggy," Colin said. He picked up the *Astronauts* album and a couple of *Vice Squad* singles, then propped them up on the floor against a table leg. Brian picked out the ones that were his, and did the same.

"The rest are for Twiglet," Stiggy said, "can you pass them on for me the next time you see him?"

Colin looked around the crowded pub. "He was here a minute ago, he must be at the bar or something."

"Really? Is he not worried about all the skinheads, then?"

Brian shrugged. "Not all skinheads are bad."

Stiggy gaped at him. "How do you know that?"

"It was a skinhead who saved his life," Colin said. "You remember Trog, that short one who was giving us loads of hassle a few months back? Turns out he knows first aid and stuff, and if it weren't for him, Brian wouldn't be here now. He's a decent enough bloke once you get to know him. We had a pint with him in the White Swan just before we came here. He said we should all go down to the Black Bull one night, and he'll introduce us to his mates. He's already told them to leave us alone from now on."

"But I thought it was a skinhead who bottled him. That's what Danny said, anyway. And he said everyone had gone down to Sheffield to batter him for it."

"Yeah it was," Brian said. He jerked his head at Sally. "And I just remembered where I've seen her before. She was with him at the *Cockney Upstarts*, only she was a skinhead back then. It was her fucking boyfriend who did it. And they still haven't caught the bastard yet."

Stiggy looked at Sally. Sally stared at Brian with her mouth open. So it *had* been Joe, after all. But at least Brian hadn't made the connection between her and the photo in the news yet. Or the smiling schoolboy with shoulder-length hair and the massive, tattoo-covered skinhead who'd attacked him.

"Yeah well," Stiggy said, "he's not her boyfriend anymore, and she didn't have nothing to do with it, so you can't hold that against her."

"I don't," Brian said. "I just wish the coppers would hurry up and catch him, so I can look him in the eye when they send him down for it." He turned to Sally. "Do you know where he lives?"

"How would she know that?" Stiggy said.

"I weren't asking you."

Sally shook her head. "No, sorry." She looked down at the table when Brian continued staring at her.

"She didn't know him that well," Stiggy said. "And he hit her too, remember? So she'd tell you if she knew."

Brian frowned, and then nodded. "Yeah, I guess. Sorry Sally, it just pisses me off that he's got away with it. I just don't see how someone like that would be so hard for the coppers to find. The guy's fucking massive, you'd think he would be impossible to miss."

"Yeah well," Colin said, "the coppers will be busy looking for that Nazi lass who killed that kid, won't they?" He looked at Stiggy. "When I first heard about it I was sure it was you who got your head stoved in. I thought them skinheads must have caught up with you or something. Especially with you being missing, and nobody seeing you anywhere. Where the fuck have you been, anyway? I went round to your flat loads of times to see if you were okay."

Stiggy shrugged. "I must've been out somewhere. I got your note, though. That was the day everyone went to Sheffield, looking for that skinhead. I saw Danny and Steve down by the river, they told me about it."

"Yeah," Brian said. "And that was a waste of time, wasn't it? The bastard's probably in fucking hiding somewhere."

"There's something else," Stiggy said. "Apparently there's a load of skinheads coming down from Sheffield to cause trouble."

"Doesn't surprise me," Colin said. "Twiglet went with them to Sheffield, he said the only skinheads they could find were a bunch hanging around outside this record shop down by the market, so they chased them across town." He sighed. "I told them not to go, that they should just leave it for the coppers, but they wouldn't listen to me. Now they've gone and started a new war."

"It's me they're looking for," Stiggy said.

"How come?" Brian asked.

"Because of what happened. You know, with the fighting and stuff. Loads of them got nicked by the coppers, and they reckon it's my fault."

"Well they do have a point," Brian said. "If it weren't for you chatting up one of their birds it probably wouldn't have happened."

"Nah," Colin said. "They were already looking for a fight long before that. Remember all that hassle they were giving

Twiglet? It would've kicked off sooner or later anyway."

Brian nodded. "Yeah, you're probably right. Stiggy didn't exactly help the situation though, did he?"

"So what are you going to do?" Colin asked Stiggy. "You know, about them skinheads looking for you?"

"Well, that's the thing." Stiggy glanced at Sally. She was watching him intently, and so were the two punk girls. "We need to get out of town before they find me."

"Is it that serious, then?" Brian asked.

"Yeah. They know I'm with Sally, and they're after her too because of it."

"So where will you go?"

"Don't know, yet. Maybe Manchester, somewhere like that. Somewhere nobody will recognise us."

"How long for?"

Stiggy shrugged. "Dunno. Maybe forever."

"When are you going?"

"Tomorrow. That's why I brought all your records back."

"Yeah?" Colin said. "Well, send us your address when you find somewhere, and we'll come down there one weekend, see how you're getting on. We could stop over, go and see some bands or something, check out the local record shops."

Stiggy nodded. "Yeah, that'd be great." But he knew it could never happen. He hated lying to Colin and Brian, but he knew it was for the best that they didn't know where he was really going. That way there would be no trail for anyone to follow if the coppers ever found out who he was.

A ginger-haired punk in a studded red leather jacket stepped onto the small stage and plugged in a guitar. A loud electrical pop came from the speakers, followed by a whine of feedback. A skinhead in a *Cockney Upstarts* T-shirt and bleached jeans joined him and sat behind the drum kit. Another skinhead, overweight and wearing a green bomber jacket, plugged in a bass and glared out from the stage while he strummed it. The punk guitarist walked up to the microphone.

"One two three four!" he yelled, and a wall of ear-splitting sound erupted from the speakers as the band started their first number. It was fast and raw, with shouted lyrics and frantic drumming, lots of guitar feedback and a steady monotone *dum dum dum dum* from the bass.

Punks and skinheads drifted over to watch. Stiggy spotted Twiglet among them and went over to shout in his ear that he'd brought his records back. Twiglet raised a thumb and smiled, then asked Colin if he could look after them for him. A couple of the Barnsley punks started dancing in front of the stage, and everyone took a step back out of their way so their drinks wouldn't be jostled. Stiggy nodded his head in time to the music. He wanted to get up and dance with the two punks, but he wasn't sure if *Razor Wire* were a Nazi band or not and he didn't want to take the chance. He decided to wait and see, and went to the now almost-deserted bar to get some drinks and a bag of salted peanuts for later. Dave stood there with his back to the bar, a pint of lager in one hand. He scowled at Stiggy as he approached.

"Thought you said it were a fucking punk pub, you lying bastard."

Stiggy shrugged. "It is, usually." He shouted his order to the barmaid and turned back to Dave. "I didn't know there'd be a skinhead band on, did I?"

Dave said something in reply, but Stiggy couldn't hear him over the music. From the look on his face it was obvious the young skinhead didn't believe him, but it was pointless getting into an argument about it. Stiggy stuffed the peanuts in his pocket, picked up the pint of cider and bottle of Babycham the barmaid had left for him, and walked away.

When he returned to the table by the stage, *Razor Wire* were on their second song and another eight punks had joined in with the dancing, while the skinheads just stood at the back with pint glasses in their hands and watched on, as if they were waiting for something. Twiglet, Danny and Steve were among the dancing punks. Twiglet's head bobbed from side to side as he leaped around, his arms flailing. Danny lay on his back on the floor, his arms and legs jerking in the air, which seemed a bit risky to Stiggy with so many Doc Marten boots close by.

Stiggy gave Sally the Babycham and downed half his cider in one gulp. He watched the skinheads for any signs of Nazi salutes when the band paused for drinks between songs, but all they did was raise their fists and shout "Oi! Oi! Oi!"

"Skinhead Army!" the guitarist yelled. "One two three four!"

The skinheads went crazy. Beer and lager sloshed everywhere as they crammed their pint glasses onto a nearby table and rushed forward. Danny, still lying on the floor doing his impersonation of a dying fly, must have seen them coming because he managed to roll out of the way just before they stampeded over him. They barged their way through the other punks and leaped around in front of the stage, using each other's shoulders to launch themselves into the air while the band thrashed their instruments and the guitarist screamed into the microphone.

"Marching down the street in our boots and braces, you better not mess or we'll kick your faces. We're in your town, not gonna back down. So you better know where your fucking place is."

The skinheads by the stage raised their arms, fists clenched, and shouted along with the chorus. "Skinhead army are on your street! The skinhead army you don't wanna meet!"

"What do you think of the band?" Stiggy yelled into Colin's ear.

"Yeah, they're pretty good."

"You reckon they're Nazis?"

Colin pulled a face and shook his head. "What, because they're skinheads? They're not all Nazis, you know. Anyway, the singer's a punk, and there's no such thing as a Nazi punk, is there?"

Stiggy thought about a *Dead Kennedys* song on the subject, but that was just in America so it didn't really count. He nodded. "Yeah, I guess."

The song ended, and the skinheads roared their approval.

"Cheers," the guitarist said. "This one's for the glue heads." He pointed at one of the punks and grinned. "That means you, Barry, I can smell it from here you filthy degenerate. One two three four!"

Stiggy smiled as the music blasted out of the speakers. He'd never heard a song about glue before, and it sent a tingle down his spine. It was like it had been written especially for him. He wanted to rush into the crowd and join in with the frenzied dancing.

"Stick it in a bag, shove it up your nose. Gotta get a buzz, every fucker knows. Glue! Glue! Stick together! Glue! Glue! Fuck forever. Life is short and full of pain, that's why we do it again and again. Fuck your drugs and fuck you too, just give us a bag and some fucking glue."

"Glue! Glue! Stick together!" the skinheads shouted in unison. "Glue! Glue! Fuck forever!"

Colin was grinning too, and Stiggy could tell he had the same idea about joining in. His head bobbed as he punched the air and stamped his feet.

Then Stiggy thought about what Danny had said down by the river. About glue being made out of murdered animals.

"Oi Col," he yelled, "did you know glue's got cows and horses in it?"

"Has it bollocks," Colin yelled back. "Who's told you that?"

"Danny said."

"He's just winding you up, mate. If there was cows and horses in it you'd be able to taste them, wouldn't you?"

"You reckon?"

"Yeah. And glue tastes more like petrol than meat, doesn't it? So that's probably what it's made from, petrol."

Stiggy nodded. Glue being made from petrol made a lot more sense than using cows and horses. Danny wasn't even a vegetarian, so what would he know about anything?

"You coming for a dance, then?"

Colin nodded, then turned to Brian. "You coming, Bri?"

Brian frowned. "What, and burst me stitches open? Nah, you're all right."

Colin smiled. "Yeah, sorry, I forgot you were still an invalid. You stay here and recuperate."

Brian grinned back. "Piss off."

Stiggy waved to Sally, then followed Colin into the melee before the stage and threw himself around, bumping shoulders with punks and skinheads alike while the raucous music washed over him. Twiglet careened into him from the side, and he stumbled into a punk with a green mohican before righting himself. He turned, ready to shove Twiglet in the chest, but before he could do so, Twiglet grabbed a handful of his T-shirt and rushed forward through the crowd, dragging Stiggy with him.

Stiggy held out his hands to brace himself for impact as he hurtled toward a row of punks in studded leather jackets. He turned his head to one side just before he smacked into one and sent him staggering forward into the row of skinheads by the stage. One of the skinheads he hit turned and grinned, then shoved the punk back and sent him reeling. Another punk grabbed him from behind and steadied him, then they both leaped around together as if nothing had happened.

Twiglet made another mad surge forward into the skinheads blocking the stage. Stiggy tried to wrench himself free, thinking even if they weren't Nazis this wouldn't end well for his black mate. But there was no stopping Twiglet, and his tight grip on Stiggy's shirt meant he had no choice but to stumble along with him and slam into the back of the skinheads.

It was like hitting a solid wall draped in green bomber jackets. Stiggy and Twiglet thudded into the skinheads and bounced off. Two of them turned and spotted Twiglet grinning at them.

Stiggy's heart sank. It was all going to kick off again, like it had at the *Cockney Upstarts*. And there was nothing he could do about it.

But then the two skinheads grinned back at Twiglet. They parted, and gestured for him to join them at the front of the stage. Twiglet squeezed himself between them, draped his arms over both their shoulders, and jumped up and down with them.

"Glue! Glue! Stick together!" they all screamed along with the band.

The song ended, and the band went straight into a cover version of *Razors in the Night* without a pause. Everyone cheered and sang along. The crowd surged forward, and Stiggy found himself flattened against the skinheads, unable to move, with everyone leaping around him.

Ten minutes later and drenched in sweat, Stiggy squeezed his way out of the heaving throng around the stage and returned to the table where Brian, Sally, Becky and Kaz sat. His arms and legs ached from the frenetic dancing, and the side of his face stung from a flailing hand he hadn't been quick enough to dodge. He grinned at Brian, feeling sorry for him that he couldn't join in with all the fun, then downed the rest of his cider and decided to get another before the band finished and everyone else rushed over to the bar. He turned to Sally to ask if she wanted another Babycham.

And gaped at the two punk girls when he realised she wasn't sitting there with them.

"Where's Sally?" he asked Brian.

"She went off with some skinhead."

Stiggy glanced at the bar, expecting to see her over there with Dave. But Dave stood alone, slouched over the bar while he ordered a fresh pint of lager from the barman.

"What did he look like, this skinhead?"

Brian shrugged. "Don't know, I weren't paying that much attention."

Stiggy turned to the two girls. "Did you see him?"

Kaz shook her head. "No, not really, we were busy watching the band at the time. I think she seemed to know him, though."

Stiggy scratched between the spikes on the back of his head and looked around the pub. If it wasn't Dave she went off with, who was it? He thought about the three skinheads from the Arndale Centre, but they were all standing at the back of the crowd around the stage and Sally wasn't with them. So who else could it be?

One of Joe's mates!

Stiggy's stomach flipped when the thought popped into his head. Blood drained from his face and bile rose in his throat.

One of the bastards must have sneaked in and grabbed her!

21

Stiggy spun to Brian, his eyes wide. "For fuck's sake, why didn't you stop him, or come and tell me?"

"I didn't know I was supposed to. Anyway, like Kaz said, she seemed to know him, so what's the problem?"

"I told you, there's a bunch of skinheads coming over from Sheffield looking for us. And now you've gone and let one of them walk off with Sally."

Brian jolted upright in his seat. "Shit, I forgot all about that. What should we do, call the police or something?"

Stiggy glared across the pub at the back of Dave's bomber jacket. So much for the baldy bastard protecting Sally. Someone must have slipped past while he wasn't looking. But why would Sally go off with him like that, without making any fuss? That didn't make any sense. Unless she thought she could reason with him, or she had been relying on Dave to intervene and save her?

Stiggy turned back to Brian, frantic with worry. "How long has she been gone for?"

"Dunno, quarter of an hour, maybe?" Brian looked at Kaz for confirmation, and she nodded.

"Fuck, she could be anywhere by now."

Stiggy imagined Sally lying unconscious in the gutter outside, beaten to a pulp. Or worse, dragged off to the cop shop for the five hundred quid reward. He had to tell Dave what had happened, get him to help. He knew those people, so he would know what they would do now they had her. Maybe he could talk them out of it, assuming it wasn't already too late. Stiggy rushed over to the bar, just as Dave turned around and staggered away from it with a pint of lager in one hand.

Except it wasn't Dave.

It was some random skinhead he'd never seen before.

"What's tha' lookin' at, thee?" the lad asked as he brushed past Stiggy and headed for the stage area.

Stiggy spun in a full circle as he searched the room once more. A couple of punk girls wandered over to the toilets in the far corner. Everyone else was near the stage, watching the band. Stiggy barged through the exit door and looked up and down the street. Passing drunks looking for a fight leered at him and shouted: "Sid's dead!" Stiggy went back inside, not knowing what to do, and bumped into Colin and Twiglet heading for the exit. A mob of Doncaster punks followed close behind.

"Are they out there?" Twiglet asked. He had his studded wristband wrapped around his knuckles, ready for action. Brian must have gone for reinforcements, and filled them all in about the Sheffield skinheads and what they had done to Sally.

Stiggy shook his head. He went over to the bar and asked the barmaid and landlord if they knew where the skinhead with the Z-shaped scar on his face had gone to. The barmaid shrugged and pointed in the general direction of the stage, where the band continued playing. Stiggy looked, but all the skinheads over there had their backs to him. If Dave was among them, there was no sign of Sally with him.

Then Becky came running over. "We found her."

Stiggy grabbed her by the shoulders. "Where?"

She pointed. "Over there, by the bogs."

"Is she okay?" Stiggy looked, but the alcove where the toilets stood was hidden from view by the edge of the bar.

"Yeah, she's just sitting on the floor talking to that skinhead we told you about."

Stiggy sighed in relief. It must have been Dave she'd gone off with all along. Then anger flared through him. What did Dave think he was playing at? Stiggy marched over, determined to find out. Sensing the panic was over, the Doncaster punks drifted back to the stage to watch the band.

Sally and Dave sat in the corner of the alcove, opposite the toilet doors. He had his arm draped around her shoulder, his mouth an inch from her ear as he shouted something. Sally smiled, then they both turned their heads so she could shout back into his ear. Dave laughed, then nodded.

"What the fuck are you doing here?" Stiggy yelled at Dave.

Sally startled and looked up at Stiggy. Her face reddened as she pushed Dave's arm off her shoulder and stood up.

Stiggy glared down at Dave. "You're supposed to be watching the door, in case Joe's mob turn up."

Dave shrugged. "Got fucking bored, didn't I? Anyway, you were supposed to be looking after her, not fucking about with your scruffy mates. Anything could've happened to her." He sneered. "Look how fucking long it took you to notice she'd gone."

Stiggy shook his head. Dave was right, he should have kept

an eye on her, just in case. But that didn't justify what Dave had done, and all the worry and panic he'd caused as a result. "She shouldn't be over here with you, she should be over there with my mates. And you should be over by the bar, so you can warn us if Joe's mates turn up. That's what we agreed, remember?"

"Where Sally wants to be is her business, not yours. You don't fucking own her."

"I never said I did. But someone's got to watch the door, haven't they? What if they all storm in and grab her?

Dave shrugged. "I'll handle it."

"What, by yourself?"

"If I have to. It's not like you'd be much use, anyway, a weedy cunt like you."

"Look, mate ..."

Dave bolted upright with his fists clenched. "I'm not your fucking mate."

Stiggy backed away with his hands raised. Great, Dave was in fucking psycho mode again.

"No, Dave," Sally said, stepping between them. "Stiggy's right, we shouldn't be over here on our own. It's not a good idea, not with Joe's mates looking for me."

Dave glared over her shoulder at Stiggy. His nostrils flared. His fists clenched and unclenched by his sides.

"I'll come and find you when the band finishes," Sally continued. "Then we'll be able to talk properly, instead of shouting all the time. You go and wait by the bar, watch the door like Stiggy says."

Dave's eyes flicked to Sally, then back to Stiggy. His shoulders slumped. "Okay Sally, but I'm doing it for you, not him."

"Come on Sally," Stiggy said. He took her by the hand and pulled her away.

"We weren't doing nothing, honest," Sally said. "We were talking, that's all."

Stiggy nodded. "Yeah, I know."

"You don't mind, do you? Only it's our last night together, and Dave's a bit down about it. I just wanted to cheer him up, that's all."

"No, it's fine. I get it, I really do. And you should spend as much time with him as you can before we head off tomorrow. I kind of feel a bit bad about taking you away from him, to be honest. Especially with ... well, you know. What happened to him and all that. If you want, we could let him stay in the flat tonight? You know, on the chair or something? That'd give you two a bit more time together, and we can figure out a way for you to keep in touch with him when we're at my uncle's house. And, you know, maybe if he promises to be a bit less of a twat to me he could come down and see us one weekend?"

Sally's mouth dropped open as she stared at Stiggy. "Do you mean that?"

"Yeah, of course. You two need each other, I can see that. After what you went through together, I couldn't just—"

Sally grabbed hold of Stiggy and kissed him. "Thank you," she yelled in his ear.

Stiggy grinned. "No worries."

Colin and Twiglet had disappeared back into the crowd around the stage, so Stiggy and Sally sat at the table with Brian, Becky and Kaz. Stiggy wanted some more cider to counteract the adrenalin still surging through his veins, but he didn't fancy bumping into Dave at the bar because he knew it would just cause another argument, and without Sally there to intervene there was no telling what might happen. So he gave Brian a five pound note and sent him instead, saying he could buy himself a drink while he was there. Brian expressed surprise at Stiggy's uncharacteristic generosity, and came back with a bottle of Newcastle Brown Ale and a shot of vodka instead of his usual pint of bitter. He supped the brown ale down to the bottom of the neck, then poured in the vodka and swished it around.

Danny staggered over a few minutes later, with a pint glass overflowing with flat lager. His shirt was ripped down one side, and his arms were covered in bruises. He swayed from side to side as he stood before the table.

"All right, Stiggy?"

Stiggy pointed at the lager in Danny's hand and grinned. "How the fuck did you manage to get served?"

"Found it, didn't I?" Danny yelled back. "Someone left a load of half empty glasses on a table over there, didn't they?" He took a sip of lager and grimaced. "You can't beat a free drink, can you?"

"You do know it belongs to them skinheads, don't you?"

Danny shrugged. "Not anymore it don't. Finders keepers, innit? Everyone knows that. Do you want some? There's plenty left."

Stiggy shook his head. "Nah, you're all right, I'll stick to cider."

"You got any glue?"

"No mate, just cider. You could try asking them skinheads, they might have some glue."

Danny looked over to the stage. "You reckon they'd lend me some?"

Stiggy laughed. "No mate, I'm just messing you about. They'd be more likely to batter you for pinching their lager. Where's Steve, anyway?"

"Dunno," Danny said. "Over by the stage, I guess. That's where he was last time I saw him, anyway." He took another gulp of lager, wiped his mouth with the back of his hand, then put the glass down on the table. "And that's where I'm going now. You coming then, or what?"

Stiggy turned to Sally. "Would you mind if I did?"

Sally smiled and shook her head. "No, you go and enjoy yourself. Don't worry, I'll stay here this time."

Stiggy glanced at the bar to make sure Dave was still on sentry duty. Dave glared back at him, his arms folded over his chest. Stiggy reached across the table and squeezed Sally's hand.

"I'll see you in a bit then, yeah?"

Sally nodded, and after a quick gulp of cider Stiggy followed Danny back into the scrum around the stage.

Razor Wire ended their song and paused for a break while they downed the rest of their beer. The drummer pulled off his T-shirt and used it to wipe sweat from his face and chest before tossing it down beside his kit. The guitarist wandered the small stage with his fists clenched, glaring down at the audience.

"Who fucking wants some, then?" he shouted.

The skinheads surged forward with a roar and waved their fists at him. "Come on then!" one yelled. "I'll fucking have you!"

Stiggy glanced at Danny. Danny's face reflected his own confusion and apprehension.

The guitarist pointed at another of the skinheads. "Do you fucking want some as well?" His finger jerked to one of the punks. "What about you, Barry, you filthy animal? You think you're fucking hard enough, do you?"

"Fucking aye," Barry hollered back. "I'll have you any day."

"We'll all fucking have you!" someone else shouted.

Danny backed away, and Stiggy couldn't blame him. What the fuck was going on?

"You fucking what?" the guitarist yelled back. "You all fucking want some, do you? Well we'll fucking give you some then, you bunch of fucking cunts!"

His fingers slid up and down the guitar's fretboard as he attacked the strings. The drummer thrashed his kit with renewed ferocity. The bass player jumped up and down while he strummed along.

Stiggy relaxed and wiped the sweat from his brow. It was just an act, and all the Barnsley crowd seemed to be in on the joke. They leaped around, their arms flailing, and shoulder-barged each other to the fast music. Stiggy grinned at Danny, then joined in, throwing himself at the nearest punks.

"Who you looking at, you two bob runt? You think you're hard but you're just a cunt! Standing on the terraces in your hat and scarf. Wankers like you make me fucking laugh."

The skinheads stopped dancing and jerked their index fingers at the guitarist as they shouted along.

"So come on! If you think you're hard enough. Come on! Show us just what you've got. Nothing! You useless fucking prick. Your cowardice! Makes me fucking sick."

Someone shoved Stiggy in the back and he stumbled to his knees. A punk reached down and helped him to his feet, then grabbed his shirt and spun him around before launching him on his way. Stiggy grinned as he slammed into Danny and knocked him flying, then staggered into a group of punks ragging each other around. Over their shoulders he caught a quick glimpse of Twiglet bobbing around by the right hand side of the stage, and barged his way through the crowd toward him. Some parted to let him pass, others closed ranks and he had to skirt around them to find another route.

He was almost there when a flailing fist hammered into the side of his head and sent his senses reeling. Stiggy's hand shot up to rub his smarting temple. He spun, ready to give the fist's owner a piece of his mind, yell at him for taking things too far and tell him to pack it in and watch what he was doing.

Dave sneered at him. "So this is how you scruffy cunts dance then, is it?" he yelled as he drew back a fist and swung it at Stiggy's face.

Stiggy darted back, more in surprise at seeing Dave there than anything else. The young skinhead didn't even like punk and oi, so what was he playing at? The fist whizzed past Stiggy and slammed into a row of spiked studs coating the shoulders of a tall punk's leather jacket. Dave hollered and rubbed his knuckles. The punk turned and glared at him. Stiggy grinned and shoved Dave in the chest as hard as he could. If the bastard wanted to play rough, that was his choice. And if he got a bit bruised in the process it was his own fault for being there.

Dave lurched forward with both fists raised. Stiggy spun and slapped him across the face with the palm of his hand. Dave staggered sideways and bumped into a punk with a red mohican. The punk turned and grinned at Dave, then shoved him back to Stiggy. Stiggy grabbed Dave's bomber jacket, thrust out his leg, and used his forward momentum to swing him over it. Dave cried out as he tumbled down among the fag ends and spilt beer.

"That's for being a wanker," Stiggy said as he reached down to help Dave back up.

"Fuck off!" Dave yelled, and slapped Stiggy's hand away.

Stiggy shrugged and turned away. Fuck him, if he's going to be like that. He swung his arms and stamped his feet in time to the music, barging into punks and skinheads alike as he headed away from Dave. Twiglet had disappeared back into the crowd, the back of his head visible now and again over by the front of the stage where the skinheads were leaping around. One of them had climbed onto the stage, and had his arms around the guitarist's shoulders while he screamed along with him into the microphone.

"Come and have a go if you think you're hard enough! We are the boys who will boot you from above!"

A hand grabbed Stiggy's shoulder and spun him around.

"Fucking cunt!" Dave yelled. His fist flew back and slammed into Stiggy's gut three times in quick succession.

The pain was incredible, much worse than anything Stiggy had ever felt before. His eyes bulged as he clutched his stomach. Dave stood before him, a sudden look of sheer terror on his face. His mouth dropped open and his hands fell to his sides. Tears welled up in his eyes and rolled down his cheeks. He shook his head slowly and backed away. His eyes were wide and staring, his mouth opening and closing.

Stiggy's legs buckled beneath him and he dropped down to his knees, still clutching his aching stomach. His shirt was soaking wet, something warm pumping between his fingers. He looked up at Dave in confusion, suddenly very cold despite the sweltering heat of the dance floor and the beads of sweat dribbling down his forehead. He caught a quick glimpse of something red with a glint of silver in the skinhead's hand, but before he could figure out what it was Dave turned and ran.

Stiggy looked down and saw blood. Lots of it pouring between his fingers and pooling on the floor between his legs, soaking into the knees of his combat trousers. He raised his hands and stared at them. Where was it all coming from? And whose was it?

Everyone seemed to be shouting at once, but they sounded far away and distant. The band on stage faded in and out, like someone was fiddling with a volume control somewhere, and then stopped completely, leaving nothing but an undulating screech of feedback.

"Get a fucking ambulance!" a voice yelled.

Boots trampled past. Someone asked what had happened. A girl screamed.

The room swayed from side to side, and Stiggy swayed with it, feeling the last of his strength draining away, leaving nothing but fatigue. All those late nights with Sally and early morning wake-ups with Dave pounding on the flat door must be taking their toll on him. Where was Dave anyway? He was there a minute ago. Stiggy tried to look for him, but everything was blurry and his eyelids felt very heavy. Why was everyone pointing at him and yelling?

Stiggy closed his eyes and toppled sideways. His head smacked down on the hard flooring, but he didn't feel anything. In his mind he was back home at the flat, hitting the pillow after a great night out. Everything ached from the dancing, but he would be okay in the morning. Just a few bruises to remind him how much fun he had. As long as whoever it was who kept shaking him by the shoulders would stop it, so he could get some sleep.

"Stiggy, wake up!"

Fuck off Dave, it's too early.

"Stiggy, you need to stay awake."

That was the last thing Stiggy wanted to do, but someone was pulling his eyelids open and forcing him back to consciousness. Colin drifted into focus above him. There seemed to be two of him, both talking at once. Why was it so cold, all of a sudden? Had someone opened the window?

"That's it Stiggy, stay with us. The ambulance will be here soon. You're going to be okay."

Colin pressed his hands against Stiggy's stomach. The sudden jolt of pain made him convulse and cry out.

Another face filled his vision. Stiggy tried to smile when he recognised Sally. She was holding his hand and saying something, but he couldn't make out any of the words between her sobs. Tears streamed down her face, and snot dribbled from her nose. Stiggy wanted to tell her he loved her, that he would always look after her, but all he could do was cough and splutter as everything faded away to nothing.

The last thing he heard was Sally screaming his name, but it seemed so far away and distant he couldn't even be sure if it was real or not.

22

... beep ... beep ... beep ... beep ... beep ...

Just a few more minutes, Mum. I'll get up soon, honest.

... beep ... beep ... beep ... beep ...

"Stiggy? Stiggy, wake up."

I don't really feel well enough for school today, Mum. I've got a really bad stomach ache. Can I stay at home with you instead? We could watch *Rainbow* and *Play School* together, like we used to when I was little. Do you remember? I liked Zippy best.

... beep ... beep ... beep ...

Can you turn the alarm off, Mum? I just want to go back to sleep. I'm really tired, and my stomach hurts.

... beep ... beep ...

"Stiggy, can you hear me?"

Yes, Mum. But I don't want to go to school today. I'm not well enough. I just want to go back to sleep.

"Stiggy, please, just wake up. For me? Please?"

... beep ...

"No, Mum. I don't want to go to school."

"Stiggy? Stiggy, wake up."

Stiggy's eyes flickered open. He squinted against the harsh light blaring down at him from the ceiling, then turned his head to one side to avoid it. Someone had attached railings to the side of his bed while he was asleep. They'd taken down all his *Sex Pistols* posters and painted the walls white, too. Everything smelled of disinfectant, and there was some weird beeping machine on a trolley next to the bed.

"Stiggy, are you okay?"

Someone clutched Stiggy's right hand and he turned his head back to see who it was. Sally's face hovered beside him, leaning over more railings on that side of the bed. Her eyes were red and puffy, like she'd been rubbing them. Her cheeks glistened with tears, but she was smiling too.

"Sally? I don't understand. Where's my mum gone? Where am I?"

"You're in the hospital. Oh God, I thought you were never

going to wake up."

A tear rolled down Sally's cheek, and Stiggy reached out with his left hand to brush it away. He found his movement restricted, and when he looked to see why he found a cannula sticking out of the back of his hand, held in place with strips of plaster. It had a tube attached, which led to a bag of clear liquid suspended on a stand beside the bed. He frowned. Sally had said he was in the hospital, but why? Had something happened to him? He turned back to Sally to ask her what was going on.

Then he noticed with a jolt that her *Vice Squad* shirt had splashes of blood down it. He gaped at her and tried to sit up, but he couldn't manage it and just flopped back down. His head was too heavy, even though it felt like it was stuffed with cotton wool.

"Sally, are you okay?" he asked. "What's happened to you?"

Sally looked confused for a second, then glanced down at her shirt and shook her head. "It's not my blood, it's yours."

"What?"

"Don't you remember?" Sally's bottom lip trembled, and fresh tears welled up in her eyes. "There was a fight, and you got stabbed." She shook her head. "Oh God, it was horrible. I thought you were going to die."

A sudden flash of memory popped into Stiggy's mind. An explosion of agony in his stomach. Dave hovering over him, a knife in his hand. Blood dripping from it. Dave's face turning from cold fury to absolute shock and terror before his eyes. Everyone shouting, and boots trampling past him. Then ... nothing.

Stiggy felt his stomach and found it swathed in bandages. There were wires taped to his bare chest. He realised the constant beeping he could hear was his own heartbeat being replicated by the machine on the trolley beside him.

"Where's ... where's Dave?" he asked. Did Sally know it was Dave who had stabbed him?

Sally frowned. "I don't know. I guess he must have run away before the police came, same as everyone else." She stepped back and gripped the top of the bed rail with both hands as she peered down at him. "Who did it, Stiggy? Do you know who it was?"

She didn't know. Fuck. How could he tell her it was Dave, her best friend, the boy who had helped her through such terrible, dark times? It would tear her apart if she knew. And what would be the point, anyway? Dave would have legged it back to Sheffield by now, terrified at the prospect of facing the consequences for what he had done. He certainly wouldn't be following them down to Cleator Moor, so they'd probably never see him again. He couldn't spoil Sally's memory of Dave in that way, it wouldn't be right. He shook his head and looked away, so she wouldn't see his face. Wouldn't know he was lying to her.

"I don't know who it was, Sally. I don't really remember much about it, to be honest. How long have I been here?"

"Two days. They kept telling me to go home and get some sleep, that there was no point me being here while you were unconscious, but I had to stay. I had to make sure you were okay."

Two days! That would make it Sunday, they should have been long gone by now. He glanced at the window to his left and saw it was dark outside. He looked at his wrist to see what time it was, but his watch wasn't there.

"What time is it?"

"I don't know. Late, I guess."

"And you've been here all the time?"

"Yeah. The nurses have been really good to me. They brought me some sandwiches, and gave me a blanket. Said to let them know if ... *when* you came round. I guess I should go and find one, tell them the good news."

"Not yet," Stiggy said. "Tell me what happened after ... after I passed out."

"Everyone ran away. People were saying someone had been stabbed, so I went to find you so we could get away before the police came. And then I saw you lying on the floor, and ... you were really pale, and there was blood everywhere." Sally bit her lip and gripped the rail so tight her knuckles turned white. "It was ages before the ambulance came. Your friends, they tried to stop the bleeding, but there was so much of it still coming out." She sniffed up a glob of snot that had trickled out of her nose, and wiped her eyes with the palms of her hands before gripping the rail again. "Then you stopped moving and I thought you were dead. The ambulance men, they couldn't find a pulse at first, but then they did. It was really weak, they said, but it was there. And then the police came and wanted to know what had happened."

"Did they see you?"

"I don't know, I think I might have had my back to them but I'm not sure. The ambulance men, they said they didn't have time to explain, they had to get you to the hospital straight away, and they took you out on a stretcher. I went with them, so I don't know what happened after that. When we got to the hospital they took you into this big room and made me wait outside. I watched through the window, but I couldn't really see anything because there was too many people in the way. And then the police came, so I hid in the toilet. And when I came out, you'd gone. I thought you were dead."

Stiggy shook his head. "You don't get rid of me that easy, Sally. I love you far too much for that."

Shit, had he really said that? Stiggy's cheeks flushed as he studied Sally's face for a reaction. She stared at him with a blank expression, then wiped her eyes again. Maybe she hadn't heard him? Or maybe she was just trying to think of a way of letting him down gently? She'd been sat beside the hospital bed for two days, so she must have some feelings for him.

"Sally, I ..."

Sally looked down. "I think I might love you, too."

Stiggy cocked his head to one side. "You think? You might? But you're not sure?"

Sally looked up and shrugged. "I don't really have anything to compare it with. I know I don't hate you, anyway."

Stiggy smiled. "Oh, okay. Then I guess I don't hate you, either."

Sally reached for Stiggy's hand and gripped it tight. "It's like ... I don't know ... weird, I guess. With Joe I was always glad when he went out, but with you I just ... well, I can't wait for you to come back again." Fresh tears welled up. "And then when I came out of the toilet and thought you were dead, I just ..."

Sally broke down and sobbed.

"Sally, it's okay, I understand. That's how it is for me, too, I don't know what I would've done if it was you in here instead of me. And I'm okay, I won't die, I promise. Once I get out of here we'll go to my uncle's and start our new life together, just the two of us. It'll be perfect, you'll see. So what happened next, after you came out of the toilet? How did you find out where I was?"

"A nurse found me crying and asked what was wrong. I told her that you'd been stabbed, and that you were dead, and I wished I was too. Then she just smiled at me and shook her head and said you weren't dead, you'd just gone upstairs so they could look after you better. Then she brought me here, so I could see for myself. I've been here ever since, waiting for you to wake up."

Stiggy thought about what she must have gone through not knowing whether he would live or die, and tried to imagine what it would be like if she was the one lying unconscious in a hospital bed for two days. She must have been frantic with worry, he certainly would have been. Dave had a lot to answer for if Stiggy ever saw him again.

"Your mum and dad came earlier," Sally said. "Someone must have told them what happened. They were really worried too, but they seemed nice. They left you some grapes, and said to tell you they'll be back tomorrow."

Stiggy nodded. It had been a few months since he last visited his parents at their flat on Beckett Road. He'd intended to go and see them before he left for the country, but things had been a bit too hectic since Dave turned up at the flat and he'd just put it off. If they were coming to visit him at the hospital tomorrow, that would save him a job. He could tell them his plans then, that he was going to go and visit Uncle Bert in Cleator Moor, stay with him for a few weeks. Uncle Bert would be sure to write and let them know he'd turned up at his house with Sally, so it wasn't like they wouldn't find out anyway. And if the worst came to the worst, and the coppers somehow managed to identify him, it wasn't like they would grass up their one and only son.

"Go and find a nurse," Stiggy said. "Then we can find out how long I'll be in here for."

Sally left the room, and came back a moment later with a young female nurse. The nurse smiled at Stiggy, then checked the heart monitor and tapped the bag of liquid suspended by the side of the bed.

"You had us worried for a while there, Mr Nixon."

Stiggy glanced at Sally and frowned. She must have told them his real name, and he was surprised she'd remembered it because he'd only ever mentioned it once. Had she given them her name, too? Anyone who'd seen the news recently would be sure to recognise it if she had.

"You lost a lot of blood," the nurse continued, "and it was touch and go for a while, but it looks like you're responding well after the surgery."

"How long will I need to be in here for?"

"We'd like to keep you in for another day or so, keep an eye on you just in case there are any complications. And you'll need to take it easy for a few months while the stitches heal, but there's no reason you can't do that at home, as long as there is someone there who can look after you."

"Yes, there is," Sally said.

"Good, good." The nurse examined Stiggy's bandages, then

smiled at him. "Well, the best thing you can do right now is get some rest. The police will want you to make a statement about what happened, but that can wait until the morning." She turned to Sally. "And the best thing you can do, love, is go home and get some sleep yourself. Don't worry, we'll look after him until you get back."

The nurse wrote something on a clipboard hanging from the bottom of the bed, then left the room and closed the door behind her. Stiggy gripped the rails at each side of the bed and pulled himself up to a sitting position. He winced as his stomach cramped. He felt drained and light-headed, and almost passed out, but he managed to hold himself upright.

"What are you doing?" Sally asked, staring at him.

Stiggy released one of the rails and picked at the strips of plaster holding wires to his chest.

"We need to go, Sally. Right now."

"What? No, you need to stay here and get better. Lie back down, didn't you hear what that nurse said?"

"Yeah, she said I'm progressing nicely. But she also said the coppers are coming to see me in the morning, and that's a risk we can't afford to take."

"But they don't even know what you look like. Not properly, anyway. And I'm in disguise, remember?"

"It's still too much of a risk. I don't want to chance it, not when we're this close to getting away."

Stiggy winced as he ripped the plasters off, taking a chunk of chest hair with them. The machine by the bed emitted one long, continuous tone. He reached across and switched it off, then clenched his fist and yanked the cannula out of the back of his hand.

Sally shook her head. "You shouldn't be doing this, Stiggy. You need to stay here and get better."

Stiggy fiddled with the rail and found out how to swing it down out of the way, then pulled off the single bedcover and gaped at the green flannelette pyjama bottoms he found himself wearing.

"Shit, where's my combats?"

Blood rushed to Stiggy's head when he realised Joe's wallet was missing along with his trousers. He and Sally needed that money to live on until he could make a fresh benefit claim in Cleator Moor. Without it they wouldn't even be able to afford the petrol to get there.

Sally shook her head. "They're gone, Stiggy. They cut them off you, so they could treat you properly. They were covered in blood anyway, so they wouldn't have been any use to you. Same with your shirt, that's gone too. I think they threw them away, but I'm not sure."

"What about the wallet? Have you got it?"

"No. They put all the stuff in your pockets in a plastic bag, along with your watch. I think the wallet was with them, but I don't know where it is now."

"Fuck."

"I could go and ask that nurse? Maybe they are just looking after it for you until you leave."

"No, it's too much of a risk. What if the coppers have got it?"

Stiggy imagined his Giro money and the remainder of Joe's cash disappearing into some bent copper's back pocket, but that was the least of his worries. They would want to know why he had a wallet with someone else's initials on it, and it wouldn't take much for someone to realise JH could stand for Joseph Hawkins. Maybe they would even know who the old woman in the photograph was and link it to him that way. And there was only one way Stiggy could have ended up with a murdered skinhead's wallet in his possession.

Stiggy sighed. Either way, the money was gone and there was nothing he could do about it. That created problems of its own. How was he supposed to escape to the country if he couldn't even afford to buy any petrol for the campervan? He had no idea how much fuel was left in it, or how far he would be able to get before it ran out. And then what was he supposed to do? Without money he'd be stranded at the side of the road.

"You don't look very well, Stiggy," Sally said. "You've gone really pale. Are you sure you'll be okay to leave?"

Stiggy shook his head to clear his thoughts. He had to assume the worst, and plan for that. The hospital knew his name, so most likely the police did too. And they could easily find out where he lived, if they didn't already. If he was lucky they would just visit him at the flat to take a statement about what happened at The Juggler's Rest. He'd either tell them he didn't know who stabbed him, or just give them a vague description of a skinhead. They wouldn't really be bothered about solving the crime anyway, so that would be the end of it. He could always postpone the trip to the country until after his next Giro came, that way they'd at least be able to afford the petrol. It would be a risk to spend another two weeks in Doncaster, but it couldn't be helped.

But what if the police started asking questions about Joe's wallet? Or they recognised Sally from the photograph they had of her? Or they noticed his own resemblance to the photofit of

Sally's accomplice? For all he knew, Dave could have gone to the police and told them Stiggy had killed Joe, like he had originally planned to do when he first turned up in Doncaster. Without Sally to hold him back there was no telling what he might be capable of. No, it was too much of a risk to take. They had to get away before any of that happened.

"Stiggy? Are you okay?"

"Yeah." Stiggy nodded, and attempted a smile. "I'm just a bit groggy, that's all. What did you have to go and tell them my name for?"

"I had to, Stiggy. They kept asking me questions, like if you're allergic to anything, stuff like that. I didn't know, so they said they would need to check your medical records before they could operate. And they couldn't do that if they didn't know who you were."

"Okay," Stiggy said. "Well I guess it can't be helped. But we'll need to leave for the country tonight, we can't risk coppers turning up at the flat before we get away."

Sally gaped at him. "Will you be okay to drive that soon?"

"I'll have to be, won't I?"

Stiggy thought again about the petrol in the campervan, and what he would do when it ran out. If they had a bit more time he could sell the camping stove at the second hand shop on Nether Hall Road to raise a bit of cash. But that wouldn't be open until ten the next morning, and they needed to be long gone by then. But he could worry about that later, maybe find somewhere to sell it on the way. The priority had to be getting back to the flat, and he couldn't do that without any clothes. If he walked the streets wearing nothing but a pair of hospital-issue pyjama bottoms, any passing cop car would be sure to stop to investigate. And if they saw the blood on Sally's shirt they would drag them both in for questioning. Once they took Sally's fingerprints they would know who she was, and that would be the end of everything.

"Sally, listen. I need you to go home and get me something to wear, okay? And you need to get changed yourself before you come back. But don't wear any of your skinhead stuff, okay?"

"Are you sure we need to do this, Stiggy? You can't just stay here a few more days until you're better?"

"Yeah, it's got to be tonight, before the coppers come in the morning. We can't risk them looking at us too closely, or asking any awkward questions. When you go home for my clothes, stay in the shadows, yeah? And keep your back turned if any cars go past, just in case it's coppers out on patrol."

Sally shook her head. "I don't know how to get to your flat from here, I don't even know where we are. I was in the back of the ambulance with you, remember? I didn't see where they took us."

"But we're still in Doncaster, right?"

"Yeah, I think so. It only took about ten minutes to get here."

"Right, well that means we're not far away from my flat. You just need to get onto Thorne Road, then walk along it past the big field. If you carry on down there you'll come to Broxholme Lane eventually. Just look out for that phone box opposite Patel's, you can't miss it."

Sally shook her head. "I'm not leaving you, Stiggy. Not again. I'm staying here, so you will have to stay as well."

Stiggy hopped down from the bed and clutched his stomach at a sudden stabbing pain. He stumbled forward, and Sally rushed over to him and held him upright.

"Stiggy, you need to get back into bed and rest. What if your stitches burst open?"

"I'm okay, honest. And we need to go, right now. We can't wait any longer."

Stiggy thought about the missing money again as he grabbed the blanket off the bed and wrapped it around his shoulders. He should have learned from the close shave with that copper at the train station and dumped the wallet somewhere, then there would be nothing to link him to Joe's murder. If only he'd left the money back at the flat instead of taking it all with him. But he'd been too worried about the flat being robbed, and he'd thought it would be safer with him, so he could keep an eye on it. Now that decision had ended up wrecking everything.

With Sally supporting him, Stiggy headed over to the door and opened it a small crack to peer out into the main ward. A row of snoring patients lay in beds, but there was no sign of any of the nurses, so he opened the door fully and stepped out to hurry across the ward and through a pair of swinging doors into a corridor. They found a lift and rode it down to the ground floor, then made their way to the exit.

A receptionist reading a paperback book looked up as they passed, but didn't say anything. Stiggy realised why when he found a group of patients smoking just outside the double doors. One woman had taken her saline drip with her. Another sat in a wheelchair with a blanket over her knees as she puffed away. A bald man with them looked like he was at death's door. His eyes were sunken, his skin an unnatural shade of yellow. He held a cigarette against a gauze-covered hole in his neck where his Adam's apple should be, and the tip glowed red. When he removed his hand, smoke billowed from the hole like his insides were on fire.

Stiggy shivered at the sight of it. Sally must have thought he was reacting to the cold night air, because she rubbed his arm through the blanket and drew him closer to her. Together they made their way across the car park, up Armthorpe Road, and onto Thorne Road. Stiggy's bare feet were freezing, and he had to watch where he was going to avoid loose gravel, piles of dried-up dog shit, and other detritus littering the pavement. Occasional taxis whizzed past in the direction of the town centre, but that was the only traffic they saw as they made their way back to Stiggy's flat.

Walking past the Town Fields, Stiggy thought about the old abandoned house that used to stand on the corner that everyone said was haunted. Kids from miles around would dare each other to venture inside and face the evil spirits who dwelled within. There was a bomb shelter in the back garden that smelled of dead things, which was probably the origin of the rumours. The floorboards of the house were rotten, and half the stairs had splintered holes in them where someone's foot had gone straight through them, but that never stopped anyone going inside to prove how brave they were.

Stiggy could still remember how scared he was the first time he ascended those stairs when he was seven years old. The house creaking around him for no logical reason. Colin and Twiglet moaning like ghosts in one of the downstairs rooms. Brian screaming and pretending he had been attacked by a crazed killer. Stiggy desperately wanting to turn back, run out of the house, grab his bike, and pedal as fast as he could back home to Hexthorpe where it was safe. But he'd made it all the way upstairs, which was more than Colin, Twiglet or Brian ever had. He grinned down at them through a big hole in the bedroom floor and called them cowards, teased them for months about it afterwards.

The council demolished the house a few years later, after a kid fell through a bedroom ceiling and broke their legs and the local newspaper made a fuss about it. The bomb shelter survived a little longer, still attracting gangs of children who dared each other to spend the night in there, before it was filled in and concreted over. Now there was nothing to show either the house or the bomb shelter had ever existed.

Stiggy directed Sally into the subway opposite where the haunted house used to be. It smelled of piss and stale glue, and the strip-lighting illuminating the interior flashed and hummed, giving a weird stroboscopic effect to their movement. Empty beer cans, cider bottles, cigarette butts, and dried up glue bags lay everywhere. What looked like an old sleeping bag and a rucksack had been dumped in the centre of the underpass, next to the right hand wall. Stiggy couldn't be sure under the constantly flickering light if he was imagining it or not, but one end of the sleeping bag seemed to twitch as he approached. He glanced at Sally to see if she had noticed it too, but her eyes were fixed on the subway exit before them.

Then Stiggy's foot hit one of the empty beer cans and sent it clattering to one side.

The sleeping bag shuddered and let out a high-pitched squeal, then one end of it bolted upright.

"Get out of it, leave me alone, you dirty bastards!" a female voice yelled.

Sally startled and stood stock still as she spun to stare at the shapeless figure emerging from the sleeping bag. Stiggy, his mind still filled with childhood ghost stories, backed away with his mouth open. Gloved hands clawed their way out. A head appeared, its face obscured by a black woolly bobble hat pulled down over it, leaving just a mouth and a hairless chin visible. Then shoulders and a chest covered by several layers of worn out clothing.

"Go on, get lost!" The woman flailed her hands in the air like she was swatting flies, then pulled off the woolly hat and glared at Sally. "I haven't got no money, so you might as well fuck off out of it and leave me alone!"

Stiggy gaped at her when he realised who it was.

"Doris? What are you doing here?"

Doris's head shot from Sally to Stiggy, then she snatched up the empty rucksack lying next to the sleeping bag and clutched it to her chest while she tried to stand. Stiggy walked over to her, one hand raised in supplication while he held the hospital blanket to his chest with the other.

"Doris, it's me. Stiggy. You know, from Broxholme Lane?"

Doris glowered at Stiggy for a couple of seconds, then her features softened. She sighed and settled back down to lean against the subway wall, her lower half still cocooned inside the sleeping bag.

"Oh, it's you. I thought you were them kids again. What did

you have to go and wake me up for?"

"I didn't mean to, it was an accident. But what are you doing here?"

Doris shrugged and placed the woolly hat back on her head. "Why wouldn't I be here? It's my home."

"What? Why?"

Doris shrugged again. "Why not? It's as good a place as any, and at least it's dry. Except when some dirty bastard pisses on me, anyway."

"Don't you have anywhere else to live?"

"Maybe I just like it here. Why do you care, anyway?"

"Because ... I don't know, I just do, okay? You're a friend, and friends help each other, don't they?"

Doris gave out a short laugh. "Yeah, right. When they want something, that is."

Stiggy frowned. Did she mean him, or just people in general?

"Anyway," Doris said, "it is what it is, and there's nothing I can do about it. We can't all afford some fancy place to live, like the one you've got."

Stiggy couldn't help smiling. 'Fancy' was the last word he'd use to describe his flat. It was more like a slum than anything else. He shook his head. "You don't need to be able to afford it, the council pays the rent for you."

Doris pulled a face. "Maybe for the likes of you."

"No, they'll pay it for anyone who's on the dole. You just need to apply for it, then they pay it to the landlord for you."

Doris shook her head. "Except you can't get no dole without an address to send it to."

"What? Why not?"

Doris shrugged. "Don't know, but that's what they told me."

"Really? That's pretty fucked up. I would've thought people with nowhere to live would need the dole more than anyone. But you must have had somewhere to live before? Can't you just give them that address, then go round and pick the Giro up when it comes?"

"Not there anymore. Funding got cut, so they turfed us all out and boarded it up."

"What? Who did? What funding? What are you on about?"

"The refuge I stayed at." Doris gestured with one hand. "Just down there, it was. Only the council said they couldn't afford it no more, so they closed it down. A few of the other women, they moved to another refuge in Rotherham, but they didn't have enough room for us all, so the ones with kiddies got priority. The rest of us, we had to fend for ourselves."

"Shit, really? That's terrible. Couldn't the council have found you somewhere else to live before they closed it down?"

"Don't care, do they? Not their problem."

"There must be someone who can help. Something you can do about it."

"Like what?"

"I don't know ... *something. Anything.*"

Doris sighed and shook her head. "Yeah well, if you think of something, let me know. Until then, I need to get some kip. So if you don't mind, I'll say good night, and maybe I'll see you tomorrow."

Stiggy watched Doris pull the woolly hat down over her face, then lie down and shuffle herself back into the sleeping bag. He stared down at her, wondering if what she'd said about the Social was true. What sort of fucked up society would deny people something as basic as a place to live, then refuse to give them any dole money because they didn't have an address to send it to? It made no sense, she must have got it wrong. Nobody would be that cruel, not even Thatcher.

Then Stiggy thought about Doris resorting to selling herself on the streets in order to survive, and he felt bad about using her in that way. He'd always assumed she just liked fucking, and it was an easy way to make a bit of extra cash. Now he wondered what sort of life she must have had before everything went so terribly wrong. What it was she needed to escape to a women's refuge to avoid. He couldn't help imagining Sally ending up in the same position as Doris if things had gone different, if she'd stayed with Joe. It didn't seem likely Joe would have let her go off with Dave when she was sixteen, like they had planned. Not without doing to her what he had done to Trisha first, anyway. And the way Dave was heading, it wouldn't be long before he ended up either dead or in prison.

Stiggy turned to Sally. She locked eyes with him and frowned, then walked away. After another quick glance at Doris, Stiggy followed her out of the subway.

"That poor woman," Sally said as they walked down Thorne Road together.

Stiggy nodded. He clenched his fist around the blanket. It was fucked up, nobody should be forced to live like that.

"She's one of the prossies who hang out round your street, isn't she?"

Stiggy felt his cheeks flush as he glanced at her. "Um ... yeah."

"You and her seem pretty close."

"Yeah, I guess. I've known her since I first moved in."

"Did you fuck her?"

Stiggy could feel Sally's eyes boring into him, but he didn't dare look into them. He shook his head and continued walking, hoping she wouldn't push the issue any further.

"You did, didn't you?"

Stiggy stopped walking and turned to face her. "Look, Sally, I'm not proud of it, okay? But it was before I met you, I haven't done it since, honest. And it wasn't even my idea, at least not the first time. My mate bought her for me as a flat warming present, and—"

"What, and you couldn't say no?"

"Well, yeah. I was only sixteen at the time, and I'd never done it before. I know that sounds really crap, but—"

"It's disgusting, Stiggy, that's what it is. It's something a dirty old man would do. And she's old enough to be your mum, for fuck's sake. That makes it even worse."

Stiggy was about to protest that his mum was a lot older than Doris, but the look Sally gave him made him realise that would be a bad idea.

Sally shook her head. "I thought you were better than that, Stiggy. I guess I was wrong. That woman back there, after everything she's gone through, and you just took advantage of her like that."

"I didn't know she was living like that, honest. If I did, I would have helped her."

An idea popped into Stiggy's mind. The rent on the flat was already paid for, and after tonight it would be lying empty. Doris could move in, at least until the rent cheque stopped coming or the landlord turned up to empty the electric meter. That would give her an address to go to the dole office with, and enough time to look for a place of her own. Or maybe even take over the tenancy. The landlord wouldn't care who lived there as long as he got his money.

Stiggy glanced over his shoulder at the subway entrance, then back at Sally, who was still glaring at him as if she wanted to kill him. It wouldn't be a good idea to go back and tell Doris the plan right now, but he could always take a detour up Thorne Road on the way north and do it then. Drop the flat keys off with her, and —

The keys!

They were back at the hospital, or wherever else Joe's wallet and the rest of his belongings had ended up. Fuck. But at least the key to the campervan wasn't with them, it was on the sideboard inside the flat. He'd just have to break in, that's all.

"Did you hear what I said?"

Stiggy blinked and looked at Sally. "Um ... you what?"

"I said you don't live in a women's refuge for no reason," Sally said. "And it doesn't take a genius to figure out what that reason would be. What you did to her was just carry on abusing her."

Stiggy's eyes widened. "What? It was hardly abuse. I gave her money, and she—"

"What, so you paid her and that makes it okay, does it? Did you even ask her why she was doing it?"

"Well no, but—"

"Is that why you buy me things? So I'll let you fuck me?"

"No, of course not."

Sally sniffed. Tears welled up in her eyes. She turned away and shook her head. "You're just like Joe."

"What? Fuck off, I'm nothing like that monster."

Sally turned back to Stiggy and wiped the tears from her eyes. "Except you are. You might not hit me yet, but that's only a matter of time."

Stiggy reached out for her, but she flinched away from him. "Sally, I'd never do anything like that to you."

"That's what I thought about Joe, as well. That he was one of the good guys. But he wasn't, was he?"

"Sally, Joe was an evil bastard, but not all men are like that. I'm not. I'd never hurt you, I just wouldn't. I'm nothing like him, and you have to believe that."

Sally shook her head. "You buy me things, but you won't let me have any money of my own in case I spend it on something you don't approve of. You let me stay in your flat, but you won't give me a key because you don't trust me with one. And you want to control me all the time, as well, just like he did. You tell me what to wear, and who I'm allowed to talk to, you even tell me what I'm allowed to eat and drink. But when I tell you to do something, like stay in the hospital and get better, you refuse."

"Sally, where is all this coming from? I haven't made you do anything, and if you wanted some money you could've just asked and I would've give you some. And I told you why we had to leave the hospital, I thought we agreed it was for the best."

"No, you decided it was for the best. Just like you decided it was for the best that I stop being a skin."

"Well it's worked, hasn't it? You know, the disguise? That's why they haven't caught you yet, because they're still looking for a skinhead bird."

"So why did we need to leave the hospital then?"

"Because ..." Stiggy sighed and shook his head. "Fuck, I don't know. It seemed like a good idea at the time. I guess I just freaked out when that nurse said the coppers wanted to question me."

"So let's go back there, then. Let them ask their questions, then you can stay there until you get better."

"We can't, they would have noticed me missing by now and that will just make them suspicious. And there's Joe's wallet, remember? If the coppers have got it, they might figure out who it belongs to. We need to get away before that happens."

"But your stomach ... what if ..." Sally's bottom lip trembled.

Stiggy reached out for her again, and this time she hesitated before she slapped his hand away. But at least she was still talking to him, and if she was worried about his health that had to count for something too.

"I'll be okay," Stiggy said. "You heard what the nurse said, I just need to take it easy for a while. I can do that at my uncle's house, when we get there. And I'll be sitting down driving until then, so there's nothing that can go wrong, is there?"

Sally sniffed. "I suppose. But it's not just that. It's all the lies and secrets. It was the same with Joe, he never told me anything."

"I guess I was kind of embarrassed about it. Like you say, it's something dirty old men do, and I was worried about what you might think of me if you knew."

"I don't mean that," Sally said. "Dave told me about the five hundred pound reward."

"Oh."

"So what else are you keeping from me?"

"Nothing. I just didn't want to worry you, that's all. It's not like it changes anything, does it?"

"Dave told me about that newspaper article as well. And I know you read it, because you knew about that kid with the brick. But you didn't tell me all the other stuff it said about me."

"That's because it was just lies. All of it. Well, maybe except for the stuff about your mum."

"Why, what did it say about her? How much she hated me, and couldn't wait to get rid of me?"

"He didn't tell you, did he?"

"Didn't tell me what?"

Stiggy ran his hand through his hair while he gathered his

thoughts. "You've got it all wrong, Sally. Your mum, she didn't hate you. She loved you, and she never gave up on you."

Sally huffed. "Well she had a funny way of showing it."

"She was ill. Depression, I think it said, or something like that. She wasn't much older than me at the time, so she must have been really young when she had you. But she didn't give you away, you were stolen from her. And she fought really hard to get you back, but the courts ... well, they just wouldn't budge, and I guess it must have all got too much for her. She killed herself, Sally. I'm so sorry."

Stiggy stepped closer to Sally and opened up the blanket, expecting her to rush into his arms sobbing. But she just stood there, staring at him. He let his arms drop to his sides, the blanket flapping open. Sally stared at the bandages coating his stomach and bit her lip.

"Sally? Did you hear what I said?"

"Yeah."

"But don't you see? It wasn't your mum's fault you ended up in that care home, it was the social workers who took you from her, and the courts who wouldn't give you back. Your mum, she never gave up on you."

"Except she did, she gave up on me when she killed herself."

"Yeah, but she was ill. It wasn't her fault."

Sally shrugged. "It doesn't matter whose fault it was, does it? I still ended up in that horrible place."

"Yeah I know, but—"

"Is there anything else you haven't told me? Any more secrets?"

Stiggy thought about John Spedding, how he knew who Sally was and what she had done. About the campervan being on its last legs, and not knowing how far they would get before it either broke down or ran out of petrol. About not having the keys to the flat. He would need to tell her about that soon, but this close to the hospital she would just use is as another excuse to get him to go back there, and that was the last thing they should do right now. For all he knew the police could already be waiting for him there, ready to pounce. He could deal with the missing keys when he got home, and the rest of it Sally didn't need to know. She certainly didn't need to know it was Dave who stabbed him. That was something that had to stay a secret forever.

Stiggy shook his head. "No, that's about it."

"You promise?"

"Yeah."

Sally stared into Stiggy's eyes for several seconds, then sighed. "Well we might as well go, then."

They walked on in silence side by side. Stiggy kept glancing at Sally, but she wouldn't make eye contact with him. He wondered what she was thinking about. The way she reacted to finding out her mother was dead wasn't what he expected. Maybe it was too much of a shock, and it would hit her later. Or maybe she was just too angry with him to digest it properly. He knew he had let her down, shattered her trust in him, and he felt bad about that. But had he really been controlling her life, like she said? Like the way Joe had done? He didn't think so. Everything he did, it had been for her own good, to keep her safe from the police. Whereas with Joe, he just saw Sally as his own property, his own personal punch bag to do whatever he wanted with. Stiggy was nothing like Joe. Was he?

Once they reached the countryside they would be able to relax, and be themselves. Joe's murder had made the national news, so people in Cleator Moor would almost certainly have heard about it, but nobody took any notice of things that happened hundreds of miles away. It would have already been forgotten about, and without any of those leaflets with Sally's photograph on them nobody would take any notice of her whatever she was wearing. They'd be safe there, and once they were settled in at his uncle's house he'd find some way to make it all up to her, show her he really was different. Regain her trust, somehow, and build a new life together free from all this shit.

Assuming they got that far, of course. And nothing else went wrong.

So far it had just been one bad thing after another. Joe coming home early before they could get away. The faulty brake light that got them pulled over by the police, which gave them enough evidence to suspect Sally of Joe's murder. The van being dumped in Doncaster, leading the police straight to them. And just as everything seemed to be going right for once, Stiggy had been stabbed by some psycho skinhead, and now all the money was gone and it was all his own fault.

If Stiggy hadn't spent so long in the toilet, they would have been long gone before Joe got home, and he wouldn't be dead. If they hadn't taken the van, or if he'd thought to check if anything was wrong with it before he drove away, the coppers wouldn't have stopped them. If Stiggy had disposed of the van himself instead of leaving it to those kids outside the Beckett Road flats, nobody would think to look for them in Doncaster.

If Stiggy had refused to let Dave tag along with them to The Juggler's Rest he wouldn't have been stabbed, and they would be safe in Cleator Moor by now with a wad of cash to enjoy themselves with.

Knowing his luck, he wouldn't be surprised if he arrived home and found the campervan had been stolen. Or it wouldn't start, or someone had slashed the tyres, or broken in and pinched all the stuff from the back of it. Or maybe he'd find an army of coppers waiting outside his flat to batter them both senseless and cart them off to jail for the rest of their lives.

The dull throb of thumping music and a buzz of drunken laughter could be heard in the distance, growing louder the closer they walked to Broxholme Lane. As they turned the corner, Stiggy saw dozens of motorcycles parked haphazardly along the left hand side of the road in front of John Spedding's trike. Either it wasn't as late as Stiggy thought, or the bikers were having an all night party. But beyond the row of bikes, under the orange glow of one of the streetlamps, was the campervan, parked outside his flat where it was supposed to be. So maybe things would be okay, after all. They'd grab the camping stove and gas cylinder, finish loading the rest of the stuff into the van, then they could be on their way.

But first they would need to break into the flat.

Stiggy rubbed the bandages covering his stomach. He didn't want to risk bursting his stitches open, so Sally would need to do it. Either kick the front door open, or go round the back and break the kitchen window so she could climb through and open the back door for him. Or maybe he should go and tell John Spedding he'd been locked out, get him to do it instead. Or bang on the front door until one of the other tenants answered it, then that would just leave the flimsy interior door to deal with. Sally should be able to kick out one of the plywood panels and crawl through. That would be the best option, the one least likely to draw any unwanted attention. The whole street would still be awake, the noise from the party would see to that, and the last thing Stiggy needed would be for someone who didn't recognise him in the dark to report an attempted burglary.

Stiggy walked up to the front door and raised his fist to knock on it. Then, on a whim, he pressed down on the handle instead and found the door unlocked. For once he was relieved, rather than angry. He didn't even care that someone had left the hall light on, too. That was something else that used to piss him off, because he knew it was his own electricity they were wasting. But now it just didn't really matter. He'd never get to use the rest of the electric in the meter anyway, because —

Still holding the outside door handle in one hand, Stiggy froze. There was someone sitting on the stairs, a third of the way up, staring straight at him. Someone with short-cropped hair and a green bomber jacket. Bleached denim jeans with red braces hanging from them. The glint of a knife in his left hand, its blade pointing straight up. And that all too familiar Z-shaped scar on his cheek.

Dave!

The bastard had come to finish him off!

23

Stiggy wanted to turn and run, slam the door behind him and get the fuck out of there before it was too late, but all he could do was stare open-mouthed at the skinhead sitting on the stairs. There was only one reason Dave would be there, and that was to finish off the job he'd started in The Juggler's Rest. He must have heard the door open, and got the knife ready. Would he do it in front of Sally this time? Or was he hoping Stiggy would return home alone?

"What is it?" Sally asked. She bumped into Stiggy from behind when he blocked her way into the hallway, but he barely noticed it.

Dave leaned forward and rose to his feet, swaying slightly as if he were drunk. He reached out for the banister and left a dark smear on its dirty white surface as he staggered down the stairs like a zombie. His eyes were wide and staring, his mouth hanging open, which both added to the effect and sent a chill down Stiggy's spine. Spatters of Stiggy's blood stained the front of Dave's green bomber jacket, as if they were taunting him.

Stiggy raised both hands and took a step backwards, his eyes locked on the knife the skinhead held as he imagined it plunging into him again and again, ripping through flesh and puncturing vital organs. The blanket fell from his shoulders and he almost tripped over it as he continued backing up through the front door, but he didn't dare look away. Somewhere in the back of his mind he registered Sally standing behind him, asking what was wrong.

Dave reached the bottom of the stairs. Stiggy expected him to lunge forward with the knife at any second, but he just stood there, dripping blood onto the threadbare hallway carpet. His mouth opened and closed, but he didn't speak. Tears of fury rolled down his ashen cheeks.

"Dave, what are you doing here?" Sally said, pushing past Stiggy and peering into the hallway. Then: "Oh God Dave, what have you done?"

When Dave finally spoke, his voice hitched with emotion. "I'm sorry, Sally. I didn't mean to do it, I really didn't."

Sally rushed over to Dave. She reached for his right hand and raised it, then rolled up the sleeve of his bomber jacket. His arm was slick with gushing blood. Two long, jagged gashes ran all the way down the underside of his forearm, from the elbow to the back of his wrist, criss-crossed with smaller cuts as if he'd tried to carve the image of a ladder onto himself. Sally stared into his eyes and shook her head slowly.

"Dave, why are you doing this again? I thought you were over all this."

Tears streamed down the young skinhead's face. He sobbed openly, his shoulders jerking. Sally released his hand and wrapped her arms around him. Dave's bottom lip trembled as he stared over her shoulder at Stiggy, his own arms limp by his sides. Still clutching the knife.

"You ... you know why. What I did ... I hate myself. Can ... can you ever forgive me?"

Stiggy glared back from his position in the doorway and shook his head. Fuck that. Dave had wrecked everything, and there was no way he'd ever forgive the bastard for what he'd done. Stabbing him was bad enough, but causing him to lose all that money, and the prospect of the coppers linking it to Joe's murder, was even worse.

"What do you mean?" Sally asked.

"What I did ... I shouldn't have done it. I'm sorry, Sally, I really am."

"Do you mean at the pub?" Sally pulled away slightly so she could look into Dave's eyes. Dave nodded, then sobbed even harder. "It's okay," Sally said, rubbing his back. "I understand why you did it. We both do."

Dave's brow furrowed as the tears continued to flow. "What? I don't understand. You ... you mean you don't mind? You forgive me?"

"There's nothing to forgive," Sally said. "You had to run before the coppers came. We would've done too if it wasn't for what happened to Stiggy. Don't beat yourself up about it, you did the right thing. You only would've got yourself arrested if you'd stayed behind."

Dave's mouth dropped open. "But ... I ... it was me who ..."

Stiggy held up one hand and shook his head rapidly. Dave must have got the message, because his eyes widened and his words trailed off.

Thank you, he mouthed silently.

Stiggy glared back at him. Dave wasn't getting away with it that easily. As soon as they were alone together, out of Sally's earshot, he'd make sure the bastard knew exactly what he had done.

"Come on," Sally said to Dave, "let's get you inside and get you cleaned up." She patted him on the back and broke the embrace. "But give me the knife first, okay? I don't want any more accidents."

Dave handed Sally the knife, and she passed it to Stiggy. Stiggy tossed it out into the front yard and picked up the blanket.

"Give me the keys," Sally said to Stiggy.

Stiggy shook his head. "I can't, I don't have them. They're with my other stuff, back at the hospital or wherever they are."

Sally frowned. "Oh. So what are we going to do, then?"

"Do you need to get in there?" Dave asked, pointing at Stiggy's flat. Sally nodded. "And you don't mind what happens to the door?"

"We're leaving tonight," Stiggy said, "and we won't be coming back, so no." He thought about Doris moving in, but if she was used to sleeping in a subway she wouldn't mind a broken door. She would just need to board it up with something, then use the back door for getting in and out.

Dave wiped his nose with the sleeve of his bomber jacket, then drew up one knee and kicked the bottom plywood panel with the sole of his boot. After a couple more attempts, the panel splintered inwards, and he kicked around the edges of the hole he'd made until it was large enough for him to crouch down and crawl through. Sally glanced at Stiggy and followed Dave inside. Stiggy shook his head and sighed, then closed and locked the front door. The hospital would have noticed he was missing by now, and if they'd alerted the police they might be already on the way to find out why. He and Sally had to get away, and it had to be before that happened. But first he would need to deal with Dave.

Inside the flat, Stiggy made straight for one of the suitcases at the bottom of the bed and picked out a Varukers T-shirt that was baggy enough to fit over his bandages, along with a pair of yellow and black leopard-print trousers and a pair of thick socks to warm up his freezing cold feet. After dressing he sat down on the bed and stared across at Dave, who was sitting on the edge of the armchair while Sally helped him out of his bomber jacket. The cuts on his arm didn't look as deep close up, but there was still a lot of blood pouring from them. Sally winced, then told Dave to keep his arm raised while she hurried into the kitchen.

Dave waited until she had gone before he whispered: "Thanks

for not telling her it was me who did it."

Stiggy scowled. "I didn't do it for you, I did it for Sally. And I didn't tell the coppers either, if that's what you're worried about. Not yet, anyway, but there's still time. What are you doing here? What do you want?"

"I didn't know where else to go."

"You could have gone back home."

"I needed to see Sally, explain what happened. Tell her it was an accident."

"An accident?" Stiggy struggled to keep his voice low. "Fuck off, you stabbed me, remember? How the fuck was that an accident?"

"I didn't mean to do it, honest. I just sort of ... it just ... I don't know, it just happened. I'm sorry, okay?"

Stiggy sighed and shook his head. He wanted to shout and scream, go over there and punch Dave's face in. He glanced at the kitchen door to make sure Sally wasn't standing there listening. He could hear cupboards opening and closing, the kettle being filled with water and dropped on the camping stove. The whumpf as she lit the gas.

"Do you even know what you've done?" Stiggy whispered. "Not just to me, but to Sally as well? We've lost all our money because of you. And we're still stuck here in Doncaster where everyone's looking for us, instead of being safe in the country like we were supposed to be by now. We can't even afford to buy enough petrol to get there."

Dave looked down, avoiding Stiggy's glare. "I know, I fucked up. And I wish it hadn't happened, I really do. Look, mate—"

"Like you keep saying, I'm not your fucking mate."

"I just want to make it up to you. Both of you. Look, I've only got a tenner on me, but you can have that if you want? And if there's anything else I can do to make it right, just tell me and I'll do it."

Stiggy was about to tell Dave the only thing he wanted him to do was fuck off out of his and Sally's life forever, but then he had a better idea. He smiled while he scratched the back of his head.

"There is one thing you can do, but you won't like it."

Dave looked up and nodded. "Anything at all, just name it."

Stiggy opened his mouth to reply, but before he could say anything Sally came back from the kitchen clutching a bowl of steaming water, a bag of cotton wool balls, a bottle of antiseptic, and several rolls of bandages.

"I'll tell you later," Stiggy said, and lay down on the bed

while Sally saw to Dave's self-inflicted injuries.

* * *

Stiggy rapped his knuckles on John Spedding's front door as hard as he could, not sure if it would be loud enough for anyone inside to hear it over the blaring music. Dave stood beside him in a plain white T-shirt, his shoulders slumped, staring down at the ground. Anxious and terrified, like a condemned man facing the gallows. It must have taken a lot of guts for a lone skinhead to go anywhere near a house full of drunken Hells Angels, never mind be prepared to enter it and put his fate in their hands. Stiggy had a little bit of grudging respect for that, and couldn't help feeling sorry for what the lad was about to endure. But it was too late to back out now, even if he wanted to.

Sally was back at the flat, curled up asleep on top of the bed. She'd been so exhausted after her two day vigil over Stiggy in the hospital that she'd almost collapsed onto it as soon as she finished off bandaging up Dave's arm, and hadn't even bothered to change out of the blood-stained *Vice Squad* shirt and jeans she wore. She looked so peaceful lying there, Stiggy decided he would risk staying in Doncaster one more night so she could catch up on her sleep.

It was while Sally slept that Stiggy took Dave into the kitchen and outlined his plan. It had been met with horror and stunned silence, but in the end Dave agreed it was no more than he deserved for what he had done. His only condition was that Sally couldn't know anything about it. Stiggy agreed instantly. He'd never had any intention of telling her anyway, because he knew that if he did she would hate him forever.

Getting no reply at the door, Stiggy tried banging on the living room window instead. That seemed to be where the loud music was coming from, and he could see light shining through the heavy drape curtains. He waited, but there was no response. He pressed his face against the glass and tried to peer through the curtains, but they were too thick to see anything. He took a step back and looked up. There was a light on upstairs too, but no sign of any movement.

"John, are you up there?" he yelled. "It's Stiggy from next door, I need to talk to you."

Stiggy waited, and when nothing happened he knocked on the downstairs window again, so hard it hurt his knuckles and made the glass rattle in its rotting wooden frame. Just as he was about to try again for a third time, the curtains parted enough for a hairy face with a crooked nose and small beady eyes to glare out.

"What the fuck do *you* want, you pair of cunts?"

"Can you get John for me?" Stiggy shouted back over the blaring music. "Tell them it's Stiggy from next door."

"No, fuck off. He's busy."

The curtains dropped and the face disappeared. Stiggy clenched his fists in frustration. This wasn't going the way he'd hoped. But he was determined he wasn't going to give up. It was too important for that. This had to happen, otherwise he wouldn't be able to move on with his life. And the more time Dave had to think about it, the less likely it was he would be prepared to go through with it.

Stiggy banged his fists on the window, one after the other, and continued banging until the curtains parted once more. The same face glared out, then the curtains opened fully and dozens more bikers, both men and women, crowded around him to see what was going on. Stiggy studied each of them in turn, but John Spedding wasn't among them. One of the men pointed at Dave, then grinned and slid his finger across his neck. Another slipped on a set of brass knuckle dusters and raised both fists. Dave stepped back, his eyes wide and fixed on the biker with the knuckle dusters. Stiggy grabbed hold of his shirt to make sure he couldn't run away. This was happening, whether Dave liked it or not. There was no going back now.

A fat woman in her late twenties inside the house hopped up onto a dining chair standing next to the window and dropped her filthy jeans and stained knickers, then bent over to press her bare arse against the glass, causing uproarious laughter from the other bikers as she rubbed it up and down with a faint squeaking sound.

"Look, it's important that I see John," Stiggy yelled. "Just go and get him for me, yeah?"

"Fuck off, you cunt," the biker with the crooked nose shouted back. "I already told you, he's busy. Now *do* one, before we come out there and fucking batter you."

Stiggy stepped back with his hands raised. Maybe it had been a mistake to confront them while they were so pissed up. Maybe he should have left it until tomorrow, after they sobered up. But that would mean delaying his and Sally's escape to the country even longer, and risk them still being at the flat when the coppers arrived to see why he'd done a runner from the hospital. Or worse, they'd want to know how he had ended up with Joe's wallet among his possessions. He decided he would give it one more try, see if he could reason with the drunken bikers.

"Look, we don't want no trouble, okay? We just need to see John, then we'll be on our way."

"Fuck off!"

Stiggy sighed and shook his head slowly. It was obvious he was wasting his time. Dave looked relieved as they headed away from the house toward the gate. Stiggy couldn't really blame him, but he was determined they would try again later in the night. Wherever John Spedding had got to, he would need to show up some time. All they had to do was wait.

Then, just as they reached the gate, an upstairs window slid open and a gruff voice called out.

"What's up, kid?"

Stiggy turned and looked up. Spedding leaned out of the sash window and peered down. His chest was bare, and beside him stood a naked young woman with long blonde hair cascading over her shoulders, her large pert breasts on display for all to see. Dave's eyes boggled as he stared up at them.

"All right, John?" Stiggy said, trying not to ogle the girl himself. "Is it okay if I have a word with you?"

Spedding frowned. "Does it have to be now? I'm kind of busy."

"Yeah, it's important."

"Okay, well give me another ten minutes or so and I'll come down."

Spedding bent the young woman over the sill of the open window and kicked her legs apart. She locked eyes with Dave in the yard below and smiled while Spedding positioned himself behind her and crouched down to his knees. His face disappeared behind her arse, and she made an 'ooh' shape with her mouth while she continued staring down at Dave.

Then Spedding reared up, his facial hair glistening, and thrust his hips into her with a grunt. Her eyes bulged and her mouth dropped open. She cried out when Spedding grabbed a handful of hair and yanked it, then gasped while he pounded against her. Each thrust seemed to propel her upper body further and further through the open window, until Stiggy was sure she would topple out of it as soon as Spedding released his grip on her hair. Her cheeks flushed. She moaned. Spedding grunted, his movement growing faster by the minute. Then he let out a primal yell and arched his back, his face screwed up in what could only be described as a grimace as he yanked back on her hair.

The woman cried out again as her head snapped up. Spedding grinned down at Stiggy, then stepped away from the girl and wiped his quivering cock on the curtains before disappearing from view. The woman straightened up, rubbed the back of her head, then smiled at Dave while she caressed her breasts with one hand and slid the other between her legs.

"Fucking hell," Dave whispered, gaping up at her. "Is it always like this round here?"

Stiggy smiled and shook his head, then turned his attention back to the bikers in the downstairs window. The fat woman standing on the chair was now fully naked, waving her arms in the air and smiling while men took it in turns to reach up and pour cans of beer over her huge pendulous breasts. One of them had his face buried between her legs, lapping up the beer as it flowed down her body.

A moment later the front door opened and John Spedding peered out, a lit cigarette dangling from the corner of his mouth. Stiggy was relieved to see he'd got dressed before coming down.

"So what's so important then, kid?"

"Um ... you remember me telling you about that skinhead who abused Sally?"

"What, the one you offed?"

Stiggy nodded. "Yeah. Only it turns out he wasn't the only one who was abusing her, was he?"

Spedding turned his gaze to Dave. His eyes narrowed, and his fist clenched. "Oh yeah?" he growled through gritted teeth.

"Not him," Stiggy said quickly. "But he knows who it was. They did it to him, too, you see. And lots of other kids. And they never got caught, so they're probably still doing it now."

Spedding took a drag on his cigarette and exhaled a cloud of smoke through his nose. "Why are you telling me this, kid? Shouldn't you be talking to the fuzz instead?"

"The coppers aren't interested, Sally tried once but they didn't believe her. I thought you might be able to do something about it. You know, warn them off or something. Maybe if they know you're watching, they'll stop doing it? There has to be something you can do. I mean, it's not right, is it, what they're doing. Someone needs to stop them."

Spedding stroked his beard, seemingly deep in thought, then nodded and turned to Dave.

"You got any proof?"

Dave gave a slight nod of his head, but refused to make eye contact. Spedding nodded once more, then gestured at the open door with the stump of his right hand.

"Well you'd better come in then, both of you."

Dave's mouth gaped open. His eyes were wide as he looked from Spedding to the cavorting bikers in the downstairs front room. "Can't we do it out here, instead? Or back at Stiggy's place?"

Spedding shook his head. "If what you are saying is true, I want the rest of the Chapter to hear it. Then we can decide together what, if anything, we will do about it."

"Will he be safe in there?" Stiggy asked. "Only they said they'd batter us if we don't go away."

Spedding nodded. "You have my word, kid. I'll make sure nothing bad will happen to either of you."

Stiggy had never been in John Spedding's house before, and he was surprised to find it had the exact same layout as the building he lived in, with a stairway at the end of the narrow hallway, and two doors on the right hand side leading into separate rooms. Except the doors were solid oak, not cheap plywood, and they didn't have locks on them.

The house stunk of cannabis smoke and stale beer. Framed newspaper front pages adorned the walls of the hallway, old reports of violent clashes between Hells Angels and rival gangs dating back to the early seventies. A mound of leather jackets with Hells Angels Yorkshire patches on the back lay strewn over the end of the banister at the bottom of the stairs. The young woman Stiggy had seen upstairs with Spedding was on her way down, wearing nothing but a bra and a pair of very small knickers, both with a leopard-print design on them that matched Stiggy's trousers. She smiled at Dave as she headed into the back room with a can of lager in one hand. Dave grinned back, but his grin soon dropped when Spedding gestured at the door to the front room where all the bikers were. When Dave hesitated, Spedding frowned at him and entered first.

"Listen up guys," he said, after switching off the music. "These people are my guests, and I want you to treat them with respect. And I want you all to hear what they have to say, so sit down and shut up."

Several of the men jeered at Dave, but Spedding silenced them all with a glare. Stiggy wondered for the first time just how high up in ranking Spedding was among the Hells Angels if he could command such authority over them. They slumped into leather armchairs and settees placed around the walls of the room and sat with their arms folded. The naked fat woman placed two dining chairs in front of the window, then squeezed herself onto one of the settees, draping her arms around the shoulders of the two men either side of her. Young women in various states of undress sat cross-legged on the floor. All eyes were on Dave and Stiggy standing in the doorway.

Dave looked at Stiggy and swallowed audibly. His hands were shaking. Stiggy gave him a reassuring nod, and nudged him through the door. Spedding pointed at the two dining chairs by the window, then sat down in a leather armchair in the corner of the room that had been left vacant for him. After another glance at Stiggy, Dave looked down at his boots and made his way over to one of the chairs and sat down with both hands clasped over his bollocks, as if he feared for their safety. Stiggy joined him, feeling uncomfortable with everyone staring at him. Even with Spedding's promise that nothing bad would happen to them, he could practically taste the hostility in the air.

The carpet by the window was sodden with spilt beer, and the chair Dave had left for Stiggy was still wet, but he didn't dare complain. He just sat down and ignored the cold and sticky dampness soaking through his trousers, then clutched his knees and tried not to catch anyone's eye.

The blonde-haired girl in the leopard-print bra and knickers entered the room and perched herself on John Spedding's knee. She smiled across at Dave as she took a sip of lager, but he didn't return the gesture this time. He picked at the bandage on his arm, his right hand still covering his bollocks, and continued staring down at the ground.

"Well go on then," Spedding said after a minute of brooding silence. "We haven't got all night."

"I, um ..." Stiggy said, fidgeting on the wet chair. "Well, we, um ... we came here to tell you ... um ..."

"I was twelve the first time I was raped," Dave said in a flat monotone, still looking down. "My best friend Sally was eleven, and it was already her second time."

24

Several of the women gasped at Dave's revelation. Stiggy's mouth dropped open and his chest tightened as he pictured the scene in his mind. He shook his head and tried to swallow down the lump in his throat, but his mouth was too dry. He knew the story of that night back at the care home, but he had no idea Sally had been so young when it happened. Or Dave, come to that. He felt his buttocks clench of their own volition, and tried to read John Spedding's face for clues as to how he would react. But the biker just sat there staring at Dave, his expression blank.

"I was trying to protect her," Dave continued, "but I couldn't. There was two of them, and they were too strong. They forced Sally to watch, then when they finished with me they made me watch while they did the same to her."

The girl with the blonde hair and leopard-print underwear jumped off Spedding's knee and rushed over to Dave.

"Oh, you poor thing," she said, and stroked the back of his head.

Tears welled up in the corners of Dave's eyes. He brushed them away and sniffed. The girl pulled his head between her huge breasts and held it there. Dave's cheeks reddened, but he didn't resist.

"Put the boy down, Sandra," Spedding said. "We want to hear what he's got to say. Stevo, get them a beer each. Mike, roll us all a few joints." He nodded to Dave. "Carry on, kid. Tell us the rest of it."

The girl, Sandra, knelt down on the wet floor beside Dave's chair and held his hand. One of the bikers tossed over a couple of cans of beer. Dave caught his in one hand and stared down at it. Stiggy fumbled his and had to rise from his chair to retrieve it from the floor. When he cracked it open foam sprayed out in a wide arc. He wasn't sure what to do with the ring pull after he tore it off, so he dropped it into the can.

The bikers listened in grim silence while Dave related his story. Most of it Stiggy already knew, from Sally's version of the events. But there were other details too, things she either didn't know, or she had kept from him because they were just too horrible to think about. Dave broke down and sobbed while he described what the fat man had done to him, about the man's penchant for sadism and torture. Sandra encouraged him to drink his beer, and when he downed it in two long gulps she got him another. Someone passed Dave a joint and he took a drag on it, then coughed and spluttered before handing it back. The bikers waited patiently for him to continue.

Stiggy shuffled uncomfortably on the sticky chair while Dave told them about Watkins, how he took money from paedophiles and watched while they abused children in their rooms, sometimes taking photographs on a Polaroid camera as a souvenir. About a house in Rochdale where selected children were taken to what were referred to as VIP weekend parties. Dave related everything that happened to him at those parties in lurid detail. Ice-cold showers and beatings. Being tied face down and naked on a bed while men with posh accents took it in turns to rape him. Then told they would kill him if he ever dared to breathe a word about any of it. Stiggy couldn't help wondering if Sally had ever attended any of those parties, but he was too afraid of knowing the answer to interrupt Dave and ask him.

When Dave completed his story he looked drained and vacant, like he'd withdrawn inside himself. Sandra hugged him, but he didn't seem to notice her presence. Some of the hardened bikers were openly weeping. Stiggy was, too. He just couldn't help it when he imagined what the poor lad must have suffered through. Others just stared at Dave, open-mouthed in shock at what they had just heard. All the colour had drained from their hairy faces. Spedding's fist clenched and unclenched. He cleared his throat, and when he spoke there was raw emotion behind his voice.

"You say you have proof of all this?"

"Oh, come on," Sandra protested, turning toward Spedding. "You really think he would make something like that up? Look at him, man. He's a fucking wreck. How can—"

Spedding held up his hand to silence her. "I didn't say I don't believe him, Sandra. I just want to know what his proof is."

Dave looked up and pointed at the Z-shaped scar on his cheek. "He did this to me. To mark me as his own property, he said, so I would always remember that he owned me. And that isn't all."

Dave stood up and peeled off his T-shirt. Sandra helped him

get the sleeve over the bulging bandage on his arm, then gasped at the long, jagged scars running down and across his chest and stomach. So many angry welts he looked like he had been sliced into small pieces and then sewn back together again, like a human patchwork quilt.

"He did these, as well. It was usually just one or two each time, but one night he got carried away, then he just left me to die. I would've done too, if Sally hadn't found me first."

Dave turned around slowly with his arms raised, so everyone in the room could see his mutilated body. More scars coated his back, continuing down beneath the waistband of his jeans. Everyone stared at him in silence. Spedding frowned and shook his head slowly. Tears streamed down Sandra's face as she held one hand over her open mouth.

Close up, Stiggy could see dozens of faded cigarette burns, too. Small, raised patches of hairless skin dotted between the scars on Dave's chest that were almost pure white. He gaped at them, wondering if it was true Dave hadn't tried to kill himself that night when Sally found him bleeding to death. From what he had learned of the fat man, and the way he fled the scene to leave Dave to die, it wouldn't surprise him. But he'd seen evidence of Dave cutting himself, too. There was no way anyone else could have inflicted those fresh wounds on his right arm. Dave even still had the knife in his hand when Stiggy and Sally arrived at the flat, so how could it have been anyone else?

Dave put his shirt back on and slumped down in the chair. Sandra hugged him once more, and promised those bastards would all pay for what they had done to him.

"Sandra," Spedding said. "Take the lad upstairs and give him something else to think about while the rest of us discuss what he's told us. I'll send for you when we're ready."

Sandra smiled, wiped her tears away, then clasped Dave's hand and led him across the room. Dave paused in the doorway and shot Spedding a quizzical glance. Spedding nodded once, then turned to Stiggy.

"You need to leave as well, kid. This is Angel business, you can't be here."

"What about Dave?"

"Don't worry about him, he'll have his hands full for a while. Wait outside, we'll call you in when we're done."

One of the women rose from the floor and ushered Stiggy out of the house, closing and locking the front door behind him. He looked up at the open window when he heard a woman's laughter, but there was nothing to see. He turned his attention to the downstairs window and peered through it, trying to make out the murmured voices from within, until someone noticed him and closed the curtains. The opening chords of a *Black Sabbath* song blared out of the front room, then the volume was turned down low enough so they could talk over it, but still loud enough to drown out their words from outside. Stiggy slumped down with his back against the front door and sat on the porch step while he waited.

Twenty minutes later the door opened without warning and Stiggy almost tumbled backwards inside. The same woman who had ushered him outside looked down at him, then gestured for him to enter.

"What have you decided?" he asked as he stood up and faced her. But she just turned away and headed back into the front room.

Dave and Sandra were on their way downstairs together, hand in hand. Dave had a huge, daft grin on his face that grew even wider when he spotted Stiggy in the hallway. Stiggy followed them into the front room. Spedding nodded to him, then gestured at the two chairs by the window. He waited until Stiggy and Dave were both seated, then smiled at Dave.

"I'm guessing you will want to play a part in this when it all goes down?"

Dave nodded. "Too fucking right, I do."

"Okay, well this is what we're going to do."

* * *

Dave was still grinning like an idiot when he and Stiggy left John Spedding's house together. He glanced over his shoulder at the upstairs bedroom as they passed through the gate, then let out a contented sigh.

"Mate, them biker chicks are fucking wild," he said. "They just can't get enough, can they? You wouldn't fucking believe the things we got up to in there, I didn't even know half of them were even fucking possible. And she licked all my scars, can you believe that? Even the ones on my arse, the dirty bitch."

"Is it true, what you told them?" Stiggy asked. "You know, about that bloke carving you up and leaving you to die? Only Sally said you did that to yourself."

Dave frowned and shook his head. "Mate, you really know how to fucking kill a mood, don't you? Yeah, the cunt did it, all right? Only don't tell Sally, she's got enough to fucking worry about."

"I would've thought she would worry about you less if she

knew you weren't trying to kill yourself. But I don't get it. If it wasn't you who did that, why did you carve yourself up like that?" Stiggy pointed at Dave's bandaged arm. "Sally says it's not the first time, either. So what's that all about?"

Dave shrugged, then looked down. His cheeks flushed. "You wouldn't understand, you've never been through anything like what I had to cope with."

"Maybe not, but Sally has, and she doesn't cut herself."

"Yeah well, she's stronger than I am. Always has been."

"But why cut yourself? It doesn't make any sense. What that bloke did to you ... I mean, fucking hell, I can't even imagine what that must have been like, but why do it to yourself as well?"

"Yeah well, that was the first time I've done it for years now. And it was only because of ..." Dave looked up and glanced at Stiggy's stomach, then looked away again. "Well, you know. Shit got on top of me, and I thought Sally would hate me."

Stiggy shook his head. "Even if I'd told Sally what you did, she wouldn't have wanted you to do that to yourself. You saw how upset she was when she had to bandage you up."

Dave shrugged again.

"Is that what you do it for?" Stiggy asked. "For the attention you get from Sally?"

"No, it's nothing to do with that."

"Well what, then?"

Dave stopped walking and crushed a discarded cigarette butt into the pavement with the toe of his boot. "Like I said, you wouldn't understand. It just helps take my mind off stuff, that's all. Gives me something different to focus on, instead of how fucking shit everything is."

Stiggy leaned his back against the campervan while he studied Dave and wondered what went through someone's mind when they decided to slice their own arm up. Stiggy had lived his entire life trying his best to avoid pain at all cost, and to deliberately inflict it on yourself just made no sense.

"Are you going to be okay after me and Sally have gone in the morning?" Stiggy asked.

Dave looked up and nodded. "Yeah. Got something to look forward to now, haven't I? Thanks to you and your biker mates."

"So you're really going to go through with it, then?"

"Too fucking right, I am. You think I would miss out on something like that? I've dreamt of nothing else for fucking years."

"But what if you get caught?"

"That's a risk I'll have to take. Anyway, it would be worth it just to see the look on that fat bastard's face when I turn up at his house with a mob of Hells Angels."

"That's if you can find out where he lives."

"Yeah well, you heard what that one-armed bloke said. Watkins is the key to it all. Once he squeals, we'll have the fucking lot of them."

"What if he won't tell you who they are?"

Dave's eyes narrowed. "Oh, he'll fucking tell me, all right. Trust me, I won't give the cunt a fucking choice."

Stiggy shuddered. What the Hells Angels were planning to do to those people once they found out who they were went far beyond what he imagined they would do. But it wasn't as if every single one of them didn't deserve what was coming to them.

"So what are you going to do now? You know, while you wait for John to organise it all?"

"Dunno," Dave said. "Go back to Sheffield and wait, I guess. They said they'll call me at the hostel in a few weeks, when they're ready." He ground his left fist into the palm of his right hand. "I can't fucking wait to get started. I might go round to Trisha's as well, see if she wants in on the action."

"What about Joe's mates?" Stiggy asked. "They'll have noticed you missing by now, and they'll know you've been with Sally. They'll probably jump you the first chance they get, then make you tell them where she is. And I know you'll do your best not to tell them where we've gone, but ... well, you know them better than I do so you'll know what they're capable of. I mean, if you don't want to risk it, you could always stay at my flat instead? You'd have to share it with ... someone else, but it'd be safer for you. And John's only next door, so he'll still be able to find you when he needs to."

After a short pause, Dave sighed and shook his head. "Look, mate, there's something I should probably tell you before you go. I only said Joe's mates were coming for Sally so you'd let me stay with her. They don't give a fuck about Joe, they never have. They only hung out with him because they were too scared of what he would do to them if they didn't."

Stiggy's mouth dropped open. "What? For fuck's sake, you mean you put me and Sally through all that worry for nothing?"

Dave looked down at his boots. "Yeah well, I feel fucking bad about that, I really do, but it seemed like a good idea at the time. You were going to send me away, what was I supposed to do?" He looked up and frowned. "You won't tell her, will you? And you can't tell her nothing about that stuff with the bikers, either. She'll only try and stop me if she finds out, and no fucking way is that going to happen."

Stiggy sighed and ran his fingers through his hair. Great, more secrets to add to all the others. But what would be the point in telling her, anyway? Dave was right, Sally would try and stop him if she knew what he was planning to do to Watkins and those other perverts. And the more Stiggy thought about it, the more he realised it was the only way to put an end to it all. A warning would never have been enough to stop what those men were doing, and he'd been naive to think it ever would be. Even after Dave nearly died, it had only put them off for a few months.

"I won't say nothing. But don't fuck it up, and don't take any stupid risks. You make sure you get every single one of those bastards."

Dave smiled. "Don't worry, I will. Look, mate, I was wrong about you. You're a decent bloke, and I realise that now." He held out his hand. "So no hard feelings, yeah?"

Stiggy hesitated, then clasped Dave's hand and shook it. "Yeah, fuck it, why not?" He grinned. "You're still a bit of a wanker, though."

Dave grinned back. "Piss off, you hairy bastard."

* * *

Stiggy drummed his fingers on the campervan steering wheel while Sally hugged Dave goodbye on the pavement outside the flat. Much to his dismay, she'd been back in her skinhead gear again when he woke up early that morning, and by the time he heard the battery operated razor buzzing away in the kitchen it had been too late to stop Dave shaving the top and back of her head. Half her hair was already on the floor when Stiggy padded into the kitchen, and there was no going back. Sally glared at him with a look of defiance, but he didn't rise to the bait. As long as they got away before the coppers turned up to see why he wasn't at the hospital it didn't really matter anymore. He wondered whose idea it had been, and whether Sally had told Dave about the argument on the way home from the hospital. How she thought Stiggy was controlling her the same way Joe did, stopping her from being a skinhead.

It was getting on for half past ten by the time they were ready to go. After breakfast, Dave helped Stiggy load the rest of the stuff into the back of the van while Sally made sandwiches for the journey. The Calor Gas cylinder and the camping stove had been the hardest to fit through the hole in the flat door, but they managed it in the end. With Sally out of the way, Stiggy reminded Dave about the situation with the petrol, and how he didn't know how far they would get with whatever was left in the campervan. Dave repeated his offer of donating his last ten quid toward petrol money, and this time Stiggy accepted it.

Back in the flat, Dave smashed the padlock off the electric meter under the sink with a hammer and a screwdriver, and after he took out enough to cover his train fair back to Sheffield this left Stiggy with an extra eighteen pounds in fifty pence coins. Which, he hoped, should get them most of the way to Cleator Moor before they had to find somewhere to sell the camping stove. And as a bonus, Doris would get free electric while she was staying there. All she would need would be one magic fifty pence coin she could use over and over again. Stiggy wished he'd thought of it years ago when he considered how much money he'd fed into that slot over the years.

Sally rubbed Dave's back and broke the embrace. "You'll take care of yourself, won't you?"

Dave nodded. "Yeah, of course I will."

"And promise me, no more cutting?"

"I won't, honest."

"Will you do something else for me?"

"Yeah, of course I will."

"Will you look after Trisha for me? Go and see her, make sure she gets back out into the world again?"

"I will, yeah. In fact I was going to go and see her when I got home, anyway."

Sally smiled. "Good. I always kind of hoped you two would get together one day. You'd be perfect for each other."

"You reckon?"

"Yeah, why not? You always got along well together, and it's not like either of you have got anyone else, is it?"

Dave smiled. "Yeah, I guess."

"Then you could bring her with you when you come down to visit."

Dave shot a quick look at John Spedding's house, then nodded. "Yeah, I will. There's some stuff I need to sort out first, but that sounds like a fucking great idea. Phone me when you get there, so I'll know where to find you."

Sally hugged him once more and kissed him on the lips. "Bye then, Dave."

"Yeah, bye Sally. See you soon then, yeah?"

Sally climbed into the passenger seat and fastened her seatbelt. She glanced over Stiggy's shoulder at Dave, and sighed.

"You okay?" Stiggy asked.

Sally looked away and shrugged. "Yeah, I guess." It was the first time she'd spoken to Stiggy all morning, and there was no warmth in her voice.

Stiggy started the campervan and raised his hand to Dave before he pulled away and drove up to Thorne Road. Dave grinned back at him and raised a thumb.

"Dave seems happy," Stiggy said, trying to coax Sally into conversation. It would be a long journey if she just carried on ignoring him like that.

"Yeah. I'm glad you two sorted out your differences," Sally said. "It means a lot to me."

Stiggy nodded, encouraged by her response. "Yeah, I guess we got there in the end. You were right, he's a good bloke. For a skinhead, anyway."

Stiggy smiled, but Sally just frowned at him. He reached for her hand while he waited for a gap in the traffic to turn left onto Thorne Road.

"It was a joke, Sally. I didn't mean it."

Sally pulled her hand away and picked up a page Stiggy had ripped from an atlas in the library a few days earlier. She traced her finger along the route he'd marked out with a red felt tip pen. "How long do you think it will take to get there?"

Stiggy shrugged. "Dunno. It depends how often we stop along the way, and how fast this thing goes. We'll need to keep to the B roads so there's no risk of being pulled over by cop cars, so it'll take a fair while. Four or five hours, maybe?"

"Oh. As long as that?"

"Yeah, probably. But it'll be worth it, you'll see. You're going to love it there."

Sally shrugged. "We'll see."

She was still pissed off with him, that much was obvious. And when Stiggy pulled up at the Town Fields to go and see Doris in the subway it would almost certainly reignite the argument again. But he was sure it would all come right in the end. Once they were safe in the country everything would be different. He'd make it all up to her somehow.

Stiggy pushed the tape with Sally's *Selector* album on it into the campervan's cassette player and turned off onto Thorne Road for the last time ever.

Epilogue

Front page of the Daily Mirror, six weeks later.

THE NAZI KILLERS STRIKE AGAIN?
The mutilated remains of Simon Watkins, manager of the
Masbury Residential Care Home where teenage murder suspect
Sally Carter spent the last five years of her young life, were
discovered late on Friday evening by a prominent Sheffield
councillor whilst visiting the premises. Detective Inspector
Brady, leading the manhunt for Miss Carter and her unknown
accomplice in relation to the brutal slaying of landscape
gardener Joseph Hawkins several weeks ago, refused to rule
out a connection.

"I don't believe in coincidences," he said at a press
conference yesterday afternoon. "And I am not ruling anything
out at this stage in the investigation."

Brady refused to speculate on claims from the police officer
first on the scene that Mr Watkins looked like he had been
tortured prior to his death, saying it would be a matter for the
coroner to decide. He did, however, confirm that several
Polaroid photographs were found stuffed inside the victim's
mouth. When asked about the subject of these photographs
Brady refused to comment, saying it would form part of a
separate overlapping investigation.

Children residing at the home, many of which have deeply
troubled backgrounds, are said to have been left traumatised
by the event and are struggling to comprehend the reality of
what has happened. One girl described with glee hearing
prolonged screams coming from Mr Watkins' office when she
arrived home from school. A psychologist we spoke to told us
this type of separation from reality can occur following such a
shocking event, and that with suitable counselling the girl in
question would come to terms with it eventually, and should
go on to live a normal life. All children affected have been
moved into alternative care homes while the police
investigation continues.

Sally Carter (above) remains at large, her current whereabouts unknown. If anyone sees her, or has any information on where she can be found, they should contact their local police station immediately. There is a cash reward of £2,000 for any information leading to an arrest. Members of the public are advised not to approach her themselves, as she is considered highly dangerous and unstable, despite her youthful appearance.

Also available by Marcus Blakeston

Meadowside

Punk Faction

Skinhead Away

Bare Knuckle Bitch

Punk Rock Nursing Home

Mama Mia